At times subtle and profou

For one day the world h
whether or not to leave th
Washington DC to the Kr
would go the wrong way.

Full of optimism and hope, this novel explores what could have happened and for some readers, imagines what still could be - an independent country, where the politicians are silenced and the people have a voice...

"In the land of fiction, independence is real. In the real world, Scotland has said no. But in the land of fiction, the Scots have gone one step further and have voted for a land grab as well as independence. Robert Castle intends to fulfil his promise to the Scottish nation, no matter what the cost. Yet again, Mark Anderson Smith has made the improbable believable. Indeed, after reading this, I thought independence would happen! Alex Salmond may have gone but there may be a real Robert Castle out there. Watch out Westminster - according to Mark Anderson Smith, it ain't over yet!" Joy Kluver

"Was looking forward to the second book in the series and it didn't disappoint. Found myself wishing that Scotland's future could really be like this. Another cliffhanger ending, that leaves you wanting to get book three as soon as it comes out." Mary Douglas

"This book was excellent, very interesting and well put together. I couldn't put it down and it certainly made me think. Well done looking forward to book 3." Susan McGrory

"Five Stars. Can't wait for the next two books Subtle and profound." Moira Currie

When Robert and Helen Castle decide to take a walking holiday in the Scottish highlands they expect stunning views, peace and quiet, but instead end up facing a lone man armed with a shotgun. Forced off the mountain, Robert determines to get justice but finds he has no rights. Faced with the fact Scotland's land does not belong to its people, the deeper Robert looks into Scotland's history the more troubled he becomes.

News that the First Minister of Scotland is missing, with only four months until a referendum on Scottish independence, challenges Robert to decide whether he will fight for Scotland's future.

Sensing that the theft of Scotland's land over many centuries has robbed the people of their opportunity to be independent, Robert fights for a modern day land grab – to reverse the clearances that stole Scotland's land from the people.

Helen fears that politics could destroy Robert and their marriage. As the campaign intensifies she faces some of the hardest decisions of her life.

Robert has a vision for a future Scotland but his determination to win this battle threatens to drive him and his wife apart. Unknown to him, there are those who are determined that he will not win and who will go to any lengths to protect the status quo.

Imagine a country without politicians, a country governed by the people, for the people. Imagine Cafe Politics and government by referendum where having your say on government policy is as easy as voting for your favourite contestant on The X Factor. The Great Scottish Land Grab is a vision of democracy, a blueprint of hope and optimism.

The
Great
Scottish
Land Grab

MARK ANDERSON SMITH

First published in Great Britain by Mark Anderson Smith, 2014
This paperback edition published in 2014 by
Mark Anderson Smith

http://my100goals.blogspot.com
landgrab@cafepolitics.net

A catalogue record for this book is available
from the British Library.

ISBN 978-0-9929883-4-0

Dedicated to Andy Wightman who has tirelessly
campaigned for land reform in Scotland and without whose
original website –

http://www.whoownsscotland.org.uk/

the seed of this novel might have remained
buried forever.

Saltire

The flag was not just cloth.
Ripped and torn by shot and sword, yet always repaired.
Even the blood soaked fibres just faded memories,
like the men who once bore the dual coloured flag.
A single battle remains. No slaughter, no weapons and no blood.
Just two strokes: A Cross.

A.J.C. 16/98/14
https://www.facebook.com/AJCWordsmith

AUTHORS NOTE

The Great Scottish Land Grab was serialized in three books over
the summer of 2014, during the lead up to the referendum on
Scottish independence.

Book two follows directly on from book one but the start of
book three occurs before the end of book two.
The original order has been left intact.

BOOK ONE

PROLOGUE – FEBRUARY 1990

Can't pay! Won't pay!

Robert Castle looked from the uncompromising placard to the slim raven haired girl who was holding it. Normally he would have given the protesters a wide berth but she was stunningly beautiful and that seemed reason enough to slow and walk towards her.

She was standing in a loose group with six, no seven other protestors; most of a similar age to himself and who had likely never even paid any tax. A small number of people were standing slightly away but most were walking on – up or down Buchanan Street – on this bitterly cold Saturday in February.

She stopped her chanting as he approached.

"Do you have time for an avowed sceptic?" He asked.

Taken aback, she frowned. "Sceptical about what? The Government's chances of continuing to oppress the poorest in society? Margaret Thatcher's likelihood of remaining in office?"

"Sceptical of people's reticence to rise up and fight for a cause even when it will benefit them. Sceptical that this cause is even one worth fighting for."

Robert saw her eyes narrow, a hint of flare in her pupils and quickly continued. "But I am open to persuasion. You look frozen though. May I buy you a coffee, or tea, while we discuss whether I should join you in this protest?"

"You want to join our protest?"

1

Her tone mocked him and he smiled in return.

"No. But if you will allow me to buy you a tea or coffee then I will stand here beside you for the rest of the day."

"You don't want to join our protest and you're offering to stand with us?"

"I'm offering to buy you coffee." He rubbed his hands together and gave an exaggerated shiver. "I'm offering to listen to your arguments and be open to changing my view on the Poll Tax. Regardless of whether you can persuade me or not, I will then also proudly hold one of your placards and out shout your loudest grandstander."

"Oh, I can persuade you."

Robert held up his right arm in invitation. "We'll see."

Ten minutes later Helen Phillips had warmed up enough to take off her coat but had only half drunk her coffee. Robert nursed his empty mug as he tried to take in her arguments. Eventually he had had enough and held up his hands in surrender.

"I don't agree with you but I would vote for you." He interrupted.

"You... What?! That doesn't make any sense!"

Robert leaned back in his seat. "You're passionate, you're eloquent, you're knowledgeable. I think you are wrong, but at the same time you have good reasons for what you believe."

"You've just contradicted yourself! How can I be wrong if I have good reasons?"

"It's not about your reasons. If everyone benefits from government then it makes sense that everyone who can afford to pays tax to provide the benefits we all receive."

"But that is the problem – hundreds of thousands of people who can't afford it are being forced to pay, while thousands who are richer than you or I can imagine are having their bill cut! That is not just!"

"I agree, but to say that hundreds of thousands of wage earners should have to pay nothing is not just either."

"The rich are only paying a token as it is. Why are you on their side?"

"Because I am rich and because I want to become richer someday. Don't you?"

"Not at the expense of others!"

"Quite right! Do you consider yourself rich?"

Helen glared at him.

"It is not a crime to be well off. It's also admirable to care passionately about anyone who is less well off than you are. Okay, my last argument – if anyone is able to work hard and make a lot of money – why should they be forced to give all of that up to help some people who are lazy? And before you go off on one, I'm not saying that all the poor are lazy but there are some and perhaps more than even I would want to admit who could do with being forced to work."

"There are far more people out there who are working damn hard every day and only managing to scrape a survival."

"I accept that."

"The poorest should not have to give up buying their children clothes and being unable to afford insurance or send their children to good schools or universities to pay such a blatantly unfair tax!"

"I accept that."

"The rich can and should pay more."

"I accept that."

"We're not asking for no-one to pay tax."

Robert stayed silent.

****

Helen sat back in her seat and studied this tall, dark young man. He had listened for so long she thought she had won him over. Right up until he had started flirting with her again: telling her he would vote for her even though he disagreed with what she had been telling him. She didn't know whether to be insulted or complimented.

He was infuriatingly arrogant and sure of himself. She was tempted to storm out but that would imply she'd lost the argument. That the time spent with him had been wasted entirely.

Had it been a mistake to leave the group? They were having such trouble recruiting people to join the protests that when Robert offered to join them it seemed worth entertaining his offer for a coffee.

Robert Castle. The name seemed to sum him up completely. A tall rugged Scot. Thick black hair that he didn't appear able to tame. He stooped a little as if embarrassed about his height.

Something she knew a little about having shot up by almost a foot from ages 12 to 13.

His eyes were clear blue yet seemed to present a paradox. There was openness there but also a guardedness. In the way he acted, in what he said, he came across as completely open and honest. He was direct, almost threateningly so but she found it a relief to meet someone who simply got to the point with such clarity.

It wasn't anything he had done or said that suggested the guardedness so why did she see that in his eyes? Eyes that right now were studying her.

He had been right not to agree with her statement. Some of the protestors were calling for an end to Government. They resented all taxes. She didn't want to concede but...

****

"Well, I'm not asking for that."

"I accept that."

"You are infuriating!"

"Can I buy you lunch?" Robert asked.

"No!"

"At least another coffee?"

"I don't want your money."

"I'm offering you lunch. No strings attached. Though I should tell you that I want to invite you out for dinner tomorrow night?"

"Why are you flirting with me?"

Robert became serious. "I find you to be the most beautiful woman I've ever seen or met. Intelligent, courageous, compassionate, well spoken, did I say passionate already? I plan to ask you to marry me."

"I couldn't possibly marry someone who would vote for the poll tax!"

"I would vote for a more just tax."

"Or someone I had only just met."

"Then allow me to court you."

"Court! Hah!" Helen laughed. "You're a dinosaur!"

"Rumbled. I also hold open the door for ladies and, well, I was going to say fight to protect their honour but I've never actually had to do that."

"Have there been many ladies?"

"I've had three short relationships in the last two years. I confess I'm not a virgin."

"Short?"

"I'm looking for something more substantial, more meaningful."

"If you're looking for a virgin bride then I'm not the one."

"In my eyes you are perfect."

"And I would have to insist on a vow of celibacy before any betrothal..."

"Consider myself chaste."

"And how would you keep your hands off me?"

"With great difficulty..."

Helen leaned back. "Campaign with me this afternoon."

Robert leaned forward. "Would you accept me standing next to you shouting for a fairer tax?"

"I could live with that." Helen nodded.

"Then I accept your date."

"Hey!"

Helen leaned forward, a look of mock outrage on her face and he kissed her before she could react. Standing quickly he announced: "Two coffees!" Before walking to the counter.

The whole way he had to force himself to keep from turning back to check she had not run out the door.

Helen finally dragged him out of the cafe at a little after One PM and by the time the sun had set, Robert had shouted himself hoarse.

****

CHAPTER ONE

As he walked over the summit of Newton Hill, Robert Castle saw the stag. Six feet from hoof to ear and another two feet of antler towering above it. It was only forty yards or so away from him. Robert stopped and – carefully moving one arm behind his back – motioned to Helen to slow down.

The stag was magnificent; and staring right at him. Robert ran through his options: stay where he was, remain still and hope the stag didn't see him as a threat; back-up slowly and hope the stag didn't charge; run, and hope the stag didn't chase.

They were not great options.

There were no trees nearby to run for. Around him in Glen Fyne, there was simply grass covering the ground. Even the small wood they had passed earlier was only of Scottish Fir. No use for climbing and with the branches of the trees all squeezed together there would have been no way to enter the woods anyway.

"What are you looking at?" Helen asked. "Whoa, look at that!"

"Be quiet." Robert whispered.

"But it's gorgeous! Have you taken a photo? No, of course not, too busy admiring it. Hold on."

She dropped to one knee and began rustling around in her camera bag.

"What are you doing? If we scare him, he'll charge us!"

"Nonsense." Helen pulled out her Canon Digital SLR and began adjusting the camera settings.

"It's not nonsense. We're in his territory and if he charges us, I..."

"It." She said emphasising the word. "Is not scared of us. You are obviously scared of it and, frankly my dear, that is far more likely to make it charge than if we simply relax, stand here and take a few photos."

Unable to relax but knowing Helen was not going to be persuaded otherwise, Robert waited while Helen began snapping away. The stag remained still, obviously wary of them, but also unafraid. Its head was erect, its ears straight up and despite a gusting breeze, it remained motionless.

Watching us, watching you, Robert thought. Who is the master here?

"Oh look, there are more of them over on that side of the valley." She waved over to her right.

Robert put a hand on her shoulder. "That's enough waving. No matter what you think about relaxing, waving at a stag on his territory is not a wise move."

Helen gave him an impish smile.

"Can we retreat now?" He asked.

Helen hoisted up her camera bag and turned round. Robert took hold of her arm and stepped backwards, keeping the stag in view. He made it three steps before tumbling to the ground. Beneath him, he felt the contents of his rucksack crush and winced at the thought of what damage he had caused.

"What are you doing walking backwards on a hillside?" Helen was now shaking her head and laughing. "The stag isn't going to charge us, look."

Robert lifted his head and they both saw the stag lower its head to point its antlers at them at the same time. Looking at Helen, he saw her face whiten. He hurriedly scrambled up off the ground, grabbed her arm and shouted: "RUN!"

He didn't look back as they crested the small hill once more and set off down the other side. It had been a lovely walk up but running down, Robert struggled to keep his balance as the uneven ground pushed his feet off kilter.

"Are you okay?" Robert shouted at Helen.

"I can hear you fine." She shouted back. "Do you think it's stopped chasing us?"

Robert risked a glance back and saw the stag standing above them, his, no – it's head and antlers raised high, proudly guarding it's territory.

"Probably. But I don't think we should stop just yet."

"Can we at least slow down? If one of us breaks an ankle we are not going to be escaping anything."

"Maybe I should leave you behind then..."

Helen wrestled her arm out of his grip and punched him. "It'll be me leaving you behind in a minute."

She slowed down and Robert carried on for an instant until he realised she wasn't beside him. He stopped completely and turned only to see her racing by him.

"Who's the tortoise now?" She yelled as she passed him.

Laughing, Robert ran after her. She was pulling ahead but he forced himself to go faster until he could almost touch her. A part of his mind warned him they were going too fast. If either of them fell, they could both end up breaking a leg or arm. He tapped her on the shoulder.

"You're it." He shouted and then slowed.

Helen glanced back and realised he was no longer there. She slowed too and once he was sure they were not going too fast, he grabbed her and wrestled her to the ground.

"Careful of the camera." She yelled.

"I'll buy you a new one." Robert kissed her before she could say anything else.

Helen resisted the first three kisses but on the fourth her mouth softened and she kissed back. Before he could kiss her again, she pulled back and looked over his shoulder.

"It's not still chasing us is it?"

"I don't care anymore." Robert kissed her again.

"I really need to put this camera away."

"I said I'll buy you a new one."

"With my money?"

"I have money."

"All your money is mine, remember."

Robert attempted to unzip her jacket while distracting her with another kiss. Helen slapped his hand away and sat up.

"What's wrong?"

"Not going to happen."

Sighing dramatically, Robert sat up. "And here I was thinking we were on holiday."

"I don't know what kind of holiday you were thinking of."

"One where we get to spend a bit of quality time together?"

"Quality time doesn't always have to mean sex."

"We didn't have to have sex. Just a quick roll in the hay."

After checking it wasn't damaged, Helen put her camera in its bag. "On a hillside? In a popular walking area? You'll be lucky."

Grinning at her, Robert stood up. "That's what I was hoping." He gave her a last quick kiss which lengthened and then turned serious before pulling away to see her sigh.

"That's more like it." She said.

Robert pulled his map out of his coat pocket. "Where to now then? I hoped we could make it up Beinn Bhuidhe this afternoon."

"After all that running about? I'll be happy to head back to the B&B and have a bath."

"That is tempting."

"On my own!"

"Disappointing. Ah well." Robert studied the map. Beinn Bhuidhe was the only Munro within walking distance. He had chosen to try a different route to the one in the guide book – heading up Newton Hill from Glenfyne Lodge. If they circled round though...

"Look at this." He said, showing the map to Helen. "If we follow the treeline round we'll reach the Allt na Faing waterfall which takes us on the traditional route up to Beinn Bhuidhe."

"Is that really how you pronounce it?" Helen asked with a dead pan expression.

"I Googled it. We can basically circle past the stag and the other deer and still reach the Munro."

Helen gave him one of her amused smiles. "How many of these Munros are you expecting me to climb this week?"

Robert blew out his cheeks. He had been hoping to bag a cluster of four slightly further North before they had to head back to Glasgow but it maybe wasn't the best time to mention that.

"You know, we have done a lot of walking so far. How about you plan the itinerary the next couple of days?"

He saw her scrunch up her eyes and give him one of those searching looks she sometimes did when she wasn't sure she believed him.

"And what would tear you away from your ambition, Robert Castle?"

"I'm simply acknowledging that this is as much your holiday as it is mine, Mrs Castle."

"Speaking of castles..."

Robert smiled. Their ideas of what made a good holiday often diverged completely. The thought of spending a day, or even worse – a week, walking round old buildings filled him with despair. Yet Helen loved to explore museums and castles; abbeys and cathedrals, whenever they went to a new location.

"Yes?"

"Well, I saw in the guide book that there's a ruined castle on the peninsula... I wondered if we could drive out there later in the week."

"Sounds like a plan. Would you like to go there tomorrow?"

He took her arm and they set off North, in the direction of Allt na Faing.

"I would like that, yes, and maybe after that we could take the ferry across to Mull and see Duart Castle. It even has dungeons..."

Robert looked up at a blue sky with large Cumulus clouds scudding across. He kept half an ear listening to Helen as they walked but allowed his mind to drift and himself to relax and simply enjoy the walk.

****

"Who's that?"

Robert looked to where Helen was pointing and saw someone walking towards them. The man waved at them so Robert waved back.

"Is that a gun he's carrying?"

"Shotgun, yes. Must be a gamekeeper."

"I thought this was public land."

"It is. I think..."

Robert was suddenly unsure. There had been a deer fence around the wood but that was to protect the wood from the deer. They had followed the fence round until it had started to head down slope and were now following the contour around to the waterfall. "Must be looking after the deer."

"With a shotgun? Maybe he's a poacher..."

"Maybe. You want to ask him?"

They both quietened as the man approached.

"Good afternoon," Robert called.

"You'll need to leave the estate, sir. This is private land here."

"I thought this was public land."

"You're mistaken. This is a private estate."

The man stopped about six feet away. He was holding a double barrelled shotgun, pointed at the ground but Robert noted that the man's right hand was gripping the stock just behind the trigger guard. His left hand holding the barrel down and away yet it would not take much for him to swing it round and adjust his right hand to the trigger. Triggers, Robert corrected as he focused on them.

Helen put a hand against Robert's arm. "We're just heading up Beinn Bhuidhe. We're not lost are we?" She asked.

Robert saw her smile at the man but her smile was not returned.

"I'm sorry ma'am. You won't be able to head up any further. Now, I'm asking you nicely, you head down to the waterfall and you can take the road off of the estate."

"Don't we have a, what is it, right to roam now?"

"That's dependent on sticking to normal routes and responsible behaviour. I saw you both on the top of the hill. You can't behave like that near deer."

"We did nothing wrong. We chanced upon the deer, took some photos and then realised a stag was ready to charge us. What were we supposed to do? Stand still and let it gore us?"

Helen's hand tightened around Robert's arm.

"This isn't up for discussion. Turn around and head back down the hill."

"Is there another way we can get up Beinn Bhuidhe then?"

"I'm not aware of routes that don't cross this estate, now I'm not asking you and I'd rather not have to tell you again. Turn around now. Head back down the valley."

Robert fought down a desire to laugh at the ludicrousness of the situation.

"Perhaps you could show us on our map where the estate ends?" Helen asked.

"The estate ends at the main road."

"Wouldn't it take less time for us to leave the estate if we just climb Beinn Bhuidhe. How big is the estate anyway? We'll avoid the deer and be off the estate faster."

"There you go," Robert gave Helen a grin. "Trust my wife to come up with a sensible solution."

His grin faded quickly as the man raised his shotgun and pointed it towards them. "You are both trespassing. Turn around and head back down to the road."

"Robert, I think we better just go."

"Wait a minute, you can't just threaten us like that! What's your name?"

"I've asked you, told you and now I'm warning you, turn around."

"Who owns this estate? Is it you? Someone else?"

"Robert! Let's go." Helen tugged at his arm.

Robert took a step backwards. He was simultaneously terrified and furious. "Who owns this land?" He asked one more time. The man simply stared back, his shotgun steady.

Robert turned and put his arm around Helen as they hurried away. "How dare he!"

"Let's not talk until we're away from him, please."

"Okay, okay."

He took one more look back and saw the man, gamekeeper or something else, standing watching them. His shotgun still pointed in their direction.

****

CHAPTER TWO

"But this is Scotland. There's never been a law of trespass! I have a right to roam, don't I?"

"It is not as simple as that, Mr Castle and never has been. There is very little public land in Scotland. Most of it is privately owned although most large estate owners allow access to popular tourist areas. There are recognised rights of way but no-one has the right to walk wherever they want."

Robert turned and continued his pacing back and forth in front of the Station desk. He gave the Sergeant an angry glance. "Well, how am I supposed to know where I can and cannot walk? There were no signs. There was nothing to distinguish the hill from any other that I've walked up hundreds of times. We walked up a hill and were threatened with a gun. I would like to report that as a crime."

The Sergeant calmly watched Robert and then turned to a filing cabinet and pulled out a form. He confirmed Robert's name and began writing.

"Where did the incident happen?"

Robert pulled out his map and showed him. The Sergeant took a copy and then told him to draw the route they had taken.

"Okay, please tell me everything that was said when you were stopped by the man."

Robert recounted the conversation, uncomfortably realising he was already unsure exactly what had been said.

The Sergeant wrote everything down without comment but when Robert finished he stood for a moment, tapping his pen on the counter.

"The land you were on is private property. Based on what you've said a man who may or may not be the landowner asked you several times to leave private land. When you refused, he told you to leave and then ultimately threatened you with a shotgun."

"That's right."

"Why did he ask you to leave the estate?"

"He seemed to think we were threatening the deer. It was ridiculous."

The Sergeant started writing again.

"Wait, he didn't give us a chance to explain. There was a stag at the top of Newton Hill. We took some photos but then I fell and it looked as if it was going to charge at us so we ran. That's all that happened."

"I see. I'm going to ask you to come and take a seat in the interview room while I call the estate owner."

Lifting the counter, the Sergeant waved Robert through and then directed him into a small room with a desk and four chairs.

"Just wait here."

Robert watched the door close and suddenly felt claustrophobic. The Sergeant was gone fifteen minutes by which time Robert regretted not taking a newspaper or book to read.

"Well?" Robert asked, standing as the Sergeant came back in the room.

"Please sit down."

The Sergeant waited until Robert had taken his seat before sitting across from him.

"The estate owner has agreed not to press charges against you."

"I'm making a complaint against him, what right has he to press charges against me?"

"His estate manager observed you and your wife and became concerned about your behaviour. Despite asking you to leave the estate several times, you refused and became argumentative."

"Because we had done nothing wrong!"

"Mr Castle, SOAC was introduced to make it clear that both land owners and visitors to the country have rights and responsibilities. From what you have said and the estate manager has confirmed, it was reasonable for him to demand you leave the estate. If you are given a reasonable request to leave private land then you have a responsibility to honour that request."

"You're saying he had a right to threaten me and my wife with a gun?"

"The estate manager felt he had no choice but to defend himself."

"Defend himself? Against what? Do I look dangerous to you!"

"Please, lower your voice, Mr Castle."

"This isn't right."

"You mentioned 'Right to Roam' earlier. There has never been a right to roam in Scotland. I strongly advise you to read through the Scottish Outdoor Access Code."

"That's not what I meant."

"I know what you meant, Mr Castle. How would you feel if someone walked into your garden or home and refused to leave?"

"That's not the same."

The Sergeant looked as if he was going to respond then stopped himself.

"I also advise you to avoid returning to the estate. What are your plans for the rest of your stay?"

Robert stood.

"We'll stay away. Can I get the incident number before I go?"

****

The B&B was set back from the main road: an old converted farmhouse that must have once belonged to a wealthy farmer. Two stories tall and with enough rooms to have held several generations of farmers at the same time. It was painted in the same white as all the houses in Inveraray even though it stood alone in its own grounds.

Leaving the police station, Robert had sat in his car for several minutes before driving off. His initial anger at being threatened had turned to frustration at the police Sergeant's reaction. Robert had a sense that there was something intrinsically wrong with what had happened in Glen Fyne but other than the threat of violence, he couldn't identify what was disturbing him.

Arriving at the B&B he parked the car in the farmhouse's vast courtyard alongside several other cars. The B&B was full as was almost every other in this small town. The good weather had seemingly brought people out to the countryside in their hundreds.

Robert had expected to meet more people earlier in the day when they attempted their walk along Glen Fyne but perhaps others had been warned to stay away. He would have to ask the B&B owner if she knew.

Letting himself in, Robert walked along the hallway, leading into the back of the house and then took the stairs up to their room. It wasn't en-suite – they had to share a shower room and bathroom with other guests on their floor. Not ideal but since it had been the first booking available in Inveraray for these dates, they had booked it rather than spend any more hours phoning round other locations.

He paused by their room door, knocked and called through: "Only me."

Opening the door he saw Helen sitting up on the bed, a mostly empty glass of red wine in her hand. She turned her head slowly to look at him.

"How much have you had." He whispered after he had closed the door.

"This is my first glass."

"Cheap date." He replied with a smile.

"Did you make your complaint?" She asked.

Robert took a deep breath and let it out slowly, then went and poured himself a glass of the wine. "You want a top up?"

Helen shook her head. "No, I could fall asleep right now."

"We haven't had our dinner yet."

She gave him a half smile and he realised she had been crying. "Helen..."

He put down his glass and sat down beside her. Putting an arm around her he gently took her glass and placed it on the bedside cabinet. "It's all right, nothing happened. We're safe."

"I know, but he pointed that gun at us. I keep seeing it. Then we turned away and I thought he was going to shoot us in the back."

Robert handed her a tissue and she dabbed her face. He thought back to their walk returning to the car and then the drive home. He had talked almost the whole way about the injustice of it, the cheek, the bloody-mindedness of the estate manager. Helen had responded, he thought, but only to what he had been saying. He hadn't once asked her how she felt, what she was thinking.

"I'm sorry. I should've asked you how you were."

"I was so scared. I thought you were going to do something stupid. Fight him, try and take the gun off him. I thought..." Helen began sobbing.

Pulling her close, Robert held her until she calmed.

"Do you want me to see if I can get some food taken up for you?"

Helen nodded.

"Okay. I'll be back soon."

****

Helen felt a lone tear fall down her cheek. She abruptly wiped it away. This wasn't like her. She wasn't someone who fell apart, who got hysterical.

She held out a hand. It was no longer trembling. Helen tried to remember if she had ever lost it so completely... Then stopped herself. She was going to get over this. She picked up the wine glass and took a tiny sip.

Normally Robert went off and climbed his Munro's on his own. They holidayed together visiting places where she could enjoy architecture and art while Robert could rest, reading, enjoying the local coffee or laze on a beach.

For several years they had travelled to Europe. Time spent in Prague, Barcelona and Venice had been amazing. Then the recession hit and while they still travelled, they stayed in the UK, exploring cathedral cities and countryside. But always South of the border.

It just had seemed right to try a week in Scotland. Try climbing together. See some of Scotland's heritage. Helen couldn't believe she had never driven North of Loch Lomond.

They were only two days into this holiday and had planned a whole week. She wasn't going to let this one dismal day ruin the rest of her time.

She set the wine glass back down on the cabinet. It hadn't helped relax her. Numb wasn't relaxed, it was dead. She didn't want to feel dead.

Helen curled up on the bed and pulled the comforter over her. Another tear fell to the sheet below.

****

Robert found Mrs Jackson in her kitchen. There was a scent of herbs and lamb along the corridor and a large pot of stew bubbling on the gas stove.

"Ah, there you are, Mr Castle. We'll be serving dinner in ten minutes."

He smiled at her. "I was wanting to ask, we had a, uh, fright while we were walking and Helen was quite upset by it. Would there be any chance I could take some food up to the room for her?"

"A fright? What kind of a fright?"

"Well, we went up Glen Fyne this morning, heading up Beinn Bhuidhe, but we detoured a bit and got stopped by the estate manager. He refused to let us past and threatened us with a shotgun."

"The estate manager? You say you detoured, where were you stopped?"

"Near Newton Hill, up from Glenfyne Lodge."

"I don't know Glen Fyne very well. It's not a popular walking route. Most people tend to stop at the Oyster Bar or the Brewery. It seems strange that you would have been stopped though. Did the estate manager say why?"

Robert thought back to his experience at the police station.

"He believed we were behaving inappropriately near a herd of deer."

Mrs Jackson tilted her head and frowned at this.

"Were you?"

"No. Of course not. We reached the top of Newton Hill and a stag was there – a magnificent creature. We took some photos but when we went to leave I, uh, tripped and it looked like it was going to charge so we ran. The estate manager must have seen us but..."

Straightening, Mrs Jackson weighed up what he had said.

"This isn't the city, Mr Castle. Landowners have a responsibility to protect the deer on their land. Visitors also have a responsibility. You can't blame someone for doing their job."

"But threaten us with a gun? That can't be right?"

Mrs Jackson turned away to stir the stew. "I can understand why your wife would be upset by that. You can always report it to the police if you feel it necessary."

"I did."

"What did they say?"

Robert was beginning to get irritated by all the questions. It felt like he was back at the police station.

"They sided with the estate manager."

"I see."

Admitting to himself that Mrs Jackson had more sympathy for the estate manager herself than with them, Robert decided it was time to leave. He was about to turn away when Mrs Jackson started speaking again.

"If I remember correctly, the Ardkinglas estate used to be over twenty thousand acres. I don't know if you were walking on that estate or not but large plots of land have been sold off over the years making dozens of mini estates. It is quite possible you were on one of the smaller estates. They often get sold off with sporting rights in which case the estate manager may have been trying to ensure you didn't scare the deer away."

"Why wouldn't he have said that?"

"I'm not the person you should be asking."

She turned back to the stove and spoke over her shoulder. "I'll put food on two trays. You can pick them up in ten minutes."

Robert thanked her and headed out of the kitchen. As he walked down the corridor he thought he heard her saying to herself. "Our land no longer."

****

"I can collect our dinner in a few minutes." Robert said as he closed their room door behind him.

Helen didn't respond and he walked over to her side of the bed and knelt by her.

"Helen?"

She made a slight sound.

"Do you want to eat?"

"Not hungry." She answered. Her eyes hadn't opened.

Robert looked round and found a rug on a shelf. After

placing it carefully over her, he stood for a moment looking down. Her breathing was relaxed. He brushed some hairs away from her face and then left. They'd only need one plate after all.

****

She woke first, suddenly, which was unusual for her even when the alarm was blaring. Beside her Robert was still, his breathing slow. She turned on her back and stared at the coving which surrounded the old high ceiling. A sign of wealth when the house had been built. All those extra stones laid for no purpose other than to show how much the family had been worth. Much like their own house.

She thought back to the previous day on the hillside and shivered. Had she ever been that scared? Even her work with the homeless had never left her feeling so wiped out. Drugged up or drunk men and women who threatened violence had just become situations to handle. Not a normal part of the work but not unusual.

Yesterday she had for the first time in her life believed Robert was going to get himself killed. She had been afraid for herself but was utterly convinced that if he did not stop pushing that man he would have been shot.

She reached out a hand and felt him move. She didn't want to wake him but wanted to hold him. To be held.

Robert turned to face her, a puzzled look on his face. "What time is it?" He asked.

"Hold me."

He searched her eyes and then leaned back, drawing her onto him, his arms secure around her. She buried her face in his chest and allowed her eyes to fill up as the emotions she had felt the previous day rose up again.

Robert seemed to know not to ask. He just held her.

After some time her thoughts began to order themselves. She had been enjoying their holiday up till then. She determined there and then that the previous day's event was not going to ruin their week away. Even if Robert wanted to climb another of those monotonous Munro's… No, maybe not that but they were going to enjoy the rest of their time.

She pulled away and looked up at Robert. "Didn't you say we could visit a castle today?"

He smiled. "You have one right here..."

She gave him a friendly punch.

"I may have mentioned it."

She sat up and wiped her eyes. "Promise me you won't go picking a fight with any of the locals."

He seemed to examine her for a minute, his eyes searching hers. He just nodded in response.

Helen extracted herself from the bed and made for the bathroom. Turning, she looked at Robert.

"Do you think we can put yesterday behind us?"

Robert sat up and ran his hand through his hair. "I want to see a solicitor when we get back."

She considered this and decided it wasn't worth arguing over. "Can we at least not talk about it the rest of the holiday?"

She could see that he didn't want to agree to it but he nodded. "Of course."

"Do you think we can be ready in half an hour?"

Robert picked up his watch and checked the time. "It's not even Six. Breakfast isn't served until Seven."

"We can find a cafe on the way."

He raised his eyebrows. "This isn't Glasgow..."

"I'm sure you'll find somewhere..."

He didn't look convinced but his eyes took on a distant look and she knew he was working through options. She closed the bathroom door and studied herself in the mirror. She didn't wear makeup so there had been no mascara to run. After a quick shower it wouldn't look as if she'd been crying.

She closed her eyes and saw the shotgun pointed at them. She forced herself to examine the scene, to accept it but also to reject it. She was not going to be controlled by fear.

****

Kildrein Castle was a castle no more – just a collection of old walls with a couple of stone staircases you could walk up to get a higher view of the surrounding countryside. Robert had separated from Helen and was walking around by himself, trying not to think about the previous day.

Hunger was not much of a distraction. He'd driven through Lochgilphead only to find everywhere they might have liked to eat had been closed. They'd stopped at a garage and bought day old sandwiches, snacks and expensive coffee all of which had helped but it hadn't been the same as a full Scottish.

There were a couple of nice cafes and a decent pub on the peninsula and he intended to make up for it at lunch.

The ruins of the castle sat in a grassy field, surrounded by a dry stone wall. Robert estimated the field was less than an acre in size. Once, when considering buying a plot of land, he had paced out an acre – to get an idea of the size of land he might be buying. It was larger than he had thought.

In the end he had procrastinated over investing the £50,000 being asked. It would have involved liquidating all his investments and taking out a £30,000 loan. He could possibly have persuaded Helen to agree to it – after all it had been in a lovely village on the East coast of Scotland. Not far from St Andrews. Very posh. He found himself smiling at the thought of them both – Glasgow East-enders – living among the pseudo-rich Edinburgh commuters.

That had been what, ten years ago and of course, there had been other considerations. That took his smile away. He closed his eyes tightly, trying to shut out the memory, then felt a hand on his shoulder.

Turning and blinking, he saw an older gentleman smiling at him.

"Everything alright, sir?"

"Yes, yes, trying to get into the spirit of vacation."

"Not always easy." The man removed his hand and offered it to Robert. "Angus Donaldson – retiree." He winked.

Shaking the man's hand, Robert introduced himself. "Are you holidaying here as well?"

"Good heavens, no. I just live down the road – in Tayvallich. But I walk up here a few times a week, when the weather permits, and enjoy the quietness. At least until the tourists arrive..." He gave another wink.

"I'm here with my wife." Robert looked around and saw her taking a close up photo of one of the castle walls. "That's her. Keen photographer."

"Not something I have any skill for, I confess."

"Nor me. I just enjoy looking at the results. Have you always lived here?"

Donaldson nodded forwards in invitation and began a gentle stroll. "Yes. All my life."

"I often wonder what it would be like to move out of the city, out to the country. But then I think I would miss all the amenities. Do you mind my asking what you do? Or perhaps did, before you retired?"

"Certainly. You might say I was a man of the land." He gave Robert another of his winks.

Robert stopped. "A farmer?"

Donaldson realised Robert was no longer beside him and turned back. "No, no." He gave a self-deprecating smile. "I own the estate. This castle in fact – at least, what's left of it." He gestured expansively at the old ruins.

"You own this?" Robert felt himself tense but forced himself to relax.

"Indeed. The castle; the land around Tayvallich; in fact, most of the peninsula."

Robert tried to visualise the shape and size of the peninsula from the map they had looked at while driving here. "You own the peninsula?"

"Most of it. There are a lot of small plots which have been sold off to tenants over the last hundred years or so. It's really not that large an estate. Only just over five thousand acres now. But I do have my castle."

There was another little wink and Robert realised how irritating he was beginning to find the man's habit.

"Do you allow people access to the land?" Robert found himself asking.

Donaldson looked confused by the question.

"To walk on. Do you allow people to walk around the estate?"

"Well, of course." He smiled. "I'm not holding a gun on you now, am I?"

Robert didn't return the smile and slowly Donaldson's faded.

"Is there something wrong?"

"My wife and I were threatened by a..." Robert was going to say gamekeeper but stopped himself. "An estate manager. Yesterday. He pointed his shotgun at us and demanded we get off his estate."

Donaldson blew out his cheeks. "Where was this?"

"On the slopes of Beinn Bhuidhe. Near Newton Hill."

"Glen Fyne... That estate isn't what it used to be. Large areas sold off over the years to pay off various debts. Belonged to the

Campbell's originally and has had a few owners since. I believe the City of Glasgow purchased a large portion around Lochgoilhead. All public land now. But Glen Fyne? I haven't kept up with all the minutiae: parcels of land sold off all over the Glen."

"So I've heard. Is it common for estate owners to threaten people who are on their land?"

"Well, not without reason."

Helen put her arm through his and gave him a gentle nudge in the ribs.

"Robert! You must introduce me."

Distracted, Robert turned to see his wife smiling at Donaldson.

"This is the most beautiful castle." She said.

"Uh, Angus Donaldson, this is my wife, Helen."

Helen held out her hand and Donaldson took it, placing his left hand over hers.

"Delighted to meet you, Helen. I'm glad you like my castle."

"Your castle? You own this? It must have been magnificent in its day."

"I've heard it was. Unfortunately burnt down in the late eighteen hundreds. I might be living here today if not for that."

"Imagine that Robert, owning your own castle? Well, it is very kind of you to allow us to view it."

"I would be happy to give you a tour."

"That would be wonderful, wouldn't it, Robert." She gave him a look which did not quite match the wide smile on her face.

"Yes, dear."

Helen wrinkled her nose in disgust at that little jab but offered her arm to Donaldson and he led her towards the Northern staircase, Robert following behind.

****

CHAPTER THREE

Robert opened his eyes and looked at his alarm clock: 06:07. He felt wide awake. For the first time since they had been stopped by the estate manager, he had slept the whole night. Maybe just being back in their own bed had helped.

He checked Helen but she was fast asleep. He lay there for a couple of minutes but it only allowed his train of thought to solidify and without conscious thought, he was sitting up and then trying to silently dress before heading downstairs.

The laptop whirred into life when he lifted the lid. He entered his password and stared at the screen while programs loaded. He was going to have to clear out some of the junk that was slowing it down. He opened Firefox and brought up the Google search page. Then began typing: trespass law in Scotland.

He tried a few of the top returned links and then went back to the search page and changed the search terms: right to roam Scotland.

****

His back was stiff from being hunched over his laptop. Robert arched his back, leaning left and right and moving his shoulders up and down. He had intended to get his head round the thoughts that were troubling him. Try and organise them;

find some order in the chaos but every strand he pursued opened up new leads and the evidence was everywhere. Everywhere and yet raising more questions than it answered.

Robert adjusted his laptop and loaded up a new document. Pausing before he started to type, Robert looked over at his Kindle. He had bought and downloaded one book this morning but had only skimmed the first couple of chapters. Still, it highlighted one of his concerns. He began to type:

Who owns Scotland?

Carriage return, new line. What else, he thought.

Do we have democracy?

What do people want?

To live in peace, he mentally answered himself. To get on with it. To be able to work... He started a new line.

Why are there not enough jobs?

Why are there so many people on benefits?

Why is our country in so much debt?

Why can't we stop our Government spending so much?

Why do we let our Government get away with so much?

Robert stabbed at the enter key at the end of that line. MP's expenses; detention without trial; forcing through legislation that no-one voted for in spite of public protests. It was almost like Britain was becoming a dictatorship.

He took a deep breath and blew it out. So many problems. So many wrongs. The SNP claimed they were giving Scotland independence but all it would do is grant the MSPs themselves more power. As far as Robert could see, the Scottish people would gain nothing and that was why he'd joined the No campaign. But it wouldn't matter if they won their campaign against independence. Nothing was going to change.

He stood up, then sat down. There was an idea. Almost formed but he'd lost it. Robert shook his head. If it was worth considering it would appear again.

He had sent several web pages to the printer already. He clicked save on the document he had started and sent that to print as well, then got up and put on the kettle.

He stood at the kitchen window as he waited. A dozen thoughts were fighting for space in his head. He'd only scratched the surface but was now aware of a history of Scotland that had never been taught to him in school.

He focused on the garden. It was just grass with paving

where they held barbeques; some lawn furniture and a couple of fruit trees. He had never had any interest in gardening, except, that wasn't completely true, was it?

Walking through to the sitting room, Robert studied their book shelf and found a thick hardback he'd purchased several years before. He'd bought it on the back of reading an article which suggested it was possible to provide vegetables all year round from just nine square metres of ground. The book gave a suggested plan for dividing the area into smaller raised beds.

He'd even bought a garden fork and spade only to gradually forget about the book as rain had blighted several successive weekends.

The kettle finished boiling and clicked off. Robert glanced at it then looked back at the garden. Then up at the sky. It was blue.

****

One hour later Robert leaned back and stretched, hoping the pain in his back would ease. He looked at the tiny plot he'd manage to dig, not even a square metre. It couldn't really take that long to dig up a garden, could it?

He liked to think of himself as fit but obviously running didn't do anything for the muscles he'd been using for the last hour.

The big question he'd had when he'd bought the book was whether providing 'enough vegetables all year round' was only supposed to be a supplement or whether nine square metres could actually provide all your vegetables for the entire year.

It didn't seem possible but then again, in centuries past in Scotland people had subsisted on less land without the techniques and technologies available today. If it was possible to grow enough vegetables to feed your family on such a small plot of land then if every family in Scotland did so, the cost savings would be immense.

Maybe it was only possible if you had a back reinforced with iron.

He'd spent a full hour digging and redigging one square metre. The results looked like what he thought a plot ready for vegetables should look like but had he gone about it the wrong way?

He now had a pile of muddy grass clods and weeds. Would he be better roughly digging the whole plot once over and then leaving the sun, wind and rain to break up the clods before he redug it over? He decided to give it a go.

****

Helen woke an hour later and padded downstairs to make some tea. She found Robert's laptop on the kitchen table next to some papers but no Robert.

She walked over to the kettle and lifted it. It had water in. She switched it on and looked up, out the window. Her hand went involuntarily to her mouth. He's flipped, she thought. Finally lost it.

A few minutes later she carried out two mugs into the garden.

"Oh, you're a life saver!" Robert went to kiss her but she shied away.

"Have you seen yourself?" She took in his mud smeared face, hair glistening with sweat. "What are you doing?"

"Isn't it obvious?"

"That you've lost your mind? Maybe. You've never shown an interest in the garden before."

"I had an inspiration."

Helen handed him his mug. "What time did you get up?"

"Six."

"You've been in the garden since Six?"

"I did some research first."

"Should I ask what on?"

"Probably best not."

"Just call the solicitor tomorrow. He'll know if there's anything you can do. You remembering it's Sunday?"

"Mmm." Robert looked at her, then frowned. "Church. Better get some breakfast."

Helen surveyed the small patch of half dug soil. "How many bodies did you bury?"

"Ha, ha." Robert deadpanned. "I'm going to grow some vegetables."

"I see." Helen sighed. One downside to marrying an ambitious, motivated man was the countless projects he managed to dream up. A few petered out but all of them took up time and energy. Well, life was never dull.

"I'll see you inside." She left him drinking his coffee and went to make breakfast.

****

"Should Scotland be an independent country?" Robert dropped his newspaper next to his empty plate on the kitchen table.

"It's better than the original. Less of a leading question." Helen smiled as Robert grimaced.

"Shouldn't be asking the question in the first place. Waste of time and money."

"Is that a hint that you're regretting signing up to campaign for the No party?"

Robert leant forward and slowly banged his head on the table. "Why didn't we stay away on holiday for another week?" He said in a muffled voice.

"Bills to pay, jobs to go to, No party to attend..."

"I wish you wouldn't call them that." Sitting up, he stretched then stood. "One of these days I'm going to end up shouting it out and that'll be the end of my political career."

"You couldn't make it in politics, you'd end up punching someone and getting arrested."

"Getting a medal possibly. Depends who was on the receiving end..." Robert yawned. "Can't believe we're back at work tomorrow. You all set?"

"Yes. What time should I prepare dinner for?"

"I'm not sure I'll be back for dinner. If the solicitor's available I'll just go and see him and will need to work late to make up the time."

"Can't you just take some longer lunch breaks?"

"Current manager is rather rigid when it comes to flexibility. I suspect he'll complain that I'm daring to book an appointment during working hours. Then I was thinking I'll just head straight to the Stronger United meeting."

"See you next weekend then..."

"I'm not doing anything Wednesday evening."

"I've got that night out with my friends."

"Ah. Next weekend then."

Helen held out her hand and Robert took it.

"Oh well..." Robert sighed. "At least I'm not going to the Big IF this weekend."

Helen gazed calmly at him. "Sure you still want to go? You could always drop out."

"I can't... Well, I could." He held her gaze. "I'm going to go. If I don't do something..."

"Hmm. You do enough."

"Not nearly enough. I saw a post on Facebook last week. This guy sitting next to Jesus. He asks: Why do you allow all the hunger and violence and abuse to exist in the world. Jesus responds: Funny, I was just about to ask you that."

Helen gave a sad smile. "I guess that sums it up."

****

Robert swiped his pass on the RFID scanner and slowed, listening for the approving beep. The range of RFID appeared to be appalling though he had once read they should be able to pick up a signal from metres away. Maybe that had adverse security implications he wondered, ignoring the lifts and heading for the stairs at the back of the lobby.

He had been working in this particular company for almost four months and was already beginning to wonder if his six month contract would have to be extended. Something he would have to discuss with Jim – his manager – that morning.

Placing his rucksack – with laptop – carefully on his desk, Robert greeted April and Ken, both of whom were always there before him no matter how early he turned up; and rarely seemed to leave. He was thankful this company had chosen to give him a semi-permanent desk. Hot desking in an environment where people worked flexible hours was always a disaster: he frequently picked an empty desk only to be asked to move once the owner turned up.

He logged into the company's network – on their computer, while waiting for his own to boot up. It didn't take long for him to forget he had been on holiday the previous fortnight and bring himself up to speed with email discussions about the project. His suspicion that he would need to discuss the project goals with Jim confirmed, Robert sent a meeting invitation and then began reviewing the project plan.

****

"Do you want the project completed in the next two months?"

"Only if you can't deliver it in the next one." Jim looked amused.

"I absolutely could complete the project in the next one month." Robert slid over his project plan. "Just tell me which components you want me to cut."

Jim sat back in his chair. "What's the problem, Robert?"

"The system is growing arms and legs. I don't have a problem with changing the scope of the project, the specification or designs but I need you to be aware of the requests I'm getting and the implications of my acting on them."

"What sort of requests?"

"The usual kind. I see this all the time. Because I go and speak with the business, I make them aware of possibilities. I was speaking with Peter before I went on holiday to clarify what reports his team would need from the system and while I've been away he's sent me a dozen emails asking if the system can integrate with a spreadsheet his team uses; if they can use the system to track what his team does; and even if the system can produce a rota for them."

"A rota? What has that got to do with..."

"Nothing." Robert shook his head, smiling to ease a tension that he sensed was building up in the room. "It is normal though. We want these teams to feel they have ownership of the new system. We want to show them this can improve the situation but the flip side is that once they start to own it, they also, quite rightly, want to direct what it does. They start to see other ways it can be used to simplify their workload, automate processes. Ways you and I never considered."

"So are you saying we should take on board what is being asked for?"

"Absolutely not. No. I made it clear when you hired me that I aim to be flexible but that you are my key stakeholder. You are the one investing in this project and you have the ultimate say in what is delivered. I need you to look at what is being asked for, look at the impact I think it will have on development time and decide whether the additions are more important to you, to the business as a whole than some of the original plans.

"I can complete the original project as agreed by the original deadline. Or I can complete a revised project by the original deadline. Or, and this is at your discretion, you can accept some or all of the additional requests and we can extend the project deadline. I would always recommend that if you choose the third option that you get a funding commitment from the requesting teams. I find being asked to pay for their requests has a way of clarifying what they are really interested in."

Robert tapped the project plan. "I've added in all the new requests and placed them on the plan as lowest priority. I've estimated how long I think they will take to complete. Currently this adds another two months to the plan."

"I see." Jim looked away towards the glass wall, staring out into the open plan office. "You know, I had a feeling when I hired you that you'd turn out like every contractor I've ever met. Only interested in extending your contract as long as possible."

Suddenly very conscious of his body language, Robert sat up straight. "If you would like me to deliver the original requirements by the original deadline I will do that."

"Did you suggest to Peter what you could do for him?"

"He asked me if the system could help with several issues his team is having. I told him there may be scope to help and that he should discuss these issues with you. Did he do that?"

"He hasn't said a word."

"I'll forward on his emails." Robert waited for a response but Jim seemed to be waiting for him. "How would you like me to proceed?"

Jim pulled the project plan towards him without looking at it and folded the A3 sheet in half. "Leave it with me." He said.

"There's one more thing." Robert told him.

Jim narrowed his eyes.

"I've arranged an appointment with my solicitor for an hour this afternoon. I'll work late tonight to make up the time."

Jim took a sharp breath. Robert waited, wondering if he was about to witness an outburst but Jim just grunted in acknowledgement.

Robert stood. "Thank you for your time." He walked out, wondering what had just happened.

****

"I hate style sheets!" Helen glared at her computer monitor, then realised her boss was staring at her. "Sorry." She said, turning to him.

Stephen Alwyn raised his eyebrows. "Cup of tea?"

She nodded.

They got up, walked two metres over to the office tea trolley and Stephen filled the kettle from the sink. He asked Sylvia if she wanted a cup too and the sole three employees of Glasgow Homeless Shelter stood round waiting for it to boil.

"Problems with the website?" Stephen asked.

"Style sheets were supposed to make websites easier to manage but even after six years of working with them I still get confused. I really need to properly document everything but never seem to find the time. I'm not a coder, never wanted to be one. Give me a poster to design and I'll be in my element but this..."

"The website's really good though." Sylvia said.

"Thanks, but it needs constant updating or it will start to look out of date. If I knew more about server side scripts... Sorry." Helen saw Stephen rolling his eyes and Sylvia start to lose focus. "If I could figure out a way to build a template maybe I could cut down on a lot of the work."

"Could we hire someone in?" Stephen asked.

Helen shook her head. "We don't have the budget. Even a junior contractor would clean us out and I doubt a junior contractor would have the knowledge to create the sort of system we need."

"Could Robert..." Stephen began to ask but tailed off.

"It's not his area. Databases sure. If this was an application, definitely but he never went down the web route. No, I just need to get my head together and figure it out."

****

"Mr Castle, take a seat." Mr Armstrong gestured to a chair in front of his desk and walked round to his own. "Now, how can I help you?"

"There are a couple of things I wanted to ask your advice on." Robert opened a leather folder he had brought with him containing his notes. "Helen and I were walking in Argyll last week. We were accused of trespassing by someone I believe was an estate manager and then he pointed a shotgun at us and demanded we leave the property immediately."

Armstrong pulled a yellow legal pad in front of him and began making neat notes. "Had you climbed over a wall or fence?"

"No. We parked the car on the main road, on the grass verge. Got out and started walking up the valley."

"Which valley?"

"Glen Fyne."

"Oh yes. A lovely area."

"It is. We, well, I wanted to climb some of the Munros around the valley and we started up one slope towards Beinn Bhuidhe, but we ran into a stag and surprised it and ended up retreating back down."

The solicitor smiled. "Surprised a stag? Did it chase you?"

"Well, it lowered its antlers and we didn't look back once we started running."

"I see. Go on."

Robert wondered how the man could write so quickly and yet produce neat notes. "We tried another route up Beinn Bhuidhe and were maybe a third of the way up the slope when we saw a man approach." Robert described the encounter, checking his own notes of the incident as he spoke.

When Robert finished, Armstrong sat back and studied him. "And you came to see me because?"

"Because we were threatened. By a man with a gun. I can see no justifiable reason why he would have needed to point a shotgun at us. We didn't threaten him in any way. We would have left, I just wanted to find out why we had to leave and who it was that owned the land."

"You said you reported this to the police. What was their response?"

"They almost charged me. They called the estate owner who accused us of behaving irresponsibly. They advised me to stay away from the estate."

"Do you feel the police should have responded differently?"

"He pointed a gun at me. I thought that was illegal."

Armstrong shook his head. "I'm no expert in criminal law but I've had some dealings with trespass in the past. There are differences even between the rights of a home owner and a land owner in this regard. A home owner may defend him or herself, with a licensed firearm if they own one. But it is still possible to be arrested for pointing a gun at someone, even if you are in your own home.

"If you are on private land however, land which you own or – in the case of an estate manager – you are responsible for, it is not considered by law to be unacceptable to enforce your rights with a firearm."

"But how were we to know that was private land?"

"That is a good question. If there were no fences; no walls, then you had no way of knowing you were trespassing. It would have been polite to ask you to leave. Sensible to have answered a few questions, to explain why you were not allowed there. But, and this is where the law is very clear – once you were asked to leave, and you refused to do so, the land owner is allowed to use reasonable force to evict you."

"Even shooting us?"

"He did not actually shoot, did he?"

"Well, no."

"Pointing a gun can be considered reasonable force. A warning if you like. Not nice to be on the receiving end but better than being shot without warning."

"Is there anything we can do?"

"In my opinion – you did the right thing in asking the questions. However, you had no right to the answers. Unfortunate but true. You also did the right thing in informing the police – but no crime had actually been committed. However, if you have been accused of behaving irresponsibly on private land then without proof that you were not, it is simply their word against yours. You may have been fortunate to get away with a warning. If the estate owner had decided to press charges it could have been very costly even if you managed a successful defence. I'm sorry, but I would not advise taking this further."

****

Back in the office, Robert found another email from Peter waiting for him. He forwarded it onto Jim after a quick read. It was a typical email and Robert wondered briefly if Jim felt threatened by Peter.

Peter managed several teams himself, all of whom used the

system Jim had brought him in to modify. He had been part of the original working group that had agreed the specification but having read through some of the minutes, Peter had wanted to go further than the agreed plan. The proposals he had made all were backed up by analysis into cost savings that would result. Even head count reduction in his own teams which was not something Robert usually found managers willing to consider. Usually managers protected their own territory fiercely, suspecting – probably correctly – that any head count reduction was likely to result in them losing a degree of power or income.

He had forwarded Peter's email on as he'd told Jim he'd do but Robert thought he would need to speak to Peter directly rather than just writing back. He picked up the phone.

****

"Thanks for seeing me this afternoon." Robert pulled a chair over to Peter's desk and sat down, conscious they were in a large open plan office with Peter's teams surrounding them. He lowered his voice. "I met with Jim this morning. He made it clear to me that he wants the project to stay on target to complete in two months."

"And no diversions from the plan...?"

"He said he would look over the additional proposals but I got the impression the goal is fixed."

"I've been trying to set up a meeting with him for a couple of weeks now but his calendar is permanently full and he won't pick up my calls or respond to my emails."

"Have you tried seeing him in person?"

"Walked down to his desk a couple of times but he wasn't there."

Robert spread his hands apologetically. "I think your proposals are worth tackling but ultimately I've been employed by Jim and he, how do I put this... He expressed concern at the idea of changing the project specifications."

"I've heard his attitude described in more colourful terms. Well, thanks for trying. Maybe we'll have to get you back after your current project ends."

Robert stood. "I'd be glad to work with you. You have my estimates and business plan? If you need me to put together a revised estimate based on a standalone project I can provide that in my own time."

****

Pulling up outside the community centre, Robert noted the four cars already there. The usual suspects: Colin; Martha; Abed; and June. It was likely Allan was also there having only had to walk across the street.

This was confirmation their holiday was well and truly over. No more castles to walk round, no more hill walking, back to work this morning and now: Monday evening and the weekly meeting of the 'Stronger United' campaign. The No Party as Helen had taken to calling them.

She had joined him once, on the first meeting. Smiled, nodded, left afterwards and once safely out of range had vowed never to return. "I volunteer at the Shelter twice a week and if I had time I'd be there a third night. One minute spent there is more useful than that entire pompous disgrace of a campaign!"

He had almost stayed away himself but before the week was out he had found himself wrestling with the conviction that if he did nothing to prevent the attempt to dissolve the Union, he would never be able to live with himself. Certainly he wondered if he would find himself unable to stay in Scotland and that was something he couldn't bear to contemplate.

Robert shook his head and walked through the door.

"Robert! Good to see you back." Colin was hovering near the entrance and immediately offered his hand.

Greeting Colin, Robert wondered if he was there to welcome strangers or turn them away. "I was only away a fortnight."

"A lot can change in two weeks!"

"Has it?"

"Well, no. But it could."

Robert smiled and clapped Colin on the shoulder before making his way to the main room. Seven chairs were pulled round a large table. Allan was there as were Abed, June and Martha. He said hello and sat down.

"First order of business." June said. "How was your holiday?"

Robert hesitated and then decided to share the events of Glen Fyne.

"...The rest of the holiday was uneventful." He finished up

by saying.

The others just stared at him.

"He tried to shoot you?" Martha asked.

"No, no. He pointed a gun at us. He threatened to shoot but that was all."

"Hardly all." Colin said, joining them at the table. "You're lucky you kept a cool head on you."

"Helen was the cool one. I'm not sure I handled the situation as well as I might." Robert shook his head ruefully. "It has made me think though, what is it we are fighting for?"

"We're stronger united!"

"To preserve the Union."

"We need each other."

"Yes, absolutely, yet why is it that I was not able to walk up a hill in my own country? If we win the referendum that won't change."

"This isn't about petty issues, Robert." Allan spoke for the first time. "Independence for Scotland will set us back decades."

"I'm suggesting that while their arguments are flawed, the Yes campaign have the positive bias in their favour. They are fighting for something."

"But we are fighting for something." Martha frowned.

"I think we need more. I value living in the UK, being part of Britain as much as everyone here but it has been a long time since this country deserved to call itself Great."

"You sure that man didn't bang you on the head while you were up that mountain."

"I'm pretty sure, Abed. I had a lot of time to think and to be honest, I'm not sure we're going about this in the right way."

"Let's talk about this later Robert." Allan said firmly. "We'll bring you up to speed on what's been happening while you've been away and get on with the agenda."

Robert nodded politely and fixed a smile on his face while Allan got on with the meeting.

****

"You need to get your focus back, Robert." Allan said in a low voice as they stood at the side of the room.

The others were returned to the table after making teas and coffees while Robert had stayed standing, Allan then joining him.

"And why is that?"

"We are going to struggle to win this campaign if we don't remain focused on the goal."

"And the goal is to keep things the way they are?"

"Yes. Of course."

"I don't like the way things are now. Millions unemployed. Millions more trapped on benefits. Government chipping away at my rights while increasing the tax burden. Landowners still have more rights than the common man: the rich laugh and hide their money away while the rest of us pay for their excess."

"Maybe you should join the Socialists."

"I'm already a card holder."

Allan gave him a double look. "You are joking, right?"

Robert took a sip of his coffee and decided not to answer. "What does it matter when all we want is to maintain the status quo?"

Allan sighed. "We need you to believe in what we're fighting for."

"I'm trying to, Allan. Trust me."

****

Instead of taking the turning for home, Robert headed straight on towards the river. Parking, he sat in the car for a moment before getting out and walking towards the river bank. Ahead of him, the lights of luxury apartments shone brightly. To his right the Casino was lit up with neon while to his left the millennium bridge stood out, reflecting pulses of light from passing cars.

It wasn't his favourite view but it was Glasgow and it was a far sight better than the views of his childhood when the whole world was grey by day and black by night.

He loved the country but would never leave the city. Too much life here. Too much buzz. The country would never be enough and yet...

There had been a time before Glasgow and he had never forgotten. Playing up the hill; climbing rocks and trees. Trying to dam the burns that flowed slowly in summer and never quite managing it no matter how many stones they threw in. If he had stayed... If they had not been forced to move...

He looked up at the sky. No clouds but he couldn't see the stars.

Robert got into his car and drove back to Helen.

****

CHAPTER FOUR

"You volunteering tonight?"

Helen stopped washing the dishes and turned to Robert. "Every Tuesday and Thursday for ten years and you still ask me that?"

"Got to have something to talk about. You were quiet tonight."

"I'm having problems with the website. It's just grown so big, I can't keep track of the pages. I've got too many style sheets and I'm in danger of making changes that will affect something without me realising. How do you deal with stuff like that?"

"Lots of lists. Long documents. Even then though, it still takes time to check through implications of making a change. The bigger a system gets, the more permutations. I don't find it easy either."

Helen arched her back to stretch before continuing washing. "I do enjoy working with the website. I like the way it looks and we get good feedback through it but all those promises that design would get easier seem to be no closer to reality."

"Can't you use a package like WordPress? That's pretty much all done for you."

"Maybe I'll have to. Maybe I'm just too attached to the graphics I've designed for the current version."

"Graphics and images you can re-use. But..." Robert stopped

to think. "You've said before you don't have time to really look into it. Then there's the technical aspect, you do have some custom stuff you've had developed in the past. I presume you wouldn't want to lose that. Then there's the financial side. You still need to integrate with the bank to collect donations. You almost need your own version of WordPress for charities."

"Well, that's not going to happen. We only get funding to pay for our salaries and the office. We can't take money out of the donations we get to pay to develop a new website."

"What if you didn't have to pay?"

"Are you volunteering now?"

Robert laughed. "No. Of course not. There's a site I've been wondering about using myself, allows people to offer a service paid for by the hour."

"Do I need to start monitoring your Internet usage?"

"Not that kind of site! More of bidding site..."

"Not sounding any better." Helen deadpanned.

"A cross between an auction site and a job site. A company says they need a database developed and people bid to do the job at Ten pounds an hour or Thirty pounds an hour." Robert paused to see if he was going to get any more flak but Helen was studiously examining her nails.

"I've considered using it but haven't had a project that it seemed relevant for. Basically individuals can advertise their skills and individuals or companies can post jobs or projects and get people on the site to bid for them. I've seen all kinds of stuff from people wanting help leafleting to companies wanting a quick website put up, or help with a coding problem. I'm sure there are even rich kids wanting someone to do their homework for them." He smiled.

"We'd still need to pay though."

"I'll donate a hundred pounds."

"I'd rather the money went directly to the homeless."

"Ungrateful wench!" He flicked her with his tea towel.

Helen retaliated with a spray of soap suds and Robert backed off.

"Okay, look at it like this. If you can get help to simplify your website then it frees you up to spend more time on marketing and design."

"Nobody's going to create a new website for a hundred pounds."

"You never know. Why don't we try it and if you get no offers you've lost nothing. In fact you'll have gained a hundred pounds that can go straight to your shelter."

"Okay. You've sold me." She kissed him and quickly turned back to the pans giving him a look. "Volunteering tonight." She said firmly.

"Don't be out late."

****

Robert headed out into the garden after Helen had gone. It was another fine evening. He bent down and picked up a clod. The earth was crumbling. He was able to break it up and pull out the grass and weeds leaving most of the soil to fall to the ground.

Looked like a rough first dig had been a good idea. He went and got the fork.

Half an hour later his back was sore again from bending and pulling out weeds and grass. He stood straight and stretched his back. He was going to have to decide what to plant. Peas for definite. Maybe carrots. He would have to check the book to see what was best.

He set to again, trying to see if there was a way to avoid bending as much. He got into a rhythm of digging, casting the weedy clods to one side to deal with later.

How did his ancestors cope, breaking up the hard soil, digging with poor quality tools? He tried to imagine working on a narrow run-rig plot hundreds of years ago but couldn't picture it. What must it have been like to have been scraping a life, trying to create a future and then to be evicted, forced to move from the country into the dirty city? Tens of thousands of Scots, all thrown off their land, well, technically even then not their land. Land that they had to rent at increasingly high rates from a few who had been lucky enough to be born in the right family or who had fought, bribed or stolen their way into power.

Had there ever been justice in Scotland?

Robert reached the end of the row he had been digging and surveyed the plot. He was not even half way. He decided to stow his tools away and called it quits while he could still move.

Once he'd washed and made himself a fresh coffee he posted the advert for Helen's charity. He took his time over it, giving as much detail as he could. He gave his credit card details and authorised £50 into escrow – to be held as proof of his intention to honour the contract, with the rest to be paid upon successful completion of the project.

Robert knew there were developers out there with ready-made templates. Ones that might only need a bit of tweaking to be suitable for Helen's needs. There was a time when he'd have been reluctant to part with £100 for something bought off the shelf but years of developing his own applications had taught him to respect the amount of time that would have gone into those creations.

If someone was able to resell the same piece of work to multiple buyers, more power to them. It was no different to a musician selling an album.

That done he got his Kindle and continued skimming through his book. It didn't take him long before he set the Kindle aside to load up Google and start pursuing a new line of thought.

By Nine P.M. the kitchen table was strewn with paper. Printouts from websites; reports and statistics. Robert was about to load another ream of paper into the printer but stopped, sighed and sat back down. Where was he going with this? He had a sense he was missing something but couldn't pin it down.

He pulled over his Kindle and continued reading.

****

Helen came home at Ten P.M. to find Robert engrossed reading his Kindle. "Did a bomb go off while I was out?" She asked, looking at the papers on the table.

"Hmm?" Robert looked up.

"Good book?"

"Depends." He shook his head, frowning. "It's long, detailed, mostly harrowing."

"Want some cocoa?" Helen said with a wide fake smile, walking over to the cupboard.

"No. Yes. I don't know." He stood and stretched. "How was the evening?"

"Quiet. Only had ten men in. It's getting warmer. And Andy said that Joe had found a place to stay!"

"Great. Would I ever have met Joe?"

44

"You must have. Tall guy. Skinny as a beanpole with a shock of white grey hair. Cocoa. Decide now."

"Yes." He sat back down and picked up the Kindle.

"What's the book?"

"It's an investigation into how Scotland's land came to be owned by the rich and powerful at the expense of the poor."

"And the papers on the table?"

"Research."

"Into...?"

"Land ownership, unemployment, government corruption."

"Should I be worried?"

"No. I just need to work this through. The incident, I know..." Robert held up his hands. "I don't want to keep going over it but it seems to sum up a whole lot of injustice." He leaned back. "Before you came in, I was reading some of the history of why the author wrote his book. He has a website as well: Who Owns Scotland. The BBC even backs him up, apparently over fifty percent of Scotland is owned by a few hundred people."

"Hasn't it always been like that? You had the Lairds and the tenants. I'm sure we did something about the Run-Rig system in history at school."

"Maybe it's been like that for hundreds of years, but it can't have always been like that. There weren't always Lairds. Weren't even always kings."

"But now you're talking thousands of years ago. Celts and Picts time. That's not really relevant to today."

Robert shook his head. "No. I think it is relevant. Why shouldn't it be relevant? How did we get from there to here? I mean, how can one person own ten thousand acres? What do they do with it?"

"Farmers own that much and they do a lot with it."

"Okay: farmers. Farmers might own a lot of land – but do even they need that much?"

"And most of Scotland is worthless land anyway. Rock or steep mountain-side. What would anyone do with that apart from walk or climb it?"

"That's not the point! Well, maybe it is – if one person owns the land and refuses access then no-one else can walk or climb on that land."

Helen just raised an eyebrow in response.

"Okay, I'm getting wound up again. I admit it."

"Did you think about anything else the rest of our holiday?"

"Hmmm, I'm sure there must have been one or two distractions..."

"Cocoa! Sleep. Those are my priorities right now."

Robert closed his laptop screen and watched the hard-drive light change from green to slowly flashing amber. "Is the cocoa ready then?"

Helen nodded. "Just going to mix it in."

"Maybe we should drink it up in bed."

"You sure you wouldn't rather stay and carry on your research?"

"There's always tomorrow." He stood and walking over to the stove gave her a hug.

"You need to post that ad on your website tomorrow."

"I already did that."

"You did? Show me." Helen pulled away and moved round his laptop.

Robert opened it back up, waited for the operating system to reload; brought up the job auction website and logged back in. "There." He let her read it.

"You really think someone is going to offer to build me a complete server side template for one hundred pounds?"

"You don't ask, you don't get. Now, are you coming to bed?"

****

Robert gave Jim till Thursday to respond to his request for feedback. He had begun developing some reports and used the excuse of emailing drafts to Jim to also ask if he'd reviewed Peter's requested design changes. By the time he went home, Jim hadn't responded.

There was no response on Friday morning either. Just before lunch, Robert decided a face to face might be better. He logged off and went to see if he was at his desk.

"Hello Jim, do you have five minutes?"

Jim turned and frowned at Robert. "No."

Taken aback by the abrupt response, Robert persisted. "Did you get the report drafts I sent?"

"Of course."

"Have you had a chance to review them?"

Jim began drumming his fingers on his desk. "Not yet."

Robert acknowledged that with a nod.

"When do you think you will be able to give feedback on the design of the reports?"

"I thought we'd agreed all the designs."

"Yes, but I often find it helpful for clients to review the drafts. At this stage it is less likely to delay the project if you decide you want something changed."

"I was quite clear in my specifications. Are you saying you didn't understand them?"

"There is always a degree of interpretation. I would simply like to give you an opportunity to confirm the project is on track."

"That's what we're paying you for, isn't it? To manage the project."

Inwardly Robert groaned. If this was Jim's attitude it explained part of his response. He'd seen similar attitudes before, a sense that employing a professional absolved one of the need to monitor progress. That there was no time cost involved in assigning a project to someone else. If he could not persuade Jim to spend time now then it was highly likely he would find some fault with the way the design had turned out even though he could have prevented it simply by reviewing the design now. He decided to change tack.

"How about the design changes based on Peter's requests?" He asked. "When do you think you can review them?"

"I don't see any reason to change the direction of the project at this stage. Peter should have been more involved at the start."

Robert resisted the temptation to push any more. "I recommend you do review the drafts and I'm happy to take the time to answer any questions you might have. Thank you for your time."

He turned and walked away. He would keep trying to speak with Jim but was now wondering whether he needed to flag the situation up with Jim's line manager. It was a last resort but with less than two months until the project deadline, there wasn't time to risk developing a design that could be rejected at the last minute.

****

Weeds were everywhere, tangled white threads that he couldn't separate. Robert tugged and pulled but the pale cords resisted. He took his shovel and tried chopping them. The roots severed and he pulled a huge clod loose. Tendrils dangled from the muddy earth. He tried shaking the clod to free the earth but the soil was too damp. He had to throw the clod to one side.

He took the garden fork and tried again to break up the soil. The fork just got entangled. He could only cut out sections of turf and throw them away.

Robert gradually became aware he was dreaming but kept his eyes closed, confused by the dream. The garden hadn't been that difficult to dig. Hard work but the turf was relatively free of weeds.

He came fully awake. He'd managed out in the garden on Friday night but it had rained most of the weekend. What was he doing dreaming about weeds? He had only managed to dig half the plot over. Still a lot of back breaking work to go. Maybe he would buy some seeds. Might give him some much needed motivation to keep going. The forecast was uncertain for the next couple of days. He might need to take whatever dry weather he could to finish.

He looked over at the clock. Almost Seven. He reached over and kissed Helen then got up.

****

Robert tried to call Jim a couple of times during the day on Monday; then again on Tuesday and sent another email asking for feedback. He knew he could just leave it but there was a part of his professional nature that insisted on getting sign off for the next crucial stage of the project.

He checked the time. Approaching Five PM. Maybe now would be a good time to drop in on Jim.

"Jim!, Hi, I've been trying to speak with you." Robert caught up with Jim as he walked towards the lift, on his way home.

"I'm finished for the day."

Fixing a pleasant smile on his face, Robert continued to walk alongside Jim. "I can see that. I'll walk you out."

"Can't it wait until tomorrow?"

They reached the lifts and Robert waited as Jim pressed the

down button. "Have you reviewed the designs I sent you?"

"I thought we'd discussed this." Jim looked up at the floor indicator, sighing audibly.

"I haven't had any feedback from you. I appreciate you are busy but I need to warn you that this is your last chance to change the design before I start developing."

"I'm well aware of that and as we already discussed, I've already made the specification quite clear."

There was a chime and one set of lift doors opened.

Jim held up his hand as Robert made to walk in. "I don't need you to accompany me down. You assured me you could deliver the project. I expect you to do so. I really don't think we need to keep discussing this."

Robert stood there in shock as Jim got in the lift and the doors closed.

****

"I keep thinking I must be missing something."

Helen nodded, amused at Robert's annoyance.

"Does he really believe he doesn't need to have oversight of the project?"

"You're asking the wrong person."

"Do you meet people like that?"

"Maybe I'm married to one of them…"

"Ouch! Please tell me you're joking."

Helen gave him a mischievous smile and waited until he shook his head. "I think you should just forget him. You've done your best to contact him, to ask for him to look at the project. There's nothing more you can do."

"It goes against the grain. My whole working life I've tried to head problems off before they start. But this guy just isn't interested in working with me. The IT industry is full of stories about projects that failed, often because the business and the developers failed to keep talking to each other. And I get the feeling he's the type of person that will conveniently forget he was the one who failed to act."

"Is it really that big a deal? You must have worked with dozens of different people over the years."

"Ever since the recession I've been wary. There hasn't been the glut of jobs we had before, what, 2007? And every single interview they always focus on your most recent role. But even with that, it just feels wrong to let a project go South because of one person. Jim might have employed me but it's his company that is paying for me."

"Well, I don't think you should worry. What if you reach the end of the project and he's delighted with the results?"

Robert gave her a look and shook his head.

****

Robert gave Jim until Noon the next day to see whether he would respond to his last email and then pulled up the staff directory on the Intranet. Jim's line manager was listed as Alastair Johnson. He quickly dialled the extension. To his surprise, the call was answered almost immediately.

"Alastair Johnson." The tone was brisk, distracted.

"Hello Alastair, this is Robert Castle. I'm working on a project for Jim... I was wondering if I could get ten minutes of your time?"

"Certainly, give Carol a call and she'll book you in."

****

Another hour digging that evening and Robert began to believe he was close to finishing. He stopped before his back started to really hurt and put the tools away. Walking inside he saw Helen writing at the kitchen table.

What are you doing?" Robert looked over Helen's shoulder to see several lists in neat handwriting spaced out over an A4 pad.

"You haven't forgotten about next weekend have you?"

"Me... Forget?" He went to wash his hands. "Remind me."

"My birthday on Saturday..."

"Oh that. I hadn't forgotten that." He got himself a mug out of the cupboard.

"We're having the Tanner family over for a barbeque."

"You want one?" He held up the mug.

Helen nodded.

"Yes. I remember. Big do."

"And then we have Karen and Julie over on Friday night and Gordon and Penny on Sunday..."

Robert turned to look at Helen. "That's all next weekend?"
She gave him an exasperated look.
"Friday, Saturday and Sunday? Whose idea was that?"
"Yours."
Robert leaned back against the units. "My idea? I suggested having all our friends over on three separate nights? What was I thinking, I mean..." He hurriedly added seeing Helen's expression. "What a wonderful idea! No, I can't do it. What was I thinking?"
"You are unbelievable!"
"I'm sure it will be wonderful. We can get divorced the following Monday." He put the kettle on to boil and went to sit down beside Helen. "Show me your plan..."

****

Robert had requested Carol book a room for his meeting with Alastair but walked up to Alastair's desk a couple of minutes before and introduced himself.
"So, how is the project going?" Alastair asked as they walked into the meeting room.
Robert waited until he had closed the door and they'd both sat down.
"The project is going well however I asked to speak with you as I'm concerned about Jim's approach to managing the project."
Robert paused to see if Alastair would want to interject but he seemed content to listen.
"I was brought in to develop a new system and as such I've been managing the project, however I know from experience that it is important for the business to have regular input and to have the opportunity to direct the design. I've been trying to get some feedback from Jim but he has refused to meet with me and has not responded to my emails."
"Jim does have a full schedule and a large team he's responsible for."
"I fully accept that and am not asking for a lot of his time, but this project has a fixed deadline and the further I progress the harder it will be to adjust if there are any changes identified."
"So, what are you asking?"
"My advice is that someone from the business reviews the

designs at this stage to ensure you are happy with the direction I'm taking. While I've interpreted the specifications based on my experience, I need to advise you of the risk that my interpretation may be different to Jim's."

"Does that happen often? Your interpretation being different to a clients."

"There are usually small areas of difference and those can all be captured through regular review, but I have a couple of times had larger differences in understanding."

"Should I be concerned?"

"Not at all. In those cases if I hadn't regularly checked that the direction I was taking the project was in line with the clients expectations it would have had a significant impact on the project. But I did check and because of the way I manage my projects I was able to accommodate change and still meet the deadlines."

"And you wanted to speak to me because..."

"If no-one from the business is available to review the progress of the project I will carry it through to completion based on my original understanding. But I have a responsibility to advise you there is an increased risk without business oversight."

Alastair considered Robert, tapping a finger on the table. "Very well. Leave it with me."

****

"Robert!"

The volume and sharpness of tone made Robert start and he looked up, mind still half on the report he was developing. Jim was walking up to him. Several people had turned round to look.

Robert eased out of his chair and stood, sensing he didn't want to be seated when Jim got near.

"Come with me."

Jim turned abruptly and Robert hesitated, then turned and logged out of his PC. Jim turned and scowled when he saw Robert wasn't directly behind him.

"Hurry up then!"

Robert followed, pacing himself. It had to be about the meeting he'd had with Alastair. Not quite the reaction he'd hoped for but at least Jim was talking to him.

Jim walked past several occupied meeting rooms until he found an empty one. He held the door as Robert walked in then shut it firmly.

"Take a seat." Jim told him.

"After you." Robert replied.

Jim did a double take. He remained standing. "Who do you think you are making a complaint behind my back?"

So it was about his meeting with Alastair. Robert drew himself up.

"What are you referring to?"

"Are you denying it?"

"You're assuming I know what you are talking about. I would like to know what you're accusing me of before I respond."

"You went behind my back to Alastair Johnson and complained I was not managing the project."

"That is incorrect."

"Don't tell me that's incorrect, I've just had Alastair question me about the project and he made it quite clear you raised the complaint."

"I warned Alastair of the risk to the project without regular review. I explained that you had refused to meet with me to review my progress. Since you refused to meet with me on numerous occasions I had a responsibility to the company to flag the situation."

"Well you don't need to worry about it anymore, you're fired."

Robert swallowed. Of all the outcomes he'd expected, this hadn't featured as an option. "You can't fire me."

"I just have. Clear your desk. I'll have you out of here in the hour."

"No, I meant you can't fire me because you don't employ me."

"What are you talking about? I've signed your timesheets for the past four months."

"I'm employed by my own company, not by you. You cannot fire me. If you no longer wish to use my services you are contractually obliged to give me one week's notice. I have not breached the terms of the contract in any way and you have no right to breach the contract so, like it or not, I'm here for the next week." Robert took a deep breath. "However, I recommend you reconsider your decision. Terminating the contract leaves you with an unfinished project that will take a new developer time to pick up. You guarantee increasing the cost of completing the project and delaying delivery. Or risk having wasted the expenditure up till now."

Jim's face grew progressively more purple as Robert spoke.

"Clear your desk, I'm calling security."

"I'll await instructions from the agency." Robert responded stiffly.

Jim opened the door and left leaving Robert to gather his thoughts.

He pulled out his phone and speed dialled the agency while walking back to his desk.

"Hi, can you put me through to Nina?"

He sat back down and logged in one handed as he waited to be connected.

"Nina speaking."

"Nina, hi, this is Robert Castle."

"Oh, hi Robert. How are things going?"

"Not good. I've just been fired." Robert talked her through the events while he also began forwarding copies of the emails he'd sent to Jim to his company email address.

"He wants me off the premises in just under an hour." Robert finished. "Can he do that?"

"I'll need to check. Can you hold?"

"Sure." Robert finished copying evidence of his attempts to speak with Jim and considered if he needed to do anything else in case he was ejected from the office. He opened a new email and began copying contact details for Alastair and his other main contacts on the project into the body of the email. That done, he sent it.

Robert had heard horror stories of dismissals in England where you were marched out of the office then and there, not even able to carry your personal effects out with you. These to be shipped to your home. He didn't think Jim could simply have him escorted from the building, not unless he was to make up some allegation of serious fraud or misconduct but he would have to have some proof of that, wouldn't he?

Nina came back on the line. "Robert?"

"Still here."

"I've spoken with a colleague and if you are asked to leave

you have to go."

"Even though I've done nothing wrong?"

"They have to give you one week's notice which you'll get paid for."

Robert sighed. "It's insane."

"You haven't been fired yet. You're right that they need to contact us. Maybe it will just blow over when Jim contacts HR. Just keep your head down this afternoon. If you're asked to go into any more meetings then request that I'm present. But if they tell you to leave the premises then just do so. You maybe should come straight here and we can go over the situation properly with you."

Robert promised to call if there was any more news. He put the phone down and stared at his monitor for a while, gradually aware of the glances from the people around him. He had been totally focused on the call and had forgotten he was in an open plan office.

Wincing, he pulled out his notepad and stared at a blank page. If no-one else had heard about the problems he had with Jim then it would be all over the company before the end of the day. All it would need would be one person passing on that bit of gossip in Jim's hearing and security might be throwing him out the door even sooner.

He started writing: Next steps...

If he was given a week's notice he'd like to spend the bulk of that time working on the documentation to ensure that anyone who came onto the project after him would understand what he'd been doing and had been planning to do. It was galling to think that someone else might be paid to finish off his work and receive credit for his design but that was a risk that came with the territory.

There was no point in carrying on any development. Without any guidance from Jim, it would just be a waste.

He'd need to call round the agencies, make them aware he was immediately available. Immediately hopefully being a very temporary situation.

He still had his SRAID token so in theory could log onto the systems network from home.

He sat back, doodling in the lower right corner of the page. His mind was blank. Was there any point in planning when he didn't know if he would be working for minutes or days. He wanted to get up and walk about but felt he had to stay put, waiting for someone to come and tell him whether he was leaving or staying.

He had to tell Helen, but didn't want to do that in front of the office gossips. Shoving his pad in his rucksack, Robert stood and walked towards the stairwell. The usual haunt of contractors – and sometimes employees – when hustling for new work.

He dialled her office number only to find it was engaged. He hung up without leaving a message. He considered texting her but decided against it. He needed to speak with her and not with the threat of someone rudely interrupting him. He'd have to wait until they were both home.

He walked back, scanning his pass against the reader to enter the office and headed to the drinks dispensers, looking ahead to see if anyone was hovering near his desk. No-one. He took a plastic cup and filled it with chilled water. Millions of people doing the same thing every day, maybe billions of cups worldwide. All of them destined for land-fill. Or were they actually recycled? Robert doubted that all the carefully sorted bins were eventually turned into usable materials. But what did he know...

He walked slowly back to his desk. Sitting down he realised he'd left the computer logged in. I'm losing it, Robert thought. Get a grip!

He checked his email. Some corporate messages but nothing relevant to the project. He pulled out his mobile and checked his company email. Nothing new. He looked at the time: 15:13. He hadn't checked when Jim had stormed off. He looked at the sent emails and saw the timestamp: 14:48. It hadn't even been half an hour yet.

He could just get up and walk out. That would solve the problem. Except they would then have a legitimate right to fire him. No. The ball was in Jim's court even though Robert wished he could make a decision one way or the other.

****

The call came at 16:45. Robert hurriedly answered his mobile and heard Nina's voice.

"I've received an email. They're terminating your contract and giving you one week's notice. Not even a full week. Your

56

last day will be Thursday next week. I'm sorry Robert."

"Does it say what I'm supposed to do? Am I still reporting to Jim?"

"No, there's nothing. I'll ask HR."

"Thanks."

****

CHAPTER FIVE

"Fired! What do you mean fired? What did you do?"

Robert put his hands up defensively. "I'll tell you the full story, okay? Just let me start at the beginning."

Helen looked around the kitchen and shook her head. "Make me a cup of tea. I'm going to get changed first." She gave him a hard look then left.

"Could have been worse." Robert murmured to himself.

"I heard that!" Came Helen's voice from the hallway. "I've not finished with you yet."

****

"Didn't you try to apologise? Say sorry?"

"It was a lost cause."

"You don't know that." Helen threw up her hands. "Robert Castle, you are the most stubborn, pig headed man I know. I can just imagine you winding him up. It's a wonder he didn't punch you."

"That's what I did wrong. I should have wound him up more and then he'd have been fired and I'd be sitting on a nice damages claim."

Helen gave him a sharp look and Robert grimaced.

"Okay, maybe inappropriate."

"Have you thought how this is going to affect you? Will you

even be able to get another job?"

"The contract ended. I don't need to say any more than that."

"The famous Castle honesty?"

"I don't need to volunteer information. If I'm pressed I say what happened. I had no choice. If I'd done nothing..."

"You'd still have had a job!" Helen interrupted.

"If..." Robert continued. "If I'd done nothing there was a real risk Jim would have found fault with the direction of the design and blamed me for it. Either way I was looking at a no win situation."

"Job beats dole queue any day."

"I'm a professional..."

"An unemployed professional."

Robert groaned. "Are you going to attack me all evening?"

"And all day tomorrow and the day after that. You better get a new job quickly or you'll have to suffer my wrath."

"Okay, I'm ordering take out. What do you want?"

"How can you afford take out?"

Robert stared at Helen and then burst out laughing. "Are you trying to wind me up?"

"Is it succeeding?"

"Yes! "

"Serves you right. I was hoping to unwind after a stressful week and you have to go and dump this on me."

"You need to eat. What do you want?"

"Chinese."

Robert went and ordered then put the kettle on. It was going to be okay, he told himself. He had stockpiled cash in a savings account in case there was another recession. With Helen's meagre income they could easily survive a full year, maybe even more if they radically cut back on their expenses. No more take outs after this one. It wouldn't come to that though, would it?

He only needed one more contract and maybe could even do something pro bono. Employers looking for a contractor usually concentrated on the last contract and while they wanted to know about the last few years, they were not all that likely to ask awkward questions about the second last contract.

Even if they did, what he'd said to Helen was right. In the long run it was better to be known for doing the right thing even if it meant difficult consequences. He could prove that by delivering documentation during the next week.

The kettle boiled and he made tea for Helen and decaf for himself. Carrying it through he set the tea in front of Helen.

"I'm sorry." He told her and waited until she was looking at him. "I'm sorry I dumped this on you. I'm sorry I got fired. I honestly don't think I could have done anything differently but... I don't know."

"Are we going to be all right?"

Robert nodded and then had to set his coffee down quickly as Helen reached over to hug him.

"We're going to be all right." He told her.

"Do you have to go away this weekend?"

Robert grimaced. The Big IF. He'd forgotten all about it...

****

Rain drizzled down and Robert shivered. He stood alone. Back from the stage in Belfast Botanic Gardens with groups of people huddled under umbrellas dotted about. Most gathered under a huge spreading oak at the far left.

He'd chatted with people on the bus down to Ayr and then across on the ferry, but now he was here he just wanted to be alone, to think and observe.

The turnout was poor, nothing like he'd seen in footage from the previous week in London. It didn't help that they'd had to come over to Northern Ireland he supposed but even then he'd hoped there would have been more people locally willing to turn out. Didn't people understand how simple it was?

Speaker after speaker paraded out on stage to preach the message that there was enough food in the world for everyone, if only the food was shared out to everyone. Robert had signed up months before to go, believing the simple message was worth supporting. Hundreds of millions of people – many of them children – still starving in a world rich with food.

Hunger was the most basic of problems and potentially the easiest to resolve. Entire countries could eradicate hunger by choosing to feed their people before exporting food.

Except the message that was beginning to come across, in-between the support bands and choirs and comedians, was that the problem was only one of many interconnected issues. Debt; taxation; land grabs; opaque laws... All combined to make it more likely the poor would starve. Cut one head off the hydra and risk another two growing in its place.

And here I am, Robert thought. Standing in a wet field. Cold to my bones. What difference does it make that I came here? What difference to those photos of starving families in some Asian or African or Central American country?

Who was I kidding?

****

"Where's Robert?"

"Belfast." Helen poured herself some more tea. The seats weren't terribly comfortable in the cafe but they did serve delicious cakes.

"Is he working over there?"

"No. He's at the Big IF event."

"Is that something to do with Stronger United?"

"Haven't you heard of it?"

"Can't say I have." Karen cut her cake with fork and took a small bite.

Helen looked in bemusement at her friend. "I would have thought everyone had heard of the campaign by now."

Karen shook her head. "So, if it's not Stronger United... How does Robert have time for all this?"

Helen sighed. "Good question. I'm just as bad. Some weeks go by and we hardly see each other."

"Are you okay? I mean, together?"

"Yes. Just too busy. I can't complain. I keep thinking that I need to cut back but there's nothing I'm doing that I would want to give up."

"It's not healthy."

"I still have time for my friends. You are coming over next weekend, aren't you?"

"Of course, wouldn't miss it for the world!"

****

On the ferry back from Northern Ireland, Robert stood in line at the bar. He desperately needed a coffee. The day trip hadn't been a total waste. He'd enjoyed most of the acts that were supporting Big IF. Any excuse to listen to good music would do.

There had been a buzz on the bus back to the ferry. He'd listened to the conversations around him and heard hope that they were making a difference. The G8 were listening. They had promised to act.

He turned to a lady standing beside him in the queue. "How do you think the day has gone?"

"It's been great."

Robert gave her a questioning look.

"You're not convinced?"

"I was expecting more."

The woman appraised him. "Is this your first event?"

"Yes. Signed up on a whim. I believe in the message but am not sure this is the way to change things."

"I've been attending these sorts of events for thirty years. World problems aren't changed quickly."

"Are you a member of one of the organisations here?"

"No. I know many of the people and we've campaigned together on many events but I'm a free agent." She smiled.

"So why great?" Robert asked. "What did you see that I didn't?"

"You have to see the wider picture. There have been increasing numbers of people getting involved since the Jubilee 2000 and Drop the Debt campaigns started. Government is slow to respond and sometimes it feels like we take two steps back for every step forward but the more aware people are, the more support we get. Also, look around you... There are a load of younger people with us. Some of us have been fighting since the 1970's. We are desperately in need of a new generation to pick up the torch and I'm seeing the beginnings of that here."

Robert looked without really paying attention. He had noticed a wide age range on the buses. Teenage girls who seemed unable to stand still; young men and women; but the majority were – he suspected – older than him and then mostly women.

"Why so few men?" He asked.

"You're asking me?" She smiled.

"I work."

"So do I..."

Robert gave her a wry smile. "Work defines me. Maybe it shouldn't, but it does. It's a struggle to put much energy into a cause."

"Kind of a weak reason."

Robert laughed. "Maybe we just don't care. Maybe women are more compassionate. Maybe men need to do something..." He stopped as something clicked. "That's got to be part of it. Offer a man the chance to build a school in Africa or dig a well and he'll raise the money and go. Ask him if he wants to attend meetings or fund raise and chances are he'll be too busy. Same guy, same day, two completely different results."

He looked round and saw he'd allowed a gap in the queue. He moved closer to the bar then introduced himself. The woman's name was Ellen Prasser.

They ordered drinks and Robert bought a sandwich then sat down at a table.

"What do you do?" Ellen asked.

"IT Contractor. Soon to be unemployed."

"You'll have plenty of time to get involved with campaigning then."

Robert winced. "I've been helping out with one campaign but I'm not sure I want to put any more time into it."

"What campaign?"

Robert took a bite of his sandwich and sip of his coffee before answering. "Stronger United."

"I've not heard of them."

"They... We've been campaigning to stay in the union with Britain."

"You don't believe in independence then?"

"I believe that for all its faults, Scotland has done well out of the existing union."

"But you're not quite convinced enough to keep campaigning?"

"Embarrassing to admit."

Ellen shrugged. "Sometimes we want to believe something so much we struggle to see the reality."

"What way are you planning to vote then?"

"I'm independence all the way."

"And do you struggle to see the reality?"

"I'm sure I do." She smiled wistfully. "Twenty years ago I wouldn't have believed it possible that Scotland could break free. I hate the idea of big government. I really hope that independence means we can move decision making out to where it actually affects people."

"I'm in favour of that."

"I think big government wastes so much money. We can trim it right back. Only provide what is really needed and reduce the tax burden."

"I agree with that as well."

"Why on earth would you campaign for Stronger United then?"

"I don't believe the SNP share your vision. I know, I know... The referendum is not about the SNP but can you admit that they'll be the ones negotiating with Westminster in the event of a Yes vote?"

"Of course they will. That's their right. If it wasn't for them we wouldn't even be having this referendum."

"Do you think the SNP are going to vote themselves onto a smaller pay packet? Give up their decision making powers to you and me?"

"They'll have to. That's why I'm voting for independence."

Robert took another bite of his sandwich and sat back, warming his hands with the coffee. "I think that if that's what you mean by independence, you'll find the fight for independence will only begin if you win the Yes vote. I can't see the SNP shrinking government. They'll just let Europe deal with most of it and claim they have a smaller government but in reality it will be just as big and twice as hard to understand with all our laws made in Europe, not Scotland."

"You really distrust Europe so much?"

"Big, unaccountable government. You're saying you do trust them?"

Ellen pursed her lips. "If it wasn't for Europe we wouldn't have human rights legislation."

"We had the Magna Carta a thousand years before the EU. That was justice. Human rights laws have just been an excuse for some people to abuse the system."

"Try telling that to innocent men and women who were unjustly imprisoned."

"Injustice is wrong and it still continues to happen, even with human rights legislation. There was an appeal process before and still is one now. All the human rights legislation in the world will not stop people making mistakes and refusing to admit it when they've done so."

"I'm going right off you."

"All my friends say that. What next for Big IF then?"

"This is the last event. We were all focused on the G8. But there will be other campaigns, you can count on it."

"Bring it on!"

****

CHAPTER SIX

Robert left the office sharp and took a detour on his way home from work on Monday. He'd spent a couple of hours on Sunday completing digging the plot and was now happy he was ready to begin planting. He'd been to the garden centre before, for their coffee and cakes. Never to buy anything for their garden but he'd seen the stands of seed packets.

He took his time looking at the packets. All of them seemed to promise colourful, healthy vegetables. How many would actually thrive in Scotland was another matter. He'd occasionally watched snippets of Beechgrove Garden which was set in Aberdeen and heard the end of Gardeners Question Time on the radio and knew it was possible to have a successful garden but how many years did it take to get the soil just right or learn all the tricks?

He'd read more of his gardening book and knew that peas and beans were a good bet. He fancied getting carrots but they seemed to need a sandy soil and he didn't think their soil was. Still, why not try them? He picked up a packet. He found some sunflower seeds and sweetcorn. He was fairly sure he'd seen sunflowers in other people's gardens and he was curious to see whether sweetcorn could work.

At the end of the row of stands were shelves with seed trays. He hadn't considered planting the seeds indoors and then transplanting seedlings, but maybe he should. He picked up a couple of large trays with individual sections. Then he checked the price and put them back. Could he justify that much money on fairly flimsy plastic?

He kept looking and found what seemed to be biodegradable pots. Reading the label it said the pots could be planted directly in the ground allowing the roots to grow through them. Helen would like the idea of that. He picked up a couple of packets noting the price was even higher than the plastic trays had been.

"Waste of money those things."

Robert turned to see a man, his thick black beard threaded with wisps of grey. "What's that?" Robert asked.

"You can just use toilet roll holders. Cut them in half. It does the same job and you don't have to pay a penny."

"The cardboard tubes?"

"That's right. Fill them with compost and put a seed in and when it sprouts you can just plant it straight in the ground. Acts as a barrier to some of the insects as well."

Robert looked again at the price and put the pots back on the shelf. "Thanks."

"You should try onions as well. They grow really well in our climate. Those can just go straight in the ground."

"Onions, huh? From seed?"

"You're probably a bit late for that. I just buy packets of baby onions. You can get a couple of hundred for a few pounds."

"Not sure what I'd do with a couple of hundred onions." Robert had a picture of his kitchen decked out like a French farmhouse with weaves of onions hanging from the ceiling.

"Give them away." The man suggested. "Do you have an allotment?"

"No." Robert laughed. "Just a small plot in my garden. This is the first year I've tried growing anything."

"I've got three acres outside Glasgow. Potatoes, cabbages, marrows, you name it, I've probably had a go at growing it."

"Three acres? That's a small farm!"

"Keeps me busy. I retired seven years ago. Keeps me fit and gets me outside. I love it."

Robert asked: "How much food do you produce, I mean, three acres, that must be more than enough to provide food for yourself all year round, right?"

"Of course. I sell most of it."

"I've been wondering, how much land do you think I'd need to be completely self-sufficient?"

The man looked at Robert with a quizzical expression. "You're not one of those nutters are you?"

Taken aback, Robert didn't know how to respond.

"Depends what you mean. Are you a survivalist? Do you want to live off the grid?"

Robert shook his head. He had a vague idea of what a survivalist was but living off the grid...

"You need some meat in your diet if you're living in Scotland. It's too hard to get all the nutrients you need just on the sort of vegetables you can grow here. Unless you're planning on using greenhouses?"

"No, no greenhouses. And just vegetables. It's just out of curiosity really. I'm not planning on trying to survive on my own.

" You need a fair bit of land if you were to keep animals but if it's just vegetables... You can produce a lot in a small area, if you're willing to work at it."

"How small? Say for two people."

The man looked away and rubbed the back of his hand underneath his chin. "Just as a guess, no, wait... Allotments used to be 300 square yards. That was for a family of four. Halve that for two people."

Robert did the calculations quickly in his head and gave a long slow whistle. "I'm only working on nine square metres. That would be fifteen times as big... I'd need a tractor!"

"Only to begin with. Once the soil has been turned over once, it's easier to work with. Anyway, I'll leave you with one last tip." He tapped his nose and moved in close to Robert. "Urine." He said in a low voice. "Don't tell anyone but it's one of nature's best fertilisers."

Then he turned and walked off, ambling slowly through the centre.

Robert looked round to see if there were some hidden cameras and a presenter waiting to jump out at him but he was alone. He found a packet of baby onions and headed for the checkout.

****

"What are you doing?" Helen had hoped to find Robert cooking dinner but instead it looked like he'd emptied the recycling bin all over the kitchen table.

"Saving money."

Robert grinned at her. It didn't help her mood. "Had you thought about starting to cook?"

"In a minute."

"I'm hungry now."

"Ten minutes then."

"That's even worse! I'm going upstairs, call me when you're done."

"Don't you want to see what I'm doing?"

Helen walked out without answering. What was with him? All that research he was doing was driving her a bit crazy. Then there was his sudden mad obsession with the garden. Which, okay, that could be good longer term but did he have to spend every evening out there? And now he was bin raking in their kitchen...

Five minutes later she was curled up in bed, trying to concentrate on a novel, when Robert walked in with a plate and mug.

"Tea and toast, just to keep you going."

She sighed. "Thank you."

He sat and waited while she ate. She demolished one slice and then took a sip of the tea, almost immediately starting to feel better.

"What were you doing?" She asked.

"Making seed trays. I stopped off at the garden centre on the way home and was going to buy some but the price was horrendous. Then this guy started giving me advice... But that's another story." Robert shook his head. "Apparently you can use the cardboard tubes from loo rolls as biodegradable plant pots. And we chuck out plastic trays all the time so I've saved a few and am going to create my own recycled seedling nursery."

"Why is it so important to you? You've never had an interest in the garden other than keeping the lawn cut."

"You're right." Robert rubbed a hand through his hair. "I need to do this. The more I find out about what we've lost as a nation when we gave our land away, the more I feel a need to reconnect with the land. I thought you'd be happy, always encouraging me to recycle and think about the environment?"

Helen didn't know what to think. He was right but the change had been so sudden and... "This all started after the incident. Everything you're doing keeps reminding me of that man... Why do you need to do this?"

Robert stretched out his hand to her and she grasped it.

"I'm sorry, Helen, I... I'm trying to turn my anger at what happened into something good. I've found working in the garden has allowed me time to think. There's been times when I've been stressed when I've gone out on long runs. It's the same thing. Doing something physical, getting outside. It helps."

"Are you saying I should be gardening too?"

Robert studied her. There were times when she hated that, not knowing what he was thinking, feeling like she was being judged.

"I think we're similar in a lot of ways." He said eventually. "I think we both benefit from exercise. Both benefit from getting outdoors. We've both been stressed by work, both shaken up by the incident. If there's something you want to do, something I can help with then tell me."

"Don't try and manipulate me." Helen told him, a surge of anger flooding through her.

Robert withdrew his hand. "I'll have the dinner ready in half an hour." He said.

She couldn't read his face. He left without waiting for a response.

Helen turned back to her book, hoping to distract herself. She read the same page three times before giving up.

****

Robert had tidied up by the time she came downstairs. He was stirring a pot of soup and had bowls and plates and bread on the table. Helen curled an arm around his waist.

"Sorry." She said.

"It's okay. We're both under a lot of pressure."

He pressed his hand over hers and reached round for a kiss.

Helen extracted herself and sat, looking round the kitchen. She saw a pile of trays and yoghurt pots. "Is that what you're going to use?"

Robert looked round and checked where she was looking. "Yes. Should be able to set those in some of the windows."

"Did you buy compost?"

Robert looked blank. "No. I was just going to use earth from the garden."

"Might have been better with compost. Should be okay though. What seeds did you get?"

"Peas, beans, sweetcorn, sunflowers and carrots." He ticked them off on his hand.

"How about canes?"

"Canes?"

"To hold up the peas, beans, sweetcorn and sunflowers..."

"Oh. No, I didn't think of that."

"You only need them when you plant the seeds or seedlings outside. We can get them later."

"I was wondering about planting half out now and half in the trays. I don't really know if it makes much difference."

"Some seeds you have to sow straight into the garden. I'm not sure which though."

"I better get reading."

Helen wandered over to the counter where the trays were and saw the packets of seeds. "Onions?" She asked.

"Oh yeah. Forgot about those. Apparently they grow well."

"Two hundred? We don't go through that many in a year."

"I'm sure we'll find some use for them. Soup's ready."

Helen sat down at the table. "Do you think you can have an evening off from, well, everything?"

"Don't you have stuff on?" Robert set a full bowl of lentil soup in front of her.

"Night off."

"Okay. No gardening, no research, no job hunting." Robert sat down with his own bowl. "What do you want to do?"

Helen sighed. "I might just go to sleep."

She looked at Robert. "It's not funny!" Then she had to laugh with him.

****

Robert parked next to Abed's car. They'd agreed to meet in this school car park and leaflet drop in the immediate neighbourhood. He got out and greeted Abed and Martha who were both standing at the rear of Abed's car, arranging bags.

"Two hundred leaflets each. 1,200 households. Should only

take us a couple of hours at most." Abed said.

"Depends how fast we walk." Said Robert.

"And how many people we stop to talk to..." Martha interjected.

"I like finding out what people think." Robert replied.

"We're trying to persuade them to vote No."

"I don't think we're likely to succeed if we're not willing to understand what people think."

Martha waved that thought away. "People can make up their own minds. We don't have time to speak to everyone."

"We have to engage with people. Have to be willing to explain why we believe in the Union. There are people out there who need to hear that argument from a person, not a leaflet."

"I wish we had the time, Robert. I really do." Martha handed him a bag. "Colin, June and Allan should be here soon. We'll go out in pairs as usual."

Robert nodded and went to get his rucksack from the car. 200 leaflets were not a lot but he wasn't going to carry a shopping bag around the streets, especially one with the Stronger United logo emblazoned on it. Even before he'd started having doubts about the campaign he'd been aware it wasn't always a welcome sight.

The others arrived and Robert paired up with Martha. They had six streets to cover. Robert preferred taking one side of the street each but Martha preferred leap frogging. "Means you can still talk to each other."

Meant there was less chance of Robert actually knocking on a door to see if someone wanted to chat, he suspected but agreed without complaint.

The first street was quiet. A long street with a mix of short terraces and semi-detached. They went up one side and then doubled back down the other before heading along to the next street. Robert checked the map as they walked.

"We would be better splitting up for the next one. If we leap frog up and down we'll just have to walk back along to get to the next street." He showed Martha.

"Very well." She conceded.

Robert thought he detected a hint of annoyance but ignored it.

He thought he was making better time separating, not getting in each other's way, until someone opened their door as he walked up the path.

"Hello." Robert smiled at the man. "I'm delivering leaflets for the Stronger United campaign. May I ask what your views on the referendum are?" Take that Martha Cunningham, he thought to himself.

"Won't make a blind bit of difference." The man said. "We'll just exchange one lot of crooked politicians for another."

"I've been thinking the same thing." Robert confessed. "I believe in the Union but I can't say I like the status quo."

"Why are you out campaigning then?" The man laughed.

Robert held his hand up to his mouth as if to hide what he was saying and spoke in a stage whisper: "Good question. Don't tell the lady over there…" He nodded towards Martha who was giving Robert impatient glances.

"I doubt you'll get much interest here." The man said.

"Why's that?"

The man screwed up his face. "Apathy. I know some of my neighbours didn't even vote in the last election. Can't say I blame them. Ten years of Labour was no different to the Conservatives before them and then the Conservatives get in and they say they're just going to continue Labour's policies. What's the point."

"So, what can we do?" Robert asked. "How can we encourage people to get involved?"

"You can't. We aren't involved. No matter what we vote, the moment they're in power they do what they like. Anyone who says you can make a difference in politics without actually being a politician is flat out lying."

Preaching to the converted, Robert thought to himself. Might as well give up now. He gave the man a half-hearted smile. "May I ask if you plan to vote in the referendum?"

"Of course. I'm Yes all the way. Don't care if that offends you."

"It doesn't. I'd rather everyone voted. Would you like one?" He offered a leaflet.

"No." The man shook his head, grinning at Robert.

Robert said goodbye and headed to the next house aware Martha was now several ahead of him. He posted leaflets through the doors and caught up with her sooner than he thought, then realised she had slowed down.

"We don't have all night, Robert." She called.

He waved in reply and gritted his teeth. He didn't think he'd mind leaflet drops if he had more time to speak to people. It was fascinating hearing other people's views. Finding out why they thought how they did.

They finished the street and walked along to the next one. They were able to leap frog again and made quick progress up and down the shorter street.

Robert thought he felt some spots of rain from a grey and overcast sky but it remained warm and otherwise dry.

They started up the last street when a couple of teenage girls came out of a house they were approaching. They both looked to be in their late teens so Robert offered them each a leaflet. Martha continued on, huffing loudly as she past him.

"Will this be your first time voting?" Robert asked.

"Stronger United, huh?" One of the girls asked, scanning the leaflet quickly and Robert just as fast.

Robert noted the other girl looking away as if embarrassed or bored. He couldn't tell which.

"That's right. Have you decided how you're going to vote?" He asked them both even though one wouldn't meet his eyes.

"Don't get her started." The bored one said, shaking her head.

"Not for the SNP, bunch of unmentionables." Her friend said with genuine anger.

Robert was taken aback.

"Would you like to remain in the UK?" He asked.

"Of course! I'm going to be in Team GB. Can't do that if they split us up."

"What's your sport?"

"Hockey. I'm too young to compete in the Commonwealth Games but I'm aiming for the Olympics in 2016."

"If I play devil's advocate, you could still compete in the Olympics for a Scotland team."

"Aren't you supposed to be convincing me to vote No?"

Robert shrugged. "I want to know what people think."

"I think we'll be lucky if we don't have a civil war after the referendum."

Robert choked down a laugh. "That's a bit extreme, don't you think?"

"You see what's happening in Ukraine right now. You really think England are just going to let Scotland walk away without trying to stir up some trouble? No way are they going to let us keep all the oil the SNP keep banging on about. No, too much money there."

Her friend pulled out her phone and started swiping the screen.

"The SNP don't even have a mandate for the referendum."

"They did get elected promising one." Robert couldn't help himself.

"Yeah, and you know how many people actually responded to that white wash consultation they had?"

Robert did but didn't interrupt. She was fascinating him.

"Less than one percent, yeah Chantelle." She said to her friend. "That's how much Scotland wants independence."

Chantelle shook her head.

"All my class say they're voting Yes but when it comes to polling day, how many of them will be too busy doing their nails to actually get out and vote? All this referendum is doing…" She rounded on Robert. "Is dividing us. You got young versus old, rich versus poor, might as well be black versus white…"

"You can't say that, Tara. That's racist!" Chantelle piped up.

Tara ignored her. "You got to remember Ukraine." She told Robert. "It don't matter which way we vote, a huge chunk of people are going to be mad one way or the other. And the way some of them keep insulting each other, it's like they've completely forgotten we'll have to live in the same country afterwards. I've had friends tell me that they're going to kick out everyone who voted No. What kind of country is that going to be? One where you're going to get bullied if you disagree with them. No… bunch of losers the SNP are, and all their supporters. Just full of hate. Not you Chantelle, you know who I mean."

Chantelle sighed. "Are we going or what?"

"I'll keep this." Tara said to Robert, a wicked grin appearing on her face. "Post it on the college notice board. That'll wind them up!"

Chantelle pulled her hand and Robert watched the two of them walk away. He shook his head and turned to see Martha was walking back towards him.

"I don't want to hear it, Martha." He said to her abruptly. "If you don't like me canvassing opinion, don't choose me as a partner."

He could see her shock but ignored it. "Did you finish the street?"

"Don't talk to me like that." She responded after staring at him for some time. "It takes two or three times as long to finish a leaflet drop if we stop to talk to people."

"If we aren't willing to speak to people we aren't going to win the referendum. The Yes campaign are going all out to win over hearts and minds. Can we really say we believe in our cause if we're unable to even have a conversation with people."

"Not all of us are good at speaking to people." She said and began to walk back up the street.

Robert followed her. "What do you mean?"

She gave him a disgusted look. "It's so easy for you. You strike up conversations with anyone you meet. I get tongue tied. I never know what to say."

"You manage fine with me, with the group."

"You're my friends. At least, I thought you were."

While he was mulling this over, a car pulled up outside a house they were passing and Robert stopped. "I'll catch you up." He said.

Martha didn't reply.

Robert stopped to talk to two other people before they had finished. Less than he'd have liked, but he knew knocking on doors would have been just rubbing it in Martha's face.

They didn't speak to each other as they finished the drop and headed back to the car. Robert was quite glad for the chance to think. Maybe if they were making an effort to persuade people, to find out what would encourage them to vote No, he would feel more enthused about the campaign. But what he couldn't admit to Martha was that if he believed the SNP had actually been good for Scotland, he would probably be campaigning for a Yes vote.

He still believed the Union was a good thing, still believed that a union solely with Europe would be a disaster for Scotland but his doubts about the referendum just got bigger. He'd heard two stark opinions. Were they the real choices facing the Scottish people? Apathy and resignation or a country filled with hate and division? There had to be a better way.

****

CHAPTER SEVEN

His last few days in the office had dragged. Robert hadn't seen Jim once. While he couldn't think how else he could have handled it without compromising his ethics, Robert did feel responsible for what had happened. He'd built a solid reputation on being able to understand requirements and deliver successful projects. There had been conflicts before but nothing that had escalated so quickly.

Part of him had wanted to challenge Jim. To seek him out and tell him how his refusal to engage with the project had been such a risk. But he kept a lid on that. Just keep your head down for a few more days, he had told himself.

He'd avoided sending emails choosing to see others who had been involved with the project in person or to call them rather than putting something in writing that he might need to share with Jim. He avoided gossip but when asked directly what had happened he gave his side of the story. There didn't seem any point in covering it up.

And now it was his second last day. The documentation was up to date and he had written up a proposal for how he thought the project should continue.

Without any communication from Jim he would be within his rights to kick back and relax for the last few hours but...

Robert drummed his fingers softly against the keyboard for a moment and then opened up a new meeting invite. He included both Jim and Alastair and titled the meeting Project handover.

He looked at the times both Jim and Alastair were available. There were slots both in the morning and in the afternoon. Tempting to select the afternoon. He chose morning, then booked a room and added it to the location.

He added links to the documentation he had created on the network and attached the proposal. Then he clicked Send.

Robert stretched, locked the PC and went to get a coffee.

****

It was still overcast with a rare muggy heat that evening. After they'd eaten, Robert went out to the garden, armed with his seeds and trays. He'd read more of his book and realised that a nine square metre plot was too big without a path through the middle.

He didn't have any spare paving stones so he decided he'd just avoid seeding a narrow gap. He could change it the following year.

He marked out squares using small stones and planted half his peas, beans, beetroot and all of his onions, leaving entire squares untouched for the sweetcorn and sunflowers and the seedlings he hoped to grow indoors.

Then he filled his halved toilet rolls with earth, placed them on the trays and stuffed seeds down inside them. He still had seeds left over so carried the packets and trays back inside.

"I hope you're not going to get earth all over the house." Helen told him.

"Just in every window sill."

****

Robert had booked the room for a longer slot than the meeting invitation. He turned up 15 minutes early and politely waited for two people who had made use of the room to leave.

He had printed out copies of the project proposal and a summary of the project documentation. He didn't need to review it but scanned it, wondering: if he had more time would he make any additional changes. Nothing came to mind.

The allotted time for the meeting passed by. Robert started jotting down some thoughts on his research into Scotland's history and the UK economy.

He checked his watch. Ten minutes late.

He kept writing, trying to keep his mind occupied.

Fifteen minutes. Robert was glad he'd only scheduled half an hour.

Just before twenty past the hour, Jim walked by the room, did a double take and opened the door. "I cancelled the meeting."

Robert stood slowly. "I didn't receive a cancellation."

"I sent it before the meeting."

How many seconds before... Robert told himself to remain calm. "I see."

"Didn't seem much point as you've provided all the documentation."

An opportunity to clarify, Robert thought. Your last chance to ask any questions. He couldn't think of an appropriate response so kept silent.

Jim came fully into the room and held out his hand, a confident smile on his face. "No hard feelings."

Robert stared at the extended hand. Instinct dictated he shake hands. Culture... tradition... He looked from the hand to Jim's face. Jim was looking at him expectantly, as if Robert was perhaps a slow, slightly stupid child.

Robert turned away and gathered up his documents. Was the right thing to do just accept humiliation? Accept the other guy had all the power and there was nothing you could do about it? He didn't know, but there were lines he just wasn't willing to cross. He looked up at Jim. He would forgive Jim. Find a way to accept that he could have handled the situation better. But he would not shake the man's hand.

"If you have any questions, I'll be at my desk." Robert told him.

Jim withdrew his hand slowly. "You are an arrogant piece of work, aren't you?"

Robert walked up to Jim. "Excuse me." He said.

"I said, you are an arrogant piece of work, aren't you."

There was silence in the room as Robert studied Jim. Fleeting memories of off-hand comments he'd made during meetings, belittling colleagues. His lack of interest in studying the project design that Robert had initially put down to Jim being too busy. And now the final insult...

Robert nodded at the door. "No. I meant, excuse me."

Robert could almost feel a wave of hatred as Jim held his ground in front of the door. Long seconds passed until Jim finally made a small step to the side, barely leaving Robert enough room to open the door.

"Don't bother asking for a reference."

Robert held his peace while carefully extracting himself from the office. He walked away without looking back, all the while wondering if Jim could be psychotic enough to turn violent.

Returning to his desk, Robert pulled up his email and began to compose a final message to the agency. While he'd avoided sending internal emails during his last week, he'd made sure to send at least one to the agency every day, providing proof he'd been in the office. He wouldn't put it past Jim to "forget" to sign his timesheet. He thanked Nina for her help and advice and promised to call her the following day.

He looked at the PC clock. 10:42. It was going to be a long slow day.

****

Helen walked into the kitchen to find Robert cooking. "Are we celebrating?"

"Hi." He turned to kiss her. "Nothing to celebrate."

"You don't have to work with that man anymore."

Robert closed his eyes and sighed, long and slow. "Well, there is that."

"You have a few days off."

"Which I'll be spending chatting up agencies and scouring the job sites."

"And I should hope so too!"

"We need to vote tonight."

"Ah yes. After dinner?"

Robert ate quickly, lost in his thoughts. He knew it was normal for him to feel exhausted at the end of a contract, having put all his creative energies to use, but tonight he just felt drained without any of the satisfaction of having completed a project.

"Who are you voting for, then?" Helen asked.

When Robert told her she threatened to tear up his voting registration card. "You can't vote for them, they're racist!"

"That's just media lies and a few oddballs. It's not racist to want to control immigration. And anyway, they've been quite clear they would let people in from all over the world, as long as they have something to contribute."

"Not everyone."

"Of course not. We couldn't afford the benefits bill."

"People don't come here for benefits, they come here to work."

"Okay, I'll concede that most people do come here to work. And most people who come are well educated and contribute a lot. But I still feel we need to control our borders."

"Well, I'd let everyone in. If someone wants to come, they can."

"And our benefits system will collapse."

"Nope." Helen said. "We'd fix the benefits budget and share it out equally to whoever needs it. If there's more people everyone would get less."

Robert barked a laugh. "That's…" He searched for words. "That's genius! Or insane. I'm not sure which but I love it. How long have you believed that?"

"I just made it up."

"I think you might have riots on your hands if you were in charge but that's an intriguing idea."

They walked to their local primary school and voted in the European elections.

****

Robert woke at his normal time. Heading downstairs he set water to boil before grinding coffee beans. He filled the coffee pot and left it to stew while he made toast, then made a pot of tea for Helen.

Helen joined him a few minutes later. Yawning, she ran a hand round his shoulders as she walked by him.

"Do you have a plan for today?" She asked.

"Fire up the laptop and start calling agencies. I emailed most of them yesterday afternoon but it will be best to follow up with a call."

"Are you remembering we have guests tonight?"

"Of course."

"Are you planning to spend any time tidying up…?" Helen

gestured at the piles of paper that had taken over their kitchen.

Robert looked round and inwardly groaned. "Consider it done."

Helen gave him a look. "We have everything we need for tonight's meal. I've ordered in groceries to be delivered tomorrow afternoon for the rest of the weekend." She put her hand out to him. "You could just take the day off... Sure..." She said looking round. "Tidy up in here but you don't have to spend the whole day trying to find a new contract. Right?"

Robert took her hand. "I'll probably be able to relax better this weekend if I've made a start. But you're right. I don't have to spend the whole day job hunting."

****

By Eleven, Robert had called half a dozen agencies and received calls from two others in response to his emails from the previous day. There was one promising lead and he'd updated his CV and emailed it in.

He made himself a new pot of coffee and studied the piles of paper that were cluttering the surfaces. Print outs from websites mostly, arranged in piles according to subject matter:

Land ownership

Economy

Government policy

Other random topics that had caught his eye while he had been researching.

He picked up one sheet and started skim reading. UK Government regularly ignored public responses to consultations. If politicians continually failed to take account of people's views, what was the point in having politicians at all?

He laid the sheet down and looked at another. The richest ten percent in the UK collectively had access to enough wealth to pay off the National Debt three times over. If they could be forced to pay off the National Debt then £55 Billion a year in interest payments could be channelled to provide full employment at a living wage.

He took a slow, deep breath and laid that sheet back down.

Wandering over to the first pile he'd started on land ownership he looked down at a single quote he'd found on the Internet: "The entire population of the world subsists on just six inches of soil."

Robert poured himself some coffee and stood at the kitchen window looking out into their garden. He hadn't dug that deep but was sure the soil went further than six inches down. Yet the soil had not been loose. It had stuck together, been hard to separate. More like clay than sand. Or was that just an average. Six inches across the whole globe. How many mountain tops had he walked on where the top had been bare rock and the grassy sides could easily be damaged revealing how little soil existed in the slopes.

There were too many facts and figures floating round in his head. It all meant something but what was he to do with it? It wasn't going to help his ambivalence over the Stronger United campaign. Wasn't going to help him find a job or help him rest.

He had lunch then decided to clear the papers from the kitchen. He had nothing else to do to prepare for the weekend until that evening. He'd bought Helen her present – tickets to the ballet – the previous month. He would go with her and make every effort to enjoy it. The food was arranged, guests were invited. It would be a welcome relief to enjoy several evenings with friends.

By Three PM he was satisfied the house was as presentable as it needed to be. He donned his boots and went to survey his plot. A couple of starlings were pecking at the soil. He waved them away and crouched. He had no idea how long it would take for shoots to appear. Did he need to get nets to keep the birds off and protect the seeds? He didn't know.

He looked up. The clouds were starting to clear. It was turning into a nice day. He got out a deck chair for himself, sat and allowed his thoughts to wander.

****

She found him dozing in his chair. Helen gently shook him awake.

"You'll get sunburn."

"Was I asleep?" He blinked heavily and yawned. "Can't believe it. I was just thinking it was getting warm enough for a cold beer. How was your day?"

"Busy as usual. I see you tidied up, thanks."

"Start of the big weekend then. Are you excited yet?" Robert put a hand up to his mouth as he yawned again. "Sorry."

"Still got tonight's meal to prepare. I might start to relax after that."

"Well, I'm second cook and chief bottle washer so just start giving the orders."

She squeezed his shoulder. "I'm going to shower."

Standing in front of the mirror she examined her face. Lines were becoming more pronounced but nothing to really show she was about to turn Forty. She watched a tear roll down her cheek, put a hand to her stomach. Not what she would have chosen but what could they have done.

She straightened and blinked to clear her eyes. This was her weekend. She was going to enjoy it. Turning on the shower she began to review her mental list of tasks to do before Karen and Julie arrived.

****

CHAPTER EIGHT

"I wasn't much interested in Geography at school but since the incident with the estate manager I've found myself researching land ownership."

Julie put down her wine glass and sat back. "Geography's a broad subject but I don't think they deal with land ownership."

"They should." Robert gestured with his own glass. "I remember being taught meaningless facts about the run-rig system but nothing about why Scotland was carved up as it was."

"That sounds more like History. How much wine have you had?" Asked Karen.

"Not enough." Robert stood and picked up the wine bottle. "Anyone?"

Julie held out her glass for Robert to top up and then Helen did the same.

"A Dutchman, a Dane and an Arab walk into a bar... Could be the start of a joke, right? Get this: There is a Dutchman, who owns 80,000 acres; A Dane, the guy who runs the Lego corporation no less who owns 50,000 acres and an Arab who owns the 15,000 acre site where Highland Spring mineral water is produced. Almost 150,000 acres owned exclusively by three non-British nationals."

"So..." Julie raised her eyebrows.

"Why do we allow land to be sold outside the UK? Our land is all we have. If we sell it, we don't have a country anymore."

"That's a bit extreme. We have friends who own property in Spain and even Eastern Europe."

"Certainly, so do we. But most countries limit the amount of land that can be sold. We don't even have a national register for land sales that can be searched online. No-one can actually state how much of Scotland is owned within the UK. But some people have tried to find out and they've been able to show three million acres are owned by non-British nationals."

"Foreigners you mean?"

"Yes."

"Are you going to tell us you're anti-immigration now, Robert?" Karen joked.

"I'm all for people moving about. I just don't think we should sell off something that can never be replaced."

"How big is Scotland?"

"Just under twenty million acres."

"So we're talking fifteen percent. It doesn't seem that much."

"If someone walked into your house and took fifteen percent of your jewellery, or hacked into your bank account and took fifteen percent of your savings, would that seem like much?"

Karen laughed. "Not of mine. Julie might feel the pain though!"

"Hey! I inherited most of that jewellery."

"Why didn't we inherit the land?"

"I guess because our parents and grandparents never owned it in the first place."

"But why not? Who did own the land in the first place? Why did the first person to claim a million acres have the right to that land?"

"Because they were bigger and stronger and managed to kill more people than anyone else."

"But is that a history that we want to accept? Just because a few people managed to grab all the land for themselves a thousand years ago do we have to keep living with the consequences?"

"I'm not sure what you can do about it. Steal it back?"

"I came across an Office for National Statistics analysis this week."

"I thought you were giving this a rest." Helen piped up.

"Maybe it was last week, anyway, half of all households in Scotland receive more in benefits than they pay in taxes. Most of our fellow countrymen and women had no choice about where they ended up. Evicted from crofts; forced into slums; moved out into the New Towns. They never had a chance to make anything of their lives. But someone got rich selling those three million acres. I would love to know how much that land went for."

"So…" Julie drew out. "Robert. How is the Stronger United campaign doing?"

Robert looked down at his wine glass, picked it up and swirled the contents. "I'm thinking of packing it in." He looked up at Helen.

"You mean the Yes campaign has finally convinced Robert Castle?" Julie gave a mock gasp. "Hold the phone! Referendum result is in the bag!"

"No, definitely not. I still dread to think what the SNP will do to Scotland if they gain complete control."

Karen leaned over. "So let me get this straight… You're not voting No and you're not voting Yes? After all you've said about people needing to be involved?"

"I didn't say I'm not voting. I don't think I can support the Stronger United campaign anymore." Robert sighed. "I think the whole of Britain needs a radical shake up. But the SNP are not offering independence, they're offering a union with Europe. They're offering a shared currency with the UK. They're offering the same style of undemocratic government."

"And how many times do we have to repeat the argument, the referendum vote is not a vote for the SNP, it's a vote for the chance to determine our future." Julie couldn't keep the exasperation out of her voice.

"But what future?" Robert asked. "How can you say we can determine our own future when it won't be us determining it, it will be 128 men and women deciding for five million?"

"Our MSPs are democratically elected."

"That's not democracy. It's not democracy when my MSP ignores me and hundreds of other constituents and votes the way he or she pleases. It's not democracy when the Scottish Government ignores the results of numerous consultations or introduces legislation that wasn't in their manifesto."

"Maybe that's enough politics for one evening." Helen tried interjecting.

Robert leaned back. "I'm sorry. I just get obsessed."

"You have to know when you're beat..." Karen said with a sly wink at Julie. "Though, Robert... You should consider standing for election yourself if you feel that strongly about it."

"It would have to be as an independent. I don't think there's a single..." Robert caught Helen's eye and stopped himself.

He got up and brought back another bottle of wine. As he offered it round he looked questioningly at Helen. "One more question?"

Helen declined the wine. "Just so long as it doesn't lead to our guests..." She emphasised the word. "...taking offence."

Robert set down the bottle and looked intently at Karen and Julie for a moment. "Okay, lets wipe the slate clean, maybe have some fun with this. If you ruled Scotland – and I mean like a king or queen, absolute power – what would you change?"

"Everything!" Julie replied instantly.

Karen gave her an amused glance. "You mean no government, right? I could make the decisions?"

"Yes. But you would be answerable to the people, just like any dictator..."

"Better make sure you establish an army then, Julie." Karen said.

"We wouldn't need an army, we'd be a full member of Europe."

"Which doesn't currently have an army..." Helen reminded her.

"Technically, but..."

Robert held up his hands. "You're assuming Europe would accept Scotland into membership, you can only have what you have the power to change."

"Well, that's no fun!" Julie responded.

"Just rephrase your statement, maybe: I would apply for membership of the EU."

"I'm not sensing I have absolute power in this game."

"You do within Scotland. Okay, let me have a go. I would establish full employment."

"And how would you do that? Wave a magic wand?" Karen asked.

"Good question. How would I do that..." Robert winked at Helen. "I would introduce conscription, then I'd have my army."

"And who are you planning on attacking?" Julie scoffed. "England?"

"How about poverty? Idleness? Attacking the benefits culture."

"Sending young men to die is NOT the way to solve those problems."

"But why do you assume an army will be used to fight?"

"What else is it going to be used for?"

"After the second world war ended Britain had conscription for years. Young men were trained to fight, yes, but they were also given discipline, they were taught real trades that they were able to use when they had served their time. Can you imagine the impact on our society if we took the unemployed neds off the streets and taught them to respect themselves and each other? Taught them discipline and gave them a trade?"

"You could do that with training schemes." Julie protested.

"The government has been trying that for decades and has failed at least two generations with that argument."

"Well, you're not king in MY Scotland... I'm implementing a training scheme."

"Ha!" Robert grinned. "Fair enough. What else? Karen?"

"Full employment sounds good. I would lower taxes. Maybe get rid of VAT."

"Nice. Julie?"

"Wait a minute." Helen interrupted. "What would you cut from government spending to fund getting rid of VAT?"

"Why do I need to cut anything? I'm queen, right?"

"You're just going to print money?"

"Sure. Why not?"

"You won't be queen for long when your subjects can't afford to pay for anything. So, what would you cut?"

"Okay, I have full employment now so I can cut spending on benefits!" Karen held up her hand for Julie to high five.

"I'm not convinced the two will balance but... My turn." Helen thought for a moment. "Homeless shelters in every town. Nothing fancy but they need to be warm and safe."

Robert reached over and took Helen's hand. "Shelters for the homeless. Maybe can take that out of the MSP expenses budget... No need for duck ponds in Scotland, right? Julie..."

****

"What time is it?" Helen roused herself as Robert sat on the bed, balancing a tray.

"Ten AM. Tea?"

"Why so early?" Helen lay back down and closed her eyes.

"You ordered the groceries. Personally I'd have picked a later time slot but…"

"You don't need me for that." She mumbled.

"I don't see why I should have all the fun. Anyway, I have your present here."

Helen opened one eye and looked suspiciously at Robert.

"Happy birthday!" He leaned over and gave her a kiss.

Helen lay still. "I don't want to be Forty."

"It's not that bad." Robert drank some coffee. "I have pastries. Maple and Pecan or cinnamon swirl."

"It's too early for pastries."

Robert smiled down at his wife. He loved the way she looked in the morning. As if a night's sleep transported her back in time. He adjusted the tray and tucked into a pastry.

After a few minutes Helen gave a fake groan and shuffled herself up. "You're not going to leave me alone, are you?"

"It's your birthday. You don't get to sleep in."

"Grrr." She took the offered tea and took a sip. "So, where's my present?"

Robert handed her a large envelope.

"You didn't get me a gift card again, did you?"

"Would I do that?"

"You did last year!"

"You asked me to."

Helen put the tea back down on the tray and slit open the envelope. As she pulled out the card two tickets fell out. She picked them up and looked at them with a puzzled expression.

Robert realised he was holding his breath and told himself to relax.

"What are these?"

"Tickets to the ballet."

Helen looked at them for a while longer.

"You bought me tickets to the ballet?"

"You mentioned it a couple of months ago. Is it okay? I could get you something else…" Robert realised Helen was crying. He put the tray onto the floor and moved over to hug her. "What's wrong?"

"You hate the ballet."

"Hate's a strong word."

"'Never want to see men dancing in tights ever again.' That's what you said after we went, what, twenty years ago!"

"I figured I could always close my eyes… I promise I won't complain. I won't make fun of them. I'll be on my best behaviour."

"You'd better!"

Helen leaned over and hugged him, pulling him in tight. "Thank you." She whispered.

"You're worth it."

****

"Don't talk to me about it, foreigners coming over here and taking our jobs. No wonder unemployment is as high as it is." Steve Tanner said.

"That's not what I'm saying." Robert adjusted a steak on the barbeque then took a sip of his beer. "I don't have a problem with people coming over here to work. We export a ton of our own people abroad and they do very nicely for themselves."

"There aren't enough jobs to go around."

"It's more than that. There are jobs but they don't pay enough. I couldn't live on minimum wage. I don't know how anyone could."

"How can there be enough jobs if unemployment is so high? That can't be right. What is unemployment now? Three million?"

"In the UK. In Scotland it's only around 180,000."

"Is that all?"

"Yeah, but it's an artificial figure, more people are on benefits."

"Still… 180,000. I doubt there are that many jobs available."

"Probably not. Need to bring back conscription."

"You planning on starting a war?"

"That's how they'd have solved the problem a hundred years ago. Kill off a million young men and your unemployment problem is solved! I think the steaks are ready, you want to round up the kids?"

Steve shouted and his three kids came running. Robert doled out crispy sausages in rolls and burgers in buns then sent them over to the table where Helen was sitting with Kathryn.

"What happened to your garden." Kathryn asked innocently.

Helen looked away, her hand hiding her mouth.

Robert shrugged and grinned. "Finally decided to see if I could grow some vegetables."

"What brought that on?" Steve asked.

"Oh, I don't know. Midlife crisis maybe. Stress of getting fired from my job last week..."

"Nothing to do with the research Helen tells me you've been doing?" Kathryn asked.

Robert looked over at Helen who was focusing all her attention on the children. "Well, come to mention it, did you know the whole world subsists on just six inches of soil?"

"Interesting fact, Robert. But why does that mean you decided to tear up your lawn?" Kathryn gave Steve a knowing look.

"I have been doing a lot of research. The more I read up on what is happening to our country, the more problems I find. You look at the economy, at how the government is mismanaging the money we pay in tax; how the poor are being brutally squeezed... Then trace it back to laws that were passed hundreds of years ago that were patently unjust then but have been allowed to determine how we live today.

"You know, I've spent four months working on a project where the guy who hired me couldn't even be bothered to check whether he was happy with the direction I was taking. I earn a good living from these contracts but sometimes I wonder why companies are so willing to spend money but so reluctant to ensure they get good value from it. Why don't people care? We are so inefficient. We waste everything: food, electricity, plastic. Then I re-read that quote and thought: I'm no different. I use disposable cups at work. I buy mangos from India and grapes from Brazil."

"The lettuce is from Stirling and the beef is from Aberdeen." Helen interrupted.

"You keep me on track." Robert took a bite of his steak.

"I'm still not hearing a reason for the lawn..."

Robert leaned back, frowning at Kathryn, and set his plate on the table. He had to admit, he didn't really know why he felt that urge to dig the lawn. But there would have been a reason. There was always a reason, even if he didn't always know at the time what that was. He kept thinking. "I felt I had to do something. I've been reading all these articles on Scotland's history: how the land was stolen; who owns Scotland now, and yet my only connection to the land is walking it."

"That's more than some." Helen said.

"You've even dragged me on a couple of hikes." Steve reached over and took a handful of crisps.

"But is it enough?" Robert asked. "I have no idea what it means to provide for myself. I've never spent time weeding or watching plants grow."

"Now there's a hobby for you! Watching plants grow..." Steve laughed. "Better get some tall beers in!"

"Anyway, Steve... I decided I needed to experience growing my own vegetables."

"He just made that up, didn't he." Kathryn said to Helen.

Helen looked puzzled and turned to Robert. "You didn't, did you?"

Robert took his plate back. "No. Though I didn't exactly know why I dug the garden at the time."

"Told you, he made it up."

"It sometimes takes me a while to know why I want to do something."

"That's not really something you want to admit, Robert."

"Studies have shown that our subconscious can often resolve decisions faster than our conscious mind."

"Bet that goes down well at the job interviews!" Steve clapped Robert on the back. "This is good steak, good beer, good company. Happy birthday, Helen!"

****

After they'd eaten too much and topped it off with cake, Helen and Kathryn took the kids inside to watch a movie. Robert stayed outside to tidy up and Steve joined him after a minute with a couple more beers.

"Dishes will still be here tomorrow, right?" Steve clinked Robert's bottle.

They sat drinking for a few minutes, Robert admiring a growing sunset.

"Tough break on the job." Steve said. "You got anything else lined up?"

Robert sighed. "Not yet but something will turn up. It always

MARK ANDERSON SMITH

does."

"So which party did you vote for on Thursday, the sleaze balls, the tossers or the nancies?"

"You missed out a few there. I chose my favourite colour."

"Ha! Now that's just about as good a way to choose between them as any."

"Did you hear, two thirds of people didn't bother to vote?"

"That's normal, isn't it?"

"How can it be normal?" Robert stood and walked over to his plot. "Did you and Kathryn vote?" He asked looking back.

"Of course. Red all the way!"

"Did you know the Government passed their gagging law this week. Hardly a mention in the news and yet we've just moved a whole lot closer towards totalitarianism. Two thirds of people don't vote. We're sleep walking our freedom away."

"So you'll be voting Yes at the referendum then." Steve grinned.

"It wouldn't be enough."

"How do you mean?"

"The SNP appear to be ideologically no different to Liberal Westminster. You told me about that GIRFEC bill. I hadn't even heard of it and now it's law. Apparently they're planning a similar bill for England. You know, some of the laws the Governments on both sides of the border have passed makes me think of laws that were passed in 1930's Germany. Taking away our right to protest; telling parents the state is now responsible for their children."

"So, what are you going to do Robert? Start a revolt?"

"Revolutions are a bloody business. I don't think Helen would let me…"

"They managed to avoid killing anyone in Iceland."

"What's that?"

"The revolution in Iceland."

"When did they have a revolution?"

"Couple of years ago, maybe longer…"

Robert took a pull on his beer and looked questioningly at Steve. "You're making it up, right? There wasn't a revolution in Iceland."

"Sure there was. Wasn't anything on the news about it. Probably didn't want to give us any ideas."

"What happened?"

Steve was going to reply when Helen and Kathryn walked out.

"Not tidied up then?" Kathryn asked. "Men, what can you do with them?" She nudged Helen and laughed. "We are going back inside and opening another bottle of wine. Robert, it's your wife's birthday so…" She made a circular motion with her finger, pointing at the table. "I seem to remember you saying you would clear up…"

She took Helen's arm and led her back inside.

"How much has she had to drink?" Robert asked once the women were out of earshot.

"I think we've got some catching up to do. Come on, I'll help you get the plates inside."

****

It was midday before Robert woke. He lay still for a while, aware the room around him wasn't entirely steady. It had been a good evening, joking with Steve and Kathryn and their kids until late.

He wanted to turn round and go back to sleep but they had Gordon and Penny coming round that evening to finish the weekend off and Robert had promised to clean the place up. And from what he remembered of the night before, there was a fair amount to do.

Gingerly easing himself out of bed he checked on Helen before pulling on a dressing gown. He probably could dance right next to her and she wouldn't wake. Not that he could dance right now…

Once in the kitchen, Robert pulled out a frying pan and started heating up some bacon. A good breakfast would help clear his head. He retrieved his laptop while waiting for it to cook and Googled "Iceland Revolution" to see if Steve had just been winding him up.

No, there were plenty of sites all with bold headlines about an event that had apparently been ignored by the UK media.

He read some of the articles while he ate his breakfast and then read some more.

Eventually he got up, the thoughts prompted by the articles making his head spin more than the previous night's excesses. He loaded the dishwasher and started washing the pans.

****

"That was an amazing meal! Thank you, Helen." Gordon leaned back in his chair and smiled contentedly.

"It certainly was!" Penny stood from the table to join Helen in clearing the dishes away. "Let me help you."

"It was a team effort. In fact, Robert may have cooked the whole thing." Helen confessed. She whispered to Penny: "I'm not entirely sure I've recovered from last night."

"It's not every weekend you turn Forty. You're entitled to let your hair down at least once a decade." Penny told her.

"What on earth possessed you to have three separate events?" Gordon boomed. "Three times the effort when you could have had us all round at the same time."

"Strangely enough that was Robert's idea." Helen cleared the last plate from the table. "Thought it would give us a chance to spend quality time with all of you rather than rushing round all evening. And you know what, he was right."

"Good man, Robert. You didn't end up doing the dishes I hope?"

"That was part of the deal."

"Letting the side down there."

"Shall we head through to more comfortable chairs?" Helen asked.

"Perhaps I could offer you a brandy... or a malt?" Robert said to Gordon.

"A malt would be excellent."

"Penny?"

"Gin and tonic, as always."

Robert led the way and got glasses out. He served Penny and Helen, then brought out a bottle of single malt. "Will this suffice?"

Gordon nodded his approval and Robert poured two healthy glasses, no ice, no water.

"Good man!" Gordon said as he took the glass. He smelled the aroma, then took a small sip. "Hint of peat and salt. A smoky finish and very smooth. Slange!"

Robert toasted him back and took a sip himself. He hadn't had this particular malt in two decades and had taken the opportunity to buy a bottle while they were on holiday. It was still one of his favourite whiskeys.

"Forgive me, Helen if I talk politics for a bit?"

"If you must, Gordon. Robert hasn't talked about much else this weekend."

"Do you think you'll be able to protect the Union come the referendum?"

Robert glanced over at Helen who had pursed her lips. "I've actually started considering resigning from Stronger United."

"Turning traitor, Robert!"

"Gordon!" Penny scolded.

"Sorry, love. Still, that's a blow. Who's going to fight for the No campaign without you?"

"I was hardly a leading light. Perhaps you should take my place?"

"I've no desire to be centre stage. I've never understood why you didn't offer to do more. You've experience of public speaking."

"In church. Preaching to a friendly audience. Not quite the same as trying to rouse a rabble or convince sceptics."

"I would have said the opposite and from what I've seen, you've got the skills to do both."

"Well, I think my views on politics have become soured throughout the campaign."

Gordon took another sip and studied Robert. "I was planning to invest quite a lot in the Stronger United campaign. Honestly, do you think the Yes vote could win?"

"It's still too early to say. Some people are keeping quiet. That could be because they're planning to vote No and don't want the aggro they'll get from Yes supporters. Others are apathetic. I've spoken to a few people who are not even planning to vote. They just don't think it will make a difference."

"Can people really believe that?" Penny asked.

"Apparently." Robert shook his head. "But I think the referendum has become part of the problem for me. Stronger United are pushing to remain strong in Britain…"

"And I hope enough people see the sense in that." Gordon interjected.

"While the Yes supporters are pushing the idea that we can determine our own future, but I've come to believe that both sides are ignoring reality."

"Careful now, Robert. I've never been one to stick my head

in the sand."

"Do you believe the current political system is good for all people. Not just for you and me, but everyone in this country?"

Gordon thought for a minute, beginning to frown. "I'm a capitalist through and through. You know that. I would cut back the welfare state. Make people go out to work. I think we've created half the problems we've got in this country by persisting with the lie the state can and should support people. But... No, I don't think Government can solve the problem. Politicians are too dependent on popularity. Too unwilling to make the hard choices the country needs."

"Would you let people starve?" Helen asked Gordon. "If you could change everything? Would you let children suffer, make people homeless just to prove a point?"

"Of course not."

"Helen would." Robert couldn't resist.

"I would not!"

"Not what you said the other day... How did you put it, 'I would set a fixed welfare budget and it would be shared out to whoever needed it.'"

"People wouldn't starve!"

"If we had ten million immigrants sharing a fixed pot I'm not sure how you'd avoid that."

Penny and Gordon exchanged looks.

"We wouldn't get ten million immigrants because long before that they'd know there would be no money for them."

"I'm winding you up."

"Well don't!"

Robert laughed as Helen glared at him. "Okay, I'll stop. But Gordon, I agree with you. Politics is broken, from parliament right down to local councils. There are massive problems in Scotland and in Britain as a whole right now and not one of the political parties has the answers.

"If it was up to me I'd cancel the national debt; use the interest saved to fund enough jobs to create full employment. I'd seize back the land stolen from the people hundreds of years ago and settle people on it. Give them a chance to create their own future. I would get rid of the welfare state by making it irrelevant. Provide enough jobs that pay enough that every person that is willing to work hard can earn a decent living.

"That's what I'd do if I was in charge."

The room was utterly silent when Robert finished and he looked around at Helen and Penny's shocked faces.

"Did I get a bit carried away?" He asked.

"Bravo!" Gordon cried out. "Now that is the Robert that should have been campaigning. So, how are you going to vote in the referendum?"

"I honestly don't know. If I thought we could remake Scotland like that, I would vote Yes."

"Maybe I would as well." Gordon seconded.

****

Robert went through the motions on Monday, applying for three roles he found on job sites and calling round half a dozen agencies. He watered the plot which was starting to look a bit dry and also the seedling trays, none of which were showing any signs of green.

That evening he and Helen collapsed in front of the TV to watch a movie. Neither felt like talking or doing anything else.

The house phone rang and Helen suggested they ignore it but Robert got up to answer it.

"Robert!" He recognised Gordon's voice. "Are you watching the news?"

"No, just having a night off…"

"Turn on the news now! Call me back." Gordon hung up.

A strange feeling in his stomach, Robert walked back into the sitting room.

"Who was it?"

Robert didn't answer. He changed the channel on the TV and searched for BBC News.

"Robert?" Helen asked again.

He said nothing as he saw the headline: First Minister missing, feared drowned.

Robert fished his mobile out of his pocket and called Gordon.

"Are you watching?" Gordon asked.

"The First Minister?"

"It's worse than that. We need to talk!"

****

BOOK TWO

CHAPTER NINE

"Maybe this will keep them happy." John Anderson flung the report onto the coffee table.

"It's just a temporary stay." Angus Carlisle mused. "Ten years isn't that long and the agitators will be using the time to keep pushing for additional changes."

"Where do they think this is going to end?" John pushed himself up from the armchair and walked over to the open fireplace. He poked at the logs, which had been starting to die down, causing flames to rise again. He took another log and placed it on top, watching as the red and yellow tongues caressed the wood. "They must know we'll fight them to the last."

"The law's on our side, John, at the moment. We need to ensure it stays that way."

"More money, more time wasted, trying to protect something that has been in our families' possession for centuries. Haven't these people had enough from us, demanding to tramp across our land, destroying the careful ecology we've worked so hard to protect?"

"They don't see it that way... I know, it should be irrelevant what they think. But we have to be careful. Hundreds of years ago we had to put down uprisings. It's no different today – just how we go about it."

"Nothing a shotgun to the back of the head won't resolve."

Angus examined his pipe, which was going out. "If it comes

to that then we've probably lost the war." He watched John get up from the fire and begin to pace back and forth across the drawing room. "Did you actually read the report?"

"I didn't need to read it. First they document who owns what land, then they question how they came to own it. All this is..." John gestured back at the report. "Is a chance for them to cast doubt on our rights as land owners. If the Scottish Government actually takes on the recommendations, it's the first nail in our coffin."

"We've still a lot of influence over Holyrood. We'll rally the troops. Start putting pressure on the right people. There are a lot of ways to bury this. The courts have been in our pockets for centuries remember. Ownership has always been nine tenths of the law."

"I don't trust them. If we let other people fight our battles we've got no guarantee that their stake is as high as ours."

"Then we need to raise the stakes. John, relax. Sit down, or better still pour us both a drink."

John harrumphed across the room to the drinks cabinet. "Glen Affric, I think." He said. "Slightly bitter. Appropriate."

He poured two glasses and turned to Angus. "Water?"

"Yes. Thanks."

John handed a glass to Angus and returned to stand by the fireplace. "You're right, Angus."

Angus gave John a disbelieving look.

"We need to raise the stakes."

"Ah, I see. Should I leave before this harmony is disrupted?"

John sipped at his whiskey. "Hear me out, Angus. If we don't act now we may be unable to act in the future."

Angus sighed and moved his hand to indicate he was listening. John told him his thoughts and as Angus listened and eventually discussed, the thoughts became plans.

****

"...Are you watching the news?"

"No, just having a night off..."

"Turn on the news now! Call me back." Gordon hung up.

A strange feeling in his stomach, Robert walked back into the sitting room.

"Who was it?"

Robert didn't answer. He changed the channel on the TV and searched for BBC News.

"Robert?" Helen asked again.

He said nothing as he saw the headline: "First Minister missing, feared drowned."

Robert fished his mobile out of his pocket and called Gordon.

"Are you watching?" Gordon asked.

"The First Minister?"

"It's worse than that. We need to talk!"

Robert kept watching the TV and slowly sank to sit beside Helen. "It's Gordon." He said at last to Helen.

"This is a game changer, Robert." Gordon continued. "The leadership of the SNP has been decimated. First Minister and Deputy both dead…"

"The news is saying missing."

"Keep watching. There's no way he survived. Reports are saying he was out of his seat, giving an impromptu speech, when the bus crashed."

Robert looked in horror at the images on the TV, which showed a bus being pulled out of a river.

Helen turned up the volume.

"…To recap, four people are missing, including the First Minister, and six people have died, after the SNP campaign bus crashed off the bridge behind me into the river Dee in Aberdeen. Witnesses report hearing a loud bang followed by the bus veering onto the wrong side of the carriageway on the bridge, narrowly missing oncoming vehicles. The bus crashed through the wall and into the water some 20 feet below. We believe there have been 23 survivors, many of whom have been rushed to Aberdeen Royal Infirmary and are now in critical condition."

Robert turned to Helen and saw she was as shocked as he felt. He placed a hand on hers briefly then stood and walked away to speak with Gordon. He was holding the mobile too tightly against his ear and eased up. "You said we needed to talk…"

"I've been mulling over what you said last night. I want you and Helen to come over to ours tomorrow evening."

"Tuesday? Helen's normally… Why?" Robert realised he didn't know where Gordon was going with this.

"This is your chance, Robert. If you really meant what you said last night, if you have ever wanted to make a major change in society, then this might be your only chance to do something about it."

The broadcast he'd just heard played through his mind: '...Four people missing, six people dead...' Robert winced, rebelling against the conclusion he was drawing.

"I've no desire to become a politician, Gordon... And the timing... We don't even know if some of these people are alive or dead."

"You're not thinking big enough. Look, cancel everything. Come round tomorrow, Seven PM. We'll feed you and talk. Just think about what this means. Think about what it could mean..."

Gordon said goodbye and hung up leaving Robert feeling shell-shocked. He walked back into the sitting room.

"This is horrible." Helen said.

Robert sat, unsure what to say. The news report switched to footage and he realised he'd seen it before. They were looping through with nothing new to say. Robert took the controller and muted the TV.

Helen looked at him. "What?" She finally asked.

"That was Gordon."

"You said. He wasn't calling to crow was he?"

"You know he wouldn't do that."

"He always hated the SNP. Surprised he never went with you to the Stronger United campaign meetings. Well?" She looked at the TV, which was again showing a reporter. "You never liked the SNP either... No jokes to crack, Robert?"

He couldn't put into words what he was thinking. Helen turned back to him with a questioning look.

"You look more shocked than I am. What did Gordon say?"

Think about what it means... Think about what it could mean... All the research he'd been doing; all the doubts he'd had while campaigning.

"They're decimated."

"Who?"

"Has it said who else was on the bus?"

"No. Just the First Minister and Deputy Minister."

"And the core SNP campaign team. People we never hear or see but who are directing the campaign."

"What campaign? What does it matter who was on the bus?"

"Why did you come with me to the Stronger United meeting?"

"What... What's that got to do with anything?"

"Please. Think back, the one time you came, why did you?"

"You dragged me along..." Helen sighed. "Okay, maybe not dragged but... You know why."

"Because, while you support the SNP, you're not sure you want independence from the UK."

"That was last year. Come on, Robert. Keep up."

"Now?"

"I have no idea." She looked back at the images on the TV, looping back to show the bus being dragged out of the water. "I might have voted Yes. Now..."

Robert gestured at the TV. "There are hundreds, maybe thousands of people campaigning for a Yes vote around Scotland but their biggest asset, or liability... has gone. The Yes campaign seems to have far more active supporters than Stronger United but the First Minister was their mouthpiece. He was their most capable speaker. He had the facts engrained and was skilled at deflecting questions he didn't want to answer.

"For all the SNP and the Yes campaign kept claiming this was not about one man, the fact is he was their leader. I have to suspect that if they had a succession plan it would have involved the Deputy. Does any organization ever seriously entertain that their entire core staff could be wiped out?"

"I don't know. I don't really care. Can we put this off? I thought we both needed a night off?"

Robert turned off the TV. "What if he's right?"

"Who? Robert, you're not making much sense."

"Gordon. What if this was the only chance we had to change the referendum debate? What if independence wasn't about staying in the UK or Europe or whether the SNP are in charge but was actually about Scotland, about what's best for us?"

"That is what it's about."

"No. It should be but neither side in the debate is really proposing anything different. Even the SNP are proposing to mimic UK law and Government for the first few years."

"That's what they do. New Labour did that after the Conservatives and the Coalition were the same. It takes time to change things. You try and do everything at once and you would never be able to do it."

"If the whole point about independence is a different direction to the failed policies of the UK then it makes no sense to replicate those failed policies. What if we could change everything? What if we could..." Robert stood abruptly and left the room. He found his Kindle and brought it back.

Helen made to get up.

"Please." Robert held up a hand. "Just give me a couple of minutes."

Sitting back down, Helen curled up on the sofa resting her arm across the back and leaning her head against her hand. "Two minutes." She said flatly.

"Maybe three, anyway, this book..." He held up the Kindle. "The Poor Had No Lawyers. Almost nothing has changed in the centuries since those first land grabs. The rich and powerful control the courts, control the government, and ultimately the whole country. You and I are told by the media that we live in a democracy but we're not allowed to do any more than vote one representative every five years. When they ignore us, when they disagree with us, when they make laws that we hate... What can we do? They've even taken away our right to protest."

"They're evil,... They're corrupt... Blah, blah, blah... Are you getting to a point?"

"I told Gordon I wasn't interested in politics. He told me to think bigger. He's right. Hundreds of thousands of us have been put off of politics because nothing we do makes a difference. But what if this accident..." He pointed at the TV. "What if the referendum on independence gave us an opportunity to organise ourselves and take power away from parliament? Take control of Scotland for ourselves."

Helen sat up. "What you're talking about... That's almost a revolution. How would you... You're not serious about this, are you?"

"I think I have to be. This is the moment. Maybe the only time Scotland will ever have to come together. If I can do something to improve life for millions of people and I don't... I'll regret it for the rest of my life."

"I couldn't be a politician's wife. I certainly couldn't be a revolutionary's!"

"Did I tell you about Iceland?"

"What's Iceland got to do with anything?"

"They had a peaceful revolution."

"In the eighteen hundreds?"

"Just a few years ago, after the government went bankrupt over the banking crisis."

Helen shook her head. "No, no, no. I don't know what happened in Iceland and I don't care. Even if they did manage to change their government, there is no way you can predict what would happen here. Anyway, you need to get a job. We can't survive on hope and dreams. And what if you get locked up, or worse…"

Robert sat down, laying his Kindle on the table. "I'm not thinking about starting riots in the streets, I'm wondering if there are people out there who want something better but don't know how to go about getting it. I'm wondering if we could use the situation we have, to make a better country. Less politics, less law, more freedom, more personal accountability."

"I don't want you to do this."

"Please don't say that."

"I don't! It isn't just about you. It will destroy my life. I'll never see you. You'll be off at meetings and rallies and seeing your supporters. When will I ever see you?"

"We'll make time."

"Don't!"

"We would, we'd find a way. I'm not signing up to be a politician."

"You think you would end up any different to all the rest? It sucks you in. All those people crying out for attention, the corruption, the greed. How would you resist it."

"You know me better than that."

"That's what worries me."

"I don't…"

"You would give everything to this. You'll pour yourself into it and there will be nothing left. I don't want to be left alone, Robert. Do you understand me? If you do this you won't be able to stop yourself. It's too big. When will you stop? When will you let go? I don't believe you know how."

"I can learn. You can help me."

"I don't want to help you. Why should I help you turn away from me?"

Robert saw Helen's eyes were starting to fill. "Please, just think about it. Gordon invited us over tomorrow. Let's go, hear what he has to say."

CHAPTER TEN

Connor MacKenzie patted his secretary on the back as she sobbed into a hankie. His own eyes were dry of tears, though had anyone been looking, they might have said his eyes were bright. He was staring intently into nowhere, thoughts firing rapidly through his mind as he analysed what he knew and weighed this up against what might also have happened.

The leadership gone. It didn't seem possible. They had achieved much in the end, but it had been so slow that Connor was sure the many delays and setbacks had indeed been the fault of some of those men and women who were either dead or – hopefully – dying in hospital. No, it was too much to ask that they had all been eradicated. They would make useful martyrs, but he had not achieved his position in life by relying on wishful thinking. No, some of them may survive and maybe they could be useful in life too.

He fixed Moira with a concerned look. "Will you be alright?"

"I'm sorry..."

She could hardly speak. It was laughable really, her distress at the loss of those people. She had no idea that he didn't feel the same way, that his apparent stoicism was nothing more than a lack of interest.

"I'll go and..." She waved a hand in front of her face and headed for the washroom.

Twenty years he had worked towards this point and now,

with the referendum only months away, he had a chance to seize power. He had thought he would need to wait until after the referendum when he was sure the problems would begin to stack up, when the First Minister was weakened, by failing to admit the reality of what was required. But instead, the opportunity had arisen, and he would have to grab it before someone else did.

Moira returned, still dabbing at her eyes.

"I need you to set up meetings with these ministers." He wrote a list of names down on a pad. "Will you be able to do that now?"

"Yes, of course." She took several calming breaths and went and sat down at her desk.

"Today and tomorrow. Whenever they're available." He emphasised.

She nodded and picked up the phone.

Turning away, Connor allowed himself a brief smile. He had always known Scotland needed a firm leader. Oh, his predecessor had the wit and intelligence but he was too willing to compromise. Not a mistake Connor intended to repeat!

****

"You're quiet this morning."

Helen looked up at her boss, Stephen. She had been going through the motions since she got in but wasn't certain she'd actually done any work.

"You alright?" Sylvia asked.

Helen felt totally drained. She shook her head.

"You want to talk about it?"

"I had a fight with Robert last night."

Stephen exchanged a look with Sylvia. "Shall I put the kettle on?" He asked.

Helen and Sylvia both nodded their agreement.

"What's he done then?" Sylvia moved her chair closer.

"Did you see the news?"

"He was in the news!"

"No." Helen looked in disbelief at Sylvia. "You haven't heard?"

"I heard on the radio this morning." Stephen told them.

"Heard what?"

Helen gave Stephen an imploring look. "You tell her."

"The First Minister was in a bus crash last night. They think he's dead, along with eight other people."

"No way!"

"It was only six last night." Helen said.

"They found some bodies."

"So, wait…" Sylvia looked from Helen to Stephen. "Why would you get in an argument over that?"

"Robert… He was talking about hijacking the referendum. Starting a revolution. He's been doing all this research into law and politics since we got threatened on holiday. It's almost all he could talk about all weekend.

"Last night, a friend called and… He seems to think this whole thing with the First Minister dying is some sort of opportunity."

"Can't imagine Robert as Che Guevara." The kettle clicked off and Stephen started making the tea. "It is a knockout blow to the SNP. Did you hear the spokeswoman on the news this morning? 'The campaign for Scottish Independence is stronger than just one person.'" Steve said in a deep voice. "She's right, but it is going to seriously make a lot of people question what sort of government we're going to end up with."

"That's the sort of thing Robert's been saying…" Helen took a mug from Stephen. "He's so disillusioned with politics. Doesn't think a Yes or No victory will be good for Scotland."

"Well, he needs to make up his mind soon." Stephen took a drink from his tea. "Only a few more months to go."

"We're going to meet with Gordon tonight – the friend that called. I just hope I can talk him down."

****

If he couldn't win over his wife, what chance did he have trying to convince thousands of people? It was impossible to concentrate. Robert had gone through the motions of looking for a new contract that morning. Checking the job sites; responding to a couple of emails from agencies, with his updated CV. He kept going over what they'd said the previous evening.

He hadn't intended to upset Helen. Gordon's call had been out of the blue. If he hadn't called… If he hadn't suggested… Well, he hadn't suggested anything really. Just told him to think.

That had been enough. Weeks of research, on top of months and years of frustration with politics, had been enough to spark something.

What that something was, he didn't know. Was that what had scared Helen? He didn't really want to set up a political party. Didn't want to start campaigning. But was there any other way?

But to do nothing, especially now...

He'd kept the TV on in the kitchen as he tried to work. Kept checking the scrolling headline every few minutes. Two new bodies recovered. Still no word on who the dead were.

They had to identify the bodies. The families had to be informed. They would be telling someone though. Continuity of government and all that.

There had been a succession of politicians and heads of state offering their condolences to the families of the dead; offering prayers. Even those who stood to benefit most from the event managed to look appropriately solemn. Wouldn't do to go dancing to a funeral...

The picture changed to an outside view of Holyrood. A spokeswoman for the SNP addressing gathered reporters. Robert turned up the volume.

"The campaign for Scottish Independence is stronger than just one person or even one party. While we will mourn the loss of men and women who have championed freedom for Scotland their whole lives, the Yes campaign will continue."

Her voice was firm and confident but Robert could see she hadn't slept. She was holding it together though. A new First Minister in the making, perhaps?

"We thank the emergency services who have..." Robert turned the TV off. He wasn't going to get anything done if he watched the rolling repeats on the news.

He made himself a coffee then went out to the garden to see if anything was starting to grow. Nothing, except possibly, some blades of grass. He plucked a few of these out then headed back indoors.

He felt in a state of limbo. What had Gordon wanted to talk to them about? Had he misunderstood? No, he knew Gordon. But he also knew Helen.

His thoughts went round in a loop until he remembered that he'd posted a request for someone to work on her charities website. He'd forgotten all about it. He logged into the server and pulled up the job request. Sixty one offers! He gave a low whistle. Why hadn't he received any emails?

He checked the settings and realised he didn't have email notifications turned on. He rectified this and then started checking through the offers. Over half were willing to do the job for £100. A few were offering to do it for less. He quickly discounted those. £100 was the absolute minimum he thought the job was worth.

The rest were all looking for a higher rate. Checking through those more slowly he was impressed by some of the quotations and references, but he needed to stick to his price.

He scanned the rest and grouped them into rejects, maybes, and definites. He ended up with eight definites and bookmarked those. The rest got a perfunctory thank you.

Maybe he could reduce some of the tension he expected that evening by showing Helen the offers…

****

Connor caught up with Maureen as she made her way to her office. "Excellent speech, Maureen." He told her.

"Thank you." She stifled a yawn. "I still can't believe it is happening."

"Neither can I." Connor placed a hand gently on her arm. "If I may say, you really should go home and get some rest, allow us to carry the torch the rest of the day."

"There's so much that needs done."

"I'll liaise with your office. I insist, you won't be any use to anyone if you are exhausted. Go home, even if just for a few hours."

Her shoulders slumped slightly and she tried to hide another yawn. "You're right. I'm finding it harder to concentrate. Walk with me to my office. I'll bring you up to speed on what needs done."

It was that simple, Connor thought to himself, half listening as Maureen ran through her checklist. He had no intention of following her instructions. He knew exactly what needed to be done.

****

CHAPTER ELEVEN

Penny had prepared a lamb casserole, slow cooked in a cast iron pot together with potatoes. Gordon ushered Robert and Helen straight to the dining room and filled their glasses with red wine.

"Robert, would you give thanks?" Gordon asked after Penny had served the casserole.

Robert did so, adding a silent prayer that he could find a way to reconcile with Helen. They had barely talked on the way over.

Robert tried the meat. It almost fell apart as he lifted the fork. It probably had not needed the slow cooking as the meat was so tender. Penny had performed her usual magic, seasoning the sauce lightly with thyme and red wine. "Delicious, Penny."

"How do you manage it?" Helen asked. "I always seem to overcook casseroles."

"Years of practice." Penny replied.

Robert noticed she gave Gordon a glance. Gordon was studying them both.

They ate in silence for a minute. Then another.

Robert tried to think of some innocuous question to make conversation but found his mind blank.

Gordon laid down his fork. "I fully expected you to be firing questions at me by now, Robert." He said.

Beside him, Helen shifted in her seat.

"You said we should talk..."

"Can I say something?" Helen interrupted.

"Of course." Penny told her.

"I don't want any part of it, whatever it is you two are cooking up." She looked from Robert to Gordon. "I'm sorry, Penny. I... We talked last night... Fought last night. I can't do it."

Penny reached over and took Helen's hand.

"I thought you would be supportive." Gordon said to Helen.

"Of what? I don't even really know what you and Robert talked about. I'm not even sure Robert really knows."

"I needed to figure it out for myself."

"Of course!" Gordon exclaimed. "The opportunity is there but it's going to be a tough haul."

"Here's what I think." Robert started. "The leadership of the SNP are in disarray. The Yes campaign will be knocked back, yet Stronger United will be unable to take real advantage for fear of turning the whole country against them."

"That's part of it."

"The question is how to use the situation. At the weekend I finally admitted that I didn't want to vote either way. Both sides in the campaign have the potential to suck the life blood out of Scotland. So, how to turn a terrible event into something that can lead Scotland in a different direction when there are still only two options on the table..."

"And?"

"And nothing. I've no idea."

"I'm disappointed in you, Robert."

"There are no options." Helen said sharply. "Robert's never wanted to go into politics. We certainly can't afford for him to give up his job."

Robert held his tongue while Helen continued.

"At the weekend you were even talking about revolution and there is no way you're going down that route!"

"Peaceful revo..." Robert trailed off as Helen fixed him with a withering stare.

"Perhaps we should discuss this ourselves, Robert?" Gordon suggested.

"Not a chance! You invited us both here, well, here we are!"

"Very well." Gordon took his fork and scooped up some potato. "Let the fun begin!"

Robert took Gordon's lead and carried on eating though Helen and Penny both seemed to have lost their appetite.

"Robert is too modest." Gordon said in between mouthfuls.

"He might not yet have put it all into words but he's close."

"Close to what?" Helen asked.

"A third way. There is always another option. Isn't that one of your favourite sayings, Robert? That and just keep thinking."

"Yes or No." Robert said. "Neither Yes nor No or... How about Yes and No..."

"Now you're thinking!"

"Yes to independence, No to staying in Europe. Yes to Union, No to being governed by Westminster. No to independence, No to Union... Would that even be possible?" Robert shook his head.

"Personally I would stay in Europe, you know that, Robert. But as part of the United Kingdom, with our sovereignty reclaimed."

"No to independence... That is what the SNP are currently offering. Breaking away from the United Kingdom to completely lose our independence in Europe. I come across as anti-Europe, I know. Trade with them, yes. Freedom of movement, yes. But to have them make our laws, no! One of the greatest deceptions pulled on the British people has been our loss of democracy by being in Europe. So, on that we're agreed. Ditch the ability of Europe to make or interfere with our laws but keep all the benefits. Like Norway."

"You're getting bogged down in the details. You had it on Sunday. No to politics. No to ever increasing laws that do nothing to protect people and rob us of the little freedom we have left. Get out from the burden of debt. Enable people to work and allow them to choose whether to prosper or not. Why should the state be responsible for my prosperity? It is up to me to work hard and when I do, why should the state rob me of what I've earned?"

"The arguments the rich always roll out." Helen said in a tired voice.

"I don't know if we're rich... Well off, certainly." Penny responded.

"I'm sorry, Penny. I didn't mean that."

"Penny's too modest. We are rich. Maybe not super rich but certainly wealthier than most. There's no reason to be ashamed of it. Hard work and planning and taking a few risks along the way." Gordon paused and looked round at them all. "Helen, until Sunday I was ready to vote No in the referendum. In one evening, without even meaning to, your husband made me reverse my view. Isn't that worth considering?"

Helen didn't make any sign she agreed but Robert saw she didn't object either.

"Robert!"

He knew Gordon was prone to theatrics but he still was caught out.

"Did you really mean what you said on Sunday?"

"Of course."

"What would you be willing to do to achieve it?"

Looking over at Helen, Robert sighed. "I'm a realist as well as a dreamer, Gordon. I would be willing to campaign. Maybe even stand as a candidate at the next election. But I do need to find a job."

"If money was no obstacle?"

Robert laughed. "Lack of money is always an obstacle. Well, then it becomes an issue of time. I have this sense that, if we could change the direction of the referendum debate, we could take control of the country back from politicians. Actually deal with the real problems Scotland faces. But we're less than four months from the referendum..."

"Then you'll need to get a move on. Money will be no obstacle, at least in the beginning. I was planning to donate one million pounds to the Stronger United campaign. The fact is that the analysis I've done suggests my investments could lose twice that if the Yes vote wins."

Robert shook his head in disbelief. "You're willing to spend a million to stop yourself losing two? What if you're wrong? What if the economy remains stable after a Yes vote. I might not think separating from the UK will be good for the Scottish economy, but my experience of the recession has been that, despite what we were led to believe by politicians and the media, there was work available, there were jobs for those who were willing to take them. The only reason for the mass redundancies was the cynicism of company directors who were looking for an excuse to cull their workforce. I think most of those jobs could have been saved with a different approach."

"And you would have that different approach?"

"I would. I'd start with full employment. The knock on effects would be substantial. An increase in self-respect initially. Longer term we could move from a benefits culture to an entrepreneurial one. People who have never known any other way than to take, can be taught to earn. Funnel the money that has been spent on enforcing benefits rules into training and we could finally drag this country out of recession.

"But, four months... Not even that. We'd need to kick-start some mass movement. Mobilise a couple of million people. Is that even possible when fifty percent of people don't even bother to vote in general elections? The Yes campaign talks of their growing support base but are they just papering over the general apathy?"

"There are grass roots organisations out there that you can tap into and work with." Penny offered.

"Who are these organisations? Why would they back me?"

"Think about it, Robert. Thousands of charities, community groups, clubs, associations. You have churches and youth groups, community councils; all of them with intertwining networks. All you have to do is make the right contacts."

Robert grimaced. "But the government have sewn it all up. Tight limits on campaign spending. You have to register in advance, and newspapers, TV, radio, none of them are allowed to show partiality without declaring an interest."

Penny looked at Gordon. "We were talking last night. The fact is that it doesn't matter whether people vote Yes or No, what really matters is if they vote, if they become involved. If the people of Scotland were all to vote in this referendum, it wouldn't matter whether the vote was Yes or No. What would matter is that they were all finally involved in the debate, all willing to have a say. That is what is revolutionary. You don't have to campaign one way or the other, you just have to get people involved. Neither Yes nor No... Yes and No! You can skate right past those rules because you're not campaigning for one side in the referendum, you're campaigning for Scotland."

"That's the weakness of the Yes campaign and Stronger United." Robert mused. "Both campaigns are divisive. Our way or the highway. Could we do that? Bring people together who disagree and get them fighting for one common purpose?"

"We do it all the time." Penny laughed. "Politicians spend so little time in the real world they don't see die hard Labour and Conservative voters campaigning together against unjust laws. They don't see Liberals and UKIP supporters turning up at a school fair and both giving to the same cause. The fact is that we, well you, work with people who each have widely different views on a daily basis. You might not agree politically, but you still work together towards a common cause."

"The beauty of it is that it almost doesn't matter what the referendum result is." Gordon said. "If you can mobilise enough people towards a common cause, whether we end up with a Yes or No result, those people can continue to work together to make sure it happens. The fact is that before the accident yesterday, the SNP only had a majority of one in Holyrood. Now they are completely dependent on the minority parties to pass any new legislation. If those parties unite together, then Scotland has a new government.

"What's more, if Holyrood doesn't elect a new First Minister within a month, there will be an automatic election."

"They'll never let that happen. Not at the same time as the referendum."

"It's conceivable they would have no choice but to postpone the referendum. I agree, it's unlikely, but who knows what could happen."

"There would be riots on the streets. No matter how people feel about independence. If the referendum was withdrawn, it would push a whole load of people over the edge from undecided, to being willing to fight for independence."

"Who do you know that would want to be anywhere near a riot?" Helen scoffed.

"Students. Several hundred thousand unemployed young people."

"I can't see it. Even so, they might only have half a brain between them, but there is no way the MSPs would be responsible for delaying the referendum. They'll choose someone."

"We'll see. They've not yet named the dead. Will there have to be by-elections for them?"

"Speculation is that four SNP MSPs are dead. Three of them constituent elected. The other a regional candidate. The regional candidate is automatically replaced with the next name on the party list, but there will have to be by-elections for the other three within three months."

"So I could stand as a candidate?"

"Robert!"

"It's one of the quickest ways to get attention. Establish a political party and challenge them."

"You'll be fighting against the sympathy vote. In danger of turning people against you if they perceive you're taking advantage of the accident."

"Which I will be."

Robert met Helen's disgusted look with one of concern. "I've never done anything major without your support."

"Don't blackmail me."

"Give me till the referendum."

"Are you asking or telling me?"

"I'm asking. Will you give me till the referendum?"

"I don't have any choice, do I. What will you do if I say no?"

Gordon leaned forward speaking to Robert but directing most of his attention at Helen. "Robert, what you said the other night was radical, it was revolutionary. You saw the statistics, two thirds of people could not be bothered to vote at all in the European elections. Fifty percent turnout for the 2011 election. The turnout for the 2007 general election was not much better. Why is that? Apathy? A belief that politics has nothing to do with people's lives? If you could persuade the fifty percent who have not voted for the other parties to vote for you you'd win by a landslide."

"That's a big ask. Persuade half the population – the half that rarely if ever vote – to support me."

"I'll ask you again, do you believe what you said the other night?"

"Of course."

"Well I'm giving you the chance to prove it. I'm giving you the chance to see if you could make a difference."

"Why, Gordon? Why would you do this?"

"Because I believe in you, Robert. I believe in you both." He said looking directly at Helen.

****

CHAPTER TWELVE

Helen said she was going to bed as soon as they got home. Robert stood alone in the kitchen thinking over the evening. They'd left without making any firm commitments but Robert had promised to call Gordon the next day. The whole thing seemed surreal. Could he really go from IT Consultant to political upstart in a couple of days?

He headed upstairs, got his running gear and told Helen he was going for a run. She watched him without saying anything.

He hadn't been running in months and so eased off at a slow pace. The air was cold but he knew it wouldn't bother him more than a few minutes. The sky was heading towards dark and the street lights had come on. He headed North and settled into a steady rhythm.

His feet pounding on the slabs, his breathing quickening, he allowed himself to relax. He slowed at each corner and checked for traffic before crossing. The streets were quiet with only one man walking a dog. As Robert passed, he lifted a hand in acknowledgement.

Houses gave way to industrial units. Robert increased his pace. Ahead he could see brighter lights. He pushed it harder, faster until he was at his limit, and held the pace until the last unit fell behind him and he could see the Clyde in front of him.

Pulling up, Robert walked to the sheer bank and looked across at the black water. Dark water had always scared him. The thought you might not be able to tell which way was up, mistakenly swimming down until your lungs burst.

Twenty years ago nothing had lived in the Clyde, but efforts to stop pollution had resulted in fish once again reclaiming the river. He waited as his breathing returned to normal, holding thoughts of politics at bay as he drank in the cold evening air.

He began to walk along the bank, heading West. Projecting his thoughts forward, he visualised the industrial units giving way to the shipyards, once the source of much of Glasgow's prosperity. Depending on who you read, Glasgow's industrial past had either been it's making or it's destruction. Glasgow had once been a garden city, a place of learning with wide broad streets, universities and museums and art galleries.

It still was that city, but much of it had been gutted to make way for shallow and temporary glass and steel structures.

Generations had lived and died in squalid tenements. Some claimed this had fostered Glasgow's drinking culture. Men, driven out of overcrowded homes into pubs. It seemed the men of Scotland were always being driven somewhere. Driven from their land by greedy landowners who destroyed the sustaining forests. Driven from tenements into the New Towns.

Robert knew he belonged in the city but he couldn't shake a feeling that he also belonged on a mountain somewhere, scrabbling up steep ground to attain the summit and a view that made the struggle worthwhile.

There was a healthy community of hill walkers, climbers and families, who took every chance to enjoy Scotland's natural beauty, but how many more had been trapped by the glittering lights of their TV's, condemned to spend most of their natural lives distanced from nature?

If these people could not be encouraged to walk heather covered slopes and marvel at Scotland's rugged beauty, then what future did they have? He had a sense that reclaiming the land would only be the start. Would he have to drive people out of homes they couldn't afford? Free them from debt they couldn't pay and sink or swim...

Robert believed it had been cruel to drive people from the land. Would it be equally cruel to drive them back? To force them to fend for themselves. There was so much injustice. Was the only way to solve it to dictate what must happen? And how would that be possible, when at the heart of what he wanted was true democracy? Yet, wasn't it true that people were willing to choose difficult and hard over easy and soft?

Present the truth to people and sometimes enough of them would rally together to overturn the previous order.

Can I do this? Robert thought. Gordon believes I can, Penny too. But Helen? She doesn't want me to, but that is not the same as believing I cannot.

Robert stopped, looking ahead at a distant crane towering over the surrounding buildings. A passage from Genesis which he'd always been fascinated by, came to mind. God came down and found mankind working together as one. To prevent them succeeding in their quest to reject God and set up their own monument to their greatness, God had confused their languages.

The heart of the story was a warning not to reject the creator who had absolute power over men, yet Robert had perversely always found one aspect of the story inspiring. God created us to work together, to pool our creativity and strength. When we did, when we do, we are powerful. We can achieve greatness.

But were there enough people in Scotland who would share his vision, would commit to making it happen?

Robert looked upwards into a sky blinded by pollution and asked God to bless him. "If this is a mad plan, protect me and guide me out of it. But, if I can do some good here, give me wisdom and courage."

He waited but God was silent. That was okay though. Robert knew God expected him to use his wit. If God actually felt the need to speak to him Robert felt that he would have failed.

Robert turned towards his home and started the long run back.

****

Helen couldn't sleep. She lay, curled on her side, thoughts firing a hundred a minute. She knew Robert was out making his decision, knew what that decision would be and how she felt about it. Why? Why now?

She had been the political one, at least when they met. She had so much anger as a teenager. Raging at the injustice of Tory rule. At the hypocrisy of politicians. But after the Poll Tax was repealed, she found the proposals being put forward by her friends were too radical for her. She wouldn't commit to something she didn't believe in and so she'd withdrawn, alienating herself from her former friends when they couldn't seem to understand or accept why she was unwilling to stay involved.

They'd both stayed involved in their communities. She'd been moved by the sight of street beggars to investigate their situations and had found a community of volunteers providing accommodation and meals for the homeless. Looking back it shouldn't have been surprising to find that so many of the volunteers were Christians. She'd thought most Christians were hypocrites, until she found herself working alongside them. Found they shared the same struggles she did. Were trying to make a difference; sometimes succeeding, sometimes failing.

When she'd told Robert she was thinking about going to church he hadn't argued, hadn't mocked her. Had just studied her until she wanted to hit him.

"Okay. When are we going." He'd said. Matter of fact, as if they were going to a concert or for dinner with friends.

If she hadn't invited him to church maybe he wouldn't be planning this thing, which terrified her. But if he wasn't the sort of person who thought things through and ended up acting on them would she ever have married him? Would she still love him?

Why couldn't he just let things go every once in a while?

She turned over. Looked at the empty space beside her. Was she wrong not to support him?

****

Robert stopped in the kitchen when he got home. Stretched his leg muscles knowing he'd still hurt in the morning. He poured a glass of milk and headed upstairs to the bedroom.

Helen was still, facing away from him. He sat on the bed and drank the milk, listening to her breathe.

"Are you awake?" He said softly.

After a while she made a mumbling sound.

"Since we've been together, I've always had your support before I've done something major. I know you don't want me to do this but I need you to at least tell me it's okay."

"Do you even know what it is you want to do?"

Robert looked at his still prone wife. "I'm going to set

Scotland free."

"That's impossible."

"Should get it done by breakfast then." He took a sudden deep breath, the enormity of what he was considering towering over him like a wave about to crush him flat. "If I try and no-one likes my ideas, the worst that will happen is I'll be a laughing stock until the news crews see another squirrel. If I don't try then we could end up with a divided country. If I could have done something to have prevented that, done something to bring people together..."

Helen finally turned to face him, her eyes glinting in the gloom.

"I don't want you to do this."

"Why?"

"I don't know. I think it's going to cost us more than I can bear. I think... I don't want anything to happen to you."

"Nothing's going to happen to me."

"You don't know that."

"I do." He caressed her hair. "How about I give it to the referendum? If I've not started to get support by then I'll call it quits."

"You won't quit."

"No." He sighed. "I won't. This feels like the right thing to do. The right time to try. I will give it all I've got."

"And us? Will you give us all you've got? Will there be any time left for us?"

"Yes. I'll make time."

"You've no idea what you're getting into, do you."

"I need you with me."

"I'm not standing in front of any crowd."

"Says the woman who caught my eye holding a placard in Buchanan Street."

"That wasn't the same thing."

"I know."

Robert held his tongue and waited. He wouldn't force her, though he had to admit he'd left Helen little choice. Was it the right thing to do? Yes. He couldn't shake the growing conviction that Scotland only had one shot at getting this right. If no-one intervened between the increasingly hostile Yes and No camps, would we be in danger of causing a split in the country that could never be repaired?

He caught himself nodding and jerked his head up.

"You can do it." She whispered, so soft he could barely hear her.

"Is that the same thing as having your blessing?"

"Don't push it." She mumbled.

****

Yes, God, bless him. Helen silently prayed. Protect him, protect us. He's going to need you more than he knows.

****

CHAPTER THIRTEEN

"We need continuity of government. The First Minister was telling me just the other day that the months before and after the referendum vote are the most critical to keep Scotland stable. I've discussed my plans with Alan, James and Stewart and it's essential that we move quickly to elect a new First Minister and maintain the momentum to convince the electorate to vote Yes in the referendum."

Charles Lawrence, MSP for the Northern Isles, exclaimed: "We don't even know for certain the man is dead!"

"The chance of him surviving is so small as to be miniscule. He would not have wanted us to falter now, for his sacrifice to be in vain."

"Even so, until his death has been confirmed, we can't elect a replacement."

"But how long do we wait? That is a fast flowing, deep river. If his body made it past the nets it is possible we'll never find the body."

Charles rubbed his knuckles against his forehead. "Two weeks. I don't think we should even discuss this in public for two weeks."

"And at that time would I have your support for the nomination?"

"You're sincere about your plans assuming a Yes vote?"

"I think you would make an excellent Secretary of State."

"You have my vote."

****

The reporters were permanently camped outside Holyrood now so it was easy for Conner to schedule a press conference. He laid his notes on the hastily erected podium knowing he would not need them.

"The police will today begin a full investigation into the cause of the bus crash. While at this moment we have no reason to suspect foul play, the fact is there have been numerous death threats made against the First Minister and other MSPs. There are individuals and groups within the UK who do not want to allow Scotland the chance to determine our own future.

"We will not allow them the victory. The Scottish government will press on to encourage the people of Scotland to vote Yes for independence.

"The search to find those missing will continue and all resources will be given to the emergency services.

"In the meantime, the Scottish government will continue to serve the people of Scotland." Conner paused and looked from the cameras to the reporters. "Do you have any questions?"

There was a hail of voices. Conner pointed at one reporter.

"Alison Carstairs. Who will lead the Scottish parliament now?"

"The SNP are still the majority party and we will continue to lead the parliament." He pointed at a different reporter.

"Kenzie McCulloch. Has the Yes campaign been derailed?"

"Of course not. We have said all along that the campaign is not about one person or party. There are tens of thousands of campaigners throughout Scotland and we will continue to work hard to secure Scotland's future." He pointed at another.

"Darren Johnstone. If the police investigation finds evidence that this was not an accident, what does this mean for Scotland's security, if it were to vote for independence?"

"Scotland will defend itself from attack whether external or internal. We will use all powers available to us to investigate the accident and, if it proves to have been caused deliberately, to prosecute those responsible. Thank you, no more questions as this time."

He strode away leaving many of the assembled reporters

with worried expressions.

****

Conner shook yet another hand and walked his final appointment out of his office. He checked with Moira who was busy fielding phone calls. She handed him a list of messages and he retreated into his office to reflect on his progress.

He now had the support of the existing cabinet and the other key MSPs he thought he would need to swing the nomination. There was no appetite to rush the appointment of a new First Minister but he was sure it would have been fatal to delay his efforts to secure support.

There was a knock on his door.

"Enter." He called.

Moira opened the door. "I have Maureen Shaw asking to speak with you."

"Send her in." He gave Moira a smile.

"Maureen, have you recovered?" He asked as she walked in.

"I'm feeling less tired, if that's what you're asking."

He gestured to a seat in front of his desk and returned to his own.

"Excellent."

"My team tell me you've transferred all calls to your office."

"It seemed to make sense. I have a bigger department so we can spread the load out more."

"We were coping."

"And doing an admirable job. I'm glad you came round actually. You realise we no longer have a majority in parliament."

"There's still a chance…"

Conner gave her a patient smile. "I think it's important we are realistic about their chances. When I spoke to the police earlier they were not hopeful. We have a short window while the opposition delays out of respect but I think it is important that we start planning for by-elections immediately."

"So soon?"

"I believe it is vital. We must retain control of parliament in the lead up to the referendum. If voters lose confidence in our ability to lead, it could cause many undecides to sway to a No vote. I would like you to take charge of the by-election campaign. Nothing public yet, just start sounding out candidates and begin to develop the campaign plan."

"Very well. If you're sure?"

Conner leaned forward and clasped his hands in front of him. "I am."

After she had gone he reflected how easy this was turning out. One only had to start giving instructions to become the de facto leader.

****

Helen caught a sound bite from MacKenzie's speech as she made dinner. The media had picked up the statement about death threats and were headlining that story. The whole thing seemed off. Of course the police were going to investigate. There was no way they would simply accept so many politicians dead or missing or injured without doing some sort of investigation.

And why was he making this speech. Wasn't it normally the police who made statements about investigations? It was a pointless statement.

It wasn't all that likely though, that it had been anything other than an accident? People made foolish statements all the time, but surely no-one really wanted to carry them through.

All the same, she couldn't shake a concern at the back of her mind that this was the life Robert was aiming for – one where any angry voter could decide to have a rant. Anyone could threaten and while it might not come to anything, what would that mean for their lives?

****

CHAPTER FOURTEEN

Robert looked round at the five people in his living room. Helen was hovering in the doorway, having asked everyone what they wanted to drink. He was glad to have her there at all.

Of the couple of dozen people he called friends, only their closest had turned up. Kathryn had left Steve looking after the kids.

"He'll help though." She assured Robert, as she had taken her seat.

Gordon and Penny had both come, claiming the sofa by the fireplace. To his surprise, both Julie and Karen had also come along.

"I'm establishing a political party." He began. "To push for a different result at the referendum."

"The maybe party?" Karen offered.

"Whichever way the vote goes, we have to live together afterwards. I want to encourage people to vote regardless of Yes or No."

"No spoiled ballot papers then?" Kathryn said.

"Absolutely not. I am proposing four main policies: Land redistribution; government by popular vote – or government by referendum; full employment and a subsequent end to government provision of benefits; and abolishing the national debt."

"Only four? You might just keep their attention." Karen

laughed.

"We did come here to talk him out of this, didn't we?" Julie said in a mock whisper.

"You can't run a government on only four policies." Penny said.

"You're right." Robert replied. "But you can campaign on a single issue if you want. I don't believe that political parties should have an opinion on every issue. You put ten people in a room and you can easily have ten different opinions. Scale that up to a whole country and I suspect that one of the causes of the problems we face is government trying to do far too much.

"My second policy is enforced democracy. Make people register to vote and make them vote on major issues."

"That would cost a fortune!" Kathryn exclaimed.

"Why? Every week millions of people vote for Britain's Got Talent; The Voice; or Dancing on Ice. That doesn't cost a fortune. And those shows don't even allow Internet voting, which would cut down the cost tremendously. There is no reason why once a week Scots couldn't be compelled to sit down for a couple of hours and decide how they want their country run!

"Remember the game we played at the weekend." He said looking to Karen and Julie. "Imagine communities across Scotland carrying that out for real. Each one deciding which policies are important to them."

"What game was this?" Gordon asked.

"Robert wants to be the King of Scotland." Julie dead-panned, a slight twist to her mouth.

"You were quite happy to be Queen." Said Karen.

Gordon looked in bemusement from Robert to Julie and Karen. "Is there something you're not telling us?"

"Moving on… I propose this party governs itself the same way I propose the country does. I've made my proposals but it's not my way or the highway. If you don't agree, or if you come up with better proposals then our policies change."

"So I can cut VAT?" Karen laughed.

"If you can get us to agree. Also, I genuinely think we should set an absolute limit on the main policies. If we come up with dozens we all agree on it might be good to start with but the moment someone starts quizzing me on the detail… I don't want a Farage moment where I wasn't aware what my party's policy on Trident was."

"But they will quiz you." Gordon said. "Quiz anyone standing for election. You have to know what the policies are."

"No. I have to know and agree what our main policies are. The detail, that's for the members to decide. A model for the rest of the country."

"What you're proposing. It sounds a bit like anarchy."

Everyone turned to look at Kathryn.

"I'm proposing democracy." Robert stated.

"Anarchy and democracy are closely related. If I understand what you're proposing, this decentralised model, where people do genuinely have the right to decide local policies and have those policies filter up to national level, you can only have that work if leadership does not intervene. The interesting thing about UKIP's 2010 manifesto was not that it contained crazy policies, it was that people genuinely want some of those policies. Whoever wrote them actually wanted those policies. Look across British politics. Even just here in Scotland you have people voting for the British National Party and others voting for the Socialist Party. Opposing ends of the political spectrum. If you govern the whole country using your model, you will get enclaves where people espouse radical views which the rest of the country will want to reject. Can you really establish a model that will embrace such views?"

"I'm not voting for anarchy, Robert." Gordon said.

"He wasn't really proposing that, were you?" Penny looked from Kathryn to Robert.

Robert looked towards Helen but she turned and left. He faced the others. "I know nothing about anarchy. I'll have to do some reading, so thank you, Kathryn. I need to be aware of this. I think that self-governance works. There are some issues where groups of people will always disagree. Why should a minority of people force others to act or live with policies which they never wanted? The impression I get from listening to most politicians is that people cannot be trusted to make decisions. Yet the majority of people usually agree on what is important."

"Are you sure about that?" Kathryn asked. "Sometimes the majority can turn on a group of people."

"I suspect that in most cases that is because a minority has persuaded the majority to do so. Most people are happy to live and let live. We just want to be allowed to get on with our lives."

"I think you'd need some checks and balances." Helen said, as she walked into the room carrying a tray.

Robert looked round in surprise. "What sort of checks?"

"If you open up policy making to everyone, you'll be swamped with thousands of contradictory views. You need some way to ensure that only policies that actually gain a majority are promoted. Maybe you should allow people to vote Yes, No or offer their own alternative. Say you propose keeping Trident, I propose getting rid of all nuclear energy, Karen here proposes a third way – we lease space in London and build our nuclear plants there. Everyone in Scotland prefers Karen's proposal so that's what we do."

"And war breaks out with England…" Julie sighed.

"Remember the game. We can propose something but it has to be possible. Nice as it would be to move Dounreay close to Westminster, I think we'd struggle to get planning permission. But, that's the model I'm proposing – someone makes a proposal, they justify it, everyone discusses and argues and debates and eventually we vote on it."

"So, kind of like an online forum." Karen said. "What about people who don't use the Internet?"

"There's no reason why politics has to be off limits anywhere. Discuss it in homes, discuss it in pubs, offices and churches and everywhere there are people. We already have hours of broadcasting and reams of print newspapers devoted to politics but what if we, the people, could determine the hot topics, what if the media were forced to start listening to what real people actually think?"

"Like they're going to start doing that!" Julie sat back on the sofa and crossed her arms.

"If people have an alternative outlet to vent their feelings and desires and wishes about how the country is run, perhaps the media would have no choice but to adapt."

"How soon are you expecting this to happen?" Karen asked. "The referendum's only a few months away!"

"112 days to be exact." Said Gordon.

"Can a whole nation be persuaded in such a short time?"

"I don't think the end goal can be the referendum. Whether Scotland votes Yes or No, people want change. We saw how divided the nation was at the European elections. Less than half of people voted. Ten percent of those voted for UKIP. Then a huge split between Labour and the SNP. No matter what the result, the fact is the current system of politics disenfranchises a huge segment of the population. Whoever wins power then feels they can ignore everyone who didn't vote for them. It's unsustainable in the long term. The fact is that some Conservative and SNP voters feel the same way on some issues. Some Liberals and UKIP voters also feel the same way on some issues..."

"He's suffering from a form of delusion, right?" Julie grinned round at the others.

"How we run our country covers a huge spectrum of issues and there will be people who feel strongly about some and are happy to compromise on others and who would be surprised to find that some of their usual opponents actually agree with them on some issues. Not every Conservative supports Fracking. Not every Liberal wants to remain in Europe. Not every SNP voter agrees we should have an open borders policy."

"So how will anything ever get decided?" Kathryn said. "If we disagree on so much... Won't we just argue and argue on and on and on?"

"I have a couple of proposals. The main discussion and voting forum would be online. Anyone can start a topic; anyone can raise a proposal. People can vote this up or down. If a proposal gets enough votes it goes to a national referendum and, depending on the proposal, there will be a period of time to debate at a national level. We could have a check whereby if the votes are split evenly it cannot go to a national referendum. Our current political system allows amendments to bills. In principle that's a good idea but since the ruling political party has all the power, it becomes meaningless. But if everyone could vote and no-one would be penalised for voting, then amendments could become a powerful way of overcoming problems that would prevent agreement."

"Wait, are you saying the votes wouldn't be in secret?" Kathryn leaned forward.

"Personally I don't see how the discussions can be. Whether the voting is in secret or not, that's – like everything else – up for discussion. But, to be clear, I propose discussion should be in public."

"Voting has to be in secret."

"I agree."

"Me too."

"You're outvoted, Robert!"

"Very well, our first proposal carried." Robert smiled. "Democracy in action!"

****

"I think we should wrap it up." Gordon stretched and yawned.

"I was just getting warmed up." Said Julie.

"I've had enough." Kathryn replied. "What are you planning to call this political party then?"

"We should be the Land Grab Party!" Julie laughed.

"The Scottish Land Grab Party."

"Why not The Great Scottish Land Grab Party!"

Helen put her hand on Robert's shoulder. "Sub sect of The Monster Raving Loonies..." She said in a whisper.

Robert looked round as Julie called: "Vote!" He turned back to see four hands in the air.

"Whoa, wait a minute!"

"Carried." Said Gordon. "Though I think we need to appoint a chairma... person before voting on other proposals."

"The Great Scottish Land Grab Party..." Robert looked round the room. "You're really sure that's what you want to call ourselves?"

"You had a better name?"

"I think it's wonderful." Helen said as she sat down beside Kathryn. She smiled sweetly at Robert.

"How do I explain it?"

"It was a community decision. Our main policy is reclaiming Scotland's land for the people of Scotland."

"We're Scottish."

"And we're going to be great!" Julie finished.

"D'you get what I said about anarchy and democracy now?" Kathryn asked.

"I think I'm starting to. Well, thank you everyone. Welcome to The Great Scottish Land Grab!"

CHAPTER FIFTEEN

"Can I take your name please... Thank you. And your account number... Excellent. How can I help you?"

"You want to place a bet on Robert Castle becoming First Minister..." James rapidly typed in the details as the customer spoke. "In Scotland. I see. Can you hold on a minute?"

James pressed the mute button and attracted the attention of his supervisor. "I've got a customer wanting to place a bet on some guy called Robert Castle becoming First Minister of Scotland in the next year."

"Is he an MSP?"

"I don't know."

"Search Robert Castle MSP."

James did so and received a Google prompt: Did you mean Robert Castle bakeries? There were several entries below for the bakeries option but nothing about an MSP.

His supervisor leaned over and scanned down the list. "There's going to be a general election in Scotland in 2016. If this guy isn't an MSP now, it's a thousand to one he'll even be in their Scottish parliament, let alone First Minister."

"What odds should I offer?"

"Hundred to one. Might tempt them to place a larger bet."

"Thanks." As his supervisor walked off, James killed the mute button and told the customer. He waited while the customer spoke, then politely put them on hold again and called over to his supervisor.

"What now?" The supervisor said abruptly.

James told him the size of the bet.

"I'll have to punt this upstairs." He held up his smartphone. "Email me the details."

James copied his notes into an email and sent it, then took the customer off hold. "We're just getting approval. Shouldn't take long." He placed the customer on hold again and looked over at his supervisor who was pacing back and forth in front of his desk, phone held tightly to his ear and speaking in a hurried manner.

It wasn't the largest bet he'd had by a long stretch, but at 100 to 1 odds it would mean a huge payout if by some miracle it was won. He stood to make a healthy commission out of it either way though.

His supervisor walked back over. "It's approved."

Of course it was, James thought. Bets were almost never turned down. The odds shortened in some cases but since they could hedge the bet, it was a win/win system for the company.

He told the customer and asked how they would be paying. The customer confirmed it would be a bank transfer but then said they would like to place another bet. James took down the detail then politely put the customer back on hold. Sighing, he called his supervisor over once more.

****

He'd resigned from organisations before and stepped down from responsibilities but never to start campaigning in almost direct opposition to that organisation. No, he told himself as he steeled himself to enter the community centre, not in direct opposition. Just a different direction. He wasn't convinced they would see it that way.

The full crowd were there, chatting round the table as he walked in. Allan rose to greet him. The others smiled and said hello.

"Very well, shall we get started?" Allan asked once Robert was seated. "First order of business, Robert asked if he could make an announcement."

"Thank you." Robert looked round at these people he considered friends. How many would still talk to him after this evening? "I've made a decision that I'm going to stand for election as an MSP."

"That's fantastic news!" Colin exclaimed.

"Well done, Robert." Said Abed.

"That will be great publicity for the campaign." Allan clapped Robert on the back.

Robert noticed Martha didn't join the others in congratulating him. She looked like she was waiting for the punchline. Well, here goes, he thought.

"I'm resigning from Stronger United and will no longer be campaigning solely for a No vote."

"You don't have to resign." Colin looked round for support from the others. "He can still be an MSP if he supports a No vote. Can't he?"

"What do you mean: solely?" Martha asked.

"I've reached the decision that the current opposing campaigns for Yes and No are divisive. What Scotland needs is to join together, regardless of how we will vote."

"But that will happen. We've always drawn together as a nation. That's why we're Stronger United!" Abed voice rose as he spoke.

"I'm not convinced we will. Some of the rhetoric from both sides has been 'my way or the highway.' Where some people have tried to debate, others have chosen insult and mockery. I've decided that I want to seek a third way – regardless of the result, I want Scotland to agree on a core set of issues."

"It's called sitting on the fence, Robert. I thought you understood that."

"I disagree, Allan. I will vote in the referendum. Whether No or Yes, I can't say any more but I will vote one way or the other. But regardless of whether I vote one way and you vote another, I still want to work with you after the result. I want to find common ground."

Allan shook his head in disgust.

Robert pushed back his chair. "I don't want to take up any more of your time. I consider you to be friends and I wanted to tell you this in person. I'm not resigning because I know which the right way to vote is, but just remember, the people you're trying to convince: your friends; your neighbours; your colleagues – you still have to live beside them after the referendum. You still have to get on together, still have to work together. It won't matter whether there's a Yes or a No vote if Scotland ends up bitterly divided after the result."

"As you said, you don't want to take up any more of our time." Allan stood and waited as Robert did the same. "Goodbye, Robert."

Robert took one last look around the room, nodded in acknowledgement and left.

****

Helen walked into the kitchen the next morning to find the table covered in a sprawl of notes, Robert's laptop at half-mast by his usual chair. She put the kettle on and stood looking over the notes as she waited.

Hastily scrawled bullet points on policies he was considering, with for and against arguments underneath. 'Full employment' caught her eye. Below he had written: How? How much would it cost? What if people don't want to work? Can we really remove all benefits? If we were independent would we end up taking on UK government debt? Could we avoid this? What would they do?

If he had this many questions now, how was he going to cope if he was actually elected? Except, he would cope. He always found a way to distil it all down to what was most important.

The kettle clicked off and she made a pot of tea. Robert was normally up by now but he wasn't working and so had shifted to staying up late and getting up later.

She moved some of the papers aside to make space and then ended up sweeping them all towards his laptop. Until one caught her eye.

She took the paper and sat down, holding it.

THE
GREAT
SCOTTISH
LAND
GRAB
PARTY
?

He'd written it out in big capital letters. Centred on the page. Below the words, a big question mark.

The name was ludicrous. She'd have to ask Julie what she was thinking. She'd hoped her endorsement of the name might have made Robert hesitate but he'd gone with it.

She read the words out loud. She might end up hearing them constantly. Seeing them too. They would need posters and flyers. Perhaps even TV ads. The name didn't really lend itself to an acronym: TGSLG...

Her eyes lost focus as an idea formed. She pulled over a blank sheet of paper and pencil and began drawing. By the time she had finished the pot of tea was cold. She sipped and made a face then got up to put the kettle back on.

While she waited she studied her drawing. It would need to be redone in ink. Maybe with oils... Or could it be turned into a resizable font? Maybe she would have to try using that website of Robert's... She folded the drawing and went to slip it into her handbag. She would have a look when she got to work.

****

Once she'd dealt with the usual batch of emails from the previous day and evening, Helen checked in her diary for the details of the website Robert had shown her. He'd given her the login and password and she decided to check to see if there had been any responses before looking to see if a font could be designed.

She still wasn't familiar with the site so had to spend a few minutes looking until she found the link to the job Robert had posted. Clicking on it revealed she'd had eight offers, each at £100.

Helen looked through the list and clicked through to CV's and examples of peoples work. She was impressed. She pulled out her phone and wrote a quick text to Robert: I've had eight offers to work on the website.

She went back to the list. Now, how do I choose which one to go with? She wondered. She ended up choosing a man who had carried out work for a couple of charities in the past. She was just about to contact him when her phone buzzed.

The text from Robert read: Oops. Sorry. Forgot to mention that.

Helen texted back: When did you know?

The reply came back almost straight away: Day we went to Gordon and Penny's

She shook her head, sighed, then took a deep breath. She hesitated over how to respond, then ended up writing: Never mind. Thanks for arranging it. Have decided which one to use.

Helen wrote an email to her chosen designer and then began searching to see if someone could help her with her idea.

****

CHAPTER SIXTEEN

Robert looked out at the assembled group in the village hall. There was one man standing with a heavy TV camera on his shoulder, a bored looking woman that Robert vaguely recognised standing beside him; there were a couple of apparent journalists sitting in the front row, notepads on knees and Dictaphones in hands; and less than ten other people sitting dotted about through the hall.

"I think I'm going to throw up."

Gordon laughed. "Excellent, just let me signal the cameraman. Important he gets it on film. For posterity of course..."

"Seriously. I've never done anything like this before. Why did I ever think this was a good idea. I don't even like giving presentations at work!"

Gordon checked his watch. "Seven P.M. I better get started." He thumped Robert on the shoulder. "Just remember – speak from the heart, stick to the simple idea. You'll be fine."

Walking out onto the stage, Gordon's voice boomed out: "Thank you all for coming. It is my pleasure to introduce Robert Castle as your next Member of the Scottish Parliament for Inverness. Robert..." Gordon clapped as Robert joined him on the stage, the noise echoing round the hall. No-one joined in. Gordon stepped backwards into the wings.

The cameraman was now pointing the camera at him and the

journalists at the front were holding out their Dictaphones, jaded expressions on their faces. Robert looked past them to the eight, yes only eight, people that were seated in the hall. They were looking up at him, one or two slightly hostile; the others curious.

Robert walked to the front of the stage and crouching down, jumped off. He walked to the side of the journalists, aware they were now right beside him and looking up at him.

Clearing his throat, "I wonder if you would mind joining me here." He said looking at the people in the hall. "It's a big place and there's no need for me to be shouting at you."

He gestured at the seats in the front and then as no-one moved, began rearranging the empty chairs in a circle. "Come on, I promise I won't bite."

At the back of the hall, one man could be heard to say: "Waste of bloody time!" As he got up and left the hall.

"Thank you for coming." Robert called after him, then turning around, shouted: "Gordon, will you join me?"

"Well, folks, not exactly what I was expecting but it makes sense." Gordon shouted, as he walked down the stairs off the stage. "Come on and join us." He waved and gestured until one white haired woman stood and side-stepped her way out of her row. The others slowly followed and warily, selecting their seats, sat down in the circle.

"Thank you." Robert said, looking round at them. "I wasn't sure if you would want a seat." He said to the cameraman who gave an imperceptible shake of his head.

"I am seeking election for one reason only. I believe that Scotland's lands were stolen from its people a thousand years ago and I intend to grab the land back and redistribute it."

"You can't do that!" Shouted one man angrily.

"I can and I will." Robert responded.

"You'll have a fight on your hands then." The man said. "I bought my land legally. No-one is stealing it from me."

"How much land did you buy?" Robert asked.

"Three acres! It took me years to save the money to afford it."

"Then what I'm proposing won't affect you. I will not take land away from anyone who owns one hundred acres or less."

"Why would you want to do this?" Asked the woman who had stood first.

Robert saw that closer up, her pure white hair made her look older than she was. She wore a long green jacket that looked expensively cut.

"From 1,000 A.D. till 1,580 A.D. a series of laws were passed that allowed a small group of people to unjustly claim ownership of Scotland's land. The laws were added to continually, to reinforce the legal status of that ownership. These new landowners drove out the peasants who had previously made a living from the land and placed thousands of others in great hardship by forcing them to pay a rent that they could not afford. It was in effect theft on a grand scale. The land has never been legally owned by anyone. It is only entrusted to each generation. Yet we now have a situation where the vast majority of the people of Scotland have no legal right to use their own land." Robert looked at each person in turn as he spoke, making eye contact and getting a sense of their reactions: universally hostile.

"I intend to change this: to redistribute the land that was once stolen and enforce in law that no-one can accumulate land at the expense of others."

"I'm a farmer, Mr Castle. I currently own and make good use of a thousand acres of land. Are you really saying you intend to take all that away from me?"

"I believe that more than one person can benefit from a thousand acres."

"I take it you've never worked on a farm then."

"That's correct."

"I struggle to make ends meet every single year. I get subsidies from the E.U. that just about enable me to survive. The price I pay for feed for my livestock keeps going up while the price I get for lambs and cattle hardly changes. I could double the amount of land I've got and still not do any better but I guarantee you – I cannot run a farm on one hundred acres or less!"

"How many people live with you?" Robert asked.

"My wife and my son. Why?"

"They will have rights to the land as well. It is one thing for an individual to hold onto land they do not need. It is different if several people are working together. Do you employ people to help?"

The farmer hesitated. "Yes, to shear the sheep; help with the harvest; other times as well."

"What if they were there permanently, all year round. Could you get more done?"

"I don't know, perhaps. But I couldn't afford to pay them all year round."

"I'm not talking about paying them – I'm not talking about you employing them either. I'm talking about lots of people, working together. Why is it that your prices are so low?"

"There are lots of reasons: foreign meat driving down prices; supermarkets refusing to pay more. But the low prices would be less of a problem if it wasn't so expensive to rear and sell the animals. Even killing them is expensive – years ago a farmer could slaughter animals on his farm. Now I have to pay to transport them and pay to have them killed. It just isn't sustainable."

"I hear what you're saying. Why do you think we as a country have allowed this to happen –it's because so few of us actually work the land. If there are more farmers, there are more voices; more votes. If we give the land back to the people I'm hoping they will start to care about what happens on it."

"But you're still talking about taking land away from me."

"I am. But I'm hoping I can give you something back – something that will allow you to earn a living, maybe even do better than you have been doing."

"Well, I'll believe it when I see it."

"Mr Castle, I own 13,000 acres. Much of the land is absolutely useless for farming: mountains and forest land. I have two deer sanctuaries on my land. Are you proposing to dismantle those?"

"Deer are animals, Ms..." Robert looked at the lady and wondered, was she? With her expensive coat, her bearing...

"Mrs. Irvine."

"Mrs Irvine. Deer are animals – just like sheep and cattle. They have no special status beyond that. I certainly want to continue to see deer on the Scottish mountains, but not at the expense of its people. As for mountains and forest land: trees can be cut down and there are lower slopes of mountains that are indeed suitable for farming. But, I am not proposing to cut down every tree like a new highland clearance. Instead, I would like to see a greater variety of uses for the land. There used to be a million acres of oak forest in Scotland. Wild apple and plum trees. Why don't we plant orchards throughout Scotland. Let us grow food that we can eat instead of just wood for burning or pulping."

"It will never work." Said Mrs Irvine.

"Scotland is not working at present, Mrs Irvine. You say you own 13,000 acres of land. There are thousands of young people in our cities who have no jobs and no hope and no future. I am not willing to let that situation continue any longer. You have land: let us use it. Let us bring our young people back out into the country. Let us put them to work. Let us teach them new skills, educate them how to grow their own food, build their own homes. Let us give them a chance at a new life. Surely that is worth a chance? Or do you have another suggestion for giving our young a future?"

****

CHAPTER SEVENTEEN

"You really laid into her!" Helen gave Robert an incredulous look.

"It wasn't like that. I was responding to her and it all just sort of slipped out."

"Slipped out, huh? You're going to have to watch that nothing else slips out."

Studying her, Robert asked: "Was that an innuendo?"

She gave her most innocent expression. "Moi?" Then punched him on the arm. "I didn't sign up to be a politician's wife. Nothing better slip out!"

"For better, for worse – remember? Okay, okay..." He said quickly as she punched him again. "Nothing is going to slip out, assuming I know what you're talking about." He leaned out of the way before she could hit him again.

"You know darn well what I'm talking about: politicians and their lady friends!"

They lay on the bed in silence for a minute, both staring at the T.V.

"Can I watch it again?" Robert asked.

"Oh, go on. This is the last time."

Robert took the controller and rewound the news segment back to the announcer, then pressed play.

"...in other news, Robert Castle may just be a name to watch out for in the forthcoming Scottish elections. Gail Charleston has the report. Gail..."

"Thank you, Lorna." The camera shot switched to the outside of the Inverness community centre he had been in yesterday evening. Gail Charleston – Political Correspondent tagged across the bottom of the screen. "Yes, it is not often one gets to see the birth of a rising star but a few voters here in Inverness may have just had that opportunity. Robert Castle has just announced his bid to become their next Member of the Scottish Parliament and caused a few fireworks in the process."

The scene switched to inside the centre focusing on him mid speech: "The land has never been legally owned by anyone. It is only entrusted to each generation. Yet we now have a situation where the vast majority of the people of Scotland have no legal right to use their own land.

"I intend to change this: to redistribute the land that was once stolen and enforce in law that no-one can accumulate land at the expense of others."

The scene switched to outside the centre and a full face shot of the farmer. "I don't know what to make of him. He's talking about seizing the land and effectively stealing away my livelihood. I don't know how stealing from me makes up for the land supposedly being stolen hundreds of years ago."

And there was another switch to Mrs Irvine, her face set in anger. "He has no idea what he's talking about. You can't settle people on the top of a mountain. I look after my estate and it's available at all times for anyone to come and enjoy. If he gets his way, there will be nowhere left in Scotland for people to walk."

And the scene switched back to Gail Charleston. "Mr Castle has certainly got people here in Inverness talking about him. Whether enough people will like his ideas to vote him into power is another matter. Robert Castle posed some intriguing questions this evening. I'll let him have the last word."

The scene switched back to inside the hall and a close up of Robert as he raised his voice. "Scotland is not working at present, Mrs Irvine. You say you own 13,000 acres of land. There are thousands of young people in our cities who have no jobs and no hope and no future. I am not willing to let that situation continue any longer. You have land, let us use it. Let us bring our young people back out into the country. Let us put them to work. Let us teach them new skills, educate them how to grow their own food, build their own homes. Let us give them a chance at a new life. Surely that is worth a chance? Or do you have another suggestion for giving our young a future?"

"It gives me goose bumps every time I hear it." Helen gave a mock shiver.

"Do you think anyone saw it?"

"I sincerely hope not!"

"This is the sort of publicity I need."

"I doubt if anyone was up. It was past midnight when they broadcast it."

"Maybe it will be on again today."

"You're not spending the whole day watching T.V. just to see if you get famous. You promised you would help me sort out the hallway cupboard."

Robert groaned. "I forgot about that."

"It's in the schedule."

"Right. I said to Gordon I would meet with him this afternoon."

"We better get going then!"

Robert climbed off the bed and switched off the T.V. Walking downstairs he studied the cupboard door as he waited for Helen.

"Come on then." She said, pulling the door open.

Robert winced as he looked at the boxes piled high, every nook and cranny stuffed with bags, odd shaped utensils and equipment.

"I think I'd rather face Mrs Irvine again." Robert announced.

"Stop being a woose. We'll start at the top. Can you lift something down?"

Robert eased out a box as a long handled paint roller fell down, narrowly missing his feet. Dust filled the air as he lowered the box and looked at the writing on the top. "Tell me this wasn't packed before we moved in?"

"This is why we need to clear the cupboard."

"I'll hire a skip. Should only take a few hours."

"Your vinyl collection is in here, but if you want to use a skip, that's fine by me..."

"I'm going to need a pot of coffee." Robert said, taking the box through to the kitchen table.

****

Robert locked the front door behind him and walked over to put his rucksack in the car. He walked past it before doing a double take and turning.

Along the length of the car, from the mirror to the boot, was a shiny gouge that undulated up and down.

Robert looked up and round. The street was quiet. Was he really expecting whoever had done this to just be waiting around for his reaction?

The scratch hadn't been there before. He was sure of it. It wasn't as if his car was on the street either and this had just been some drunk or random angry ned. Their driveway was deep, with hedges in between the pavement and a parking area. Someone had walked in off the street to do this. Or was he just being paranoid? Did drunks and angry neds occasionally go out of their way to cause trouble?

Would his insurance cover it? He would have to check. If not it would be an expensive repair bill. Three full panels to re-spray. Why had he gone for the metallic paint option?

Robert unlocked the car and got in as he began to calculate the potential costs of the repair.

****

"Any calls?" Asked Gordon.

"Nothing. I watched the lunch time news and it was all about the economy, the banks, football. Not a mention."

"That will change. I've booked you to speak in Shawshields tomorrow. Invited everyone back again."

"And by everyone you mean...?"

"The media. Local, national, T.V., print, radio. The works. I want to talk about your message."

"My message? Do you mean my speech? I have to admit, I just kind of winged it last night. I had no idea what to say."

"I would never have guessed. And yet, you did manage some eloquent statements. We need to work on those. Focus on what it is you really want to say."

"I thought that I did that last night."

"The problem is that you also wanted to discuss last night. You started answering questions."

"Well, that's something I hate that politicians don't do more – get into conversations with people, listen to them."

"Certainly, but some people are going to hate what you have to say. When you get into discussions with them, you give more ammo for the media to use instead of spreading your message."

"I can't avoid people not liking what I have to say. I need to face it head on."

"I didn't say like, I said hate. What you faced in Inverness was tame compared to what's coming your way if you continue with this plan. There are a lot of powerful people out there who stand to lose a lot because of what you are proposing."

"Okay, so what are you suggesting?"

****

CHAPTER EIGHTEEN

Gordon had arranged for posters to be put up outside the community centre in Shawshields:

Vote for

The
Great
Scottish
Land Grab
Party

We're fighting for you

Robert studied them before walking into the centre. Plain white with green writing. In the glow of the street lamps it took him a while to work out why the font was fuzzy – then he realised the letters were made of grass.

Gordon had hired students to distribute leaflets in the town centre. They had worked on the wording late into Saturday evening. Helen had been asleep by the time he got home. Sunday was usually a lazy day for them. They occasionally attended an evening service at City Freedom church but tonight he was going to be preaching his own message.

The hall was packed. Robert walked in through the doors

and realised a throbbing noise he had heard in the corridor was the combined sound of over a hundred people all talking at once.

He looked around and saw Gordon standing at the front. Making his way over to him around the people seated in rows, Robert became aware of stares and a lowering of the over-all volume. Then he began to hear one or two louder voices:

"That's him, ain't it, from the photo."

"He's going to give us the land."

"Hey, Mister!" A voice called out. "Gies a job!"

There were a few laughs from those old enough to get the joke.

"Still sure this is a good idea?" Gordon whispered when Robert got close enough.

"Why Shawshields?" Robert asked.

"If you can deal with this crowd you can deal with anyone. Good luck, and remember to smile!" Gordon put his arm around Robert and turned him to the crowd. "Ladies and Gentlemen..."

"Ain't no ladies here." A man at the back called and was promptly slapped by a woman next to him.

"Thank you for coming along tonight." Gordon raised his voice. "I would like to introduce Robert Castle, your next Member of Scottish Parliament."

No-one applauded and a large proportion of the seated and standing people carried on their conversations as if nothing had happened.

Robert forced a smile. "I am Robert Castle and I am here to give you back Scotland's land."

"I'll take the High Street!"

"First dibs on the shopping centre!"

Most of the audience laughed. Robert felt his smile becoming harder and harder to maintain.

"How many of you here have jobs?" He asked.

The general laughter died away and a few people looked around.

"Not many. Not as many of you as would want to be working."

"Can't afford to work, mate!"

"I understand that. The government has trapped you in a situation where you can't afford to give up benefits. I want to set you free. But you are going to have to work hard. Most of Scotland's land belongs to no-one. Sure there are people with legal documents who claim the land as their own but it doesn't belong to them and never has."

"I am going to carve up the land and parcel it out to anyone who is willing to work on it. I'm going to provide basic housing, tools and equipment. Seeds to enable you to grow your own food. I'm going to give you a chance to make your own future."

A young man stood up, his face unshaven with uneven patches of blond stubble. "Look, mate, I just want a job. Can you give me that."

"Yes I can." Robert responded. "If you vote for me. I am going to create two hundred thousand new jobs – more than enough to give full employment to everyone who currently signs on. But there will be a cost. Everyone will be able to work and will be paid for that work, but benefits will be stopped."

The room went completely silent.

A woman stood up, supporting a baby that rested on her. "You're going to take away my benefits?"

"I am going to replace them with paying jobs and provide anyone who wants it – a home and an area of land that will enable you to be self-sufficient."

"I can't work. I have three wee-uns to support."

"There are ways round any difficulty. Child-care would be an option."

The woman shook her head. "That's mince! He's havering."

"What if we can't do the jobs? What if they won't give them to us?"

Robert searched for the voice and saw an older man sitting near the back. "You will be able to work. I will create the jobs – if you will vote for me."

"I ain't voting for anyone who's going to take away me benefits!"

"No-one will need benefits when everyone has a job." Robert persisted.

"I think you're full of shit." A young man stood up from the front row and walked towards Robert.

Stepping forward to meet him, Robert found himself tensing as he saw anger in the man's eyes.

The man took a swing at him and Robert dodged. It was followed up by a quick blow with the other arm which Robert only just managed to block. As the man drew back his arm for a third punch, Robert decided he needed to end this. Instead of backing up, he stepped in as the man threw another roundhouse. Only the man's arm could connect at this distance and before he could withdraw, Robert grabbed at his jacket, twisted and pulled. At the same time he reached out and grabbed the man's lapel, pushing the man off balance while stepping inside the man's leg and using his knee to buckle the other man's.

Twisting his own body, Robert used the momentum of the other man's punch to turn him and throw him to the ground. He held on as the man fell and threw himself forward in a break fall, which took him to a crouching position facing the wrong way. Robert spun himself around and checked the man was still down. Fortunately he seemed dazed.

Standing and taking a step back, Robert looked round in case he would have to face the man's friends but saw two other young men being held in their seats by those who had been sitting behind.

"I'm offering you a choice." Robert said in a loud but shaky voice. "You can remain in poverty, dependent forever on a government that despises you, always taking charity and never in control of your lives. Or you can vote for me and I will fight for you and with you.

"You've seen how the government has treated you over the past years: cutting benefits, taxing you if you have a spare bedroom; sanctioning you for every possible reason. If you believe, like this man, that I'm full of shit, vote for the other guy but make sure you stop complaining about how little you have. I'm giving you the chance to change your future. If you take it, you can improve your life. It is completely up to you."

"My name is Robert Castle and I am standing to be your MSP in Shawshields."

He turned to the man lying on the floor beside him. "Am I going to have to knock you down when you get up?" He asked him. The man shook his head.

Robert walked round and offered him his hand. Helping him to his feet, Robert offered: "Those were strong punches you threw."

"How d'you do that?" The man asked. "It was like one second I was standing, the next I was on the ground."

"It's a Judo throw. Takes a lot of practice to use it properly.

Are we good?" Robert asked holding out his hand for the man to shake.

The man took it warily. "I think so."

Robert saw he was still shaken by the throw.

"Have a seat for a minute while you get your breath back." Robert led him to his seat, ignoring the stares of the man's friends who were still being held down.

Stepping back he looked up at the crowd, most of whom were now on their feet, he supposed to get a better view of the politician getting a beating. Sorry to disappoint you he thought.

"I am not going to campaign to lower taxes." He shouted over the noise of people talking. "I am not going to tell you that I will improve your children's education. I am fighting for one issue – to grab back the lands of Scotland that were stolen from us and return them to the people. I believe that to make this happen I will need people who are willing to work. If you are only interested in receiving your benefits – don't vote for me – I will take them away so I can pay your children a decent wage.

"To prepare the land for you to work on it will take effort; it will take courage. Some of you will be injured. Some of you will slip and fall on those steep highland mountains. Some of you will die. If you are too scared to leave your false security blanket; if you need a government who gives to you while taking with the other hand then vote for the other guy.

"If I am elected, I will work for minimum wage. If my party gains power – I will force every Scottish MSP to work on minimum wage. I've heard it said that if the politicians and leaders were forced to work for this pittance – then you can watch how quickly the income of the poor rises! I will set in law that no company director can earn more than twenty times the lowest paid employee in their organisation. I know some of you are looking at me now thinking – twenty times! Why not ten? Why not five?

"Currently, the highest paid company directors earn two hundred times more than the lowest paid employees – and those employees are not even on minimum wage! I am proposing to either reduce director's salaries by ninety percent or force those companies to increase pay for ALL employees to be in line with their director's salary.

"Yes, some companies will choose to leave Scotland – those that do – we will stop buying their products. They will take their jobs away but we will replace those jobs with companies that pay everyone the profits of success.

"I am fighting for one issue and yet this issue is so central to Scottish law that by changing it, I will force change across society. If you want to benefit from this change – vote for me; vote for The Great Scottish Land Grab Party."

****

"Minimum wage! What were you thinking?"

"I wasn't, really…" Robert leaned back against a wall. "Must have been hyped up on adrenaline."

"You can't make policy on the hoof like that." Gordon paced back and forth in front of Robert. "If you don't think through what you want to say you'll keep saying things you regret."

"I don't regret what I said."

"Seriously?" Gordon stopped and looked intently at Robert. "You honestly think that any other politician would be willing to vote their salary down to minimum wage."

"No other politician, perhaps. But we've almost two hundred thousand unemployed, many of whom would be willing to run the country for that. As a start anyway."

"How long before they voted a salary increase?"

"We take away their right to do so. This can only work if we give Scotland real democracy. If politicians have all the power then nothing will ever change. If the people have the power then maybe, just maybe, we can turn this country around. I've been thinking about that actually."

"I should hope so. You need to be one hundred percent focused on this."

"We need to model what we're proposing."

"Democracy?"

"Yes. These meetings aren't working. You said it yourself – I can't make policy. We need the people to start making policy."

"You sure you're ready for that?"

"I better be. No. I am. You've seen me in church. I hate standing up and preaching, would rather run a marathon than do that. But I can teach…"

Gordon smiled. "Café Politics!"

"Yeah, Café Politics. You know, the more I read about other

countries political systems, the more ashamed of our own I become. Did you know the Swiss have a constitution that expects citizens to challenge politicians and call for nationwide referendums? Think about some of the laws that have been passed by the Scottish Government recently. If each one of those could have been challenged and the people had the right to decide whether to accept them or not... How many would have been passed into law?"

"The Scottish government might actually have listened to the objections raised at the consultations..."

"Yeah." Robert pushed himself away from the wall. "Next public meeting we have, let's introduce them to a new way of doing politics."

****

CHAPTER NINETEEN

"Not often we get to see a politician really getting to grips with the public, is it Gail?"

"Certainly not, Lorna." Gail adjusted her hair and looked across the studio desk at her colleague. "Castle defended himself well, holding his own and almost throwing that young man out of the park."

"Do you think that Castle over-reacted?"

"Let's watch the footage again, shall we."

Lorna smiled. "And again, and again..."

Gail gave a running commentary: "Our camera was behind the man as he stood and went for Castle, but even from our poor angle, we can see – there – he swings his fists and Castle dodges, once, twice and then he appears to turn and, oh my..."

The man's body was a blur as Robert picked him up and threw him down.

"Every time I watch that, I get goose-bumps." Gail confessed.

"Not a man to be messed with?"

"He gives as good as he gets and in this case, better."

"You spoke with the young man afterwards..." Lorna prompted.

"Yes, here is what he had to say." Gail turned to look at the wall screen behind them.

"He's alright. Thought he was full of himself before but he's offered me and the boys a job. Was happy to talk with us."

"He still seems a bit dazed." Lorna commented.

"He does, yes. But, no bones broken, maybe we should all take up Judo?"

"It seems unbelievable that Castle would offer him a job after the man attacked him."

Gail appeared to consider this even as she read from her teleprompter script. "They do say: keep your friends close and your enemies closer."

"Well, I hope Castle knows what he is doing. He certainly has started to make a name for himself. Thank you, Gail."

"Thank you, Lorna."

****

"You what!" Helen sat up in bed.

Robert continued undressing. "I offered them a job." He repeated. "It was Gordon's idea and you know, I think it's a good one."

"They attacked you! You have the man on camera throwing punches at you. You could have them locked up."

"You know, maybe it would be good if more of us got into fights occasionally. Punches aren't that bad."

"He hit you, didn't he? You have concussion. I'll take you to A&E."

"No-one hit me. I dodged. They were pretty wild punches. Okay, if I hadn't had training he'd have decked me but, you know, how many times have you wanted to see a politician getting punched out? Be honest."

"I can't say I've ever wanted that." Helen said.

"Really?"

"Anyway, this is different."

"And why is that?"

"It is you they're trying to hit. I don't think I can watch another news programme and see someone take a swipe at you."

"This is only the first time."

"But will it be the only time? You said, Gordon said – this would be dangerous. Wouldn't it be better to back out now?"

"I believed what I said this evening. What I'm proposing is dangerous. If I'm not willing to face some danger myself, then what kind of man am I? I couldn't live with myself knowing I'd not even tried."

****

"Some people will be asking how one man can be standing for election in two different places."

"Rumour has it that Robert Castle intends to put his name forward for all three by-elections."

"That can't be legal can it?"

"He certainly can't be elected in more than one seat. Here's what a spokesperson for the Scottish Parliament had to say…"

The background sound changed to that of a busy street. Helen reached out and turned up the volume.

"MSPs can only be elected to one seat. They have to resign from an existing seat before they can put their name forward for election in another. No-one can be elected to more than one seat. A situation like this where three by-elections are being held so close together has never occurred in Scotland. Technically there is nothing to stop an individual from being on the ballot on all three seats but were that person to be elected in the first seat, they would either have to resign immediately to continue contesting in the other seats, or would have to remove their name from the ballot for the others."

The background noise faded out. Helen frowned at the radio as she thought through what she'd heard.

"So, let me get this straight… Robert Castle can actually be on the ballot role for all three seats?"

"That's what I heard."

"And if by some miracle he was to be elected in the first seat and he resigned… Would there have to be another by-election?"

"Well, I asked that and the spokesperson said they'd have to get back to me. However, I think there would. We have had cases of MSPs resigning their seats to stand for election in other places. They will only do this if they think they have a safe seat and usually a candidate from their party is elected in their place."

"Is this a tactical move by Castle then? Does his political party – if you can call it that – even have any members? Let alone potential candidates?"

"They're remaining tight lipped about that, though a spokesperson for Castle did say they welcome everybody to sign up…"

"Well, I for one will not be signing up to a land grab."

****

Robert opened the door to see a whole crew standing behind Gail Charleston. "You need this many people to do an interview?"

Gail forced a smile. "Where would you like us to set up?"

"How about in my study." Robert left the door open and turned and walked through to the kitchen.

"Where's the study?" Gail asked, stopping just inside the room.

"This is it. Is there enough room?"

Gail turned and shouted: "We're in here."

Robert allowed himself to be directed, made up, sat down, stood up, moved to a 'better position' and then sat down again. Through it all, he watched and tried to understand what was happening. It was organized chaos. Every one of the five member crew – including Gail – seemed to know exactly what they should be doing and when. They didn't need anyone to direct them, they just did it.

Eventually Gail was seated in front of Robert. Acutely aware of the large camera now pointing at him, Robert saw her smile and then she asked him if he was ready. He managed a nod.

"I'm here with Robert Castle in his Glasgow home. Robert, you've made quite an impact over the last two weeks with your Land Grab Party but do you think you have any chance of gaining wider public support?"

"Why are all weather girls called Gail?" He responded.

Gail's smile seemed to freeze slightly and Robert wondered if he could detect a slight flush under her make-up. "I'm not a weather girl."

"Did you lose the application form?"

Gail's smile disappeared altogether. "Mr Castle..." She began again. "You are one man with a crazy dream. Why should anyone vote for you?"

"No-one should vote for me – they should vote for themselves." Robert leaned forward. "When we vote for the Scottish National Party, for Labour or for Liberal Democrats in Scotland, we are voting to keep the thieves – who stole our land in the first place – in power. A vote for The Great Scottish Land

Grab Party is a vote to say we will not put up with this theft any longer. Did you know that in Scottish law – if you steal anything and sell it on – the buyer has no rights to keep those goods. Anything: money, jewellery, your T.V., what-ever you can think of – except land."

"Our laws were first created to justify the large scale theft of commons land. Over hundreds of years, the laws have been added to, by the politicians you would have us vote for. You no longer have the right to walk on, or farm, anywhere in Scotland where the land is currently unused."

"But that's not true, Mr Castle." Gail interjected. "Only last week I walked up a mountain near Inverness. No-one tried to stop me."

"But you did not have the right to." Robert smiled sympathetically.

"Of course I had the right to. Thousands of people climb and walk in Scotland every day."

"Did you own the land, Ms Charleston?"

"Well, no."

"Did you have permission from the owner to walk on the land?"

"I didn't need permission."

"How do you know?"

"Of course I didn't need permission, everyone knows that."

"Perhaps you should consult with your solicitor when you get back to the studio, Ms Charleston. We only are able to walk across much of Scotland's land because the 'legal owner' has given us permission. It is not a right. At any point, that 'land owner' can remove that right and you can find yourself at the wrong end of a gun."

"Is that what happened to you?"

"I was accused of trespassing in Scotland while trying to climb a mountain. There were no fences or signs between the road and the land and yet both the police and solicitors have assured me I have no rights to protest."

"So this campaign of yours is simply a way to get back at the man who pointed a gun at you?"

"Investigating the situation made me aware of how Scotland has lost its land. I am angry about our nation being deceived. I am angry that our lands were stolen from us. I am angry that today in Holyrood politicians, who I voted for, are fighting to suppress the Scottish people."

"That is surely not true. What about the report on the land of Scotland and the common good... Are you accusing the Scottish Government of deliberately working against the Scottish people?"

"All our politicians are culpable in this theft of our land. No law has been overturned. Vote for The Great Scottish Land Grab Party and I will repeal these laws and return Scotland's land to its people."

"You appear to be a single issue party. What about the other issues affecting Scotland today?"

"Scottish society is gubbed."

Gail looked confused. "Is that a technical term?"

"Sure." Robert assured her. "It comes in the manual right after FUBAR. You know what that means, right...?"

"Not on air." Gail said hurriedly.

"You were in Shawshields. A town similar to many in Scotland. High unemployment. The young men of that town have little to be proud of. In fact, that is a term I hate – pride. We talk about being proud of Scotland but what do we have to be proud of? Our so called nobles colluded with each other to carve up our land. If only our ancestors had truly fought for Scottish freedom. Pride... I am not proud of our high unemployment. I am not proud of the hundreds of thousands trapped by benefits. I am not proud of the women who are forced into prostitution to feed their drug habits. I am not proud of our education system that still churns out thousands each year who are unable to read and write. I am not proud of thousands being trapped in polluted cities with no rights to the beautiful land that surrounds them.

"I am not proud that I intend to do something about this. But I will."

Gail leaned back. "Well, Mr Castle, we are out of time. Thank you."

"Thank you, Ms Charleston."

"And that's a wrap." Gail took a deep breath and then appeared to compose herself. "As you can see, we only have the one camera. I need to take some footage of me asking the questions."

"I've seen that movie, I get it." Robert assured her.

He stood and backed out of the way while the crew adjusted

large white umbrella shaped objects and recording equipment and then watched while Gail was prompted and she re-asked the questions.

He had not intended to insult the woman but the question had been tugging at the back of his mind since Ms Charleston – he found himself becoming more and more comfortable with the formal title as the interview had progressed – had called him to request the interview.

If they used it – it could make him look arrogant, uncaring, and yet, Robert thought it was worth the risk. He had no respect for the media. They edited and twisted everything to suit their own agenda. There was no journalistic integrity that he was aware of. Not any more. At least by the remarks he had forced her to reveal her real attitude. He would have to try and follow a similar pattern in future interviews.

It was perhaps ironic – a wanna-be politician accusing journalists of having no integrity. I don't want to be a politician he told himself, for the hundredth time that week.

"All done." Gail walked over. "Thank you for the use of your home."

"My castle."

"Pardon?"

"My wife and I joke this is our castle. Perhaps if every Scot felt the same way about their home, we would be more willing to fight for the land that surrounds us."

"Do you really believe that, Mr Castle?"

"With all my heart."

She studied him for a minute but then shook her head. "We'll get out of your way now."

He watched as they packed their equipment, followed them down the hallway and shut the door behind them.

****

"Karen."

Her abrupt answer told Helen all she needed to know but she asked the question anyway. "Hi, its Helen. Would you like to get together for coffee?"

"Oh, hi! I'd love to but..." Helen could hear Karen sighing. "I just don't know when. I'm up in Aberdeen with the team the next couple of days and Gordon's keeping us all pretty busy most of the time anyway. Can I take a rain check?"

"Of course. I forgot you were all going up there. Well, give me a call sometime, okay?"

"Sure. I'll make time soon, I promise. Bye."

Helen listened to the dead tone for a few seconds before she disconnected the call.

Her best friends were all completely wrapped up with the campaign. All of them up in Aberdeen with Robert. Who was she supposed to talk to?

Maybe she'd just order take-out and watch a movie this evening. She had a sudden urge for Thai. Was there even such a thing as a Thai take-away? She pulled out her mobile to check.

****

CHAPTER TWENTY

"As the Aberdeen by-election draws closer we're here tonight outside the Bon Accord Community Hall where Robert Castle is to announce his intention to stand in yet a third Scottish seat. They are just getting ready to start inside but I managed to speak with some members of the public as they went in…" Gail Charleston held her smile for a few seconds until the cameraman made a cutting gesture.

"Okay, we'll segue into the interviews." She said. "Then cut back to me rounding up. We keep it under three minutes, we might make the top of the hour. Ready?"

"Need to wrap it up quick. Still have to finish editing those interviews."

"Okay, let's go. Ready on one, two…"

****

"Final briefing everyone." Gordon called.

Robert sat on a table mid stage and watched as his friends and three new members of their party gathered round. He checked his watch. Five minutes to the hour. Had he been this nervous before the last two meetings?

"First off, thank you to Denise, Kirstie and Angus for joining us tonight, the newest members of The Great Scottish Land Grab." He joined in while the others applauded. "The format of this evening may be new to you but it's incredibly simple. Our job is not to lecture, not to preach, it is to encourage discussion. To make sure that everyone has an opportunity to contribute. Not everyone will want to but ask them anyway. If someone or two or three are hogging the time, cut them off. No-one gets more than a minute to speak. We've got over three hundred people out there and there are only nine of us. That means we need to split into groups of about thirty to forty. Think about a school teacher managing an unruly bunch of kids for the first day. That's what we'll be facing.

"Some of these people will have genuine grievances. Some will just be out to agitate. Some just won't get what we're trying to do. However, on our side we have the fact that most people have never been asked how they would change things. People will respond to that. You will get support as people in the group realise we are acting democratically. I'll start by asking the questions, however, if the people decide they want to discuss something else, we'll vote on that. I'll ask you to feedback what has been discussed or decided in the groups." He looked round again. "Any questions?"

They all shook their heads, most of them looking as nervous as he felt. "Try and relax. The people out there have no idea what we're about to do. Most of them will be far more nervous about being asked to talk in front of strangers than you feel right now."

Robert stood and walked over to the side of the stage. "Curtains." He asked and they were drawn aside. Walking into the centre of the stage, he looked down at the rows of people who had been noisily chatting but now gradually stopped as they realised it was starting. What are we starting? Robert wondered.

"Thank you for joining us here tonight." He projected over the remaining chatter. "My name is Robert Castle and with me tonight are members of The Great Scottish Land Grab." He gestured and they filed down off the stage and stood in a row in front of him.

"You may have seen some of the footage of earlier meetings we've held. May have an idea of what to expect from tonight." He paused and looked at the faces, some open, some looking as if getting ready to jeer, others hostile. "Tonight we're going to introduce you to Café Politics. I'd like you to break up into nine groups of around forty people each. Take your chairs and form circles as best you can."

As he half expected, no-one moved. Robert jumped down off the stage and walked to the front row. "Okay, ladies and gentlemen, up you stand." He smiled at the frowns. "It's okay, I don't bite."

"You have been known to throw people around though." One woman told him.

Robert laughed. "Hopefully there'll be none of that tonight. Come on, sooner we get moved sooner I can start to hear what you have to say." He stepped back and looked around at the others behind him and nodded. They spread out around the hall and began to encourage people to form circles.

****

"Are we at the right event?" The cameraman asked Gail.

She shook her head, not knowing herself. "Are you recording?"

"Of course."

"I'm going to call the studio. Tell them we might be late with our piece."

****

One man finally stood and lifted his chair. "Where do you want me?" He asked.

"Start over by the stage. We'll need to use up the whole hall I expect."

Others joined him and gradually the whole hall became a mess of people as they all stood and lifted or dragged their chairs into place. He'd instructed his people to avoid trying to manage the process. Self-organizing teams were what they wanted to encourage. Act as a focal point and let people figure the rest out for themselves. As the circles formed he encouraged a few who seemed unsure which circle to join.

Noticing the news crew filming, Robert went over to them. "Hi Gail."

"What are you planning to do tonight?"

"You're welcome to stay and find out. Could you give people space though, respect their privacy. We want to encourage people to discuss freely and I'm not sure being filmed will enable them to do that."

"Of course. We'll keep out of the way."

After Robert had walked away, Gail asked: "How much of this can you film?"

"I've only got enough tape for another hour."

"Okay. Once they're set up, film some short segments and then hold off. This guy seems to attract controversy so let's see if we can capture any of it."

Once everyone was in place the noise in the hall increased, as people started questioning what was happening. Robert made sure that every circle had a member of the party to oversee it.

"What is Café Politics?" Robert raised his voice. "Quite simply it is an opportunity for you to discuss issues and then vote on how to deal with them. What we're modelling here tonight, you can replicate on a smaller or larger scale wherever you want.

"We're here representing The Great Scottish Land Grab Party. We have four policies we'd like you to discuss and vote on. Reclaiming our land; introducing full employment; writing off the national debt; and government by referendum. We've only got the hall for three hours and we want every one of you to have a say on at least one of these policies, so you'll only have a minute each to speak. If you go over your time you will be stopped. If you can't say everything you want to say in a minute you may get a chance at the end, depending on how much time we have. Once we've each had our say, we'll vote on whether to accept the proposed policy or to amend it. You have a chance to influence our party's policies.

"Right, let's kick off. Should we seize back Scotland's land and use it for the people of Scotland? Discuss!"

Robert turned back to his own circle and looked expectantly round the group. "Who wants to go first?"

"I don't understand what you're asking." One man said.

"What's your first name?" Robert asked.

"Neil. Are you saying that homeowners would lose their land? Farmers? If not, why not?"

"Thank you, Neil. Good questions. I propose that anyone who owns land over 100 acres would lose that extra land. If there is a family working that land, husband, wife, children – they would each be entitled to one hundred acres each."

"Farmers don't talk about acres, they talk about hectares."

"And your name is…"

"John."

"How many hectares are in an acre, John?"

"It's the other way around. Roughly two and a half acres to a hectare. What you're proposing would put thousands of farmers out of business. You can't keep large flocks of sheep or herds of cattle on a tiny plot of land when the grass barely grows all year round. That might work in England where they have better weather and sheltered fields but in the highlands, where the soil is so thin you can scrape it away with your boot, you need a large hectarage just to survive."

"Are you a farmer, John?"

"I am. Farm's been in my family for three hundred years."

"Thank you. To be honest, I've been thinking more about crops than keeping animals. Does anyone else in the group have experience or knowledge about farming?"

Lots of heads shook but the woman sitting next to John leaned forward. "I'm Eileen. We manage the farm together."

"Can I ask how many hectares your farm is?" Robert asked.

Eileen and John exchanged glances. "Just over one hundred hectares." John replied. "That's over two and a half times as many acres as you're proposing to leave us."

"If there's two of you, that would be two hundred acres."

"We barely scrape a living as it is. Do you know how many farms would be loss making if it wasn't for grants and subsidies?"

"I don't." Robert had to confess.

"Almost all of them!"

Several people began muttering.

Robert pointed at one person. "Speak up, we want to hear what you've got to say."

"Farmers seem to do pretty well for themselves. I've never seen a skinny farmer."

"Your name?" Robert prompted.

"Donnie."

"Thank you, Donnie. And you…" He pointed at another person who had whispered something to her neighbour.

She shook her head. "It's not important."

"Okay. You?" He pointed at the final person.

"Sheona. I did my thesis on farming profitability. It was a few years ago but from news reports I've heard the situation has

173

gotten worse not better."

"Farming's a business, Mr Castle." John said. "Land is an asset that hopefully doesn't depreciate over time, but without it we couldn't run our business. As it is, we scraped £25,000 last year – that's between two of us."

"More than I make." One young man interjected.

"Twelve and a half thousand each. And that's only because we get EU grants and subsidies. Without those we'd have made a loss every single year we've been running the farm. We might be well fed but we still have to buy clothes and maintain our home and have all the other costs every person does. We pay the same taxes you do and yes, we pay taxes on the grants and subsidies as well!

"I'm not saying we're poor and I'm not asking for your sympathy but you take away land from us and we'll get less grants than we do currently and have less land to produce on. Our income will go down but our costs will probably stay fairly static."

Robert didn't need to check his watch to realise this conversation was taking up more time than he wanted to allocate.

"John, Eileen, Sheona, thank you for sharing. We'll come back to this but we need to give others a chance to contribute. Who else has a view on the proposal to seize back control of Scotland's land?"

The discussion that followed veered between picking up on whether it was right to take land off farmers and what would be done with the land. Robert asked them for their ideas. He was impressed that several came up with suggestions he hadn't thought of:

"I've got no sympathy for estate owners but most of them do live on their land. Why should they lose their homes? At least leave them with the same acreage, hectarage or whatever, as the farmers."

"The land should become common land once more - if you've taken it off one person, why should it be given to another!"

"You need to establish communities. You can't parcel up land and give it out, separating people who're used to living in a neighbourhood. People will need others close by so they can help each other."

"Good point - if you're going to offer people the chance to move out of the cities and to the land, you probably need to give them the choice to live together - with people they already know and trust, or to move somewhere different because they know and don't trust the people around them."

"Who is going to get the land? What criteria are you going to use? There isn't enough land in Scotland to give everyone a decent size..."

"People used to only have a tiny plot of land to survive on. If you're going to make people live off the land - you have to provide enough for them to do more than survive off of..."

He'd intended to allocate half an hour to each proposal but with the larger groups he allowed the time to run on to make sure everyone had an opportunity to speak.

Once he felt that everyone had taken an opportunity to add their view or had indicated they didn't want to, he thanked the group and stood up.

"Thank you to everyone who has participated so far. There will be more opportunities to share in a few minutes. Just now we're going to round up by voting on the proposal to seize Scotland's land for the people of Scotland. Also, you have an opportunity now to propose amendments to that proposal within your groups.

"As we've already said, the proposal before you is: should we seize back Scotland's land and use it for the people of Scotland. If you want to propose amendments to that proposal, do so now in your groups."

He returned to his circle. "Well, do you have any changes you would like to make to the proposal before we vote on it?"

They looked around each other, uncertainty evident in their expressions. He looked round and could see that most of the other circles were similarly silent.

Standing once more, Robert raised his voice. "If you're unsure about how to make amendments, start with some of the suggestions that you made during the earlier discussion. For example, our group suggested that once seized, the land would remain common land in perpetuity. We're going to vote on that as an amendment to the original proposal. Once you've finished voting on whether to add amendments, vote on whether to accept or reject the proposal with any passed amendments."

Sitting down again, Robert smiled. "We have an amendment

on the table – if land is seized, it will forever remain common land – all in favour raise your hands…"

Robert raised his and waited while others did the same. He quickly counted.

"Thank you. Opposed, raise your hands." Some of the others raised their hands leaving a few who hadn't voted.

Robert counted again and thanked them for voting. "I make that fifteen for the amendment, twelve against. The amendment is carried."

"Wait a minute." One woman interrupted. "Why didn't you vote?" She looked round at those who had abstained.

"I don't support the proposal. There didn't seem a lot of point in voting for the amendment." One man replied.

"We don't have to vote, do we?" Another woman said.

"No." Robert told her. "Though I would encourage you to."

"But if you don't vote for any amendments and the proposal is voted in, you've lost your chance to improve it." The first woman insisted.

"This isn't what I was expecting. Come on love, I think we should go." A man said before standing.

The woman next to him crossed her arms. "You go on if you want to. I'm staying."

The man hesitated then pushed his chair out of the way, left the circle and walked off towards the exit.

"I'm afraid we don't have time to discuss the benefits of whether or not everyone should vote." Robert interjected as he sensed the first woman was about to say something else. "Does anyone else have another amendment they'd like to make to the original proposal?"

"Scrap it." The man who'd abstained said.

"Fair enough." Robert smiled. "Best way to decide how we all feel about it. All in favour of scrapping the proposal?"

Ten hands went up.

"All in favour of continuing to amend the proposal?"

Robert felt a shiver run down his spine as twenty hands went up. Twenty one including his own!

He looked round at these people, complete strangers an hour ago but some he now knew their names, others he was beginning to recognise.

"This is democracy." He said. "This is something you have never seen in Holyrood, have never seen in Westminster. We can change that though. Take away this power from the politicians and reclaim it for ourselves. Some of you don't like this proposal. That's okay. You have a chance now to persuade us why you don't like it and why it would be better to do something else. Take that chance." He took a breath. "What we decide tonight is not set in stone. We want to show you what's possible, how you could take control back from the politicians. So, does anyone else have any more amendments?"

He let them discuss and argue and debate and vote for another five minutes before calling time on them. Addressing the whole room, he said: "We're going to vote on the proposal with whatever amendments you have agreed in your groups. What you vote for tonight will not become law but we will use your decisions to draft our policies."

Robert polled his group and the proposal was carried, twenty two votes to six. He thanked them and then stood to ask his team what the other results had been.

One group had rejected the proposal. Another had been undecided. The rest had carried the proposal with varying degrees of support. He called for a five minute break and for his team to gather together.

"So, how did it go?" He asked them.

"It was amazing!" Julie said. "There was such a buzz once we got into it."

"I wouldn't go that far, but people generally seemed to enjoy the chance to share what they thought." Said Kathryn.

As the other shared, they all related fairly positive experiences, until...

"I don't want to do this any more." Penny said.

"Why not?" Gordon asked.

"I don't think I'm the right sort of person to do this."

"You've led discussions before..."

"Not like this. I just... I don't know how to deal with..."

"Would you like to swap groups with me?" Robert offered. "Would you be willing to try that?"

"I don't know. I'll try it."

"Okay. I'll introduce you." Robert checked his watch. "We took an hour for the first proposal. I can't see us taking any less for the next. Let's do full employment. We can maybe let them vote on which one to do last."

Robert walked Penny over to his group and introduced her.

Leaving her, he went to her former group. "I'm going to join you for the next debate." He told them as he sat down.

"So you're the big man are you?"

"And your name is?" Robert asked him.

"Free country, right?" The man smiled under a challenging look.

"In a democracy I believe it's important we know each other's names." Robert told him. He looked around and quickly saw frustrated looks and boredom. "Are you willing to share your name?"

"Sorry excuse for a political party if you have to ask this lot to write your policies for you." The man replied.

Robert decided to ignore him. "Our next proposal is to create full employment in Scotland. Would anyone like to comment?"

"Never work." The man quickly said.

"Is that your policy?" Another man said angrily. "Just another benefits scrounger?"

"Let's keep it on track." Robert said, raising his voice. "Does anyone have a comment on the proposal?"

Across the hall, Gail heard the change in tone. "Start filming." She told the cameraman.

"What?" He asked.

"Film Castle. Now!"

There was silence for a minute. No-one seemed to want to speak. Finally one woman started but she was quickly cut off by the nameless man.

"Finally got a voice have you? Too good to speak up during the last debate?"

"Let her speak." The man sitting beside her said.

"She can speak for herself, can't she?"

"Can't you just shut up for a minute!"

Several others echoed him with similar pleas. Robert stood and asked them to wait a minute. He walked over to Ollie and Gareth who were sitting by the entrance.

"Could you both come with me? I might need you to escort someone out."

"Someone getting violent, chief?"

"Hopefully not but watch yourselves, okay?"

"We've got your back."

Robert hoped they had. It was one thing winning a fight.

Quite another if he had to repeat it on a regular basis.

"Can I have your attention!" Robert shouted over the discussion that was taking place throughout the hall. He walked back into the group but remained standing, leaving enough space for Ollie and Gareth to stand beside him.

"Democracy is worth fighting for and you had better believe that you will have to fight for it. I want to introduce you to a man. A man who will not give us his name." Robert looked at the man. "A man who will not let others speak. Who happily insults others who want to debate and shuts them out."

The man leaned back and crossed his legs, appearing to enjoy the attention.

"We are demonstrating democracy here tonight and so our group will now vote on whether to exclude this man from further debates. If you are in favour of this man being evicted from our meeting, raise your hands…"

"Hold on a minute!" The man sprang to his feet. "This is a public meeting, you can't…"

Robert counted twenty nine hands raised with just one abstention – the woman who had apparently been silent during the last debate.

"Got your bully boys to back you up? Too scared to take me on yourself?"

The man started towards Robert. Ollie quickly stepped in front with Gareth joining him.

"Can I Tase' him, chief?" Ollie asked.

"If he threatens anyone else."

"I haven't threatened anyone!"

"Will you leave willingly?" Robert asked the man.

In response, the man sat himself back down on his chair.

"Very well, Ollie, Gareth, this man has disrupted a public meeting and a democratic vote has called for his removal. Would you escort him out and call the police once he's outside."

"Could you move aside folks." Gareth told the people sitting behind the man. They got up in a hurry and moved away.

Ollie and Gareth quickly stepped forward, picked up the man by his arms and marched him out of the hall. He shouted and swore the whole way, his voice only fading once the hall doors closed behind them.

Robert walked over to where seats had been knocked over and began picking them up. "We will call the police and ask them to caution him." He told the silent hall. "If anyone would like to give evidence either to defend him or against him you are welcome to do so. Otherwise I hope you can continue where you left off."

Looking around, Robert realised the television crew was filming him. Had they captured the whole incident? He looked back at his group and invited them to return to their seats. "Sorry about that. Had he been like that the whole time?"

"I think he was getting worse."

"He interrupted everyone who tried to speak. Insulted us when we did manage to make a point. I was ready to walk out of here."

Several others nodded their heads at this last statement.

"You stood up to him though, just now. And if you want democracy to be real in Scotland, we're all going to have to be willing to stand together against people like that who will try and shout us down. But, he's wasted too much time as it is. Does anyone want to give feedback on the proposal to create full employment?"

Almost all of them did. Pent up feelings erupted and Robert had to act quickly when disagreement threatened to get out of hand. Fortunately they all seemed to recognise their anger was mostly directed at the unnamed man and yet again, Robert heard new ideas being voiced that he knew he would be able to use.

He was just about to ask everyone to vote on amendments to the proposal when he saw two police officers walk in.

"Excuse me." He said to his group and he went over to meet them.

"Are you Robert Castle?" One of the officers asked, looking young enough to have only just graduated and been placed on the streets.

"Come with me." Robert told them. He walked over to his group before they could tell him otherwise. Standing in the centre of his group and aware the hall had again fallen silent as they watched what was happening, Robert addressed the officers. "Thank you for coming. We had to evict a man from our public meeting earlier. These men and women are witnesses to the events. It is up to them whether they choose to give a statement. However, we are in the middle of a vote and I'm sure these people would like to finish what they've started…"

Several of them signified their agreement.

"Mr Castle, would you come with us?"

"Without interviewing witnesses?"

"I think it would be best."

Robert turned to the woman who had tried to speak earlier but had been cut off. "Will you lead them through voting for amendments and then a final vote on the proposal?"

She shook her head.

"All you have to do is ask if anyone has an amendment and then ask everyone to vote on it…"

"I'll do it." One of the men offered.

"Thank you." Robert told him. He looked across and found Gordon who was standing, looking concerned. "Step in for me while I'm out." He called across. Gordon nodded.

Robert turned to the police officers. "Lead on."

They took him outside and led him to their car. He could see the nameless man with Ollie and Gareth, all sitting in the back.

"We found the man in the middle being restrained by these two men who claim to work for you." The other officer said. "Are they acting under your orders?"

"The man – has he given his name yet?"

"No."

"He was being abusive and disruptive and so we held a vote on whether to evict him from the meeting. The vote was almost unanimous to remove him and so I asked Ollie and Gareth here to do so."

"The man has made a complaint that he's been assaulted by these men."

"He made a threatening move towards me inside the hall. I asked Ollie and Gareth to call you in case he continued his aggressive behaviour."

"I think we'll need you to come down to the Station."

"I'm in the middle of leading a public meeting and there are several hundred witnesses to the events inside the hall. Are you sure you want to do that?"

****

CHAPTER TWENTY ONE

Seated inside a police interview room once more, Robert fought an internal battle to remain patient. He had sat through long project meetings many times; presentations that could put anyone to sleep but at least there he was being paid and could choose to take notes to maintain interest.

Being forced to wait inside a sterile room without knowing what was being said or planned outside was torturous to him. It was all the worse having to miss the discussions that hopefully were still going on back at the hall. Gordon would have kept the meeting on track and they would feed back to him what happened but it wasn't the same as being there. Meeting people and seeing and hearing them.

Still, there was no way he could run all the campaign himself. No way he could discuss with every possible voter. He needed to let go and trust his team.

He'd texted Gordon while being driven to the police station: Will need a solicitor. Being taken to Bon Accord Police Office with Ollie and Gareth.

They hadn't arrested him, yet. But there was no guarantee that wouldn't happen.

Finally the door opened and two officers entered. They sat down opposite him and took out notepads.

"We have some questions for you."

"Your names are?"

"Officer Clarkson and with me is Officer Nair."

Nair had been the older of the two officers who had initially responded to their phone call. Clarkson was a new face.

"I would like to speak with my solicitor." He told them.

"We need to take a statement from you."

"I've given you a statement which Officer Nair has already taken down. Before I answer any further questions or give any additional statement I will speak with my solicitor."

"Mr Castle, a serious allegation has been made that you incited two men to assault Mr McAllister, it will be in your interest to answer some questions now."

The man did have a name then. Robert sat back in his seat and crossed his arms.

Clarkson persisted in asking several questions but eventually gave up and they left Robert alone in the room. He had been tempted to ask if he was under arrest but did not want to risk forcing that possibility, by leaving without a solicitor's advice.

It was after Ten PM when the door opened again and a stranger walked in accompanied by Officer Nair.

"I will need five minutes alone with my client."

So that was the solicitor. Robert wondered where Gordon had managed to find him.

Once Officer Nair was out of the room the solicitor sat down opposite Robert and held out his hand. "Franklin Davies. Gordon asked me to represent you."

"Robert Castle. Thanks for responding so quickly. I take it you are also representing Ollie and Gareth?"

"Mr Barclay and Mr Lennox, yes. Though I am more concerned about their situation."

"Let's talk about that then."

"They are accused of assaulting Mr McAllister. That's a serious allegation. Also of threatening to use a Taser on him."

"Neither of them possesses a Taser."

"Regardless, threatening to assault someone is considered a crime."

"The police have no sense of humour."

"Would you like to have someone threaten to use a Taser on you?"

Robert shook his head. "No."

"Fortunately neither man has said a word to the police. It seems they have had prior experience of being interviewed."

Robert restrained a smile. "They were acting on my orders and we have dozens of eye witnesses to the McAllister's disruptive behaviour."

"Abusive and threatening behaviour. Be consistent on that. I should be able to get you all released but there may well be follow up investigations and you will likely have to return to answer questions. I understand the officers didn't interview anyone at the hall?"

"I was taken away so I don't know, but certainly I suggested they did and they preferred to take me outside."

"That was a mistake. We can prove there were hundreds of people there and for the police to fail to take witness statements at the scene means any case they have is seriously flawed. It's not as clear cut as I would like but we will use it."

It took an hour but Robert was walking out the police office with Ollie and Gareth before midnight. He counted that a blessing. Checking his mobile as he left the station he found three missed calls and ten texts from Helen. He looked up to see a full dozen flashbulbs go off in sequence, blinding him. The solicitor took his arm and steered him towards a waiting car as questions began to be shouted in his direction:

"Are the allegations you assaulted another member of the public true?"

"Have you been granted bail?"

"What have you been charged with?"

Robert tried to see past the flashes that kept going off but his vision had been compromised.

Someone opened the car's rear door and Robert was bundled in, Ollie and Gareth piling in behind him. It was no limousine and Robert had to quickly move over. The solicitor jumped in the passenger seat and the driver started moving the car immediately, despite photographers surrounding the vehicle.

"Welcome to the underbelly of politics, Mr Castle." The solicitor said, turning to face him. "We don't normally get as much of this as they do down in London, but the media everywhere are whores for a potential story."

Robert looked out at grey granite houses as they sped past. "Where are we going?"

"Your hotel."

"Is it going to be as bad as it was at the police office?"

"I don't know. Assume it will be."

"Ollie, Gareth, how are you?"

"Just a normal Friday night for us, chief." Ollie cracked.

"I hope not any more…"

"We're reformed characters we are, ain't we Gareth?"

"Aye. When we're not on duty anyway…"

Gareth elbowed Robert, he presumed in jest, but the lad still had no idea of his strength.

There were no reporters or photographers at the hotel. Obviously he wasn't quite important enough to merit that level of attention.

Gordon was waiting in the reception. Robert thanked him for arranging the solicitor.

"What next?" Robert asked as they all gathered together.

"It's all dependent on the COPFS – Crown Office and Procurator Fiscal Service." He went on to explain at Robert and Gordon's blank looks. "You have not been charged, arrested or bailed so you are free to act as normal. If a Procurator Fiscal decides to advise the police they should investigate the situation further, you may be called back for questioning and you will need to make yourselves available. I have to advise that given the current political situation and upcoming referendum there is a risk pressure will be applied to publically investigate you and so use you as a distraction. Alternatively, the powers that be may decide they don't want any more harmful attention directed towards politicians and the case could be buried."

"They have no case though, do they?"

"Member of the public assaulted by candidate's body-guards… I would say there is potential for a public and messy case. It is unlikely to succeed given all you've told me but that wouldn't matter. It is the publicity you would get regardless of the outcome that would do the damage."

"We didn't assault him." Gareth told them.

"Just carried the bawbag out." Ollie confirmed. "Didn't even tap him when he bit me."

"He what?" the solicitor turned to Ollie.

"Bawbag bit me on the hand after we got out the door." He held out his hand and Robert could clearly see bite marks.

"Did you show the police?"

"Wouldn't show the polis anything."

"We need to get his hand photographed at once. And get medical attention."

"Of course…" Robert shook his head. He wasn't at all sure the marks on the hand looked that serious. He felt suddenly exhausted, the adrenaline of earlier collapsing. "I'm sorry… Why?"

"This is evidence of McAllister's behaviour. He will be unable to show similar evidence of violent treatment. Also…" The solicitor smiled. "We wouldn't want your man to catch rabies…"

As the others laughed Robert forced a smile. He caught Gordon's eye.

"I'll sort it out. We can debrief in the morning."

Robert thanked Ollie and Gareth once more and then headed up to his room. Shutting the door, he pulled out his mobile. It was just short of One AM. He braced himself and called Helen.

****

The phone rang causing Helen to start. She hadn't been sleeping but, even though she'd been trying to reach Robert all night, she wasn't expecting it.

She picked up her seven year old Nokia and accepted the call.

"Helen?"

"You're out then."

"Just got to the hotel."

"Didn't think to call me from the police station?"

"It was kind of a media scrum."

"I saw."

"Oh. I'm sorry."

Helen fought back tears. Gordon had texted her to let her know Robert had been taken by the police for questioning. When she'd texted back she got no response and when she eventually called him she just got an engaged tone. She'd resisted turning on the news for a couple of hours but then had given in and, looking online, had found a report that Robert had been arrested after a member of the public had been assaulted.

"Were you… Arrested?"

"No. Of course not."

"They said… After last time I didn't know what to think."

"It wasn't the same. I haven't been charged with anything."

She heard him sigh. "I'm travelling back tomorrow. Do you want the details now?"

"I'm supposed to be working tomorrow!"

"I know. I can tell you tomorrow... I love you."

"I know." It was all Helen could bring herself to say. She said goodnight and hung up. Lying back down on the bed she stared at the ceiling. Did every politician's wife have to go through this? Live with this kind of pressure? Could she cope? Before sleep finally took her she still hadn't reached an answer.

****

CHAPTER TWENTY TWO

"Twenty new applications for membership after last night! All of them wanting to get involved."

Robert looked across at Kathryn who was in charge of party membership. "All of them from the meeting?"

"Every single one! I had several people ask how they could get involved and I told them to join up and they would get information packs sent out. Speaking of which… Karen?"

"They're almost done. Top priority this weekend."

They were all seated round a table in the hotel restaurant, plates or bowls in front of them as they held a breakfast conference. Robert held on firmly to his coffee mug. He hadn't slept all that well, kept up thinking through the implications from the previous evening.

"How did it go after I left then?" Robert asked.

"It took a while for us to settle back down." Karen told him. "Our group was at the other side of the hall and so we weren't aware there was any problem until Penny had said. I hadn't told the group after that and so they were quite shocked when you announced that vote. Then you didn't announce the result… It just all seemed to happen so fast and even I was shocked when Ollie and Gareth dragged him out the hall.

"But, after I explained what had been going on, several people said they wished problems they're facing could be dealt with that efficiently. The impression I got is there is a real frustration with people in power who seem to be absolutely powerless to do anything that's really important to us."

"My group was right beside Penny's and we could hear what was going on." Julie said. "We tried to ignore it but some of my group clapped when he was taken out."

"People clapped? I don't remember that." Robert thought back to the previous evening. He only remembered a stunned silence.

"You were quite intense." Kathryn told him. "You had your scary face on."

"I have a scary face…"

"When you get angry about something, you tend to get tunnel vision, Robert." Julie agreed.

"Franklin!" Gordon called. "Gareth, Robert, move over to let Franklin in."

Robert turned to see the solicitor approaching. He stood and pulled over a chair but Franklin remained standing.

"Have you heard the news?" He said, looking round at the group.

"What news?" Robert asked, wondering if the fallout from the previous evening was about to get worse.

"They've found a body. Rumour has it might be the First Minister."

No-one spoke for a minute as they looked at each other.

"Good riddance. Never trusted him." Julie said.

"He was one of my heroes." Gareth said, frowning at Julie.

"Oh. I didn't know that."

"If it wasn't for him, we wouldn't be having a referendum."

There was an uncomfortable silence until Franklin cleared his throat. "You don't know the implications of this, do you?"

"What implications?" Gordon asked.

"The SNP no longer have a majority in government. A First Minister has to be elected within one month or parliament is dissolved."

Robert felt he must still be drained as he wasn't seeing the apparent importance.

"There may be a general election before the referendum." Franklin summed up.

"No way!" Julie exclaimed.

"They'll never allow that to happen." Penny said.

Robert and Gordon exchanged a look. With the enmity

between the Yes and No campaigns at an all-time high, Robert thought it was a strong possibility they may be unable to agree on a new First Minister.

"Could an election be delayed until after the referendum?" Gordon asked.

"This has never happened before so it's possible but it would mean Scotland was without a parliament during one of the most important periods in our history. I can't see that being allowed to happen."

"Very well, we can discuss this later." Robert gestured to the empty seat he'd pulled over for Franklin. "Could you give us your advice on how to handle last night's events?"

Franklin and Robert both sat down. Franklin pulled out a notepad and opened it up.

"First off, Ollie doesn't have rabies…"

Ollie waved his bandaged hand and there were cheers around the table.

"We were able to get some good photos last night. I doubt you'll be able to claim compensation from McAllister given the circumstances, but it makes it less likely there can be a successful prosecution against you."

"Do we need to look at having indemnity insurance as an employer?" Robert asked.

"Absolutely." Stated Franklin.

"I'll sort that out." Gordon promised.

"As I said last night, I don't think there is a likelihood of a successful case against you. Normally, if there had been an allegation of assault, my advice would be to keep your head down and avoid situations that could be used against you if an investigation was to be carried out.

"However, since you are trying to establish a political party, you are going to attract people who either want to cause trouble or who want attention. Your policies, if I may say so, are controversial – making it more likely that you will be unable to avoid adverse publicity and possible re-occurrences of similar events.

"Legally, the situation is a grey area. You cannot bury this event since anyone who wants to use it against you will do. In some ways your best defence is to be consistent. If you honestly believe you had a democratic right to evict McAllister, then campaigning on that platform will either cause people to speak out in your favour or against you.

"I don't know what the ramifications for Scots law would be if you were actually elected but on behalf of the legal profession – we also get frustrated at times with the glacial speed of justice in Scotland."

****

"Have you heard about this man, Robert Castle and his Land Grab Party?"

"You know I don't have time for comics, Maureen."

"He's been getting a lot of attention from the media. Mostly mocking him but they're still giving him air time."

"Is this another UKIP wannabe?" Conner asked, reluctantly giving his full attention.

"UKIP did get ten percent of the vote."

"It was just a protest vote against Westminster. People always vote differently in European elections."

"Shawshields is a marginal seat. Even a two percent change in the vote could count against us."

"Keep an eye on him then. How are the polls looking otherwise?"

****

"He thinks what!"

"There's a possibility there might be a general election before the referendum." Robert leaned back against a unit as he watched Helen making coffee for him. He tried not to wince as she banged down his coffee pot on the counter and slammed his favourite mug down beside it.

"You've been away most of the week! That's just campaigning for three seats. What is it going to be like if you start campaigning for the lot of them?" She turned and looked at him. "How many are there again?"

"One hundred and twenty nine." He braced himself.

Helen surprised him with a smile. "One hundred and twenty nine... Less three... And you have how long to campaign for the rest?"

"Possibly two months..."

She tilted her head to one side, her smile wide but her eyes hard. "So should I just divorce you now and get it over with?"

She didn't bother waiting for an answer, just turned and hit the switch on the kettle.

"I could do that." He offered.

"No, no, I insist. You must be sooo worn out with all that travelling and talking and… What else is it you do when you're campaigning?"

"That's pretty much it."

"Oh yes, getting yourself arrested."

"I wasn't…"

"You might as well have been. Good job your mother isn't still alive." She looked away and Robert could see she was fighting back tears. He went to her but she held out a hand, palm facing him.

"No." She shook her head. "I'm making you coffee." She wiped her eyes in that strange way women did, as if pretending everything was okay.

"So what's next." She asked. "You said it was just a possibility."

"We keep campaigning. Maybe they will manage to elect a First Minister. Who knows. If so, then I stand in the three seats."

"And lose."

"It's a long shot, I know."

"You'll lose."

"And raise awareness of the party. Regardless of whether we win or lose, there will be a referendum in September and someone has to stand up for Scotland."

"It doesn't have to be you."

"The more I listen to people around the country, the more I think it does. Regardless of whether there's a Yes or No vote, we have to work together afterwards. That's getting lost in the debates."

"I went online while you were away."

"Oh?"

"Found a few forums on Facebook. Asked some questions and got called a troll."

Robert couldn't help himself, he laughed.

"Why would they call me a troll?"

He was unable to keep a straight face as he said: "Because of your hairy feet."

She threw a dish towel at him.

Wiping his own eyes he was relieved to see her expression had softened slightly. "It's a term for people they think are just there to cause trouble."

"All I did was ask some questions."

"People on both sides are blinkered. Unable to recognise they're turning people away who have genuine questions. What we did in Aberdeen though, we enabled people to discuss, to raise their doubts. We're going to do it again, see if we can encourage others to start up Café Politics around the country." He hesitated. "I'd love it if you'd come along to the next one?"

Helen turned away. Poured water into the coffee pot and dropped in a spoon of filter coffee. As she stirred it she looked round for a brief glance. "I'll think about it."

****

CHAPTER TWENTY THREE

The next weeks passed in a blur. The impending police investigation remained pending. Robert hoped that no news was good news and had no time to worry about it anyway as Gordon arranged meeting and event and discussion, one after the other.

He gave one speech to journalists the following day.

"I need to be true to myself." He told them, looking from the men and women with their tape recorders out to the cameras pointed at him. "If I'm attacked I will defend myself. If I see someone else being attacked I will defend them.

"I believe in democracy. I believe that if a group of people are being harassed or abused by an individual that they have the right to join together to remove that person. Last night we acted that out. Unfortunately we have allowed the police, the courts and politicians to claim that we don't have that right. The police felt they had the right to take me – against my will – for questioning.

"Some people will claim that if communities are given the right to police themselves that they will persecute minorities. I find that to be a disgusting claim. It has resulted in a perverse society where minorities persecute the majority.

"If you elect me and The Great Scottish Land Grab Party, we will fight for your communities, we will fight to give you rights to defend yourselves, to remove people from your communities that refuse to live in peace.

"If you have men and women in your neighbourhoods that are selling drugs, always getting drunk and threatening others or vandalising property; if you have people who steal, people who threaten, people who attack; you should not have to wait months for the police to do nothing.

"The Great Scottish Land Grab Party will enable you to protect your communities, to make them safer."

The response from the media was full of derision and outrage.

"With this announcement, Robert Castle has taken his party from the fringe to the extreme. Attacking the police, claiming that he can do away with the current justice system."

"We have important checks and balances in our current justice system. No-one wants to see an innocent person go to jail and the reason justice takes so long is to ensure that only the guilty are punished."

"Can you imagine what would happen if communities were given these rights? I can imagine people being hounded out of their homes just because a group of people had taken dislike to them. What if a community was to pick on a family because of their race or colour? Would Castle's party defend their 'right' to do that?"

Robert stopped reading newspapers, watching TV and listening to the radio.

The response from the public also had outrage and derision but Robert was relieved to see that as many people supported his handling of McAllister as condemned him. It seemed that there were a lot of people who felt just as abandoned by the justice system as he did.

Initially it seemed that a new coalition would form in the Scottish parliament but the smaller parties could not agree on some core issues and nothing was decided. Rumours started circulating that the SNP were trying to woo other parties into a grand coalition but, in the opinion of some commentators, the treatment of the Liberal Democrats at the European elections was apparently making all smaller parties wary of signing up to be a junior partner.

Robert travelled from Shawshields to Inverness to Aberdeen and back again. He stopped holding rallies and instead turned every meeting into Café Politics, inviting the participants to either discuss and vote on his proposals, or to come up with their own.

Their membership grew to five hundred people in two weeks. As one person told him after a particularly late night: "I came for the show but wasn't expecting to be asked my opinion. I really hope you pull this off. Scotland needs this."

Finally Helen came along to a meeting that had been organised in the centre of Glasgow. Penny had suggested the idea. Robert had written to the charities that worked with the homeless; to food banks; to agencies that supported people at the margins and had invited them and their workers and volunteers to discuss and suggest policies they should adopt.

Robert now had enough members of the party that he could sit in on a group without having to lead it. He made sure he was far enough away from Helen that she could take part without feeling he was watching her.

The discussions he took part in had the usual buzz. As people became more familiar with the concept and especially if they'd attended more than one Café Politics, they became bolder at sharing, more willing to say what they really felt.

Afterwards Helen was subdued. Robert didn't want to press her so they drove home in silence. It wasn't until they were in bed that she finally spoke about the meeting.

"I want to try leading one of those groups."

Robert turned over to look at her. "Okay."

"The woman who was leading ours wasn't experienced enough. She let some people speak for too long and cut others off because we'd run out of time."

"It's a difficult juggling act when you have so many people."

"You said at the start that everyone would have a minute to speak. You need to enforce that. At least until everyone has had a chance to share something."

"Okay. I'll do that."

"She also missed out on several opportunities to lead the discussion. Most of the people were leaning towards one point of view and if she'd just addressed the concerns the others were raising, she could have won over the others."

Helen's eyes were fierce and bright in the half light of the room.

"I'd like to see you lead that group." He said.

"Not a chance. I don't want you in the same room as me. That'd put me right off." She took a deep breath and let it out slowly.

Under the covers he felt her hand clasp his.

"Thank you for taking me." She told him.

He leaned over and kissed her.

"I'm going to sleep now." She insisted.

He held her until her breathing softened then turned over and stared at the ceiling. Could they make it through this? He didn't know.

****

Robert learnt how to retain people's names in short term memory, refined his views so he could adapt them to questions raised and direct the answer towards one of his proposals. He began getting requests from members to run their own Café Politics.

The core working group expanded as they got to know more enthusiastic members. There was a management trick as old as Moses he began to apply, assigning ten new members to a group to be led by a seasoned member who had shown ability and a willingness to be involved.

Reports came back of discussions which began to be more focused on local issues with groups asking if the party would consider adopting a wider range of policies.

"You need to be careful, Robert." Gordon warned him. "Get too bogged down in detail now and you will struggle to manage it."

"We need some way of managing these policies and allowing people to share their views online." Robert replied.

"Focus on the goal. We can look into that once you're elected."

"That is the goal. Getting elected is only a means to an end. Even if we never made it into power, if we could help the people of Scotland demand democracy and get it, that would transform this country."

****

CHAPTER TWENTY FOUR

The by-election for Aberdeen was held first. Gordon had ordered rosettes: blue on the outside, white on the inside with the grass green font spelling out The Great Scottish Land Grab. Gordon delivered them in person that morning.

"I'm not going to be able to join you in Aberdeen." He said after he'd handed the box over to Robert. "We had a break-in yesterday. Didn't even realise it at first, they hardly disturbed anything."

"How's Penny taking it?"

"On the chin. We're both shaken up by it though. They got some of her jewellery. Tried to get into my safe but obviously not professionals. Could have been worse though."

"It's never good, is it." Robert had commiserated. He'd thanked Gordon for the rosettes and promised to call after the result.

Over thirty new members turned up to the count, all of them eager to hear what progress they were making in the other seats and offering more suggestions than Robert could keep track of.

The night dragged on and by the time the count was finished his nerves were frayed. He allowed himself to be guided up onto the short stage and looked out at the array of TV cameras and reporters.

The media attention on this by-election was bound to be greater given it was the First Ministers home town but even so…

His mouth went totally dry. He forced a smile at the woman standing next to him and the man beside her. Both representing well known political parties that he suspected stood far more chance than he did of retaining their deposit.

Robert could imagine Helen at home, laughing at his terrified expression as he was forced to wait, while the Returning Officer left the stage to confer with her assistants.

A poll the previous day had shown only one person out of two thousand voting for his party. Another two elections with similar results and Helen wouldn't have to ask him to quit, he'd be glad to admit defeat.

The Returning Officer finished whatever discussion she'd been having and returned to her podium. She then spent some minutes adjusting a pile of papers in her hands and making notes while Robert decided that posing as a politician was definitely worse than having his photo taken at weddings.

"The result for Aberdeen having tallied all votes and had the result confirmed is as follows." She finally began. Robert took a long slow breath.

"With a total of Thirty Thousand votes including two hundred and five spoiled ballot papers, Roger Harper, Conservatives, two thousand, five hundred and thirty two. Mary Ellinton, Green Party, three thousand, four hundred and nineteen."

The names and numbers began to blur for Robert as he waited and then…

"Robert Castle, The Great Scottish Land Grab Party, seven thousand, eight hundred and ninety three."

He felt himself sway. Seven thousand. That was more by far than he had hoped to get. He looked for and found his team below and saw them cheering and clapping. He vaguely heard: "SNP, nine thousand, four hundred and ten." He'd lost, but by nowhere near as much as he'd feared.

Hands were offered and he shook them and congratulated the SNP candidate who had obviously won. Then stood back and waited while the speeches took place. He had prepared two, his expected losing speech and long shot victory one but suddenly realised he didn't know who had placed where. Was he second, third or fourth? Not fourth as the vote for him had been too high. He relaxed when he heard the Labour candidate called next. Speeches were in order of votes gained. Finally it was his turn and he strode to the podium, discarding both speeches as he did.

"Congratulations to Andy Manson. Thank you to Gordon and all new members of our fledgling party who have worked so hard to give people an alternative to traditional politics. Thank you to the people of Aberdeen who have embraced Café Politics and have found an opportunity to make their voices heard.

"We have lost this vote but we have won your support and we will continue to fight for you and for all people throughout Scotland, to bring democracy back to our country. In a few short weeks we will be voting again in the referendum. I will never tell you how to vote but I will tell you that the fight for Scotland's future starts here. It starts now. Either you can claim the right to decide what laws should be passed in this country or you can leave it up to crooked politicians to decide for you.

"Yes, I am now a politician and I don't want you to trust me. I want you to stand up for your own rights, demand the right to determine your own fate, not just on one day in September but every single day. Whether Scotland votes Yes or No, you need to decide to make your voice heard. Come along to one of our Café Politics and find out that you can take back control of your life."

****

"Seven thousand votes! How does a complete unknown who's only been campaigning for a month manage to get seven thousand votes!" Conner stopped shouting into the phone as Moira opened the door into his office.

"I'm fine." He said brusquely. He waited until she'd closed the door before continuing. "Get me everything you can on this Robert Castle."

****

The vote in Inverness had a similar result. Robert didn't get as high a percentage of the vote but still managed to scrape third place.

"This is a fantastic result, Robert." Gordon told him later. "Remember, Scotland has partial proportional representation. In a general election, if you consistently polled in third place, you would gain several of the floating seats."

"But would we have any influence?"

"You would have the right to bring bills before parliament, to persuade the other parties to commit to them. It would not be an easy road but if you can persuade this many voters in just a few short weeks, imagine what you could do in a year!"

"Still no word on a First Minister?"

"They're taking it to the line. If they're not careful there will be a general election."

"We're going to need to be able to field candidates!"

"Have you thought about that?"

"No politicians."

"None? What about councillors?"

"None at all. We start with a clean slate. Ordinary people who aren't tainted by the current system."

"You lose out on experience and risk the party opening up to a lunatic fringe."

"We do. But we can follow models from Iceland and elsewhere, where candidates need to show that local people trust and support them before they can stand. It's not a perfect system but it is democratic."

****

Conner watched the by-election in Inverness on his own. The Aberdeen result could have been a fluke. Unlikely but perhaps there was a strong UKIP presence who had found some commonality in Castle's message.

He was not pleased with the result. Castle had failed to gain the same percentage as Aberdeen but had still significantly eaten into the SNP vote. Once could be ignored. Twice could not. He called Maureen immediately and ordered her to start bussing people into Shawshields.

They could not afford to lose that seat.

****

Robert made the headlines between the Inverness and Shawshields by-elections. He had some warning when a reporter called their media line to ask if they would like to comment on the punch up that had taken place at a Café Politics in Shawshields.

He had been forced to surrender his phone as he couldn't cope with the volume of calls he was getting and had been assigned a new one with strict instructions not to reveal the number to anyone except family.

The call came through as he was leading a discussion on uses of land at a Café Politics in Glasgow. He didn't answer it but checked the phone and saw two text messages from Julie, one marked Urgent! Call Back! Excusing himself, he asked a party member to take over the group while he made the call.

"What's up?"

"There's been an incident in Shawshields." Julie answered.

He couldn't have placed who was running Café Politics in any other city or town but with the Shawshields by-election only a few days away he knew Karen was there.

"What's happened?"

"A fight broke out. Media are all over it. We had a reporter there who was quick off the mark and managed to capture some of the fight on his mobile. It's up on YouTube now."

"Anyone hurt?"

"Not seriously. The two guys involved knew each other apparently. Neighbours. There's been some bad blood between them from what I can work out. They've cooled down but it really freaked some people out. We had some kids there tonight. Teenagers and a couple of babies. Karen said she had mothers screaming at her for letting it happen."

"What do you need me to do?"

"Can you give the reporter a call? He wanted a quote from you."

Robert gave a half grunt. "I'm sure he does. Okay, text me his number."

He walked over to Mel who was now regional co-ordinator for Glasgow. "Can I borrow your phone?"

"What's wrong with yours?" She nodded down at his phone.

"Gordon will be furious if I burn another number."

"Ah. Sure. Don't speak too long, I'm not on an unlimited contract."

"I won't." He took her phone and checking his own, punched in the number.

"Gavin Flowers." A curt announcement, busy with important tasks.

"This is Robert Castle. I understand you wanted to speak

with me."

"Ah, Robert. Yes…" Robert heard the sound of things being moved about. No doubt a recorder being switched on. "Do you feel your experiment in social democracy has failed?"

"Absolutely not."

"Two men fighting at one of your meetings."

Robert waited.

"Don't you have a response?"

"I didn't hear a question." He heard Flowers sigh.

"Why do you allow people to get into fights at your meetings?"

"Why do you allow people to get into fights at your office?"

"We don't."

"Really? How do you prevent it?"

"We don't have to, it just doesn't happen."

"That must be nice for you to live in your media bubble. In the real world people sometimes get into fights. You want me to condemn those men, I'm not going to do it. I don't know the circumstances or the reasons. I hope they can reach a compromise that allows them to live together, that if one of them has done something wrong that they will make recompense, but I'm not going to judge them."

"Members of the public were put in danger tonight."

"Are you going to ask me a question?"

"Why do you allow members of the public to be put in danger?"

"We're bringing democracy to parts of Scotland that have never known it. That's going to uncover conflicts and problems. I don't yet know all the facts about tonight but I'm confident both the volunteers who ran tonight's event and members of the public intervened to protect others from getting involved. However, I note that one individual did fail in their duty to protect others around them, that wouldn't happen to have been you Mr Flowers, would it?"

Robert killed the connection and handed the phone back to Mel. "Thanks."

"Who was that?" She asked.

"Just some reporter."

"You going to be front page again tomorrow?"

"Aye. Unless they can pull a picture off the video they took."

CHAPTER TWENTY FIVE

"Castle has had some bad publicity."

"I hadn't heard."

Maureen gave Conner a doubtful look. The man seemed to know almost everything that was going on at times.

"A fight at one of his meetings. Scared quite a few of the participants."

"Can't say I'm sorry."

"It made headlines on several papers. However, any benefit from that may well be lost by the effort Labour are putting into the campaign. They seem to have fielded as many canvassers as we have."

"We have to win this seat, Maureen."

"I don't know what else to do. We've got as many volunteers as we can out on the streets. I've used up the budget on advertising and leaflets. Thomas is holding nightly meetings in the area."

"If we don't win this seat then we can't elect a First Minister and there will be a general election. It will be chaos."

Maureen didn't know what to say. She left the meeting with Conner and sat at her desk for several minutes before finally picking up the phone.

"Hello, this is Maureen Shaw, could I speak with Elaine Wear?"

Maureen waited while Elaine's secretary connected her.

Elaine was one of the two independents in the parliament and a friend.

"Maureen, what can I do for you?"

"Support our nomination for First Minister?"

"Ah. That. Your Conner MacKenzie has already asked and been declined I'm afraid."

"Really?"

"Oh yes. Last week, after the result in Aberdeen."

"He hadn't said."

"All very hush, hush. Anyway, it wasn't exactly the nomination he was asking for, he initially wanted to sound out the possibility of forming a coalition."

"And you said?"

"And go the same way as the Lib Dems? Not a chance. I wasn't voted in because I belonged to a political party, I was voted in because I'm independent. There's no way I'm turning my back on my constituents."

"Of course not." Maureen thanked Elaine and chatted for a minute before saying goodbye. She rang the other independent and then the MSPs who led the smaller parties. All said they'd been contacted by Conner the previous week. Why hadn't he said anything to her?

****

Julie persuaded Robert to release a YouTube statement after the incident. His team had been taking short segments of discussions taking place around the country and they had several media students willing to put together a brief film.

Robert recorded a voice over for the intro showing animated conversations: "Many of you will have seen the clip of a fight breaking out at our Café Politics. What our media failed to show you was scenes from hundreds of other meetings where people like you and I have found we can discuss our hopes for Scotland's future and agree or disagree in peace."

The scene cut to a headshot of Robert with the Clyde in the background.

"We would like to tell you that every meeting we hold will be safe but we cannot. We are opening up politics to every person and the fact is that sometimes, rarely, people get into fights.

"We have volunteers at every Café Politics. These meetings

are run by your neighbours, people you work with, commute with. These meetings are run for you.

"Where people behave inappropriately, we will take immediate action. You'll have heard that I was questioned by police for daring to throw one man out of one of our meetings. However, we need your help.

"The first step to reclaiming your community is to turn up, to make your voice heard. If you allow a few individuals to scare you away you will never get to see that you are not alone. There are dozens of people living near you who face the same problems, hundreds of people who are asking the same questions, thousands who want something to change.

"My name is Robert Castle and I'm fighting for Scotland."

The scene cut to a montage of short clips of party members: students, housewives, an older man in a wheelchair, two business women each holding up one of the party's posters, several men in boiler suits, all of them saying the same thing: "We're fighting for Scotland!"

The film was released immediately and viewed ten thousand times within twenty four hours.

****

The count in Shawshields was a boisterous affair, all the volunteers chatting and joking as the evening wore on. All of his core team turned out along with thirty local members.

Robert gave interviews when asked and otherwise chatted and got to know the people who had committed to the party.

Although he wasn't comfortable on the stage the third time round, he did feel relaxed enough to chat to some of the other candidates. Mostly they were friendly enough. He was surprised that the Labour and SNP candidates were on such good terms. Having been first and second for as long as there had been a Scottish parliament, he'd assumed they would be clear rivals but the more he met with politicians and their hopeful replacements, the more his assumptions were being challenged.

The returning officer had less apparent issues to deal with and launched into the results without any paper shuffling. The first few names on the ballot were low as expected but even Robert was surprised just how low they were.

"Thomas Carlton, SNP, Five thousand, four hundred and

seventy nine."

There was a communal gasp at the low figure for SNP. A safe Labour seat until 2011 when the SNP had snuck in on a slender margin. Robert looked at Andy Patrick, the Labour candidate, who was trying to restrain a smug look. He must have won a landslide victory, Robert thought. All their campaigning had paid off.

"Andy Patrick, Labour, Eight thousand and thirteen."

The figure was lower than Robert had expected. Both the SNP and Labour together had gathered over twenty thousand votes at previous elections.

"Robert Castle, The Great Scottish Land Grab Party, seven thousand, five hundred and sixty seven."

Second place! He looked down at his team who were cheering. Julie and Karen had broken off into a whirl. Labour was announced the winner.

Robert did the math in his head. The SNP had needed to win every seat to regain the majority. They'd failed to do so by just one seat. Parliament was tied.

****

"Who is this guy!"

Angus Carlisle turned from the window where he'd been examining the sky. He had a shoot planned for later that day and it looked highly likely they would need raincoats.

"John." Angus greeted him with a nod as he saw his old friend. Then he saw the newspaper John was holding up.

Angus crossed the room and took the paper. John Anderson took off his jacket and hung it over a chair then sat and poured himself some tea from the pot at the centre.

"Make yourself at home." Angus told him. He studied the picture of a row of candidates at an election count – one man at the end raising his arms in what looked like a gesture of victory – then skimmed the story.

Labour had won in a town called Shawshields – not somewhere he had heard of. But the real story of the night had apparently been a new political party gaining second place. As Angus read the name he felt a coldness run down his back.

"Second place?" He asked.

"Yes." John stirred sugar into his tea, clinking his spoon

against the fine china.

Wincing, Angus made a mental note to start leaving mugs on the breakfast table if John was going to show up more often.

"Apparently they came third in Inverness as well. And Aberdeen."

John finished skimming the story and confirmed what he'd just heard. "Why didn't we hear about this?"

"Why would we? I don't care what happens in Inverness and I don't imagine you do. I don't read the newspapers every day, mostly they just get used for polishing shoes and starting the fire."

Angus did read a newspaper most days, but couldn't recall seeing anything about... He closed his eyes and calmed his breathing. "Do you know what they stand for?"

"Isn't it bloody obvious?"

It probably was, Angus decided. "How could a party like that reach second place in an election?"

"This is why I don't trust politics. Get rid of the lot of them I say."

"If only it were that easy. Is this connected to the report on land reform?"

"How would I know? I hadn't heard of them until I picked up the paper this morning. My maid got a right scare." John's eyes took on a distant look as he smiled.

"We need to find out." Angus returned to the window and saw to his dismay that drops of rain were beginning to attach to the glass. "A land grab party coming second place in a by-election... We might not have ten years."

****

Just a few days later Robert spent the whole day watching the broadcast of an emergency session of the Scottish parliament. Several attempts were made to nominate and gain support for a First Minister but each attempt failed with the smaller parties refusing to align with the SNP.

Gordon called him during the afternoon. "They've nothing to lose from a general election and possibly everything to gain." He said. "The SNP was always going to risk losing its mandate once a referendum was announced. However Scotland votes in September, they've completed their main objective. All the smaller parties stand to gain additional votes and possibly a greater share of power."

"And our party? Will the same be true of us?"

"I don't see why not. Three by-elections have already shown an appetite for our policies. We'll have our work cut out for us but there's no reason we can't perform at a similar level, especially the way Café Politics has taken off."

****

CHAPTER TWENTY SIX

"I want to sell the house."

Helen turned slowly. "No."

"I've been thinking about what I'm trying to do. I'm going to force landowners to give up their land – but what do I lose? Nothing. I think if I own land and have to give it up as well, it gives me a stronger case."

"You're proposing we sell our home so you can buy some land and then give it away? You're mad!"

"Probably. But I still want to do it."

"We've put our whole lives into this. This is who we are, I can't imagine what it would be like, I don't want to imagine what it would be like without this place."

"We're more than this house. You and me, we're not defined by where we live."

"Aren't we? Castle's castle... This is our home, Robert. We've lived here for twenty years! We don't need to move. You could take out a loan if it means that much to you. Cash in your savings, your pension..."

"It wouldn't be enough."

"How do you know? Have you researched this? Is that what you're doing late at night? Dreaming up ways to evict us?"

"I thought you'd get this. Your work with the homeless..."

"What? You think I need to make myself homeless so I can identify with them? Newsflash! You don't need to sleep on the streets to do that!"

"That's not what I'm saying."

"It's a big gesture all right! A grand, great big gesture. The cameras will lap it up, you might even get some positive coverage in the papers if they don't tar you as a lunatic. What has my work with the homeless got to do with this?"

"We have tens of thousands homeless in Scotland. If we get elected then we can provide homes for them all. Will you think about it?"

Helen shook her head. "No. I won't, Robert. You're not taking our home away as well."

****

"He wants to sell our home. Penny, you've got to get Gordon to talk him out of it."

"Helen, calm down." Penny adjusted the phone. "What do you mean?"

"Robert. He says he wants to sell our home and buy land so he can give it away."

"I'm not following you. Why would Robert do that?"

"He thinks he needs to do it. That he can't tell other people he's going to take their land away if he's not willing to give up something himself."

"I see... I think. But give up your home... Where would you live? And it's been your life's work – such a lovely building. No, of course, I'll speak with Gordon.

****

"Sell your home and buy a plot of land to give away... Robert, that's inspired! I have to warn you, I'm under strict instructions to persuade you not to do this but... Yes, absolutely, you have to do it! I will support you one hundred percent – in private, of course. In public I'll have to attempt to persuade you not to..."

****

Helen almost didn't go to Café Politics the next day – she was still furious with Robert. In the end though, she went because she wasn't going for him, she was going for herself, and for the people she was meeting.

Volunteering at the homeless shelter gave her a sense of fulfilment but that was always tempered by the knowledge it was just a drop in a very big bucket. So many people out there with so many problems.

It was no different at Café Politics – so many problems, no less people and yet, every discussion was an opportunity to change the future. The enthusiasm of the other volunteers was contagious. It didn't matter that life was hard, that people were struggling, that there had been no hope. Every time she went, someone came up with some suggestion that turned things around. The suggestion might be impractical, might be borderline insane, or might just be ridiculous, but the fact that strangers were debating how to build a better Scotland was inspiring in and of itself.

She had to control arguments, steer heated debates and sometimes try and keep herself from laughing but it always gave her hope that maybe, just maybe, they could turn things around.

It was in the middle of one of those heated debates, after she'd listened to two women clash over whether benefits should continue to be paid out, that she started crying.

One of the other women in the group shushed the others and asked if she was alright.

Helen couldn't speak. Someone offered her a tissue but it wasn't enough and then someone put their arm around her.

"Do you want to talk about it?" She was asked.

She shook her head but who else was she going to talk to? "Robert wants to sell our house." She started and once she started, she found the words came pouring out. "He wants to sell our home and buy some dirty field in the middle of nowhere so he can give it away and..." A sob rose up but she kept on going. "Here I am, last to the party. All my friends bought into this long before I did. Robert almost had to force me along here and you're here and you care so much about everything and I just don't know if I can do it. I don't know if I can give it up. Do I have to? Do I really have to?"

"No!"

"Of course not."

Helen looked round at heads shaking and sympathetic expressions. She couldn't stop sobbing.

"I do, don't I." She ignored the protests and brought herself under control. Wiped her eyes and walked over to where Robert was leading his group.

"Robert..."

He looked at her and his expression changed immediately to one of concern. "Helen?" He asked as he stood.

She held out her hand and after he'd taken it, led him out of the hall.

She felt herself starting again so spoke quickly. "You can do it. Sell the damn house." Then she had to grab him, as all the emotion rose up again, and bury her face in his shoulder.

He held her tightly and whispered fiercely to her: "I'll build you a new house. I don't know how or when, but I will. I promise."

****

The drizzle wasn't wet enough to deserve the name. Helen stood outside nursing her mug of tea and looked blankly at the weed infested plot that Robert had dug only weeks before. Some of his seeds had sprouted but neither he nor Helen had found the time to tend the garden and so the grass had grown and Robert's careful rows had disappeared under layers of leaves.

Fortunately the rain was warm as well as weak. She closed her eyes and allowed the emotion to rise up again. Having told Robert he could sell the house she didn't feel she could let him see how she still felt about it.

She had agreed to sell the house but neither she nor he had thought about the work that would be involved. She had an estate agent coming round later and had all but decided to arrange for everything to be put into storage until they could decide what they were going to do longer term.

Looking at the garden she realised she would also need to employ a gardener. She shook her head. It would all work out, somehow. And well, there was always a chance no-one would buy the house...

Helen walked inside and put the kettle on before wandering through to the front of the house with a watering can. While they hadn't been looking after the garden, Helen had been watering the seedlings. They had thrived and would need to be planted out soon. But not just yet...

****

"Just because I agreed to sell the house doesn't mean I agreed to sort everything out! You want this to happen you're going to have to make time for it." Helen put her hands on her hips, intentionally mimicking one of Robert's favourite poses.

"I'm due to lead Café Politics in Edinburgh the rest of the week." Robert walked round the kitchen, opening cupboards and scanning the contents. "How much stuff do we have anyway?"

"More stuff than you or I can deal with if you still want to go ahead with this. I think we just need to hire movers and let them sort it out."

"That'll cost thousands!"

"Do you honestly think we can sell this house in a week?"

"We've got to."

"Then you've no choice."

"I've got no choice?"

"That's right. You are hiring the movers and sorting out storage. You can hire a gardener. I've already booked an estate agent... and don't think I'm hanging around here managing movers! I've still got a job to go to."

Robert tapped his fingers on the counter as he looked into the distance – somewhere far beyond the microwave.

"Okay. I'll get someone else to lead the meetings, or cancel."

"Good. You can also start looking for somewhere else to stay. I'm not living in a B&B for the next three months."

****

She'd felt really down the last couple of months but whether it was panic or serenity, Helen was becoming aware that she was rising to the challenge of the move. The estate agent had put the house on the market immediately, valuing it even higher than Robert had estimated. Robert had delivered on his word and the movers and a gardener were arriving the next day.

She'd persuaded Robert to pack suitcases assuming they'd be living out of them for weeks if not months. He'd reviewed a list she'd written and added a few things to it and now they had a plan. There wasn't going to be any cooking for a few nights while they concentrated on sorting and throwing out. Then they would label some boxes and cupboards that would be kept off limits to the movers.

Carrying a black bag out to the newly hired skip – she had hired it – Helen threw it in wondering how full they'd manage to make it in the short time they had. If it all got too much she could always roll up Robert's body in a carpet...

She stopped and looked out at her neighbours houses. They'd been friendly with all of them though she couldn't say she knew any of them well. Would they ever find somewhere as peaceful as this home had been?

A car drove past, slower than normal and appeared to slow even more as it passed their house. Someone checking it out already? She couldn't make out the driver but waved anyway. The car sped up and was gone.

Maybe selling wouldn't take as long as she feared.

****

Helen phoned Robert to tell him. He hadn't said much, just lots of silence on the other end of the line. The offer had been exactly what the house had been valued at and apparently the buyer didn't need to arrange a mortgage and were keen to speed up the process themselves.

The solicitor had expressed astonishment even though he had assured they would do their utmost to "expedite" the sale. "I've never seen a property sell this quickly." He'd said when he told her the news. "There was hardly time for the property to be advertised."

She didn't know what she wanted Robert to say but whatever he said, it wasn't enough. Her energy from the previous day had dissipated and she just wanted to go home, shut the door and sleep. Stephen and Sylvia were being understanding, but she still had work to do. Even so, she wanted to make one more phone call and didn't want to do it in the office.

Excusing herself she grabbed her mobile and jacket and went out to walk around the block.

"Hello."

"Penny, it's Helen. We've got a buyer."

"Already..." There was a long pause on the other end of the line. "How are you feeling?"

Helen swallowed and blinked away tears. "Coping." She couldn't stop herself sniffing.

"My dear... Have you even got somewhere to move into yet?"

"No. It's all happening too fast, I don't think Robert's started looking yet."

"You must stay with us – as long as it takes. You certainly don't need the cost of renting somewhere right now and I can't imagine either of you being able to take the time to look for a permanent home."

Helen stopped walking. She had to lower the phone while she composed herself. Putting it up to her ear she heard Penny asking: "Helen? Are you okay?"

"Yes." She whispered. "Yes, I think I will be."

****

"That's the last one."

Robert took the case from Helen and carried it downstairs and out to the car. The boot was full and he had to insert it into the back, next to several boxes that Helen had finished packing the previous evening.

She walked out of the house, a jacket carried over one arm and handed him a key. "I'm just going to stay with Penny." She said. "We might go out and get some coffee."

"Okay." He didn't know what else to say. It had been like that all week. He wanted to apologise for putting her through this but couldn't because then he might back out. He had wanted to explain but would that just be rubbing salt in the wound? She'd said yes but even though he thought he'd known what that would mean, he felt like he'd erected a barrier between them and had no idea how to tear it down.

"I'm going to do a last check." He told her.

Leaving her at the car, Robert went back into their house. Going upstairs he checked the sockets in their bedroom. All empty and off. Window closed. He checked the other rooms, bedrooms that they'd hoped would one day be used... Maybe now they would.

He ran a hand against a wall, remembered the week they'd painted and how many coats it had taken before they finally couldn't see the previous colour.

Returning downstairs, Robert did the same sweep, noticing the indents in the sitting room carpet where the sofas had stood. He ended up in the kitchen, their favourite room. Large enough for a big table where they could cook while they talked to guests, where the sun shone through wide windows first thing in the morning.

He was making them give up their castle and he doubted they could ever replace it. It would be worth it, he told himself. It had to be worth it.

Robert went outside and locked up. Laid his hand on the door for a brief moment before turning and walking away. He couldn't look at Helen.

He dropped her off at Gordon and Penny's with their cases and then went to the solicitor's.

****

CHAPTER TWENTY SEVEN

"This is quite irregular." Dawkins solicitor seated himself at the conference table, alongside his client, Neil Dawkins.

"We know that. Thank you for agreeing to meet with us." Robert looked at his own solicitor, Christopher Turnstall, and then back at Dawkins. "I take it you know who I am?"

"The nutter from the Land Grab Party. Kind of ironic you're here to buy my land."

"It is, isn't it." Robert forced himself to smile.

"If you would like to make an offer then there is an established procedure which should be followed." Dawkins solicitor interjected. "Your solicitor should have advised you of that."

"He did." Robert nodded at Turnstall and fixed his smile in place.

"By all means, make an offer and we will be happy to note your interest and set a date for other offers to be in by."

"Perhaps it would be best if I explained why we are here."

"Please do."

"As you know, my party intends to seize all privately held lands and return them to the use of the Scottish people. What you may not be aware of is that I am currently working on the detail of that proposal. Specifically, it is my intention to seize all land over one hundred hectares. As your land is one hundred and fifty hectares, it will be divided and fifty hectares seized."

"You are assuming you win the election." Dawkins laughed.

"I will win."

Robert calmly looked from Dawkins to his solicitor until he saw one of them twitch.

"Now, knowing this information, you could divide the land. Perhaps sell it in two lots, but I warn you that when I take power, I will seek to arrest anyone who has attempted to avoid returning land and will also seize all profits from those attempts."

"Threatening my client will have serious consequences, Mr Castle."

"At no point was your client threatened. A fair warning was issued." Turnstall said.

"Gentlemen, if I am allowed to continue then perhaps we can avoid any unpleasantries. I want to offer you fair price for your land – the going rate. I see you have asked for offers of over one hundred and fifty thousand. I also see that a similar area of land was sold for one hundred and eighty thousand last month in Perthshire. I am willing to offer you the same. Your solicitor will be aware that sales of land have dropped substantially since I began campaigning. I suspect that as people are very aware of my policies you will find it incredibly difficult to sell your land until the election is over… Of course, if I gain a majority, your excess land will be seized."

"Why would you want to buy this land knowing you're going to give it away?" Dawkins solicitor asked. "Or will it be one law for us and one law for you?"

Robert hesitated as he weighed up how much to share with them. "As soon as the papers are signed and the titles transferred I will be gifting the land to the people of Scotland. All of it."

"You are insane. That's good land, that is."

"Excellent land. The people of Scotland deserve nothing less."

"I will need to consult with my client in private."

Robert stood and he and his solicitor left the room.

In a hushed voice, once the door was closed, Turnstall asked Robert: "Do you play poker?"

"Used to. Every Friday."

"You haven't lost your skill."

****

Helen was silent the whole drive up to Aberdeenshire. Robert navigated himself, slowing down as he reached B roads. Eventually he reached a turn off and slowed to a crawl as he drove onto a rough track. He pulled to a stop.

"This is it."

Helen looked away from him, her gaze distant, unseeing.

Robert got out of the car. It was hard to get a scale of how large the land was. In front of him pine trees rose to a height of twenty feet. But it was a strip of trees and he could just make out the land beyond.

He went and opened Helen's door. "At least get out and get some air. We have a long drive back."

Reluctantly, she climbed out. Robert put his arm in hers and tugged her along. He didn't say anything as she sniffed and wiped at her nose.

The track detoured slightly as it went through the trees, preventing them from seeing directly ahead. Robert kept walking. Wanting to speak but realising it would only make things worse.

Out of the trees, the land rose to a low hill. They walked up, Robert noticing the grass was greener, thicker than it had been near the road. Above them, a cloud shifted and he felt the sun directly warming his back. The colours brightened around them and Robert had a sense of what it might be like to live on the land.

They reached the top, only as high as the trees they had walked under, but enough to allow them to see much of the land he had just bought. Robert held out his map and traced the boundary line. An older group of trees in one corner. Oak and willow he had been advised. Some old ruins in the centre, where a crofting village had once stood.

"You bought this to give away?"

Robert nodded.

"It's beautiful."

He held her and together they cried.

****

Gordon wrote the press release. Just a short teaser: Robert Castle of The Great Scottish Land Grab Party will be making a major announcement. Directions were provided together with GPS coordinates.

Members of the party were mobilised to print, laminate and place signs along the winding roads leading to the place Robert planned to give his speech.

Not as many reporters turned up as he'd hoped but there was one television camera and several were already using their mobile phones to film the view.

They had erected a small platform, complete with podium, in the clearing near the ruins of the crofting village. Two hundred party members had been invited to attend and from the look of things, they'd brought friends.

Robert took to the platform. "Thank you all for coming." He laid his Kindle on the podium, checked his speech was visible, and looked out at the crowd of supporters and reporters.

"I've said all along that our primary goal as a party is to return the land of Scotland into the hands of its people. But it never seemed right to demand others to give up land when I was not able or willing to do so myself."

He paused and page forwarded his notes. Cleared his throat.

"Last week my wife and I sold our house. We bought the land you are standing on. The land you can see around you. A 150 hectare plot of land that is suitable for small holding farming.

"This is my land. I invite all of you to walk it. To explore it, to see how beautiful Scotland's land is.

"But, I didn't invite you here to tell you that. I cannot ask land owners to give up their land if I am not willing to do the same. Therefore, I am today gifting this land to the Scottish people.

"It is my intention to reverse the clearances that devastated Scotland. Once our country was industrious, with small crofts and fishing communities throughout the land. It can be again.

"I have a vision to raise up new communities, to reclaim the abandoned crofts, to allow people who have been trapped in our cities their whole lives to experience the freedom of living in the country.

"If our party is elected with a majority in the general election, it is my intention that this land…" Robert gestured around him. "Shall become the first settlement."

Robert looked down. He had been unable to reach an ending

to the speech that he was happy with.

Pointing at the ground, he looked towards the television camera. "This is your land, Scotland. I urge you to reclaim it, first by voting for The Great Scottish Land Grab in next week's election, then by voting in the referendum. Thank you."

****

Conner paced back and forth in the conference room while Maureen and her election team debated their response to Castle's announcement.

"It's just a cheap stunt." He finally interrupted. "He's a clown. Offering a patch of land, as if that's going to solve all of Scotland's problems."

"I disagree with you." Maureen responded. "We need to take this seriously. What he has done is symbolic. We can't just hope people won't see that. The papers are full of it and some of them have even shifted in their tone towards the referendum."

"In large part because of the campaigning we've done…"

"Whether or not the media have finally begun to accept that independence is a good thing, it's the people who will be voting in the election I'm worried about. Castle is in first place in some polls now, second in others and never less than third. His party could disrupt the whole election. I'm not just talking about marginal seats either. If he manages to steal SNP votes as well as Labour or LibDem, then it could be anyone's guess who will win."

"Let's bring him into the televised debate."

"That could be suicide!"

"He's a clown and a fool. Every policy he has is paper thin. He admits himself he doesn't have any detail. It's all very well promising full employment but if you can't spell out how you're going to do it, why would anyone vote for you."

"Because he does have a clear vision for Scotland. The whole referendum debate is about vision. You give him another platform, you give him the acceptance and respectability of being included in the televised debates, then his message will reach far more people. Personally I believe that UKIP did so well in Scotland in large part because the LibDems foolishly agreed to public debate with them. Don't make the same mistake."

"We have always been the party with a vision for an

independent Scotland. Put us together in a studio and I'll tear his policies apart."

"We've already agreed who will be taking part. The same four parties as always. You can't exclude one of them now and trying to have a debate with five people will just be unmanageable. It's tough enough with four."

"Then just set me up one on one with him. I'll destroy him and the image people will be left with, is of a strong SNP leadership."

Or he'll destroy you. Maureen kept her thought to herself. If Conner MacKenzie wanted to go down in flames, so be it.

****

CHAPTER TWENTY EIGHT

Two months since he had stood in front of the crowd at Shawshields and Robert thought he would rather be back there than here. Two large television cameras were pointed forward at himself and Conner MacKenzie. A third camera was directed at Lorna Travers who was to lead the debate.

Despite leading in some polls, he had not had any hopes of another party leader offering to debate him. He had been mocked by party representatives in the press and on T.V. and the media had published every word spoken against him while granting him less and less air time.

The call from the SNP had been a shock and Robert found himself unprepared. Gordon's advice had been to treat it as any encounter or speech. He was at his best when unprompted, when he set the tone and pace.

"They will try and trip you up." Gordon had told him. "Try and derail you and change your focus. Don't let them."

The main parties had already had two televised debates. They were to have their final one just a few days before the election. This was his only shot. If it went badly tonight, well… No-one had said going into politics would be easy.

"Live in ten, nine, eight…"

Robert watched one of the television crew hold up a hand, fingers splayed. A quick glance showed him MacKenzie was composing himself, straightening his back, looking at his respective camera. The count went silent after four with just the fingers changing: three, two, one...

The studio lights brightened causing Robert to blink.

"Welcome to this special live televised debate between Conner MacKenzie of the SNP and Robert Castle of The Great Scottish Land Grab." Lorna Travers said confidently and clearly. She introduced each of the participants in more detail. Robert looked steadily into the camera as the light went red indicating it was live.

"In this debate each side will have the opportunity to present their party's agenda. One minute each, gentlemen, and no more." She said, turning to smile at them. "Then we will pose questions that you, our audience have submitted, allowing the candidates an opportunity to discuss their responses before giving each candidate a final opportunity to sum up."

"Firstly, Conner MacKenzie."

On his podium, Robert had a copy of his own notes, which he fervently hoped he would not need to refer to, an a4 notepad and several pens, and his smartphone which he'd turned off earlier. Live this debate was not. Robert had only learned that morning that the feed was delayed by five seconds which would allow the producers to edit out any incident they felt unsuitable for public viewing. He wasn't sure what sort of incident might merit deletion – perhaps an attempted assassination. He held back a smile at the thought.

MacKenzie expertly summed up the SNP mantra: they were the party that had promised and delivered a referendum on independence. They were the party that had released a vision for an independent Scotland. They were the party that even now was seeking the public's views on how an independent Scotland should be governed. Robert began taking his own notes on what was being said.

Robert felt tense. His breathing slowed and he found his hand was gripping the pen tighter. He let his face remain a mask though. He hoped he was displaying calm and confident but may as well have been nervous and sweaty. Would this be a Nixon moment? Hopefully his makeup had been sufficiently applied.

"And now, Robert Castle of the Land Grab Party."

Robert smiled at Lorna before turning to his camera. "Thank you Lorna. I ask you to vote for me and The Great Scottish Land Grab Party. When elected I will repeal existing land laws and introduce the Scottish Free Land Act. I will make Scotland's land available for use by any Scot who wants it.

"This is something that will provide life and hope to many in Scotland who currently have none, but it is only one policy and I know you are eager to hear how I will govern.

"Those of you who have attended one of our Café Politics will know exactly how I will govern: by letting you have a voice, by letting you decide what is important for your community and for Scotland. I will establish a system similar to that used by the Swiss where every Scot will have the right to set government policy and challenge legislation.

"Also, my government will eradicate national debt and use the money saved on unjust interest payments to bring about full employment throughout Scotland and end the culture of reliance on benefits."

He looked across at Lorna.

"Thank you." Lorna said. "We now move to questions sent in by the electorate. Firstly from John Smith of Kirkcaldy: What are your plans to take Scotland out of recession? MacKenzie."

Robert listened as MacKenzie gave his stock answer. Robert and his team had prepared by trying to predict potential questions; coming up with their own responses and then trying to counter them, attacking and shooting them down. Yet it was one thing to discuss with friends, another to face a seasoned opponent in front of several million people.

"Castle." Lorna said.

"We are responsible for the situation we are in. If we as a nation can accept that, then we have grown in maturity and will be able to do something about it. We blame our largest bank for being the primary cause of our financial woes but our problems as a nation go back decades and even centuries. For too long we have blamed the English for our problems. It is not the English who are to blame. Do you want Scotland to climb out of recession? If so, then you will have to man up Scotland! Are you willing to work hard? Are you willing to put some effort in? If you are, then we can turn things around. I will bring manufacturing back to Scotland. I will create hundreds of thousands of new jobs. I will use the benefits that are currently given out to pay men and women a living wage. Anyone who is willing to work will be given a job. Anyone who is unwilling to work will receive no more help from the state.

"These are my proposals but you will have to vote them in. If you do not – then you can carry on trapping people in poverty, continue carrying a chip on your shoulder, and blame anyone but yourselves for your predicament. But I believe you are capable of greater things Scotland, I believe you can transform yourselves and be the people you know deep down you want to be."

"MacKenzie, first response." Lorna directed.

"There are thousands of people who are unable to work and yet you have just said you will cease paying for their care. Will you really let thousands starve?"

"We currently have tens of thousands claiming disability benefits who are perfectly capable of working. They may not be able to do heavy manual labour but they are able to contribute."

"But what about those who have been hospitalized? Those on life support? The genuinely sick?" MacKenzie looked incredulous.

"All these people have something to contribute, even if for a time their contribution is simply to allow someone else to take care of them. Our current law provides for people to be sick while in work and to be supported while they recover. There is no reason that principle can't be extended. If we change the emphasis from receiving help from the state to an expectation that anyone who can, does work, I believe thousands will be encouraged to use the skills and abilities they have. But regardless of what I think, ultimately this is for the people of Scotland to decide, not you, nor I."

"We are a generous nation and we can't let the mob turn us into savages. Decisions like this need to be impartial."

"Our people are generous, but they are not fools. We have been misled by our governments into thinking that we have to provide for the lazy and incompetent. We do not! I believe the man and woman in the street are capable of discerning who genuinely needs help and who is capable of contributing something."

"Next question." Lorna said before the debate could continue. "Shona Baxter from Dunrossness: Will you keep Scotland's university education free? Castle."

"There's a referendum for that." Robert smiled at the camera. "That may seem like a glib response but it is heartfelt. I personally will campaign to keep free university places but to limit funding to essential skills only. I see no reason why the Scottish people should fund students who research the arts. We all have some free time – if an individual wishes to read Burns or Shakespeare – they may do that without being paid by the taxpayer. However, I believe this is a policy that should be decided by the people of Scotland and not just by government."

"MacKenzie." Lorna said.

"Scotland has the best universities in the United Kingdom. It is imperative that we enable our young people to continue to educate themselves and maintain our high standards. An independent Scotland will be able to increase funding for education instead of being limited by Westminster."

Lorna directed the first response to Robert.

"You claim Scotland has the best universities in the UK and yet studies show our schools are still churning out thousands of pupils each year that cannot read or write or perform basic arithmetic. Parts of Scotland's education system are prospering, but there are thousands who are being short changed. Our education system is far too complex and expects too much from every student. We can change this but it will require funds being taken away from other areas. I will give the people of Scotland the choice."

"MacKenzie." Lorna instructed.

"I think I know which studies you're referring to and those are seriously flawed. We have higher rates of basic literacy and numeracy than other parts of the UK but despite that, we have not remained complacent and the Scottish government has encouraged greater focus on the key skills of reading, writing and arithmetic."

"Comparing Scotland to poorly performing education systems will not encourage improvement. Today one in six pupils will leave primary school unequipped to read, write or calculate. Fifty years ago that would have been one in a hundred! Scotland's education system is in radical need of overhaul."

"That figure is out of date and does not reflect the broad range of skills that primary school pupils are now taught. Children today leave school with a far greater range of skills and abilities which are suitable for today's modern world. The SNP will not roll the clock back to the 1950s, we are looking forward to what Scotland needs in ten and twenty years time."

"Next question." Lorna quickly said before Robert could

respond. "Alison Carmichael, Carnoustie: How would you make an independent Scotland more democratic? MacKenzie."

"As we've set out in our white paper and in our proposals for a new constitution, we will establish a parliamentary democracy and ensure continuation of democratically elected local government. By asking the Scottish people for their views on creating a constitution we have given them the chance to decide what kind of country Scotland should be."

"Castle."

"There's a referendum for that. In fact, The Great Scottish Land Grab Party will give the people of Scotland a thousand referendums. A hundred thousand if necessary. The concept of parliamentary democracy is one of the biggest lies we are told. Only being allowed to vote for one person who can ignore you for the next four or five years is not democracy.

"As well as allowing the Scottish people to challenge unjust laws through referendums, we will also give the electorate the right to recall MSPs and councillors who fail to represent them. We will decrease the power of the Scottish parliament and local councils and allow local communities to make their own decisions, following the model of our Café Politics. Only The Great Scottish Land Grab will give real democracy to the people of Scotland!"

"MacKenzie, first response."

"Referendums take months to arrange and cost millions. It is physically and financially impossible to hold that many referendums!"

"Asking a question takes a minute. Collating the responses a few minutes more. Every week we watch television shows where referendums are held on the most innocuous of issues. It is bordering on the criminal that previous governments have withheld this now standard technology from the electorate." Robert held up his smartphone. "Millions of people vote every week for their favourite contestants on The X Factor, Britain's Got Talent and shows like I'm A Celebrity or Strictly Come Dancing."

"There have been numerous scandals where these telephone voting systems have been shown to be abused. The technology just isn't secure enough. To develop a secure system that could ensure every vote was authentic would cost a fortune – money, even you say, the budget does not have."

"The technology can and will be developed for free."

"That's ridiculous. A voting system like this would cost millions to develop and more to maintain."

"Scotland's own students will develop this system. They will do it at no cost to the taxpayer and in doing so, will help justify their own continued free education."

"We looked into electronic and online voting at the beginning of our term. It was going to take a minimum of six months to develop and each of the three companies that bid for the project said it would require a hundred people and a minimum of six million pounds development and millions each year just to run and maintain."

"They lied to you."

"These were highly respected software companies. That is a serious allegation."

"It may well require a hundred people to develop but it need cost nothing either to develop or run or maintain – at least to the tax-payer. We have highly intelligent students who are perfectly capable of designing a simple and yet secure voting system. I'm sure there are many who would happily earn their doctorate for their work on this. As far as running costs go – the BBC have a long history of getting the governments message out to the people. The hardware technology required is simple. A server that can accommodate millions of hits per hour. Access can be online and through mobile phones. I'm sure we can persuade all the mobile networks that it would be within their best interest to assist us and provide access across their networks for free. We have libraries in almost every community, most of whom now provide PC's with Internet access. These can be made available to those who neither have their own computer nor a mobile phone."

"MacKenzie, wouldn't such proposals be worth investigating, especially given your parties commitment to democracy?" Lorna asked.

"We have asked the Scottish people to tell us how they want Scotland to be run through the consultation on a constitution for Scotland. I hope that every Scot will respond to the consultation."

"The consultation runs until October. Scotland has an opportunity next week to tell you how they want their country run and then a referendum soon after."

Robert hid his surprise at Lorna's statement. MacKenzie's expression didn't flinch apart from a possible narrowing of his eyes. He didn't respond though. Just waited until Lorna asked her next question which she directed at Robert.

The questions kept coming and Robert and MacKenzie took turns to answer and attack until finally Lorna told them they each had a minute to sum up.

Robert was asked to go first. He looked into his camera and his mind went blank. He had prepared a closing speech but it didn't seem relevant now.

"This election…" He began. "In many ways, is more important than the forthcoming referendum.

"I don't personally care whether Scotland votes for independence or not. Until a few months ago I was campaigning to keep Scotland in the union. Now I'm campaigning for Scotland to reclaim her land and her freedom. Many of you will have very fixed views on how you will vote and many of you are still undecided.

"I believe though that all of you care as I do, and even Conner MacKenzie here cares about our future and I am determined that whether Scotland votes Yes or No, that Scotland will be a free country, that we will be a democratic country, that we will be in control of our own destiny.

"If that is as an independent country, so be it, I will fight to make it happen. But if you, the Scottish people, decide you want to remain in union with Britain, then I will also fight to ensure that union gives Scotland no less freedom than we would have as an independent country.

"Westminster had better watch out. One way or another, Scotland will change for the better and we will not be held back.

"Vote for us next week and we will reclaim your stolen lands, Scotland. Vote for us and we will give you full employment. Vote for us and we will give you democracy."

"Conner MacKenzie."

For the second time that evening MacKenzie laid out his party's policies. He ended with: "While you have heard a dreamer talk about giving power to the people, the reality is that decisions need to be made every day in government and require clear leadership to direct the path we take. The SNP has served in leadership for many years in Scotland and we are willing to do so again. A vote for us is a vote for Scotland's future. A prosperous future, full of hope for every man, woman and child in Scotland."

****

CHAPTER TWENTY NINE

"You are a joke, Castle. I mean, I can't say this in public but you standing for election has made my job ten times easier. Everywhere I go people are laughing at you. You have taken the spotlight away from Labour and made this into a two horse race. Of course, we will win the election but it wouldn't surprise me if you lost in every seat and won't be able to show your face outside your door. They are going to talk about you for years to come."

"Well, MacKenzie." Robert said as he stood. "As sure as I am that we could trade insults all evening, I would rather get home to my wife. Good evening." He walked stiffly out the door.

Walking along the corridor, Robert found himself churning over the statements he had made, the accusations and laughter there had been. He had booked a hotel room for the night in Edinburgh but could not face the evening alone. He pulled out his phone to call a taxi.

"Not staying for drinks?"

Robert whirled round to see Gail Charleston. He lowered the phone.

"There didn't seem to be a lot of point."

"Did you get a glimpse of your own reflection?"

Robert found himself smiling. "I deserve that."

"I find you politicians a terrible bore. All you seem to want to talk about is yourselves. Or your policies – though that usually boils down to the same thing."

"Would you prefer talking about the weather?"

Gail cocked her head to one side. "Why do you... why did you do that?"

"Change the subject?"

"You know what I mean. At the interview. I've had people be rude before. Deliberately insulting, but never at the start of an interview. Why do that? Why risk me turning on you?"

"How do you know that's not what I wanted?"

"But that makes no sense."

"Did you feel the interview went well?"

"My producer liked it. Said it was one of the best I had given."

"Maybe you should trade insults with all your interviewees before you start." Robert lifted the phone and selected the taxi company again.

"Have you really had enough of the action tonight?"

His thumb over the dial button, Robert looked up. "I'm not sure how I should interpret that."

Gail just gave him a steady look.

Robert pressed dial and slowly lifted the phone to his ear, keeping eye contact as he did.

"Castle Cars, what's your destination?"

Robert smiled. "Waverly station. I'm at the television studio."

"Be five minutes."

"Thank you. My own personal cab company." He said, ending the call. "Take care of yourself, Gail." He turned quickly and walked away.

****

"Bumped into Gail Charleston as I was leaving."

"Oh?"

"She wanted to know why I insulted her at the interview."

"Did you? I don't remember that."

Robert thought for a second. "No, of course. They edited it out."

"You insulted her? What did you say?"

"I asked her why all weather girls are called Gail."

234

Helen gave him a quizzical look. "That's not really an insult."

"No, well, she didn't like the question. Said she wasn't a weather girl."

"Touched a nerve then."

"And I followed up with: did you lose your application form."

Helen punched him.

"Ow. Find your own punch bag. I'll report you for husband abuse."

"That will do your campaign the power of good. Candidate beaten up by timid wife. So, you like her then, Gail Charleston?"

"What do you mean?"

"Don't play coy. You have the romantic capability of a Neanderthal. I seem to recall your idea of sweet talking was to tease me mercilessly. You still haven't changed."

Robert thought back to that evening. "I did wonder if she was flirting with me."

"Be careful. I'm not going to be the forgiving wife standing next to you on stage. I'll be more likely to be chasing you off it with a baseball bat."

"Received and understood. Actually, I've been thinking."

"Not your strongest talent, but do go on."

"Are you flirting with me now?"

"You should be so lucky at this time of night."

They lay silent for a minute and then Helen turned over and reached her arm around him. "I miss you." She said.

"Miss you too."

****

CHAPTER THIRTY

"This election has certainly been hard fought. And one of the most interesting in years. No-one expected Robert Castle to land on the scene and upset the electoral applecart, but does he have a chance? Gail?"

"Conventional wisdom would say no but there is nothing conventional about Castle or his Land Grab Party. I was out speaking to voters in Edinburgh today."

The scene cut to a windblown school parking lot and a face shot of a young woman. Off camera Gail's voice was heard: "Who did you vote for?"

"The Land Grab Party. He's promising me a job, saying he'll cut his own salary to match mine. I've never heard a politician do that before."

The shot cut again to an older couple. The woman spoke: "We're Labour supporters. Always have been and always will."

A suited man: "The Land Grab Party is just a joke. They have no policies, no vision. The SNP is the party that delivered on their promise to hold a referendum and I trust them to do right by Scotland."

The scene switched back to the studio. "So there you have it, Lorna. We spoke to a cross section of voters in every major city in Scotland and there was no consensus anywhere. It is looking like this will be a close race."

"Well." Lorna said, turning to look at her camera straight on.

"As you will know, the polling booths have now closed. We'll go to a special report by Tom Durnhill on the counting process being used this year. Tom..."

****

At his new party headquarters, a run-down floor of an office building that Gordon owned the lease to, Robert looked out over a team of close to a hundred people. He had not conceived that so many people would be willing to help and it wasn't only them. In every town they now had volunteers: students mostly but also a sizable number of unemployed. Robert was amazed by how many professional people were currently unable to find work. Engineers, experts in IT and telecoms, scientists.

Over the last few weeks, their numbers had swelled as the word had spread that he had promised to create full employment. But it was not just students or those out of work. People currently in a secure job, parents with children, had come up to him and asked if they could help. There was something about the promise of change; of opening up the land – that had grabbed them as much as it had grabbed him.

"So, what do we do now?" Asked Helen.

"I don't know." Robert confessed. "Never been in this situation before."

Gordon turned to them and placed his hand over the phone he had been speaking into. "You both have a drink – but only one. Then switch to coffee. It's going to be a long night."

"I need to mingle. Come with me?"

Helen screwed up her face but took his offered hand.

****

"The results are coming in from Edinburgh South!"

Everyone in the room stopped what they were doing and clustered round the television. Robert gripped Helen's hand.

"Darren Cloud of the Green Party, 103 votes. Emily Bright of the Conservative Party, 289 votes. Claire Johnstone of the Land Grab Party, 12,876 votes."

In the room, someone hollered but was quickly shushed.

"...of the Scottish National Party, 13,009 votes. I declare George Rankin of the Scottish National Party the new member of the Scottish Parliament for Edinburgh South."

"So close." Said Helen. "What is that?"

"133 votes." Robert told her.

"Well, that's good though, isn't it? You were never going to win in every seat but better to lose by a close margin."

****

The night rolled on slowly. They won Glasgow East by a huge margin but lost Glasgow West by 500 votes. Every victory was tempered by a loss elsewhere.

At midnight Robert and Helen were driven over to the count for Glasgow South, the seat Robert had contested. They drove past familiar streets in silence.

As they drew up outside the school where the count was being held, Robert took Helen's hand. "This could be the moment you've been waiting for. I lose here and my political career will be over."

Helen stared ahead. "You won't lose."

"Would you be happy if I did?"

She turned to him. "I voted for you."

"You did?"

"Don't act so surprised. Better get in. You don't want to be the last one on the podium."

"Don't I need to make a dramatic entrance?"

"Feel free to trip on the way up."

They were instantly surrounded by party members as they walked in. Their exuberance rubbed off on him and Robert felt some of his tiredness dissipate. He made his way to the podium to find he was indeed the last person to arrive. Robert shook everyone's hand and took his place at the end of the row.

The count had finished before they arrived but last minute checks were taking place with some ballots being recounted with several witnesses. Finally the Returning Officer made her way to the podium.

The SNP had just beaten Labour in 2011, a swing from the traditional Labour vote. With fourteen political parties on the ballot list, Robert had a long wait for the result. Labour received just under seven thousand votes, down on their last result. The SNP eight thousand, one hundred and two.

The previous election had seen a turnout of less than fifty

percent of potential voters. Robert cast his mind back over the results. Five parties had each received more than one thousand votes. Each of them so far seemed down on 2011. It was believed that there had been an increase across Scotland in voter turnout, but would that increase in turnout and decrease in party votes translate into votes for him? Robert couldn't be sure.

He looked down at Helen who took the hands of the two people nearest to her and raised them above her head.

"Robert Castle, The Great Scottish Land Grab Party, eight thousand, one hundred and twenty three."

A hand clapped him on the back. Helen was jumping up and down. Robert turned and shook hands once more, muttered thank yous while the last results were read out. A small part of him had secretly hoped this would be the end, but it wasn't even the beginning.

He was invited to give a speech and remembered to thank the other candidates, returning officer and everyone he was supposed to. "This is not the end. It is not the beginning. Thank you to everyone who has placed their trust in me. Regardless of how you voted, we all have work to do to rebuild Scotland into the country we want it to be. If you want things to change you have to get involved, stand up, speak out. I do not intend to let Scotland slip back to being a country where politicians make all the decisions, but if you agree with that vision, I need you to get involved.

"The referendum is your next opportunity. Whether you vote Yes or No, I want you to vote, to show that you do care what happens in and to our country."

****

They were driven back to their party headquarters and entered to cheers.

"Are there further results in?" Robert asked Gordon.

"It's a three way split at the moment. SNP are ahead, with Labour next and then ourselves. Only a couple of seats in it though. Still half the results to come in so it's all to play for."

By Three O'clock, Robert had had enough.

"I need to get some sleep. Even if only an hour."

"I had them set up some camp beds on the floor above." Gordon told him. "I'll give you a shout if there's any change."

Robert took Helen upstairs. There were clusters of air mattresses and sleeping bags dotted about the otherwise empty floor. "How do professional politicians cope?" He asked.

"Maybe you should ask them."

****

Feeling himself being shaken, Robert opened his eyes. Gordon was crouching beside him. He looked round and saw Helen's eyes were closed.

"It's over. You lost the Islands. Incredibly tight voting but in the end that's what counts."

"There's no-where else?"

"Only three seats left to declare. It just isn't enough. You won forty five percent of the seats. Even if you win these, you are still below fifty. I'm sorry, we didn't get a majority."

****

Robert woke Helen once Gordon had left and told her. She hugged him but didn't say anything.

Together they walked back downstairs to a room full of exhausted people.

Robert climbed up on a table and waited until he had their attention.

"I am so proud of you. Gordon tells me we won forty five percent of the seats. That is an incredible achievement. How many did the other parties win?"

"The SNP is currently on thirty one..." One of the volunteers stated. "Labour on twenty seven with three seats still to declare."

"How many seats have we won?"

"Fifty eight. Seven short of an overall majority."

"Thank you... James, isn't it?"

"Yes sir."

"I'm not royalty. You can use my first name."

A few people chuckled.

"We gained the same number of seats as the SNP and Labour combined! That is a fantastic result. It means that we will have to try and form a coalition government but given what we are trying to achieve, that is no bad thing.

240

"Make no mistake, this is a huge victory. We went from one man with a foolish dream to thousands of people working and fighting together. You are responsible for all the success tonight. You put in the hours to win people over. You are my heroes. Thank you."

He waited while they politely applauded and then began to shake hands. He would thank each one in person and then insist they all got some rest.

"Wait a minute!"

Robert looked up to see James holding up a laptop.

"We didn't lose! I was so focused on the number of seats I didn't check the number of votes cast. We didn't lose."

Robert pushed his way through. "What do you mean? We failed to win a majority."

"In terms of seats, but not in terms of votes. I haven't worked out the percentage, but even without the last three seats, you're three hundred thousand votes ahead."

"That doesn't matter though, does it? Legally?"

Gordon made his way over. "Show us what you mean."

"I've made a note of all votes cast for each party. I was just punching in numbers as they were read out. I was planning to do some analysis after the election but then when you were talking just now I was curious… Anyway…" He said, realising the others were growing impatient. "It looks like almost ninety five percent of the voters turned up. That in and of itself is amazing. There are approximately four million registered voters in Scotland and by my count, you have won two million, three hundred thousand. The closest in terms of votes is the SNP with seven hundred thousand and then Labour with six hundred thousand. By any standards, you have a clear majority."

"That can't be." Robert said. "How can I fail to win a majority in terms of seats and yet still win more votes?"

"It makes sense." Gordon said. "Even if you lost a seat, you did so by a small margin, but almost each seat you won, you destroyed the competition. I think he's right. We need someone to check this though."

Gordon arranged for two of the volunteers to run their own tallies.

"This happens in a lot of elections though. Isn't it common for one party in Westminster to win a landslide victory but only have thirty or forty percent of the vote?"

"It is even worse than that. In most elections a large proportion of the electorate don't turn out so in reality whoever wins only has a mandate of twenty or thirty percent. You can argue it both ways – whoever wins will say that those who did not vote were happy for them to win; I've sometimes heard people say they were abstaining because none of the parties represented them. This is incredible, Robert. This isn't an argument about who had a minority of the votes. You clearly won the election and by a sizable majority."

"I've won but I haven't won?"

"Yes!"

"Why are you so excited?"

"Because you can prove you won and you can challenge the election result and take power. Don't you see it? This is Scotland – we have proportional representation. A number of seats are allocated simply on the basis of the peoples vote – you can claim all of those and you can legally take seats away from those who lost the peoples vote."

"I doubt that will hold up in court."

"Robert – what are you standing for?"

"What has that..." Robert tailed off in confusion. Gordon was obviously excited but he wasn't seeing it.

"Do I have to spell it out for you? Okay – you were seeking election on the basis that the law is rotten. That the courts assisted in the theft of Scotland's land. Why do you care what will stand up in court? This is just another example of a rotten system – an election where you can win but are relegated to the side-lines. Did you really stand for election thinking that once you won you would not still have to fight?"

"No, of course not."

"Scotland has elected you. Scotland has chosen you. You said you would return the land to her people, are you going to do it or not? If you need to fight to keep your promise – will you? Are you a man of your word – or just another politician?"

"I'm not a politician!"

"Then what are you and what are you going to do about this?"

"I'm going to fight."

"Who here is with us?"

There were shouts of Aye and Yes.

"Don't go anywhere." Gordon told Robert. "I'm going to

check on the recount."

Helen came over. "Could this really make a difference?"

"If we've won the vote then yes, maybe."

"They'll fight it. It won't be easy."

"I know. Will you support me?"

Helen took his hands in hers. "All the way."

Robert felt his limbs turn to ice as he heard his name being chanted: "CAS-TLE." Again and again.

Helen pulled him through and then he was being pulled and pushed until he reached Gordon.

"They confirmed it! Just over sixty percent majority!" Gordon had to shout to make himself heard. "Now get up on that table. You have a rabble to organise!"

Standing precariously, Robert looked over his people. His people! They were still chanting his name. He raised his hands to quieten them and they broke into applause.

Shaking his head he began: "This is not my victory – it is not even our victory – it is your victory!" They began cheering and applauding before he had finished and he was shocked at how quickly he felt this was normal.

"We said that our land was stolen and Scotland agreed with us. But we haven't won the fight yet. I don't yet know what we are going to do about this but I know one thing – I didn't win this election – you did! I could not have campaigned or worked a fraction of the amount you did. You did not have to be told what to do – you just got on and did it. I am counting on you – that you will know what to do, that you will have the courage and the perseverance you have shown until now."

"We've said all along that the fight for Scotland does not end with the referendum, well it doesn't end with this election either. Scotland has voted for a Land Grab and Scotland is going to get one!"

****

BOOK THREE

CHAPTER THIRTY ONE

The contract came as it usually did: a text to his phone, giving a link to a website which was open to the public. Nothing incongruous for him to be checking someone's profile should he be in a public place. The photo was a typical head and shoulders, grayscale image, posed shot. The target was not smiling, fairly common for these sorts of photos. You want to sell your professionalism, not your sense of humour.

He had a secure account with an online storage provider. Actually secure, unlike most of the offerings the public received for free bundled with phones and operating systems. The folder he checked next was only accessible by one other person, a cut out whom he trusted implicitly and who didn't know fully what she was part of.

The dark web had made it slightly easier to sell his services but he was still at risk if any authority penetrated the veil he hid under.

What was unusual was the location of the target. Tam Frost would be going home.

****

She sat watching the TV, the volume loud enough to hear but it was just background noise, with moving pictures to distract her. Shifting slightly to stop her legs going to sleep as she lay on the leather sofa, Irene heard the familiar noise of something being pushed through the letterbox.

"Billy!" She called.

No answer.

"Colin!"

No response.

Grimacing, she eased herself up off the sofa. Standing was painful but once she was up, she could make her way without too much pain. She put a hand out to an old wooden wall unit to steady herself and felt the dust under her fingers. Two weeks recovering from hurting her back and neither one of those lazy, good for nothings had done a single bit of house work except make her sandwiches and tea.

In the hallway she could see envelopes had fallen to the dirty floor. Steadying herself, she put a hand on the wall as she carefully lowered herself down, keeping her back straight. The pain had lessened considerably in the last week but every now and then she moved in the wrong way and regretted it.

She scooped up the envelopes and, in one smooth movement, stood. Light-headedness threatened her balance and she almost dropped the envelopes.

Closing her eyes, Irene breathed slowly until the sensation passed. If those boys were asleep upstairs she was going to give them a hiding, pain in her back or not.

She made her way back down the hallway and went into the small kitchen. Plates were piled up in the sink, a loaf of bread sat opened on the table with a tub of margarine next to it, a dirty knife abandoned on the table.

Laying the envelopes on a more or less clean bit of table, Irene checked the cupboard for a glass – none. Probably all up in the boys rooms, those that weren't in the sink or left sitting out collecting rain in the garden.

There was a sole mug in the next cupboard. She checked it before filling it with water, then carried the mug to the table before heading back into the sitting room for her tablets. The doctor had prescribed co-codamol which was supposed to be stronger than paracetamol. It hadn't seemed to make much difference at all the first day but by the second she had been able to sleep for an hour or two at a time.

Irene slowly took these back into the kitchen and gingerly sat down.

She wasn't supposed to take more tablets for another fifteen minutes but all that walking around must have used up the chemicals in her system.

She palmed two and swallowed them down with the water, trying not to gag on the size of the tablets.

That done, she picked up the first envelope – a bank statement. Time was she didn't need one or have one. Her benefit check would come and she'd head down the post office to pick up her cash. All this rubbish about bank accounts... It was just a way to trap you in their system.

Opening it she stared at the statement for a while. Numbers had never been her strength. Nothing much had ever been her strength, except getting pregnant. That she had been pretty good at. First time she had sex was age fifteen. Nine months later Billy was born. Eight months and twenty nine days after the last time she saw that scum bag who had screwed her and walked away without even a thank you.

The next time she had been more careful. Made Jimmy Roper wear a condom. They hadn't mentioned in sex ed that condoms weren't reliable. Colin baked away real easy for the next nine months.

She'd never risked it again. Reasoned that some people caught pregnancy like others caught colds.

It had been tough at the start. Friends turning their back on her, even though several of them were themselves pregnant within a year or two. The benefits system hadn't been as good back then. She'd got by, somehow. Her own Mum had basically looked after her.

When Colin had finally gone to school she'd tried to find a job but few places wanted to take on a twenty year old with no qualifications or work experience. She worked as a cleaner for a while. Had even been offered a job in a factory but they wanted her to do shifts and she couldn't do that with the kids.

Then the benefits system changed and she was offered a house of her own and income support. She had enough to live on, to bring up Billy and Colin. Nothing extra. Nothing for emergencies, for times when they tore their trousers or lost a shoe. How could you lose a shoe? Somehow Billy had... And Colin, more than once.

But there had always been people willing to lend her money.

Irene stared at the bank statement. There seemed to be

plenty of money in the account. She'd never really understood why they put a dash in front of the numbers. Or why her card no longer let her take money out.

****

Seeing the sign for the coffee shop ahead, Helen slowed and checked her reflection in a window. She'd only just managed to squeeze into the trousers she was wearing that morning. It had been getting harder and harder over the last couple of weeks to find pairs that fit. The stress of the campaign and not eating properly were finally beginning to affect her.

She would just have to cut back, find some time to exercise. After this morning...

Lunchtime was always busy but Helen was able to see an empty table as she ordered for herself and Karen. The girl at the till said she would carry the Panini over when they were ready.

Helen negotiated her way to the table with a tray balancing two large cappuccinos. After she'd taken a sip of her coffee she checked her phone, saw a message from Karen: running a few minutes late. That was okay. Give her time to get her breath back.

That was another thing. She had found herself being short of breath occasionally. She had put it down to stress, more stress than she had thought possible over the last couple of months, but she couldn't be that unfit already, could she?

She needed a proper break, her and Robert to get away, though when that would be possible she had no idea. If he was actually elected would things quieten down or just get busier? MSPs did take holidays, didn't they? They must do, that was when the paparazzi caught them on some millionaire's yacht or bathing topless on some secluded beach.

She suddenly looked around, was anyone watching her? She'd been lucky so far, had very little to do with the election campaign. Robert had taken the brunt of the media attention and she'd been able to mostly get on with her job. Would that change? Did she want it to change?

Everything had been all about Robert's vision, his priorities up till now, but at the Cafe Politics she'd started discussing issues she dealt with at work; tried to see if anyone else cared about the homeless. She was relieved that many did. Not everyone, but she already knew that. Enough though, that she had begun to wonder how they could use Cafe Politics, use Robert's proposed referendums to change government policy.

It wouldn't even need to be as if she was using undue influence. Robert wanted every citizen to have a voice. That included her, didn't it?

****

Karen saw Helen and walked over. Helen stood and Karen gave her a quick hug and then sat down, able to relax for a short while.

"How are you coping?" Karen asked.

"I'm not."

Helen had said it jokingly but Karen saw her look away. Saw her face tense slightly as her smile faltered for an instant.

"You?"

Karen took a sip of her cappuccino as she thought. "I work normal hours and then am out most evenings at Cafe Politics. If it wasn't for weekends I don't know what I'd do."

"I really need to go shopping. I just don't know when I will have the time."

"Maybe we should take a Saturday off? Go into town."

Helen nodded. "I'd love that. Hardly any of my clothes fit me anymore. The stress must be getting to me."

"To us all. Not long now though..."

****

251

CHAPTER THIRTY TWO

The last two weeks she'd sent Billy and Colin to the food bank but today Irene wanted to go with them. The doctor had said her back would heal quicker if she gradually did more walking.

By the time she reached the end of her street, Irene thought her doctor must have been having her on. She was in agony. Billy stood impatiently tapping his foot while she rested, leaning against a lamp post. She didn't know what he was in such a hurry for. When they got back home he'd just disappear in his room.

She'd stopped suggesting the boys think about getting their own place when the bedroom tax came in. Her boys living in the same home as her was the only thing enabling her to survive on the little benefits she still got. That and the food bank.

Colin offered her his arm but she didn't want to look like a cripple. Though, as she set off again she thought back to the doctor's advice about using walking sticks to take the load.

There was a bus into town but the cost of tickets was as much as a bag of food and even in pain, Irene couldn't bring herself to use the bus.

She saw Billy and Colin exchange glances but gave them each a look that told them to keep their thoughts to themselves.

She'd allowed half an hour to walk in but by the time they approached the church hall it had taken them over an hour. The queue of people outside had long since gone in and Irene felt a momentary panic that they'd taken too long and there would be no food left.

Somewhere back on the street she'd started feeling light headed and had finally taken Colin's arm. Then a minute later she grabbed Billy and ended up carefully walking into the hall with both her boys held close.

Irene was relieved to see there were still lots of people inside. Most of them sitting on benches around the hall with cups of soup, tea or coffee, and paper plates with sandwiches.

Tim was on the door. Over the months Irene had gradually learnt most of their names. Tim was okay. Some of them she suspected were secretly judging her behind fake smiles. He gave them a ticket. Billy took it. They were in the queue.

The boys walked her over to a free bench and helped her sit down, then went to get some soup and sandwiches.

Irene focused on the floor. This was the worst part of her week. The rest of the time she could shut out the worry, the fear. But here, in this hall, she couldn't lie. She had no future, no way to change the mess she'd made of her life. Thirty eight years old and all she had to show for it were two boys who had never worked and maybe never would.

"Irene, is it?"

Irene looked up.

"I'm Sylvia. We've spoken once or twice when I've been handing out the parcels."

Irene remembered. She didn't come here to get sympathy, tried to avoid speaking to people, ate, took what was offered and left. But she couldn't be rude. What if they didn't let her come back?

"You seemed to be in a bit of pain when you came in...?"

"My back. I slipped a disc last month. Still hurts."

Sylvia's expression grew concerned. "Are you travelling far to get here?"

Irene looked away. They took addresses when they gave out the parcels, she supposed to stop families getting more than one but even so, she was reluctant to say where she lived. "Takes me half an hour normally to walk. Took longer tonight."

"I can imagine."

Irene doubted that. Then she saw Sylvia smiling.

"Don't believe me, huh? Fair enough. I was helping my husband move our sofa. Lifted it wrong or bent wrong or something and my back went pop. Couldn't move for two days."

Irene saw Sylvia's smile fade as she described it. Then Sylvia shuddered. "Took me six months before I felt I was walking normally. Probably a year before I stopped worrying about how I moved. At the time I didn't think anyone understood how much agony I was in."

Irene looked away as she felt her eyes fill up.

"Do you have anyone to talk to about it?"

Not since Mum died. Irene desperately wanted Sylvia to go away. She just needed to get the food and go.

"It's okay." Sylvia sighed. "If it would help, I or someone else here is willing to listen. You only need to ask."

Irene managed to nod.

Sylvia sat in silence until Irene began to wonder if she'd ever leave.

"Let me give you a lift home." Sylvia suddenly said.

"No. We'll manage." Irene didn't know why she didn't want to accept the offer. The thought of having to walk back being helped by Billy and Colin was horrible. She saw Sylvia studying her.

"Do you know why we help out here?"

Irene shook her head.

"Any of us could be in your position. If we were we would want people around us willing to help. We don't buy extra groceries for this place because we are rich, we don't go without ourselves because we don't need, we give because we see ourselves when we look at you and we hope that when we need, someone else will be willing to help us." She paused. "Don't go. Wait until I'm finished helping and I'll drive you home. Okay?"

Irene fought an internal battle without knowing why she was fighting it. Sylvia waited and eventually Irene agreed.

The boys brought over soup for her once Sylvia left.

"What was that all about, Mum?" Colin asked.

"She's giving us a lift home."

Billy frowned. "They don't do that."

"Well she is." Irene snapped at him.

"Do you think they do deliveries?" Colin joked.

"Don't push it." Irene carefully stretched her back. She was due more co-codamol but had been starting to leave it longer than the recommended four hours. Too many people she knew were addicted to one drug or another. She'd never wanted that for herself.

They ate in silence until their number was called up. Billy and Colin helped her to the desk where a couple of the volunteers sat. One of them got up and brought another seat so all three of them could sit.

"Irene! Good to see you."

The cheeriness of the greeting grated on her. She didn't want to be here. Didn't they realise that?

"Have your boys been looking after you?"

Irene frowned at Billy and Colin who hadn't seemed to hear the question.

"We're getting by." She said.

"We've still got several programs you'd be welcome to join: the job club meets on Mondays, CAP Money course on Wednesday, and drop in centre every Friday afternoon."

Irene shook her head. "Thank you." She forced a smile.

They took down the usual details and then one of the volunteers got up and fetched several shopping bags filled with essentials. It was often a strange mix of own brand, basic range and expensive brand: cereals, pasta, rice; tins of meatballs and spaghetti. They usually included a loaf of bread and carton of milk. It had been a weekly lifesaver.

Irene thanked them and let Billy and Colin carry the bags while she made her way back to the bench. Normally she would leave straight away but the offer of a lift home was definitely worth waiting for.

Most people arrived early and queued before the food bank opened and there hadn't been many people arriving after Irene. After about twenty minutes Sylvia came over and said she could leave.

Sylvia took some of the bags allowing Colin to hold her arm. The walk out to the car was painful enough for Irene. She planned to down a couple of co-codamol and lie down as soon as she got home.

The journey that had taken them an hour earlier only took ten minutes in the car. Sylvia drove slowly. Irene directed her to their street. When the car stopped outside, Sylvia turned to Irene.

"Tomorrow you'll likely hurt all over. Get up and get outside. Even just a short walk to the end of the street. Your back will heal itself but it will be faster if you exercise a little every day."

"You really hurt your back?"

"Five years ago. It does get better, I promise."

****

Sylvia drove Irene and the boys home from the food bank for the next two weeks. The walk there had got easier but Sylvia had been insistent. Irene fought an internal battle as she was driven home. As Sylvia parked outside their house, Irene turned to her.

"Would you like a cuppa?"

"Thank you, yes."

So much for her fear Sylvia would turn her down, would make some excuse. Irene made the boys carry the bags but the moment she walked in the house, she regretted making the offer. Scuff marks on the hallway wallpaper. The floor itself was unsurfaced, just bare concrete after the lino had been chewed up by a dog they'd had for a while.

Irene walked through to the kitchen and realised the sink was overflowing with dishes. Sylvia followed her in and Irene suddenly felt ashamed at how she was living. Admittedly everything had got a lot worse since she hurt her back, but why could she never get the boys to help?

"Sorry about the mess..." Irene trailed off.

"It's difficult when you're not well." Sylvia frowned at Billy and Colin who had set the bags down next to the table and were now walking back out the kitchen. "Hold on, you two. Where do you think you're going?"

Billy and Colin stopped and looked back with uncertain expressions.

"Billy and Colin, isn't it? I'm going to make your Mum a cuppa while you both do the dishes. Billy, you're on washing. Colin, you're drying." Sylvia looked at Irene. "Why don't you take a seat here. Something tells me we're going to have to keep an eye on these two."

Irene watched in amazement as her two boys who usually ignored her requests for help, who insisted that cleaning was woman's work, both followed Sylvia's orders.

Sylvia made them clean up two mugs first of all and then got the kettle on to make tea. When she sat down, Irene whispered to her: "How did you make them do that?"

Sylvia looked puzzled. "I don't really know. Why?"

"I can't get them to do anything."

"I struggle to get my own kids to pick up after themselves. Maybe it's easier with other people's kids."

They watched while the boys finished the washing up, Sylvia giving them directions every now and then. As soon as they'd finished they both fled the room. The two women sat in silence, drinking their tea.

Irene's thoughts were conflicted. The battle she'd had with herself in the car hadn't been resolved by inviting Sylvia in. Eventually she stood and walked out of the kitchen. She returned a minute later with a piece of paper which she handed to Sylvia.

Sylvia took it but didn't look at it. Instead she gave Irene a puzzled look. "What is it?"

"A bank statement."

"No, I meant, what's wrong?"

Irene shook her head. "I don't know. I've never been good with money, never good with numbers. The bank won't let me take any more money out. I don't know why."

Irene watched as Sylvia looked at the bank statement. Watched her frown. Turn the piece of paper over briefly, then turn it back. Then she took a deep breath and blew it out.

"You owe the bank money."

"Not just the bank."

"Who else?" Sylvia asked.

"I've been borrowing money from a guy in our neighbourhood."

"A loan shark?"

"I don't think so."

"Can you tell me how much?"

"I think it's five hundred pounds."

"Is he charging you interest?"

"Yes. But it's only ten percent."

"Is that by the day, week, month or year?"

"He didn't say."

Sylvia hesitated, then gave an uncertain smile. "You did the right thing telling me. This is..." She held up the bank statement. "This is going to be difficult to sort out, but we can help you. It will be easier if we get you back to talk to someone with more experience but just looking quickly at this, you've reached the limit of what the bank will lend you – that's why they won't let you take any more money out. Looking at the statement, it seems you've more money going out than is coming in. That needs to change otherwise you'll never get out from this."

Again Sylvia hesitated. "Have you any cash left?"

Irene shook her head. She'd been wondering about going back to ask for another loan now her back was starting to recover.

"Don't go back to the man who lent you the money. I'll come back tomorrow... It'll be evening but, do you think you can wait till then?"

They had the bags from the food bank. Irene nodded. "I think so."

****

It had taken several weeks to sort out the money. Irene still wasn't totally sure she understood but Sylvia had summed it all up into one thing that made sense: she could only spend what she had.

The CAP Money course the church ran hadn't been enough. They'd referred her to CAP Debt Help who had spent a whole day with her going over purchases she'd made, the payments and interest she was expected to make; how much income she had; how much she owed; who she owed money to.

Then they had taken copies of everything, went away and came back with a plan. It was going to take several years to sort out but even though it made her scared to think about, she would start having money coming back in. As long as she stuck to the plan, they would survive.

When Sylvia had come back the previous evening she'd brought several more shopping bags bursting with supplies. "We've an emergency fund." She explained. "It's not just food, there's cleaning materials and toiletries."

CAP Debt Help had also applied for an emergency grant on her behalf. When they brought round an envelope with £200 in cash she couldn't stop crying.

It turned out that the friendly man who had lent her £500 had neglected to tell her he was charging ten percent interest every week. The amount she owed him had more than doubled since she first had started borrowing money. He'd demanded she start paying him fifty pounds a week.

The two people from CAP Debt Help who worked with her were Chris and Shona. They both came to her house when she called Neil.

"Hello?" His voice didn't sound as friendly over the phone.

Irene was sitting in her living room, Chris and Shona next to her with a piece of paper on her knee that had written out what she needed to say.

"This is Irene Wallace, number 54 Burns Road. I'm not going to be able to pay you the money I owe." She bit her lip.

"The hell you're not! I'm not running a charity here. You need to start paying, and now!"

"I've got no money. If you want to come round and talk about it, I'm at home now." The first part would have been a lie but Chris had insisted she say it. Irene had made them take the money she had left so she wouldn't be lying. "We'll give you it back when he's gone." Shona had promised.

Irene hung up before Neil could say anything else. She gave back Chris's phone. She hadn't been able to top up her own in months.

"You head upstairs." Chris told her.

As she hurried up to her room, Irene hoped they would be okay. She didn't know what to do with herself. She sat on the bed for a few minutes. Lying down didn't seem right. Eventually she went and sat on the floor with her back to the door. Every sense heightened as she waited to see if Neil would come.

The knock on the door made her jump. She looked at the clock next to her bed. It had been more than an hour. She heard someone walk to the door.

"Who're you?" She heard Neil say.

"My name's Chris. Come in."

"Where's Irene?"

She heard Neil's voice get louder as he came into the house and then the door to the living room closed and the voices became muffled.

She could tell who was speaking but not what was being said. Then Neil was shouting and swearing and she heard something crash. She pulled her legs close to her and wrapped her arms around them.

More speaking with Chris doing most of the talking. Then Neil swore loudly again. She heard the sitting room door bang against the wall, someone walk out into the hall and the front door also hitting against the wall. Then there was silence.

"Irene?" She heard Shona's voice. "You can come down."

Opening the door to her room, she saw Billy and Colin looking at her from their rooms, worried expressions on their faces. Both looked so young.

She didn't know what to say to them so just went downstairs.

Chris was standing in the far corner of the room, a black object in his hands. Shona stood by the TV, her arms crossed and a frown on her face. Irene looked at each of them in turn.

"He's a nasty piece of work." Shona said. "Doesn't care at all about the lives he's destroying. Ten percent interest every week... If you let him get away with that, you'd be paying him for the rest of your life!"

"He shouldn't come back." Chris told her. "If he does though, don't answer the door. Call the police. He's broken the law and has no right to chase you for the money. You need to get some credit on your phone so you can call me as well, but first call the police."

"Don't I have to pay him the money?"

"I've told him that I'm dealing with all your debts now. If he wants any of his money back he has to provide me with all the paperwork. The problem he's got is that he's breaking the law by not being licensed to offer loans. Also, he never provided you with paperwork. Never got you to sign anything, did he?"

Irene shook her head.

"It should be against the law to charge you such a high rate of interest but the law as it stands is broken. Pay day loan companies and the place you got your TV and sofa from are almost as bad as blokes like him." Chris sighed. "He threatened us and you. I need to warn you of that. If you want, we can take you somewhere safe tonight. Help you get re-housed somewhere else."

"This is my home. I'm not going to let him scare me away."

"He broke one of your ornaments." Shona pointed at the fireplace where pieces of a china dog were scattered about.

Irene looked up and saw its twin was still on the mantelpiece.

"We got that on film." Chris came over. "Got the whole thing. Him threatening you, us, demanding his money. He's damaged your property... Maybe could claim that was an accident but from where I was, it looked deliberate. If you change your mind, even if you just feel worried, call us. We'll get you out of here, okay?"

"What are you going to do with the film?"

"Give it to the police. He's threatened you, damaged your property, illegally lent you money and threatened us into the bargain. The safest thing for you is if he's taken off the street. As he's made multiple threats there is a good chance he won't get bail."

"I feel so stupid."

"Don't put yourself down." Shona came over and put an arm around her. "He lied to you. Now, I'm thinking we could all do with a cuppa. What do you say Chris?"

"Good idea." He walked into the hallway. "Billy! Colin! Put the kettle on..."

****

CHAPTER THIRTY THREE

Rain fell, vaguely discernible as shifting grey against the building opposite. Helen looked above the building to a mottled white sky. The heaviness of an earlier downpour had passed on, taking darker hues with it.

She turned back from the window to watch Robert as he paced back and forth, his mobile pressed tightly to his ear.

She caught his attention and mouthed 'conference call' at him. He stopped and looked round at the others in the room.

"Hold on a minute." Robert said into the phone then laid it on the table before changing the speaker setting. "You're on loudspeaker now with Gordon, Helen, Kathryn and Julie. Could you repeat what you just told me?"

"Certainly." Helen heard the voice of Christopher Turnstall who she'd never met but had spoken with once when they had sold their house. "I've discussed the situation with colleagues and we're in agreement that you are in unchartered waters. Legally, you have no claim against the election result. To all observers, you won in a transparent process with no evidence of manipulation."

"Yet we didn't win an outright majority." Gordon said, leaning forward towards the phone.

"As I understand it, the Scottish electoral system is designed to prevent any party gaining an outright majority." Turnstall replied. "However, seeing as you managed to win a majority in the popular vote and the SNP previously gained a majority with only a fraction of the votes you achieved, I can understand your frustration."

"Legally, what are our options?" Robert asked.

"The simplest course of action would be to accept the result and try and build a coalition government. You are not far off being able to do that."

"We tried calling the smaller parties this morning. None of them would take our call."

"It's only the day after the election. Negotiations take time."

Kathryn leaned forward. "We won the election yet didn't achieve a majority. Surely we have a right to challenge that."

"You do, though there is no guarantee any court would hear your case. The Scottish Parliament exists as a result of an act of Westminster's parliament. You could appeal to Westminster but I'm doubtful of the likelihood of success. Also, bear in mind the referendum is only a few weeks away. In the event of a Yes vote, you may not need to appeal to anyone."

"And in the event of a No vote…" Julie left the question hanging.

"Christopher, thanks for investigating this." Robert said. He looked at Gordon as he continued: "Will you be available if we need to speak with you again?"

"I will be finishing up for the day shortly and am going fishing tomorrow but I'll email you my mobile number if you need to contact me over the weekend. I should have coverage."

"Where are you fishing?" Gordon asked.

"Culter, on the River Dee."

"We'll try not to disturb you." Gordon turned to Robert as he said goodbye and ended the call.

"What are you two thinking?" Helen asked.

"Am I missing something?" Julie looked round.

"They're up to something." Kathryn confirmed. "Care to share it?"

Robert sat down at the table. "Last night… This morning, whenever it was…" He shook his head. "We were talking about a legal challenge but how can we challenge when the courts don't have jurisdiction over the result."

"You're not going to accept the result, are you?" Kathryn asked.

"Of course not." Robert looked at Helen "But we only have

a few days before Parliament is sworn in. We can either waste months or even years trying to change the system or…"

Helen looked from Robert to Gordon. "Or what?"

Robert didn't answer, just kept looking at her.

Gordon placed both his hands on the table, palms down, and pushed himself up. "Or we force change."

Helen studied Gordon and Robert. Both looked tired though Robert more than Gordon. Despite his age, Gordon seemed to have coped with the strain of the election far better and if anything he seemed to have had a new burst of enthusiasm following the result. She suspected Robert just needed a couple of proper nights of sleep. He had been waking earlier every day, working on speeches and responding to emails from their teams across the country. Yet there was an edge to Robert at the moment.

"What are you proposing?" Kathryn asked.

"Robert?" Gordon prompted and went to get a glass of water.

"We stood for election promising radical change but if we don't have a majority in parliament, we can't guarantee to deliver anything. Regardless of the referendum result, without a majority, we can't negotiate on Scotland's behalf."

"The parties will have to join together after the referendum." Kathryn said.

"But we shouldn't need to worry about whether or not other political parties will work with us. Sixty percent of Scotland voted for us… Most elections now struggle to get sixty percent to vote at all, let alone for one party." Robert stood and began pacing once more.

Helen decided she needed some water herself. She pushed herself up and began walking when she realised the room was spinning slightly. She slowed, suddenly very aware of her breathing. Stopping at the unit where they had jugs of water she waited until everything steadied before taking a glass and pouring the water. Must have stood too quickly, she thought.

Robert had continued speaking. "We have a mandate to change Scotland, whether or not Holyrood or Westminster recognizes that. I don't think we can wait until the referendum or even another week. We need to assume and act like we are a majority now."

"But what does that mean?" Julie asked. "We only have 45%

control of Holyrood."

"We have sixty percent of Scotland." Robert replied. "Holyrood doesn't stand a chance."

****

"They're not happy." Robert said to Gordon after the others had left.

"They're women. You can't expect them to feel the same way."

"The majority of our supporters are women. Majority of our MSPs come to think of it. If we can't convince the women closest to us, how can we convince the rest?"

Gordon sighed. "You just need to find the right way to sell this. If we're going to do it, it has to be this week."

"Monday, Tuesday, Wednesday… Do we still register our MSPs?"

"Yes. Whatever happens on Wednesday, you want everyone there for the opening of parliament."

"Four days to prepare." Robert shook his head. "It had better be enough time."

****

"What you're proposing sounds like civil war." Helen nursed a mug of tea, her legs tucked under her as she leaned back on the headboard of their bed.

They had returned to Gordon and Penny's after sending everyone else home for the night. Robert sat by an ornate writers desk. He had switched to decaf coffee for the evening as he was beginning to wonder if the amount of coffee he was drinking was keeping him awake.

"Without the guns or tanks or street to street fighting." He said.

The remains of a Chinese takeaway sat on trays between them. Both had been famished though they had also agreed they were getting tired of fast food.

"You're going to call on all our supporters to march on Edinburgh. What are you going to do if this doesn't work out? What are they going to do?"

"It has to work, there is no plan B."

Helen shook her head. "You don't want the media getting hold of that quote. Have you really considered what would happen if a million people turned up? One million angry Scots, furious that their election has been stolen from them?"

"It's a powerful motivator. How many politicians or judges have really had to face the people they are supposed to serve?"

"How will you face them if you can't deliver what you promised?"

"I have to deliver. We can't have made it this far to be beaten by a corrupt political system."

"The legal system might do it for you. An illegal march. One that could easily descend into riots. You as the ring leader. You could spend the next few weeks in jail if this turns South."

"That's another reason to go ahead."

Helen gave him an exasperated look. "If you want to go to jail, there are easier ways."

"I meant that protesting should not be illegal. Just another example of a corrupt political system that has systematically tried to stamp out any form of disagreement over the last decade. The government watches every move we make through CCTV, spies on our emails and phone calls, has made it harder and harder to organize any popular movement. And even when we get a majority of the vote, we still cannot change parliament."

"There's got to be another way."

Robert shook his head. "If you can come up with a plan B, C or even F, I'd love to try. I think we have to use the momentum we have from the campaign now though. If we try and work within the system our support will dwindle as people see nothing change."

"Cafe Politics was always plan C."

"I know. But sometimes in life we have to stand up for what we believe, even fight for what we believe. Otherwise evil wins."

"What happened to turning the other cheek?"

"I've never been very good at that. I seem to remember Jesus making a whip and using it in the temple. Telling his disciples to buy a sword..."

"Don't you go buying a sword." Helen laid her mug on the bedside table and lay down on the bed.

"I could wear a kilt, paint my face white and blue..."

Helen screwed up her face and put her hand up in protest. "No, no, no!"

Robert moved the trays off the bed and joined Helen, turning to look at the ceiling. "We've got this weekend to organize it. We make it clear we're looking for noisy but peaceful protest."

"Then you bluff your way through?"

"A bluff only works if you're half intending to go through with it."

Helen placed an arm round Robert. "Be careful."

He didn't reply, just stared at the ceiling trying to plan his attack.

****

CHAPTER THIRTY FOUR

By Nine AM, Robert and Helen were back at headquarters and on the phones. Every volunteer had been called back in. Those who didn't have desk phones were on their mobiles.

Television, radio and newspaper journalists were calling asking for quotes and interviews but they were being politely yet firmly turned away.

Trying to reach more than two million people in one weekend should have been an impossible task, but the network of Cafe Politics that had grown during the last month enabled them to quickly spread the request out to every part of Scotland. By avoiding the media, they hoped to keep their plan a secret as long as possible, yet by Sunday morning they had one journalist asking them about the planned protest march.

Julie took that call and hurried to tell Robert.

"It could never stay secret for long. There are too many people." He told her.

"Do we need to alter the plans?"

"We actually want the media there. It's just best if they don't know for certain what's going on. They can't twist our words if we don't comment."

"They can speculate though."

"That's ninety percent of what they call news now – speculation and opinion. No, our supporters will hear from us what we are planning. The rest of Scotland will hear on

Wednesday. Which reminds me, who's arranging the streaming broadcast?"

"Kathryn is sorting it out."

"Good. Last thing we want is people unable to view the action."

****

Robert led his fifty seven MSPs into Holyrood. Thirty women and twenty seven men. The timetable was fixed in advance though there was some flexibility over this stage – the registration of MSPs.

Robert had decided to register on mass, in part to prevent any of his party being cornered by a journalist and being tricked into revealing their plans. Also to make a clear statement to the watching media and the country – we are united.

There was a delay when one of the men realised they didn't have all the necessary proof of identity documentation on him. Fortunately he'd just left it at his hotel and a volunteer was dispatched by taxi to collect it.

It was normal for party leaders who had gained a majority to receive calls of congratulations from the other parties but whether simply gaining more seats than the others was not considered a majority or because there was general uncertainty over what the huge popular vote would mean, Robert had received no calls.

Robert was standing in a corridor, chatting with a group of his MSPs he didn't yet know well, when he saw a group of people walking towards them.

"What's the hold up?" Robert heard, recognizing the voice. He stepped out, blocking the group's progress.

"MacKenzie. Congratulations on your victory." Robert said, keeping his expression neutral.

"What? Who is... Castle!" Connor MacKenzie pushed his way to the front of the group.

"We shouldn't be too long." Robert said. "I think we're half way through. You might want to come back in a couple of hours."

MacKenzie glared at Robert but didn't reply.

Robert stepped back and turned to the person who had been speaking, now standing with an amused expression on her face.

He concentrated for a second. "Colleen, you were saying..."

Behind him he sensed the group move away slowly. Robert resisted the urge to turn and look as they stopped outside the office being used to register MSPs. There was muffled discussion, silence and then more discussion. Colleen and the others exchanged glances. Then the group quickly made their way back up the corridor.

Once out of earshot, Colleen asked: "Victory?"

"He retained his seat in spite of a determined effort by Tom Whinnie. Managed to beat our candidate by all of five hundred votes. Bit of a change from his landslide in 2011 but a definite victory."

"Rather childish of you. Tell me this isn't how you plan to act in parliament." Colleen crossed her arms.

"I plan to strip parliament of much of its power and hand that power to the people."

"The Scottish parliament still doesn't have much power."

"For now."

****

The Kirking of parliament the following day took place without any upset. Robert and Helen attended along with all their MSPs and spouses or partners. Robert was not convinced by protestations of the inclusiveness of the service but chose not to comment. Following the service, they headed back to the hotel they had booked into and changed before going to Waverley station.

By the time they arrived they could see groups of people greeting each other. Some had travelled from as far away as the Shetlands, Lewis and Harris while others from the relative closeness of the Highlands.

It was a logistical nightmare with nowhere near enough accommodation available in Edinburgh and the likelihood that public transport wouldn't cope if as many people as they hoped would turn up the following day.

Some volunteers were opening up their homes while others said they had room for a tent in the garden. Headquarters had been manned every day since the weekend, sending out advice on where to park, what trains or buses to take.

Everyone was advised to be in Edinburgh as early as possible and be prepared for delays. For some it would make as much sense to walk in from the suburbs as try and take public transport.

Robert and Helen separated and started asking people if they needed advice on where to go. The first group Robert approached were genuine tourists and he found himself struggling to answer what the best attractions in Edinburgh were. Looking around for help he saw a sign pointing the way for Information and recommended they go there.

Fortunately one of his team came up with the idea of printing large cards with the words: Castle Tours. The cards were hurriedly printed out and distributed that afternoon and texts and tweets were sent out to look for the cards.

They had advised people to avoid any direct mention of the march through social media but whether news got out through the journalist or someone made a complaint, the police sent officers to their headquarters that evening.

Robert was directing a group from the Borders up to the Taxi rank when he got the call on his mobile. He excused himself and answered.

"We've been cautioned." Gordon told him abruptly. "Advised that if we attempt an illegal gathering or march, that arrests will be made."

"Did they know what we're planning?"

"They know it's happening in Edinburgh and have seen an increase in the volume of people arriving."

"Kind of hard to hide that." Robert looked round as more people made their way to volunteers. "Anything else?"

"They believe we're marching on Holyrood."

"Okay. Nothing we can do about that. Any news from volunteers?"

"No news is good news, hopefully."

Robert looked across at Helen. He didn't want her there tomorrow but she refused to talk with him about it. "Someone had to keep an eye on him." She had said.

"Okay. Thanks for letting me know. See you tomorrow." Robert said.

"Wouldn't miss it for the world!"

Around him volunteers were smiling, waving and greeting. What they were about to attempt was dangerous and while he had not emphasized the illegality of their plans, he had spoken to enough people around the nation to know the people who were travelling were no fools.

Let the police seal off Holyrood. Obviously it had been a while since they'd last had to deal with a revolution...

****

CHAPTER THIRTY FIVE

At a Quarter to Ten Robert and Helen were waiting at the Western end inside the cathedral. Helen was studying a stained glass panel. A scene at the top of the panel depicting the crossing of the Jordan had caught Robert's eye. He was very aware they were about to cross a line that they could not retreat from.

"An alien, a prophet and a victim."

"What?" Robert looked at Helen.

"The three women." She indicated at the stained glass panel.

Robert had only glanced at the three women in white underneath the Jordan scene. He had presumed they were saints and lost interest. "An alien?"

"Ruth. At the right. She gave up her family, her homeland and said she would follow Naomi's God."

Robert looked more closely and realised the woman was standing in a field of wheat, even holding the 'gleanings.'

"In the middle is Miriam. Without her Moses would have been killed with all the other infants. Was she a prophet even as a child? Willing to risk death herself to save her baby brother?"

"What's she holding?" Robert had assumed the brown, box like structure in her hands was a wash board. "I thought... Wait, it's a musical instrument, isn't it?"

"What did you think?" Helen asked, her eyebrows raised.

"You don't want to know. Who's the other woman?" He

said quickly.

"A child really. I forget the father's name but he made a vow before he went into battle that if he won, whatever came out of his house first would be sacrificed. What an idiot!"

Robert vaguely recalled the story, one that still made him uneasy. "His daughter. How could anyone kill their own child?"

"Abraham was about to. You could say that God did. Yet even though God intervened to save Isaac and must have known Jesus would overcome death, that man stands alone as an arrogant fool."

It wasn't often that Helen spoke so passionately. Robert instinctively put an arm around her, unsure if he wanted to protect her or hold her back.

She took a deep breath. "Though, I did read recently that maybe we've misinterpreted the story. That even such a fool wouldn't have dared sacrifice his daughter and instead would just have condemned her to remain in solitude – a virgin for the rest of her life."

Helen caught Robert's eye and he could see a sudden change in her expression.

"Think of him as an extended Darwin Award winner..."

Robert chuckled as he got the joke.

"Why right to left?" He asked.

"I like Ruth. I find her story more inspiring, her willingness to risk everything, her ability to see hope even after she had known such heartbreak. She worked so hard, was so faithful and in the end God rewarded her."

Neither of them said it out loud but both asked the question, would God reward them.

They stood together for a while, Robert still holding Helen until they saw Christopher Turnstall walk through the door into the cathedral.

Robert checked his watch. It was Five to Ten.

They shook hands and then Robert led them outside into the square. Across the Royal Mile was the High Court. In the square he could see groups of people with white armbands.

He took three out of his pocket and handed one to Helen and then Christopher before putting his own on.

"If this doesn't get me disbarred I'll be astonished." Christopher said.

"I'll settle for not being arrested." Robert looked at Helen who looked pensive. "You don't have to be here." He told her.

"I'm not letting you out of my sight." Helen pointed at a group of young men. "Your brown shirts have arrived."

"Don't call them that." Robert replied looking at the group of young men with Ollie and Gareth. While they had only employed the two men as effective bodyguards for Robert, Cafe Politics had also attracted hundreds of young men with the promise of full employment. Some had started self-policing events, leading to Helen's nickname.

Robert had made it clear they were not above the law but he shared Helen's concern about the potential for a worrying direction. The sooner they could actually implement their planned policies, including full employment, the better.

However, he had asked for volunteers to assist them today in a move that, he had to admit, fully justified Helen's concern.

Robert walked over to the group, looking round at faces that were older than they should have been.

"No violence in the court room." He told them. "You can restrain people if they act violently towards you but otherwise don't react, is that understood?"

"It's going to be difficult not to fight back if they start something." Ollie said.

"I know. But how we act today will determine whether we are justified or not."

"You said we needed to fight for Scotland, chief." Gareth said. Several of the group nodded.

"Let me do the fighting. We have Scotland on our side now but if we let today descend into violence then we've lost the battle."

"Whatever you say, chief." Ollie looked round the others. "No banging heads, alright?"

They nodded.

"One more thing. When we're all inside, no one leaves the courtroom until we're done."

"Going to be hard to enforce that without someone getting hurt."

"A couple of you at every door should discourage most people from leaving. If you aren't able to show restraint, don't enter the courthouse. Is that understood?"

It didn't matter how many times they said okay or nodded, no matter what was promised, he had no way of controlling the outcome. Robert looked round seeing that more and more people were arriving in the square, white armbands clearly visible. A lone police officer, walking up The Royal Mile, stopped and looked across at the assembled people. He saw her raise her microphone.

Robert looked over at Christopher who nodded an affirmative.

"Okay!" Robert said in a loud voice. "Follow me."

Without having to ask them, Ollie led his team to the police officer and formed an impromptu barrier in front of her as Robert made his way to the High Court. Looking down The Royal Mile he could see many more of their supporters making their way up. He waved and then checked to see that Christopher was with him.

"Lead on." Robert told him.

Christopher sidestepped a security guard and Robert followed, ignoring his protests. The plan was to use the volume of people to keep the doors open and then barricade themselves inside. Robert knew they had to move quickly though before the court was sealed off.

Christopher led the way until they reached a large set of double doors with another guard. These doors were open with people entering the court, the guard checking passes. Christopher moved to the front of the queue.

"Solicitor for the prosecution." He said to the guard, handing him a bit of paper.

Before the guard had time to react, Christopher carried on into the court. Robert followed close behind and from the reaction of the guard, knew there was a crowd following them.

Both the solicitors for the prosecution and defence stood and began protesting as Christopher and Robert stood in the centre of the court. Their supporters filled remaining spaces in the gallery and kept pressing in until they were standing then began to fill the floor of the court itself.

Ollie and Gareth pushed their way through the crowd.

"That police officer called for backup. I don't think it will be long before the police are trying to get in." Ollie said.

"Are there any people still outside?" Robert asked.

"They just kept coming." Gareth said.

For the first time since Robert had known him, Gareth's normal jaded expression had been replaced by what looked like amazement.

"Could you organize them to form a human shield round the court? To link arms?"

"I'll try."

"Good man. Ollie, can you take one of your men with Christopher and bring the judge here?"

"Of course."

They all left and Robert turned to the solicitors. "You will need to step back. We're taking over this court."

He turned and ignored their continued complaints.

The guard that had been on the door pushed his way through. "Are you in charge of this mob?"

"I wouldn't call them a mob." Robert said. "They might not like it."

The court could hardly contain any more people. They had stopped moving in and he could see the press of people continuing into the corridor.

"It's a serious crime to disrupt the court." The guard told him.

"It is a crime to deny the democratic will of the people. Are you attempting to do that?"

"I've no idea what you're talking about..." The guard turned and Robert heard the judge before he saw him.

"An outrage! How dare you threaten me. What the..." The judge was pushed through the crowd into the court.

"Take your place." Robert told him, gesturing at the Bench.

"I will not! Clear this court at once!"

"Ollie, if the judge does not make his own way to the Bench, would you pick him up and take him there?"

The judge and Robert stared at each other until Ollie grabbed the judge's arm. The judge jerked his arm out of Ollie's grip.

"Very well. Whatever you're planning to do here today, there will be serious consequences."

Robert just gestured towards the Bench and waited while the judge squeezed his way through.

"Christopher?" Robert said quietly.

Christopher nodded and turned towards the judge. In a loud voice he said: "Court is in session. Seal the doors."

Ollie's men, with some difficulty, cleared a way so the doors could close then posted two men in front of each door.

"You are to hear the case of the Scottish people versus the Scottish Government, brought by Robert Castle of The Great Scottish Land Grab party." Robert addressed the Judge.

"This case has no legal basis." The judge responded.

"The law only exists at the will of the people and it is the will of the people that you hear this case." Robert cleared his throat. "Your honour, this case need not take long. The Scottish people elected my party and myself to lead Scotland. Over sixty percent of the electorate voted for the changes I propose. I have a clear mandate to take power and force through the changes the people have voted for. I seek legal recognition of our mandate, the dissolution of the current electoral and parliamentary systems, and the creation of a temporary constitution to allow us to proceed."

"You're right, Mr Castle, this case need not take long. Your request is denied."

"On what basis are you denying the Scottish people their request?"

"I am not denying the Scottish people anything. I am denying you the right to throw our nation into anarchy. I am denying you the right to set yourself up as dictator. But I thought you did not want to go into detail on this matter, or did I misunderstand you?"

"I have been elected by a clear majority of the Scottish people. They have elected me to speak on their behalf. I caution you that both you and I now serve at their pleasure – and will be removed at their displeasure."

"I have every right to have each person here arrested for the threats you have made in my court."

"This is not your court, your honour. You serve at the pleasure of the Scottish people."

"I serve at the pleasure of Her Majesty the Queen. Be very careful, Mr Castle."

"Her Majesty also serves at the pleasure of the Scottish people. There is precedent for the removal of both monarch and unjust judge in our long and inglorious history."

The judge frowned as he saw Christopher Turnstall standing next to Robert. "Mr Turnstall, are you with this man?"

"I am your honour. I counsel you to do as he says."

"I have to advise you both that you are not only risking imprisonment by threatening this court, you are also risking a charge of treason, the penalty for which is much more severe."

Robert decided to change tack. "Your honour, look around at this court. These people here are only a small sample of the two million, three hundred thousand Scots who clearly have said they want... No, demand a change to our society."

"You have organized a mob." The Judge took a quick look towards the windows behind which chanting could be heard. "They will need to disperse."

"Who elected you?" Robert said.

"I was appointed. Appointed to serve at Her Majesty's pleasure."

"The Scottish people are no longer inclined to blindly accept Her Majesty's appointments. I will seek discussions with Her Majesty over such matters but in the meantime I asked you to recognize my mandate and dissolve the electoral system to allow me to replace it."

"I cannot and will not."

"Then you will face the charge of treason."

"How dare you threaten me!"

"How dare you ignore the command of the Scottish people! I will hand you over to the people outside. I do not call them a mob but I advise you to heed their wishes otherwise you will answer to them directly. I am offering you one last chance – recognize I have been given a mandate to recover Scotland's land; to change the electoral system and to lead Scotland!"

"How are you going to change the electoral system? I cannot simply give you Carte Blanche to make change without knowing the details!"

"I will introduce government by referendum. All major policies will be decided by the Scottish people who may also introduce new policies as they see fit. If a majority of one hundred thousand Scots petition for a change – it will go to a full referendum. If decided by the Scottish people it will be implemented.

"To force this through – I need recognition that my majority applies in parliament. It is neither just nor acceptable to the Scottish people that a minority of politicians should continue to decide Scotland's fate. I seek that seats in Parliament be allocated on the basis of votes won. I will not haggle over whether individuals or political parties decide who keeps a seat. I have a clear majority and more important work to do than please politicians who have only won through a corrupt and unjust electoral system.

"I will abide by the current terms of office and do not intend to seek any extension. I am happy to be limited to four years in office."

"You do realise that any judgement I make has been made under threat and cannot be enforced?"

Robert smiled. "Your judgement has been requested by the Scottish people. If they wish to challenge it, they may do so under our new electoral system."

"Very well, I will need an hour to draft this."

Robert turned to his solicitor. "Christopher, take Ollie and Gareth and make sure he follows through with this."

Robert turned to his supporters. "We may as well take a seat, it looks like we'll be an hour."

****

CHAPTER THIRTY SIX

There were people everywhere. Robert held onto Helen as they, Gordon and Christopher pushed through the crowd who clapped them on the back and cheered. There were people holding onto lamp posts, standing above the crowd; sitting on the sculptures; all the way down the Royal Mile and along the road towards Holyrood.

"Should we be worried about people getting crushed?" Robert shouted towards Gordon.

"Good point." Gordon shouted back. "Hold on."

Robert stopped and waited while Gordon talked with the people nearest him. "Okay." He said to Robert a minute later. "I've asked them to spread the word out to the crowd."

Robert felt his phone vibrate and pulled it out. A new Tweet from @BigJoeLoon: Look out for anyone hurt in the crowd and help #landgrab #holyrood.

Democracy in action. He showed Helen and they shared a smile.

As they got closer Christopher caught hold of Robert's arm. "The police have a cordon around the entrance. I'm not sure what their intent is."

Robert nodded. "We're going in, with or without their permission."

"They have marksmen on the roofs. This is for real now."

Looking up and around, Robert saw a couple of small black

outlines. "Watching you watching us." He whispered to himself. To Christopher he said: "There was no going back once I threatened the Judge. He probably put a warrant out for my arrest as soon as the crowd left the court."

"I had a few people stay behind, just in case."

"No-one who will do anything rash I hope?"

"I think you can trust them."

"Okay." Robert turned back to Holyrood and began pushing his way through again. The crowd tried to part but there were just too many and he had to squeeze through. Reaching the police line he held up the judgement he had received in the court.

"My name is Robert Castle, I represent the Scottish people. Let me through."

The police officers in the line almost seemed to ignore him. Robert made his way along the line until he reached the entrance. "Let me through!" He demanded. The officers stood still, large transparent shields held in front of them making an impenetrable wall. With their helmets and protective glasses on, it was hard to see their expressions.

Robert saw an officer behind the line, talking with a colleague. He shouted over, "You! Are you ranking officer?"

The officer walked up to the line. "This crowd needs to disperse right now. Riot police are on standby to clear the area."

"My name is Robert Castle."

"I know who you are. Tell the crowd to disperse."

"The people behind me demand the right to enter their parliament."

"That is not going to happen. I have orders to protect the building while parliament is being sworn in."

"Parliament is currently standing outside the building demanding to be let through."

"You lost the election, Castle. I will have you placed under arrest if you do not order this crowd to disperse."

"The Scottish people elected me with a clear majority. I have a court judgement here that recognizes the majority and grants me extraordinary powers to dissolve parliament. You will let me through or you will set the police against the Scottish people."

"Don't threaten me, Castle. I will give you five minutes to send this crowd away. Then you will be responsible for the consequences."

Robert turned and held out his hand. Turnstall handed him a bull-horn and raising it, Robert turned back to the police line.

"My name is Robert Castle! I have been elected by sixty percent of the Scottish people to bring change to our land." Behind him he heard the crowd grow silent. "Each of you police officers here today have sworn an oath to protect the Scottish people. Yet you stand here against the people you swore to protect. None of the men and women who are in parliament today received a mandate to govern Scotland. I did. You will let me and my people pass through now or you will have declared war on Scotland's people. You work for us. Honour your oath now or I guarantee you, by the end of the today each one of you will be placed on trial for treason."

"CASTLE!" The senior officer pushed through the line of officers. "Stop this now! Would you really bring Scotland to civil war?"

"Look behind me." Robert told him. "I abhor the use of violence but I will not allow you or anyone else to deny the people of Scotland – the people whom you serve – the change they have demanded. You need to decide – right now – whether you will honour Scotland's people, or the broken and corrupt system that this building stands for."

Robert turned away from him and again raised the bull-horn. "Scotland! Are you with me?"

There were a series of shouted 'Ayes' and one loud 'Freedom!'

Robert saw Gordon push his way to him and standing beside Robert began to chant: "Scot-Land, Scot-Land!"

It was taken up by the people nearest and swept across the crowd until a wall of sound was beating on the police line.

Robert turned back to the senior officer. "Let us past!" He demanded.

The officer stared wide eyed back at him. Robert pushed him aside and then pushed at the nearest riot shield, looking the officer holding it in the eye. Robert gently shook his head as he applied more force and the officer stepped back, a look of fear in his eyes.

Behind him, the chanting dissolved to a roar and he sensed the crowd swell beside him as suddenly the police line dissolved and Robert and the crowd walked through into Holyrood.

CHAPTER THIRTY SEVEN

Inside the main chamber, Robert found the politicians he had been debating with for the past few months. Connor MacKenzie stepped forward and Robert halted in front of him.

"What do you think you're doing disrupting the procedure? We are being sworn in!"

"There has been a change in electoral policy. We are assuming the role of government and instigating an immediate change."

"Have you gone mad? You didn't win a majority, Castle. You can't change anything!"

"I seem to have had a lot of people try to tell me what I can't do. I'm not asking your permission, MacKenzie." Robert pushed past him and walked down to the centre of the chamber. He waited while people continued to pour into the chamber and waved at Christopher to join him.

"Are the speakers set up?"

"Yes. I'm not confident we can get a good signal out of here though."

"We'll just have to hope it works. What do we need now?"

"We need the Presiding Officer to recognize the Judge's document and swear you in. We need this recorded on camera together with your planned speech and for this to be distributed as quickly as possible to avoid further confusion. I have two people with broadcasting experience and equipment in the crowd. They are making their way through now."

"Okay, find them. I'll get set up here."

Robert pulled a bundle of wires and a black box out of his coat pocket and, attaching a microphone at one end of the wire to his jacket, he turned on the broadcasting unit. Speaking now, he hoped, to the crowd outside: "This is Robert Castle. Could I have your attention?"

From outside, Robert heard his words being repeated.

"There is no more room inside Holyrood and I ask that you wait where you are. We will broadcast everything that is said and are now making a recording that will be distributed shortly. Thank you for your support today. I ask that you will treat the police with respect and allow them to now leave. We are going to uphold the law and will continue to need their help."

"I am waiting for the Presiding Officer to swear me in. Earlier this morning I obtained a legal waiver that acknowledged I have been duly elected to serve as a majority leader in parliament. I am acting on this now. Ah, I see her approaching now."

Turnstall led the Presiding Officer up to Robert. Robert held out his hand but could see the woman holding clenched fists at her side.

"This is outrageous, Castle. You have no right to disrupt the proceedings when parliament is being sworn in."

"I was elected and yet you tried to prevent me from being sworn in. I would say that is a criminal act."

"I had no idea you were prevented from entering."

"A police cordon surrounding parliament denying access to the people and you had no idea?" Robert looked away and forced himself to calm down. He still needed the woman. "Please read this." He handed her the waiver.

Reading hurriedly she shook her head. "This is irrelevant. A Judge cannot force a change like this on parliament."

Robert switched off his microphone and leaned in close. "Do you see those people standing around the chamber? They have already blockaded the High Court, breached a police cordon and invaded parliament. The only thing preventing them from turning into a mob and tearing this building apart is a belief that you are going to swear me in. Do I have to give them the bad news?"

Her eyes darting all over, looking at the gathered crowd, the

Speaker drew herself up. "Regardless of your threats, you cannot force me to go against the law."

Robert allowed himself a wry smile at the woman's stubbornness. He turned to Turnstall. "Do we need her?"

"We need a Presiding Officer, but not necessarily this one."

"Does it matter who replaces her?"

"Hold on..." She spluttered.

Robert held up his hand in her face.

Turnstall considered and then shook his head. "The Presiding Officer is elected by parliament. Any MSP can be chosen. I would advise choosing someone able to grasp the complexities though."

"Or someone able to cut through them."

Robert looked up, searching for his MSPs in the midst of his supporters and saw a face he recognized: Ellen Prasser who had stood in the borders. He shouted up to her to come down.

"Ellen, I need your help. Would you be willing to become the Presiding Officer here in parliament?"

The activist looked round at the chamber. "What would that mean?"

"The Presiding Officer manages parliament." Christopher explained. "You would chair the debates, ensuring members get a chance to say their piece and that they do not over-run and so prevent others from talking. You would be expected to remain impartial at all times."

Ellen screwed up her nose as Christopher continued explaining.

"Also, you would chair the Scottish Parliamentary Corporate Body and Parliamentary Bureau. Finally you would represent Parliament at home and abroad. It is quite a responsibility."

"Impartial?" Ellen asked. "Me? I stood as an MSP expecting to change Parliament, change Scotland."

Robert heard some shouts from outside. "Does it have to be a permanent position, Christopher?"

"Anyone can resign a position at any time."

"Ellen, with your help we can start changing Parliament and Scotland right now." Robert said.

Seconds seemed to stretch as Ellen stood debating with herself.

"Very well." She eventually said. "I'll do it."

"In that case." Robert said, turning back to the current

Presiding Officer. "You're fired."

"You can't fire me!" She protested.

Robert gestured for his bodyguards to come over. "Can you please take her out of the chamber? Thank you."

"Christopher, talk us through what we need to do."

Taking out his notebook, Christopher flipped to a page. "Ellen, I need you to repeat after me..."

As Ellen was sworn in, Robert switched the microphone back on. He did not want the crowd outside to get restless. He felt a tap on his shoulder.

Turning round, Robert saw two men with large head phones round their necks.

"Do you want us to record this?" One said.

Robert looked round at his own people who were recording Ellen being sworn in.

"Who are you?" He asked.

"We're the Holyrood broadcast team."

"You have a TV camera?"

"Yes, just back there."

"Can it broadcast live?"

"Of course. Though it is rarely used. We've been recording everything up to now," The man hesitated. "You came in while proceedings had started."

"Everything?"

"Yes." The man lent in close and whispered. "Though with your backs turned to the camera and standing so far away from the mikes, I doubt we picked you up threatening the Presiding Officer."

"Let's assume you did." Robert winced – aware of the live microphone. "Release the tape as soon as you get a chance. I'm not going to apologize for forcibly removing bureaucracy. Now, can you arrange for the rest to go out live?"

"I'll call the stations." The second man offered.

"You do that. Let's get them broadcasting me being sworn in."

The first man gave Robert a second clip on microphone.

"Hopefully we won't get feedback or interference with the signals." He said.

Robert explained the situation to Christopher and Ellen. They waited until they got an okay signal from one of the men.

With Christopher prompting her, Ellen swore Robert in as

First Minister.

The crowd in the chamber began cheering as he finished taking his oath but Robert could hear a louder crowd outside.

Taking care to switch off both mikes, Robert leaned over to Christopher. "We did it. Now what?"

"You are leading the government, Mr Castle. Lead your people."

Stepping forward, he turned on the mikes again.

"Last night I was elected by over sixty percent of the electorate. MacKenzie, your party received eighteen percent of the vote. McAllister, you will be aware you received only sixteen percent. I trust you will not attempt to rob the Scottish people of the result they expected?"

Neither of the men looked ready to challenge him with so many people watching. The politicians who had been waiting to be sworn in were now huddled together in one corner of the chamber.

"Each of you was elected to serve the Scottish people." He said to them. "However, you were elected under an unjust system that attempted to deny democracy to the Scottish people. Within the next two months there will be additional elections under a new system and you may all stand in those elections. However, until that time parliament will be operating under emergency powers. You will have the opportunity to elect representatives on a pro-rata basis in the meantime but until you have done so, you will have no hand in decisions this parliament makes."

Robert held out his hand to Christopher who passed over his note pad, opened at the correct place. Robert quickly scanned the large clear writing.

"I have several changes to our laws that I intend to put in place immediately. These were promises I made and expectations the Scottish people have. Firstly, every elected official will work for minimum wage. This includes myself, all other members of the Scottish Parliament and all local councillors. I realise that councillors have had no warning of this change and so they shall continue to receive their current salary for two months from today. If any elected official objects to this change they must give one month's notice of their intention to stand down to allow us to appoint someone in their place."

"I realise that there are often expenses incurred by elected officials and that no-one can currently afford even basic expenses on such a low wage but it seems unjust to me that thousands of people receive no help and that the expense system is available to be abused by those in power. Beginning today, all expenses by elected officials must be published online within one week. Failure to do so will invalidate any expense claim. We will set up a website to allow elected members to record their expenses and details will be made available."

"I also announce a consultation on expenses to be made by the Scottish people. There will be a referendum within two months at which you – the people – will be given the chance to propose your solution and vote it in."

"We will commission a referendum system that will allow all citizens to propose government policy, to debate it and vote on it. This will be available within one month."

"I am introducing the Land Grab act. All privately held land larger than one hundred hectares will be immediately confiscated by parliament. I have already announced that I willing give over my own land in Aberdeenshire as a gesture of my own support for this law."

"The land is to be held by parliament and to be allocated for use to any Scot who wants it. I intend to abolish the current benefits and unemployment systems and replace them with a Land Grant. We will enable any family who wants to work to do so. Land will be allocated, along with a basic housing unit to enable families who are currently trapped in poverty to make their own future. There will be no-one left in Scotland who can legitimately say they have not been given a chance. Anyone who is willing to work hard will be given the opportunity."

"We will guarantee full employment for the Scottish people. Anyone who does not wish to work will be free to refuse work. But they will receive no further help or support from the Scottish people. I realise there are those who are unable to work, but these people are few and far between and you will be given a chance to propose how best to support them and enable them to contribute in some way to society."

"We will introduce full employment in Scotland. Currently the Scottish parliament does not have sufficient powers or budget to make this reality but it is my intention that regardless of the result in the referendum later this month, that Scotland will have the ability to provide full employment."

Robert paused as he scanned the next paragraph. Everything they were doing was revolutionary but how would Scotland take what he was about to say?

"I have made it clear until now that I neither support a Yes or No vote, I will fight for Scotland regardless. However, it has become clear to me over the last weeks that to make the changes needed in Scotland it will be far easier as an independent country."

Several cheers were made in the chamber and echoed outside. Robert saw many more concerned and uncertain expressions.

"I realise that many of you believe passionately that Scotland will be better off as part of the UK and if that is the will of the Scottish people I will uphold that decision. But, to implement full employment, to set Scotland free from debt, to reclaim our land and transform this nation will require more powers than I believe Westminster will concede."

"I have decided to campaign for a Yes vote. Everything you have fought for to enable us to transform Scotland can only be helped by making the final step towards independence. I urge you all to vote considering what we have achieved and can achieve in the future."

"I will publish a full set of proposals in the next month and you – the Scottish people – will have the chance to vote these into law over the following weeks and months."

Robert stopped and scanned the room. Many of his supporters still looked uncertain. Whether because of his announcement he would campaign for a Yes vote, or because they could not take it all in he could not be certain. The unsworn MSP's looked distinctly hostile. He addressed them.

"You have just received a pay cut and been told your job security is now uncertain. This has been the reality for many of the people who voted for you for too many years. If any of you no longer wishes to serve Scotland, you may leave now."

Robert paused. "If you choose to stay and try and work for the Scottish people, even if you are not re-elected I will guarantee you the chance to work for Scotland. You will have a different purpose to the one you expected. You are no longer here to tell the people what they must do – you are here to listen to the people and enact what they want. Are you willing to do this?"

Robert waited a minute while responding calmly to the angry stares he was receiving.

"As I said a moment ago, you may leave if this is not acceptable to you. If you are willing to serve the Scottish people then step forward to be sworn in."

Robert turned on his heel and walked down to the centre of the chamber. "Are none of you willing to serve?"

"I'm willing." Came a shout from the crowd. There was general laughter.

"How can you threaten us and then expect us to respond willingly to you?" Asked MacKenzie.

"How have you been threatened Mr MacKenzie?"

"You lead a mob into parliament, you threaten the Speaker!"

"How have you been threatened?"

"Every act of yours has been a threat. You have thrown away our democracy..."

"No!" Robert shouted. He strode up the chamber to stand in front of MacKenzie. "This is democracy!" He gestured round the chamber. "The Scottish people for once are a living democracy – every person acting together to make a change, to take responsibility for their future. This is real democracy and I am proud of my people.

"Since you will not serve with us you may all leave. We will hold further elections at which you may stand though I doubt many will forget your rejection of the will of the people today."

Finally some of the group stepped forward and said they would serve.

They held a brief ceremony where a much reduced set of MSPs were sworn in.

Gordon came up afterwards. "You need to go outside. Address the crowd in person."

Leaving them, Robert headed out of the chamber, slowed every step of the way by the crush of people. Arriving outside he was cheered as people saw him and then lifted up and carried to one of the sculptures and allowed to stand there.

"Let today be a day of celebration!" He shouted. "Scotland has fought to regain her land and has been successful!" He waited, but the cheering did not die down. Raising his voice again he cried out: "Tomorrow the real work begins but for now enjoy today, enjoy your victory!" He stood there clapping the crowd, even as they cheered him.

CHAPTER THIRTY EIGHT

The following morning the whole country knew they had a new government. Helen woke early. She couldn't seem to sleep late any more. Strange dreams had made her restless during the night and she'd had to get up to use the bathroom, something she never normally had to do.

Robert was completely out of it as she padded round their small hotel room to make herself a mug of tea. Taking the tea back to bed she curled up against the headboard and read the headlines.

Revolution in Scotland was top of the news on BBC. She checked The Guardian and Sky and found similar reports with commentators speculating wildly about what would happen next.

The speculation was in stark contrast to the peaceable way people had dispersed after the events in Holyrood. Robert had said there had been two reports of fights that evening, both outside local clubs, and as likely due to drink or drugs than anything to do with politics.

Let the media have their headlines. Everyone she knew had become far more sceptical of what was churned out as the media had twisted and distorted the election campaign and referendum debate. Maybe Robert's planned referendum software would enable people to share news without relying on biased commentators...

THE GREAT SCOTTISH LAND GRAB

Robert saw Helen on a train back to Glasgow at Half Past Seven and then headed into Holyrood for his first day on the job. He expected all of his experience as a project manager was going to be called upon.

He didn't expect that the first person to meet him would be a police officer.

"Chief Constable Allan Gillies." The officer introduced himself but did not offer a hand.

Robert looked past him to two additional police officers who were standing at the Holyrood reception desk. There was no-one else about apart from the security guard.

"Chief Constable."

"May I have a word in private?"

Robert shrugged. "Certainly. I don't know my way around the building yet though."

"Not a problem, follow me."

The two other officers fell in behind as Robert followed the Chief Constable. He pulled out his phone and quickly texted Christopher and Gordon. If he was going to be arrested first day on the job he didn't want to be behind bars for too long.

Robert was led into a small meeting room and the door closed behind him and Allan Gillies.

"Take a seat."

Robert pulled a chair out from under the table and sat warily. "I'm not familiar with ranks in the police force. Chief Constable is..."

"The highest ranking officer. I'm at a loss as to what title to give you. Your supporters are calling you First Minister but you and I both know the title carries no legal weight, given the circumstances in which you acquired it."

"Legality is defined by those in charge."

"Indeed. And those in charge of the United Kingdom have sent me to arrest you."

Robert sighed. "I see. Quite a low key arrest."

"They were concerned not to risk upsetting the natives."

Robert frowned at the slur but took note of the hint of humour in Gillies tone. "Go on."

"Westminster has no idea what to do with you. They could charge you with treason but given the level of fervour your supporters displayed yesterday they are worried just how far people would be willing to go."

"I was concerned about that myself."

"Yet despite threats and people being manhandled, no one has been reported hurt or missing. The crowds dispersed and this morning Edinburgh seems remarkably normal."

Robert bit back agreement. He decided to just let Gillies continue.

"The threats and manhandling of my own officers are not something I am willing to overlook."

Robert's phone started buzzing but he ignored it. "I see. Actually... I don't. How is that relevant?"

"Several of my officers were either held against their will by your supporters – at your orders – or they were threatened. That is not something you will allow again. Is that understood?"

Gillies tone had lost any hint of humour and his expression was one of utter focus. Robert's phone went still.

"Understood." Robert told him.

"We cannot enforce the law if politicians publically flout it."

"And... What does this have to do with an order to arrest me?"

"Absolutely nothing. I wanted to make it clear what my position is."

"I support your position."

"Good."

Robert waited for a follow up statement but Gillies simply studied him for a minute.

"Why exactly are you here?" Robert asked.

"As I said, Westmin..."

"I know." Robert interrupted. "So why are we having this conversation?"

"It seemed the appropriate time. I refused Westminster's order. They don't know that yet. I may leave them hanging for a while longer. We have a referendum in two weeks that may render Westminster's authority moot. Given the level of support you have currently, I personally didn't think it wise to challenge what appears to be a democratic movement, if one that has crossed several lines."

Robert swore. "The officers outside the door?"

"My driver and assistant."

Robert's phone started buzzing again. He took it out and

looked at it. Christopher was calling him. He let it go to voicemail and studied Gillies. "Would you send a message back to... Whoever it was at Westminster?"

"Tell them yourself. I don't do errands." Gillies stood and held out his hand. As Robert shook it, Gillies said: "You had better achieve all you're intending. Scotland is in dire need of change."

"Will I have your support?" Robert asked.

"Unless I'm fired."

"That will only be a temporary situation, if it occurs."

After Gillies had left, Robert called Christopher and Gordon. Neither was particularly happy when he explained what had happened.

Christopher summed it up: "We absolutely have to get a Yes vote on the 18th. A No would justify Westminster trying something like this again. In the meantime, you had better make a phone call."

****

Robert had hoped to find out where his office was and other practicalities the previous day, but eventually he'd had to admit it was never going to happen.

Not knowing where else to go he headed back to the debating chamber and pulled out his laptop. He made a stab at prioritizing his next actions before people started arriving.

"Mr Castle?"

Looking up, Robert saw a young woman with incredibly straight black hair, cut at her shoulders. "Yes?"

"I'm Carla Watson. I was Personal Assistant to the last First Minister."

"This must have been a difficult few months for you."

"The staff here have kept his office running." Robert noticed she raised her right hand up to hold her other arm. "You, of course, can choose your own staff but until you do, we work for you. Would you like to see your office?"

"That would be good, thanks." Robert stuffed his laptop into his rucksack and stood.

Carla held out her hand and Robert shook it.

"Actually, I was offering to take the rucksack." She told him.

"Oh. No, I can carry it. You're my PA, not my butler, right?"

"I guess you pass the first test then." Carla gave a small smile and led the way out of the chamber.

Tested by his staff... Almost arrested by the police. This was turning into a first day to remember, Robert thought as they walked down another corridor.

It turned out he had two secretaries as well as a PA, a large office which doubled as a meeting room and even his own private bathroom with shower.

"So I can cycle to work..." Robert said to Carla.

"So someone with odour problems can freshen up before meetings."

"Ah. Hopefully not an issue."

"We'll tell you if it is."

He couldn't tell if she was joking or not.

Back in the front office he addressed his new team. "I'm happy to work with you. It will be good to have your experience as I'm learning how all this works. As you'll know, I've set several difficult challenges for the government and I expect the next months to be busy. What you may not know is that our overlords down in Westminster tried to have me arrested this morning."

That statement brought a reaction from the three women. Why was it always women in these roles, he wondered. Were men just not organized enough, or was it some conscious or unconscious bias?

"I need to call the Prime Minister. Can you set that up for me?"

They said they would and Robert went back into his office to continue working on priorities.

At Five minutes to Nine, Gordon walked in. "We did it!"

As Robert stood, Gordon wrapped him in a bear hug. "I never doubted you, my boy." Gordon said, as they separated.

"We've still a lot of work to do."

"But the foundations have been laid. You have the country behind you."

"There is still the referendum. Even if we win that, it's not going to be easy."

"Easy's for wimps. We will get there. Now tell me about this attempt to arrest you."

"Yes, do tell us." Christopher walked in as Gordon finished speaking.

Christopher gave Robert a more restrained handshake but also quietly told him: "Well done."

"Thank you. I couldn't have done any of this without either of you. I don't know how I'll ever repay you."

"You're in charge of the government's budget now..." Gordon grinned. "I'm sure you'll find a way."

Robert shook his head and invited them both to sit. "Carla, my PA, is trying to set up a call with the Prime Minister. Whether he will be willing to speak with me or not is debatable considering he ordered my arrest." Robert told them the full story.

"Well, at least the police haven't turned against you after our actions yesterday." Gordon said once Robert had finished.

"Gillies sounds like a canny man." Christopher thought out loud. "Whether he genuinely supports you or not, he's aware the nation does and he isn't willing to go against them. Sounds a bit like my partners. They weren't at all happy with my increasing involvement with you, but they seemed to have decided to let the situation play out before making a firm decision."

Carla opened the door. "The Prime Minister will be available in ten minutes. You will have five minutes of his time."

"Should be long enough, thank you." Robert turned back to Christopher and Gordon. "I'm looking forward to this call."

****

"Two police officers to see you, Robert."

Robert looked round at the others and groaned. "Gordon, you're in charge."

Carla showed two men into the room. Both dressed in smart but plain suits.

Robert stood. "Why are you here?" He asked abruptly.

"We're your protection detail, Sir."

"Protection detail? What do I need protecting from?"

"It's standard practice for the First Minister to be assigned a detail for his or her protection."

"I've already got a team of volunteers acting as my bodyguard and I've just had most of Scotland vote for my party, I don't think I need any more protection."

"With all due respect, Sir. I've seen your bodyguards and they lack the training and discipline you need. We've been sent by the Chief Constable, Sir."

Robert sighed. "Very well. If I must. You two are going to have a cushy job doing nothing all day."

****

"Mr Castle. You asked to speak with me."

Robert glanced at Christopher and Gordon over the spider phone on the desk. "Prime Minister, let's keep this formal. My title is First Minister. As I have been elected with over twice the majority you gained to win your election, I expect there to be no more attempts by you or your office to arrest me or in any way disrupt the referendum."

Robert waited for a response, then said: "I'll take your silence as acknowledgement your office did order my arrest. Let me make it clear, Scotland may currently be part of the United Kingdom but as of today, we are asserting our democratic right to govern ourselves."

"Mr Castle, don't overstep your abilities. Holyrood has a limited budget and..."

"Scotland's budget is only limited by what we can achieve. My government will recognize the current limits on our powers until the referendum. After that point I will be heading our negotiating team and I warn you, I will not be waiting until 2016 for you to cede powers to Scotland."

"I don't take kindly to threats, Mr Castle."

"Neither do the Scottish people. I have a clear mandate in Scotland. If you attempt to interfere with that mandate or attempt to reverse the change that is taking place, I will not be able to prevent the people rising up against you. Scotland has been divided but if there is one thing likely to unite us all together it will be continued foolish intervention by your government.

"Yesterday we had one million Scots march on Edinburgh. Trust me when I say you do not want four million angry Scots descending on London."

"Are you threatening civil war?"

"I am warning you that the patience of the Scottish people is wearing thin. There are still a few people who believe the country is united but that number grows less every day that Westminster curses the people it is supposed to serve. We have two weeks until the referendum. Allow us to hold that referendum in peace and you will save yourself a world of trouble."

"I have always been committed to allowing Scotland the chance to decide their future."

"So committed that you won't make any promises until after the next election. If Scotland votes No you can arrest me as a traitor and hang me outside Holyrood and deal with the consequences. But until then, Scotland has elected me leader. I'm sure we'll talk after the result."

Robert killed the call and took several deep breaths, unclenching his fists as he did. "Do you think he got the message?"

"He has the option to send in the army." Christopher offered. "I've no doubt that would end up worse than Northern Ireland ever did. No, if he has any sense – debatable I know – he'll back off."

"First priority then." Robert said. "Referendum software. I've been working on a design for weeks..."

****

CHAPTER THIRTY NINE

Jane Irvine crouched down on an outcrop of rock that overlooked her largest valley. On her left the valley rose until it joined with three other mountain valleys, the peaks popular with Munro climbers. To her right the valley grew shallower and broader as the ranges lost height until the valley ended and a sea loch began.

Her Land Rover was parked some six hundred metres below. She could easily make it out on the track that wound its way up the valley, giving easier access to the higher forests and one of the two deer sanctuaries she managed.

Above her a deep blue sky was filled with fast moving white clouds. A harbinger of faster winds that right now were only lightly tugging at her scarf. It had been warm down in the valley but even with the wind only light it was still chilly. Jane wrapped her coat around her.

This had always been her favourite place. When as a girl, her father had taken her to climb the Munro behind her she had stopped at this rock and stared for ages at the view.

"One day you will be responsible for this land." He'd told her.

She struggled then to grasp how big it was. It had taken what seemed like forever to climb this high. And the valley just kept on rising until it seemed lost in the clouds. Had she really thought that as a girl? She supposed she must, it was such a strong memory.

She had scorned the advances of teenage boys as she grew older, not believing them capable of accepting the responsibility she knew was hers. Until she met Derek at a New Years Ceilidh. He'd actually courted her, taken the time to get to know her family, shown an interest in the estate and farm. He was training to be a lawyer but was open to the idea of working in the highlands.

She wished he was with her, able to give her advice.

13,000 acres of land. Much of it only useful for climbing or painting. Yet there had been small communities spread out across the valleys. She had read all the histories of her family and done further research when she attended university. There had been good reasons for moving people off the land: disease and famine had been a problem throughout Scotland at different times. But there had also been greed and opportunism. Those communities had not been allowed to reform. No help had been given to enable the tenants to survive temporary troubles.

With modern knowledge and efficient farming techniques, the land could support many more people than it ever had. She'd always admired mountain communities in Asia that practiced terrace farming, making use of every available piece of land, no matter how steep the slope.

Some countries advertised tourist trips round abandoned cave dwellings that had been carved in cliff faces. The astonishing thing about those caves was not that people had once lived in them but that people were living in them until modern times.

Looking across the valley now she could picture a community living in tunnels and caverns blasted out of the rock leaving all available land free for growing crops. Would that constitute a Grand Design? She was no architect but she had always had imagination. She had allowed her childhood dreams for the land to be crushed by adult realism and practicality. Was this a time to return to those early dreams, to imagine even more creative ways to enjoy the land?

While some assumed early man was an unintelligent cave dweller, the fact was that drilling into rock was an efficient way of living. Almost zero maintenance costs – no need to paint the cladding or replace roof tiles every few years. Spray insulation on the walls and you could maintain an even temperature with little power.

Whether anyone would fund it was debatable, but even with villages spread out over the valley, there was room.

Jane carefully stood. Her joints were not as flexible as they once were. She looked around but could see no deer today. It was one of her greatest joys to see the majestic creatures patrolling the estate. She decided to drive up the valley before returning home.

****

There was a message waiting for her when Jane reached home. She hung up her scarf and shrugged off her coat before reading it. John Anderson was calling a meeting of all estate owners. No reason given but he didn't have to.

Strength in numbers, strength in shared wealth, in shared power. That was the only way to fight the threat they faced. Some would go, others would decline but pledge their support. It had always been the same and always would. She had picked her side many years ago. Her father had impressed on her the responsibility she held, the need to protect the land, to protect the future.

Only once had someone dared to question her and she had been outraged. One arrogant man...

She took a deep breath to settle herself and picked up the phone.

****

John Anderson placed his phone back down and ticked another name off his list. Most had pledged their support but a worrying number had declined to help. There was a fatalism growing that change was inevitable. He had attempted to persuade them to at least attend the meeting. There was strength in numbers and he was certain that once together they would see how strong they still were.

He checked the next number and dialled. "Harold! How are you, old chap?"

****

302

The food bank had an unusual buzz to it when Irene and her boys turned up. She was looking forward to telling Sylvia how she'd got on the previous week. She'd stuck rigidly to the plan that had been agreed and actually had a couple of pounds left over. For the first time she felt like she understood why she had money left over, maybe more importantly, how she could have spent it without realising.

Irene had cut up her bank cards. Once the debt was paid off she might consider opening a new account but for now she was happy to rely on Chris and Shona making sure she actually got some cash each week and the rest going to pay off the debt.

There had been nothing from Neil. The police had taken the video Chris had shot but he hadn't heard whether they were prosecuting him or not.

Irene hadn't slept well for a couple of nights but the more days went by, the less she thought about it.

"What's everyone talking about?" Billy asked one of the men in the queue.

"The Land Grab party are in power. They've promised full employment."

"What? We could get a job?" Colin asked.

"Everybody. That's what they said."

"I'm going to join the police." Billy said.

"I always wanted to work on TV." Laughed Colin.

"I don't think that's how it works, boys." The man shook his head. "We'll be lucky to get a labouring job I should expect."

Irene had heard people talking about this Scottish Land Grab party but apart from hoping they wouldn't cut her benefits even further she doubted anything would change.

The doors opened promptly at Six PM. While they waited, Irene and the boys ate. The church had made pasta with a bolognaise sauce and gave them paper bowls to eat out of. Billy and Colin both finished theirs before Irene was half way through. They sat impatiently while others queued, waiting for them to offer seconds.

Irene saw Sylvia was on the desk. She'd have to wait until it was their turn to go up before she could tell Sylvia how the week had gone. After a while she noticed people seemed to be taking longer than normal at the desk. She hoped there wasn't a problem.

Eventually it was her turn and Irene walked up.

"Good to see you. You look like the pain has gone." Sylvia gave Irene a smile as she sat down.

"It almost feels normal. I still get sore if I'm in the same position for too long, or if I slouch, but other than that... It's so much better. That's not all, look..." Irene held up two pound coins.

"What's that?"

"Money I didn't spend this week!"

"That's fantastic! Well done."

Irene held out the money. "I want to give it to the church."

Sylvia's smile became hesitant. She turned to the volunteer sitting next to her, a questioning look on her face, then back to Irene.

"That's very generous of you but, are you sure? You do need to start saving..."

"You've given us so much. I know I've a long way to go, but just this once, I want to give something back."

Sylvia nodded and took the money from Irene. "We'll use it to buy supplies for the food bank. Thank you."

The other volunteer leaned forward. "Have you heard what the Land Grab party are proposing?"

Irene shook her head. "They're going to offer everyone a job?"

"That's part of it. They are also going to stop benefits. If you don't work, you won't get any money from the State."

All her happiness seemed to drain out of her. Irene searched Sylvia's face to see if she'd misunderstood. "But I... How can I pay off my debts if I... I don't know if I can work. Who would employ me?"

"I don't know, Irene. They haven't given any detail yet. We'll still be here and will help as much as we can but... We thought it was important you know.

For the first time in weeks, Irene turned down Sylvia's offer of a lift. She made Billy and Colin carry the bags while she tried to think what would happen to them all. She had just started to feel she had a plan for her life and now someone else was turning it upside down.

****

Across the street stood Tam Frost. He wore a charcoal

woollen suit, suitable for keeping the sometimes cold wind at bay. His grey shirt was unbuttoned at the neck revealing a wisp of thick black hair. If any of the assembled politicians and their retinue had noticed him, they might have thought he was one of the many businessmen that could be seen around Edinburgh, watching, slightly star-struck at the sight of the new leaders of the nation.

Tam hadn't lived in his native land for thirty years and had little love for the place, other than accepting the good will that often seemed to come his way when he revealed his heritage. He'd never even worked here though, as with every other location, finding the tools he needed hadn't proved all that difficult.

The target was in a good mood. Having just won a major election it wasn't surprising. The result of the imminent referendum would have been in the bag, he suspected. Was this the reason he had been called in? He didn't think too deeply on it. Curiosity had a habit of leading to questions that he didn't need. Distractions that were better forgotten.

Though some questioning was important.

He was being used. Being paid well for it too. But if he ever suspected he was being set up he would walk and the client would find that while the cut outs and secrecy protected Tam, they offered no protection in the other direction.

There seemed no risk of that here. The target had upset some powerful people. He had been arrogant, had not been careful and would pay the price.

The target's schedule had not been difficult to obtain. There was a location Tam thought he would use. And soon. That had been part of the contract.

Satisfied he had imprinted the target's face and mannerisms, Tam turned away from the scene in front of him. It was time to get ready.

****

CHAPTER FORTY

Tam had walked in under cover of darkness, wearing a carefully applied pattern of makeup that would confuse the best facial recognition system if he had failed to avoid a CCTV camera. The location was not ideal. 1250 metres out from the planned site for the stage wasn't an issue for him. He routinely shot at longer distances but next to the Firth of Forth, the unpredictability of the wind concerned him.

However, even with the fitted silencer slowing the bullet's velocity, the speed of the bullet should be sufficient that the distance wouldn't be an issue.

His hide was in a third story flat with a FOR RENT sign pasted on the windows. He'd picked the lock and closed the door at Four AM. There was a risk that creaking floorboards would wake a light sleeper below so he took his time walking over to the window. If he stood on a noisy board, it was usually better to quickly follow through than retreat or stop which created an unnatural sound, but he was fortunate and made it without any potential disturbance.

Once at the window he carefully took off and laid down his rucksack and then turned and looked at where he'd walked. There was no point in trying to hide the fact he'd been here. Ballistics would pin point his location yet he had no intention of leaving any clues that he could prevent.

He crouched down under the window and set his alarm for

Seven AM. Double checked his sidearm was in its holster at his back and lay down to get some sleep.

****

He'd woken before the alarm. Pulled a bottle from a side pocket in the rucksack and drank some water. Eating on a job was never an easy task. Food left crumbs. Crumbs were clues pointing to eating habits, purchase locations, and sometimes even providing DNA traces.

Early on in his career he had found a company that sold food in a tube. The selection wasn't great and he would never choose the tubes of paste over a real meal normally, but it stopped hunger and kept him going during these long waits. A tube of cinnamon flavoured porridge was his breakfast.

From downstairs, Tam heard movement. A TV or radio went on. Ideally the occupant would be heading out to work but he couldn't count on the flat being empty.

He unpacked his rucksack, a specially designed piece of kit in itself that silently unzipped along the back to open out providing easy access to the dismembered rifle inside.

With years of experience, Tam assembled the components and checked they were secure. The Steyr HS .50 rifle was multishot but he wouldn't be firing more than once. One impact from a .50 calibre bullet was usually enough to kill most people. Anywhere in the centre mass of the body, which is where he planned to aim, and the shockwaves would fatally damage all internal organs. Hit someone in the head and there would be nothing left to identify them.

On the rare occasions he hadn't hit the target the first time, the confusion that resulted from being fired on usually resulted in a mess of potential targets that prevented a clean shot. He wasn't being paid to go on a shooting spree.

There was no furniture in the flat and there was no way he would rest the bipod on a window sill, with half the barrel visible to the world. Fortunately he also carried an extendable tripod that could replace the bipod attachment and allow him to stand inside the room.

With the window open, Tam attached his Nikko Nighteater scope and stood in the centre of the room. He set up the rifle on the tripod and looked through the scope. He adjusted the settings and looked over the scope a couple of times while he focused on the location.

Once he was dialled in he stood looking through the scope for several minutes, watching the activity as a stage was hastily erected.

The speech was due to take place at Nine AM but the target may turn up early and if he did he would terminate him. There was no requirement for cameras to be rolling.

He disconnected the rifle from the tripod and locked in the scope settings in case they got knocked. Checking his watch he saw it was now approaching Eight AM. He took another drink of water and downed another tube of paste. He might be standing for a couple of hours so he clipped on a utility belt and placed the water bottle in a pocket.

Then he reattached the rifle once more and settled in for the wait.

Jobs like this were mostly boredom with a sudden opportunity that had to be taken instantly or lost forever. He settled into a rhythm of scanning over the activity. As new cars arrived he checked each person exiting the vehicle against his mental memory of the target.

He'd watched several online videos of speeches and events and had a good feeling for the target's way of moving, his posture, what he looked like from behind and the side.

Media crews arrived and set up cameras. They would be in for a show they didn't expect.

He expected the target to turn up between ten and five minutes before the speech was due to take place and he wasn't disappointed.

Tam got a glimpse of his head as he exited the vehicle but someone else was in the way. A security officer? There was an immediate rush of reporters surrounding the newly arrived car, all shouting pointless questions that wouldn't be answered, Tam expected.

He kept his scope centred on where he thought his target was. The group dispersed but the target headed back behind the stage and out of sight. No problem. He would be front and centre soon enough.

Eventually his patience was rewarded. A group filed on stage and he had a clear line of sight.

Tam breathed out, held his breath and fired.

****

The timing was off. A gust of wind caught the bullet, slowing and pushing it away from the target.

On the stage Gordon coughed. Distracted, Robert moved to his right. Had he stayed still or moved left, the bullet would have hit him. As it was, Robert felt a rushing sensation by his temple followed by a strange tearing noise.

The bullet passed between him and Gordon who had turned and bent to his left as he coughed.

Robert saw his security team start running towards him. He turned towards Gordon who now was looking up, puzzlement evident in his expression.

Robert ran towards Gordon and all but picked him up and bundled him down the back of the stage, all the while shouting for the others to get down. By the time he reached the bottom of the stage he was himself being picked up and forcibly pushed towards the car. He felt his head being pushed down and then he was in the back seat, a man on top of him.

There had been no time to think.

****

Tam didn't see the expected movement from the bullet's impact. Instead his target appeared to move just as the trigger had activated the firing mechanism. He could have taken a second shot as his target was still in the clear but blurs at the edge of the scope told him others were converging on the targets location.

He'd failed this time. He had to ensure a quick extraction as the next priority.

The rifle was quickly disassembled and stowed in the rucksack. The tripod next. Tam removed his utility belt and packed this before zipping it all up. Next he closed the window. Putting on the rucksack his last task was to run a towel over the floorboards where he'd slept and walked to remove any imprints in dust.

Tam opened the front door and exited, turning round to close the door behind him. Too late he realised there was someone else in the corridor. He turned, his right hand straying behind him to where his holster was snug between his back and the rucksack.

In front of him was an old granny. That was his first impression. Female, short, wispy white curls with traces of grey. She had a patterned woollen shawl over her shoulders, covering a jacket. A shopping bag in one hand and a climbing stick in the other, the loop around her wrist.

She frowned at him.

No witnesses. That was the rule...

****

Robert was being crushed by the weight of the officer on top of him. "Can you let me up?"

"Sorry, Sir. Not just now."

"At least let me breathe." Robert felt the weight ease as the man lifted himself.

"I didn't imagine that, did I? Someone just tried to shoot me?"

"Looked that way to me, Sir."

"Stop calling me sir."

"Yes, Sir."

Robert sighed. "Gordon, the others? Are they alright?"

"I don't know, Sir. It's not our top priority right now."

Robert felt sick to his stomach. "Stop the car."

"No, Sir."

Robert moved his hands underneath him and levered himself up until he could look the officer in the eye. "I said stop the car!"

The officer was going to speak but then his eyes narrowed as he looked back at Robert. "Mike, I uh... I think you'd better stop the car."

"Let me up." Robert told him.

Reluctantly, the officer moved and Robert was able to sit up.

"Are you Mike?" Robert asked the driver.

"Sir, you really should get your head down."

Robert looked behind them and saw cars that had moved out of the way onto pavements. He became aware of the siren.

"Do you have to obey my orders?" Robert asked.

Mike glanced at him in the mirror but didn't respond.

"Turn the car around now and head back to the bridge."

Another glance, a hesitation and the car slowed slightly.

"If it will help, give me your radio and I'll tell your commander I've ordered you back."

"It doesn't work like that." Mike shook his head.

"It's either that or lose your jobs."

Mike swore. "With all due respect, Sir, you are full of yourself."

"So I've been told."

"Our job is to protect you. We take you back and you get shot we won't just lose our jobs, we'll be arrested."

"You honestly think the shooter hung around once you drove me off, just on the off chance I would come back?"

"I'm not paid to think, Sir. Just to follow orders..."

Robert saw him wince as Mike realised what he'd said. Robert sat back. "Turn the car around." He said in a quiet voice. "If you hide me away you might as well shoot me yourself. The press will eat up the fact I ran off and left my team in danger."

The car slowed even more as Mike kept glancing at Robert in the mirror. "Why do you really want to go back?"

"I need to know my friends are safe." Robert looked from Mike to the officer beside him. "What? You thought I was enjoying myself back there?"

Robert clenched his fists as he realised he was shaking.

"Are you alright, Sir?" The officer next to him asked.

"Fine."

The car abruptly pulled to the right and Robert saw Mike was doing a U turn. "Thank you."

Mike just shook his head.

They sat in silence as Mike retraced his route. Robert looked out the window at ordinary streets, houses with people unaware that someone had just tried to take out the First Minister. Was this the future of Scotland? Someone angry enough at him they would try and kill him? Not all that different from parts of Glasgow. He could try and rationalize it to sound like it was a different scale but was it really any different to an argument between neighbours or family, that escalated to the point where one person lay dead.

"I'm sorry." Robert said.

The men both glanced at him but neither of them said anything.

"I'm sorry I didn't ask your names. When we first met. It

probably came across as arrogant but I thought... I still think that if I need security then I've failed. If I need you to protect me from the people out there then I've not done my job."

Robert saw an ambulance, it's lights flashing blue, as they pulled back up to the site. He jumped out of the car before the officers could stop him and ran over to a paramedic.

"Who was hurt?" Robert asked as he kept walking until he could see in the back of the ambulance. It was empty.

"A journalist grazed his knee when he tripped. Far as I know that's all."

"No one else?"

"Pretty much everyone was gone when we got here. Just a few police officers and journalists hanging about." He looked closely at Robert. "Someone really try to take a pot shot at you?"

"It looks like it." Robert headed back to the car where the officers were looking off into the distance.

"Your staff are all on their way back to Holyrood, Sir."

"Thank you. What are you looking at?"

"Trying to work out where the shooter was. Must have been a long shot. Gusty day like this, you were lucky."

Robert looked but had no idea where someone might have hid. The thought that really had him worried though, was what Helen would say...

****

Reaching his car, Tam threw his rucksack in the boot and quickly got in. He held out his hands and watched them trembling. He gripped the wheel for a minute until he felt in control.

It didn't matter whether a job went well or went South, he was always wound up afterwards. Encountering that old woman had done nothing to help.

His own Gran had been similar, from what he could remember. She'd died when he was a teenager and his only memories of her were from living in Scotland, but they were good memories.

A rule was a rule... Except when you had to break it. He didn't know why he'd said it...

"It was only one night. The door was open."

Her frown had deepened.

"I had nowhere else to go."

"Don't you be coming back. I'll tell the landlord he had a guest."

"I won't." Tam promised, keeping his eyes down. He thanked her once he was past and then was off down the stairs before she could change her mind.

If, when the police canvassed the area, she remembered the stranger with his rucksack, she wouldn't be able to give an accurate description of his face with the makeup he had on. It was a risk, but probably less so than risking other potential witnesses being created if they heard him shooting her.

He took a deep breath and turned on the ignition.

If an observer had been watching as he drove away they would have seen his modified licence plate read N0 THNKS.

****

CHAPTER FORTY ONE

Helen was struggling to concentrate. It had been good that Robert had introduced her to the job site as their website was now far cleaner and easier to manage. Still, it seemed to be taking her just as long to get things done.

Stephen and Sylvia had been incredibly patient with her, allowing her extra time off to help with the campaigning and allowing her to work at her own pace when she was in. She felt bad though that things were not being done.

If Robert had still been working, well, if he was still earning his contractors salary then she might have considered quitting, but there was no way they could survive only on Robert's reduced income. If only he hadn't made that stupid promise...

The phone rang. "Helen Castle... Oh, Hi Robert."

As she listened, the first words he said seemed to circle round in her thoughts, getting louder and louder as the room turned grey. "Everything's all right, everything's all right, EVERYTHING'S ALL RIGHT."

Then it all went black.

****

There was something wrong. Everything smelt different and the room was too bright. What was Robert doing opening the curtains this early?

314

Helen tried to move her arm but it felt heavier than normal. She struggled to open her eyes and looked about in puzzlement at the strange room.

"She's awake." Someone said. A woman's voice. Helen turned and saw a young woman, smartly dressed who was just standing up. She cradled a laptop in one arm.

Then Robert came through the door, followed by several others.

"Am I in hospital?" Helen asked.

"You gave us a scare."

Then she remembered and all at once felt light headed. She closed her eyes and clenched her fist, trying to hold onto something stable. She felt someone take her other hand, hold it firmly. She squeezed back.

"Can you get a doctor?" Robert's voice, close to her.

The feeling passed and Helen again felt able to open her eyes. Saw Robert holding her hand. She extracted her hand and then punched him in the leg.

"Hey!"

"That's for having someone shoot at you." Helen saw that everyone else had left the room. "You can tell me later. I don't think I can cope with it just now." She offered her hand and Robert again took it.

They sat in silence until the doctor arrived, a clipboard in hand. She shut the door behind her. "Mrs Castle, Mr Castle. There's no cause to worry." The doctor said, obviously in a rush. She came over and checked Helen's pulse and shone a light in her eyes. "Not that unusual a case but everything appears to be in order. We'll have to run a few more tests and give you a scan but that's quite normal."

"A scan? What, like an MRI?" Robert asked.

"MRI? No, no. I should have said an ultrasound. Sorry, quite a few cases on the go today. Anyway, your baby's heartbeat was healthy when I checked you earlier. I'll get one of the nurses in to see you."

The doctor smiled and walked out the door. Helen felt Robert's grip tighten and then he jumped up and ran out the room. She heard him call the doctor back.

"...Of course I have questions." Robert ushered the doctor back in and shut the door. "What do you mean baby? Helen and I can't..." He looked at her and she saw her own pain reflected in his eyes.

"I don't know your history but your wife is pregnant."

Robert slowly walked over to Helen's side and kneeled down beside her, taking her hand. "But she's not... You're not..."

Helen put her hand on her flat belly. She'd felt tired for months, had put it down to coping with Robert's campaign. She had felt hungry but had little appetite. Could it...

"Can I borrow your stethoscope?" She asked.

The doctor nodded, put it in her own ears first and moved the cold metal cup round her belly for a few seconds before leaving it still. "Here." The doctor gave the earpiece to Helen first.

The sound of rapid thudding filled her senses. Helen gasped and gripped Robert's hand tightly. She eased off the earpiece to let Robert hear. She saw him start to cry and then realised she already was.

She didn't notice the doctor gently take the stethoscope back or hear her say she would give them a minute alone.

****

Outside, Carla heard sobbing as the doctor came out looking fairly pale. Her hand came up to her mouth as she looked at the others. All of them looking as worried as she felt. Someone tried to kill the First Minister and now his wife was seriously ill. Could things get any worse?

She called the office and told the secretaries. "I don't know if he'll want to put out a press release but you better prepare one... No, I don't know what's wrong with her yet. We'll have to fill that in when we know."

Carla tried to do some more work on her laptop but her mind kept turning possibilities over and over. Eventually a nurse came down the corridor wheeling a metal cart. Carla followed the nurse into the room and beckoned to Robert.

Out in the corridor, Carla didn't know what to say. "Would you like me to put out a press release, Sir?"

Robert seemed to have calmed down but still seemed distracted. "That's a good idea. Maybe hold off just now."

"Certainly. Can I just say... I'm very sorry."

Robert looked confused. Then she saw him looking round at his security detail, all of whom looked as sombre as she felt.

"Sorry..." He gave a short laugh. "No, no need to be sorry." He reached out and held her arms. Carla saw tears fill his eyes but he was forcing a smile. "Helen's pregnant. We didn't know. Didn't think we could have children. It's okay. It's all going to be okay."

He went back into the room and closed the door. Carla stared in shock for a minute and then pulled out her phone. "Cancel the press release. I got it wrong... I'll tell you when I get back."

She ended the call. I was wrong, she thought. It could get worse.

****

She'd sent Robert home when they told her she'd be kept in overnight for observation. In truth she wanted to be alone. She found herself holding her belly, willing for some sign there was life in there. It didn't matter she had heard the heartbeat, seen the limbs move during the ultrasound, she needed to feel it.

The nurse who had carried out the ultrasound had explained the placenta was at her front which usually made it difficult to feel movement – like a huge cushion between her and her baby.

When they'd finally given up trying to conceive she'd put all her focus into her work, finding joy and satisfaction as she saw people who had been homeless helped into accommodation. She didn't want to give that up.

Once she'd let the desire go, it hadn't seemed like there was anything missing in her life without children. Now she wasn't sure there'd be space. How was Robert going to cope with what he was planning? How was she going to cope if he was always away, too busy to help?

Was she even going to be any good as a mother? She was going to be sixty when the child was twenty! What kind of childhood would that be, having two grandparents instead of parents?

Helen smoothed her top. Wondered what it would feel like to have a proper bump. There had been so much she'd planned to do…

They'd attached a drip while she'd been out but had removed it when she obviously wasn't taking any more liquids in. She was still wearing her work clothes and needed to change but first…

She walked out to the desk and asked if she could borrow a pad and pen.

She needed to write it down. She didn't know if she could tell Robert everything that was going through her head.

****

Robert took the pad. "What's this?"

"My terms and conditions."

He frowned but started reading. She picked at a nail while waiting.

He turned over the first page, raised his eyebrows and gave her a quick glance.

She watched his eyes scanning quickly from side to side. She didn't know how he could read like that, almost as if he was memorizing whole sentences. He wasn't of course, but he could skim a document quickly while it had always taken her ages to go through methodically.

It used to annoy her. She would read something and because of how she read she'd understand the detail, but Robert just went straight for the big picture. Then they'd argue because he'd missed something important or because she was so focused on the detail that she wasn't ready to think about the implications.

He finished the four pages but sat looking at the last one for a time.

Eventually she'd had enough waiting. "I thought I'd have more time. I didn't want to distract you now and thought we could introduce some of this later but... I don't think I can leave this any longer."

"This is what you want?"

"Of course it is." She bit off any more. Why would she have shown him her plan if she didn't want it?

"Okay."

"Okay what? Okay you understand? Okay you think it's possible?"

"Just okay." His eyes took on a distant look. "It fits. No less radical and takes us on a slightly different direction but it does fit. We reclaim land, why not buildings that are unused? We'd need to propose it and definitely need it ratified by the people but we can come up with a way. In fact, maybe it's even better than some of my plans."

She hated it when he was being condescending.

"Not everyone is going to want to relocate to the country and if we can use existing buildings, that cuts down tremendously on cost. And factories and warehouses…"

"You remember the Grisham novel?"

"Yeah… And you going on and on about it for days afterwards. It seemed too easy but we can try it and if there are problems we can fix them. I reckon there must be premises that have been built using funding from government that are now standing empty. You and I paid for those buildings, why shouldn't we reclaim them?" He studied her. "Are you sure you'll be up for this?"

"What do you mean?"

"This is going to involve a lot of work. We'll have to bring you into the civil service, but that should be doable as long as we keep it transparent what is happening and why."

"No, wait…" He'd misunderstood! "I want you to do this."

"Me? This is your dream. Why should I get all the fun?"

She couldn't stop the blasted tears. "I can't… How can I?"

Robert took her hand. "I was imagining you with a little papoose, ordering people about with a bottle in one hand and nappy bag in the other."

She took her hand away. "I'm not using a papoose!"

"You'd look so cute…"

"You wear it if you like them so much!"

"I might just… Can you imagine the press conferences we could have? Look, you can delegate all of it, can pick and choose parts to manage when you feel able, but this was always and will always be your dream. I can make it my own but why would you give up something you've given your life to work towards?"

She placed her hands on her belly. "Because maybe something more important will need my time."

Robert nodded. "Okay. I'll try and make it work but at any time you can take over. Is that alright?"

She breathed out. It would have to be.

****

"Mr Castle."

"Baroness Irvine." Robert held out his hand, not knowing if he'd be rebuffed. Jane Irvine shook his hand with a firm grip.

"Thank you for coming. This way." She led Robert and his team through into a large room with more than enough armchairs to seat them all. "Tea? Coffee?"

A butler was called who then took their requests.

Robert sat and waited until everyone was settled. "The last time we met, you introduced yourself as Mrs Irvine."

"Baroness is a rather unwieldy title. It tends to make people uncomfortable... And less honest."

Robert smiled. "I've never been much of a respecter of titles." He looked round at his team. "We're here at your invitation."

"You asked if I had a different suggestion for giving young people a future." Jane thought back to that evening in the village hall. "You didn't know I had already tried. Groups of youth have been invited to the estate. We've made the estate available for camps, for events. People need wide open spaces. They need to be able to run and climb and swim."

"I agree." Robert said. "I've never wanted to take that away."

"You may think that because I live on this estate I have no idea what life is like in the cities but I sponsor several children's charities. I'm a patron of one. I travel into Inverness regularly. I also spend a significant amount of time in the House of Lords and debate legislation to improve people's lives.

"But, until your rude appearance in Inverness, I had forgotten some of my own dreams for the estate. As a child I once wondered about building castles, establishing my own town, wondered how the land could be better used. As I read up on how difficult life was for early crofters – how disease swept through small villages, times of famine – I focused on practicalities.

"You've said you intend to seize all land in private hands above 100 hectares. I am willing to give up everything outside the grounds of this house, if I'm allowed to manage the rest of the estate."

"I didn't come here to negotiate. The land belongs and always has belonged to the people of Scotland."

"I made a commitment to my father that I would take care of the land, Mr Castle. I don't make promises lightly."

Robert sat back and studied the woman before him. "How would you manage the estate?"

"I've worked and looked after this land my whole life. I

know which land may be fertile and which can be used for grazing or forest. You could... You have the power to seize everything and strip all I've worked for away but then you face a similar situation to Zimbabwe. Productive land being given into the hands of people who don't know how to use it and the output collapsing. People with no experience of managing a large area of land who destroy the careful work of generations."

"There are reports that output has risen in Zimbabwe."

"But at what cost? A decade of famine?"

"A quarter million of Zimbabwe's citizens may feel it has been worth the pain."

"But there didn't need to be any pain, that is my point, Mr Castle. I didn't want to give up this estate. In truth, I still don't. But if you are serious in your promise to share this wealth with everyone, to bring life to these valleys, then I can help you."

Robert turned to Carla. "What is our policy on land grabs?"

"All privately held land over 100 hectares is the property of the Scottish people. Title deed holders of land in excess of 100 hectares will receive a grant to 100 hectares in perpetuity."

"This policy is non-negotiable, Baroness Irvine."

"I'm offering to help..."

"I will not take more than I've committed to. I made a promise myself. However, we need... I need help to turn the land into something that will sustain hundreds of thousands of people. I would be glad to have your help."

****

She drove them out to the largest valley and then up the dirt track until the sea loch was almost on the horizon. Jane pointed out features in the valley that could be utilised. Places where the soil was shallow that would be better for building on; areas where crops had once been grown; how the wind would be constant on one side of the valley while leaving the other side untouched.

"Set up wind turbines there to generate electricity and solar panels high up on the North side to capture the maximum sunlight."

"It will be expensive to run cables that far." Robert said.

"Less distance than taking cables from the nearest grid line. These communities could be self-sustaining given the right help at start up."

"They need to be, otherwise the whole venture will have collapsed in ten years."

"We need to build in the ability for them to give something back." Jane's eyes lost focus as she stared down the valley. "Each community should be capable of not just surviving but prospering."

"Any ideas you have to enable that would be appreciated."

"Oh I have plenty of ideas... But what you really need is to get the whole country involved. Scotland is a land of dreamers. The reason we produced so many inventors over the decades... Put the request out to your Cafe Politics. Get people talking about how to make small communities prosper. Stop us griping about what we can't do and start imagining what we can. Then see what Scotland can become!"

****

Robert cut back on his campaigning and Helen took indefinite leave of absence from her work. Parliament was in effective limbo until after the referendum and, while there were still decisions that needed to be made, Robert found that the announcement of his wife's pregnancy – and the leaked news of her collapse – had resulted in far less questions being directed his way.

Robert had asked Carla to do some investigating and she found out there was a property owned by the Scottish Parliament in Edinburgh that was sometimes used to house visiting guests. He asked permission to use it until they could arrange somewhere more permanent.

Penny insisted they could stay with her and Gordon but Robert knew he and Helen would need some space before and after the baby was born.

During the week leading up to September the 18th, no-one could get away from the speculation. While a Yes vote had overtaken No in the polls after the election, there was still a significant portion undecided. Robert knew it could swing either way.

He gave one last speech, to a packed stadium that had been highly secured. To the annoyance of many in the Yes campaign, he shared the platform with a dozen others, trusted men and women from around Scotland – some of whom supported Stronger United – giving what Robert hoped was a final balanced presentation to the Scottish people.

As he shook their hands afterwards he hoped they would all remember that however the vote turned out, the next day they would still need to work together.

Robert and Helen were still registered to vote in their old neighbourhood. There had been a day of panic when they realised they hadn't received polling cards but fortunately the new owner of their house had forwarded them on.

As they were driven to the polling station Robert turned to Helen. "I never asked how you were going to vote."

"Think you can change my mind?"

"I have been known to in the past."

"And how do you know that I wasn't just playing hard to get?"

Robert laughed. "I have no idea. Are you going to tell me?"

"I've always harboured a secret desire to vote Yes."

"No!"

"Yes."

"All those times I tried to get you along to Stronger United..."

"The question you really ought to be asking yourself is, did I change your mind..." Helen joked before wincing.

"You all right?" Robert put his hand out to her.

Helen grimaced. "I think she is stretching. Not a lot of room in there."

Robert looked in amazement at his slim wife. The doctor had told them that this type of pregnancy was rare but not unknown. Maybe some seven thousand women would not know they were pregnant until they actually gave birth. In Helen's case, some strange positioning inside that caused the baby to grow just under the rib cage; slightly tougher stomach muscles that resisted the expansion of the womb. The baby's growth had forced her other organs out of the way and somehow she had just kept going.

"I'm not ready to buy pink baby grows just yet." Robert said.

"She's not wearing yellow."

"She could be a tomboy..."

He enjoyed the banter, but at the back of his mind was the thought that today was his last day of freedom. Whatever the result, he would have to work to build the Scotland he envisaged.

In the ballot booth, Robert held his pencil over the paper. He'd campaigned against independence longer than he had for it. He made his choice and then placed his vote in the box.

Helen gave him a mischievous smile as they walked out. He held her close but didn't ask. This was her decision to make. If she wanted to share it she would.

****

Neither of them got much sleep that night. Unlike general elections, the result would not be announced locally until it had been authorised centrally by the Chief Counting Officer in Edinburgh. The CCO had advised that in the event the votes tallied were conclusively for Yes or No, regardless of any remaining local authority areas, that an announcement on the outcome would be made.

Robert and his team would know what the result would be a few minutes before the rest of the nation and the world, though given the distance of the more remote islands and communities, the result still wasn't expected until morning or afternoon on the 19th.

Helen stayed in their hotel room in Edinburgh, 24 hour news on low volume while Robert camped out in a large conference room that had been prepared for the long wait.

The early results made it clear there would be no early announcement. There was a clear Yes/No divide between Glasgow and Edinburgh but the majority was slim both sides of the nation.

As expected, the Borders favoured No while as results came in from central areas, Yes caught up.

By Seven AM it was still too close to call.

"Only four more areas to report." Gordon updated Robert who had been dozing in a chair.

"I should make an announcement. People will be waking up and wanting to know the answer."

Gordon studied his print out. "Let the CCO give the news on the tally. Concentrate on the peaceful vote and desire of all Scots to work together after the result."

Robert gave his face a quick wash in his office bathroom.

For nights like this it was a useful perk to have. After a brief session in front of the journalists camped outside Holyrood he returned to the conference room.

The last areas reported in quick succession and Robert received news of the final result just after Nine AM. He gripped Gordon's arm, suddenly overcome with emotion. "I need to tell Helen."

"There's no time. The CCO will be announcing the result and you need to be ready to speak after her."

"Call her for me. Tell Helen... Her vote swung it."

Robert walked out into a new world.

****

CHAPTER FORTY TWO

"Robert, I've Chief Constable Allan Gillies to see you." Clara interrupted Robert's meeting with Gordon.

"Send him in." Robert turned back to Gordon. "Do you want to stay for this?"

"Certainly."

They stood as the Chief Constable was shown in and introduced themselves.

"We've completed our preliminary investigation." Allan told them once they were all seated. "The shooter had broken into an unused flat over a kilometre away. A female resident in the flats saw him leave, thought he was homeless and had been squatting.

"She is working with officers to try and produce a description. Other officers are reviewing CCTV footage in the area to see if we captured an image we can use and to find out where he went.

"Other than that, or barring a lucky break I don't think this will be an easy case."

"Why not?" Robert asked.

"We won't have ballistics. The shooter was firing at you from above with the Firth of Forth behind you. We'll never recover the bullet."

Robert thought back to that morning, remembered the rush of air past him and felt a shiver.

"We don't know who, do we know why?" Gordon asked.

"No-one has claimed responsibility. Unfortunately, I have to assume they will try again. We need to talk about how we will manage your security."

Robert stood and walked over to the window. "I'm not hiding out in Holyrood indefinitely."

"Of course not. But you will be travelling down to London for the negotiations. The Metropolitan Police will be happy to assist with your protection while you are in England."

"It does get you out of the way for a while." Gordon said.

"I'm not driving around in a bullet proof car."

"Don't worry, Sir. We don't have one..."

****

Robert was indeed well guarded as he travelled through London. While the Scottish police force did not possess armoured limousines, the Metropolitan police did. He and his team were driven to Westminster where the negotiations were due to start.

The Prime Minister met Robert for a photo shoot in front of journalists on the first morning. "You know, it was always my hope Scotland would choose to remain in the UK." He said while shaking Robert's hand and smiling.

Robert decided quickly that his impression of the man had been correct. "You know I campaigned originally for Stronger United." He said, smiling back.

"I did. I don't understand why you changed your view."

"Neither did Stronger United. That's probably why they lost the argument."

"Our team has been well briefed. Scotland is still our largest trading partner and we do not want to lose that."

"I'm sure you don't."

They were shown into a large, ornate room that could have easily held a dance for two hundred. A long, wide table was centred in the room with a dozen seats on each side. Off to one side were additional tables with stacks of books, some ancient leather bound volumes. There were also piles of more recent print outs and folders.

On the opposite side of the room tables held trays of sandwiches, cakes and biscuits with bottles of mineral water and pots of tea and coffee. "Do you think we should have brought a food taster?" Robert whispered to Gordon.

The team representing Westminster filed in to the room and made their introductions.

A new member of the cabinet was heading up the Westminster team, Charles Grosvener. He explained there would likely be several people taking his role over the next year. "The negotiations are likely to take a considerable amount of time and it is likely my duties will change."

Robert frowned at this but said nothing.

It took until Eleven AM before they were all finally seated.

Grosvenor thanked them for coming. "Her Majesty's Government recognizes the will of the people of Scotland to seek greater powers of self determination. We will accommodate you as far as we are able though will need to refer back to the cabinet for approval in all matters. It is expected this will be a long process. Accommodation will be provided and it is suggested that we limit ourselves to three days each week as I am sure you, like myself have other responsibilities."

Robert found himself gritting his teeth. The thought of spending three days a week for the next year in a room with this man might just provoke him to murder.

"We suggest two sessions of three hours each day." Grosvenor continued. "You may refer to any document on the tables behind us though you will not be permitted to remove them."

"What are those documents?" Gordon asked.

"The Act of Union from 1707 and all relevant legal agreements and laws passed since."

Robert looked once more at enough paper to fill a small room. "We can take copies though..." He asked.

"I'm afraid many of these documents are confidential. We cannot permit copies to be taken."

"Documents relating to the union of England and Scotland? How are we supposed to refer to them when we cannot study them?"

"You will be able to view them during the day."

As the morning drew on it quickly became clear to Robert just how far they would be accommodated. When they broke for lunch, Robert took Gordon aside.

"We can't let this drag out a month, let alone a year."

"I know you're keen to get this resolved but it is a

complicated task, unpicking two nations."

"We have hundreds of thousands of people who are expecting change now. They can't wait a year for negotiations that might not even deliver what we want."

"Then we have to ensure we do deliver."

As Grosvenor had led the morning's talks, Robert was allowed to lead the afternoon.

"The Scottish government's position has been clear and I do not intend to change it, we expect to take on ten percent of the debt of the United Kingdom in exchange for ten percent of the assets."

"We would expect nothing less." Grosvenor replied.

"We have compiled a list of assets we expect to be broken up and shared at the agreed ratio." Robert indicated and Carla handed over folders containing identical sheets of closely typed text.

Grosvenor breathed in sharply as he scanned down the list. He quickly reviewed the other sheets. "A comprehensive list. My team will have to take time to review it."

"Of course. We would however like to begin working through the list this afternoon. See how far we get." Robert smiled. "Shall we start with the gold held by the Bank of England?"

"As I said, our team will have to review this list."

"It is my understanding the total gold reserves held by the UK Government are only 310 tonnes. Can you confirm if this is true?"

Grosvenor shook his head. "I will need to confirm that figure."

"In order to save time, I suggest you advise the cabinet we seek full physical patriation of ten percent of your gold holdings to Scotland as part of any settlement."

"The Bank of England has a highly secure vault. There is nowhere in Scotland that can offer the same level of security."

"Some would say Faslane is the most secure location in the UK. Perhaps you should also discuss the matter with the MoD. Let's move onto the Falkland Islands and surrounding territorial waters..."

Tension in the room ratcheted up as Robert read out each item. When Robert started reading out the intention that space be allocated in each embassy and consulate around the world,

Grosvenor interrupted.

"Some of these buildings only have one room, Castle. You can't seriously expect us to allocate you space in them."

"Scots taxes and Scots oil have provided an equal or greater level of funding than our ten percent ratio for each and every one of these locations. Sharing consulate or embassy space is standard practice for many countries. This is not an unreasonable request."

"I think that is enough for today." Grosvenor replied.

On their way out, Robert whispered a message to Carla and asked her to tell the others on their team.

On their way to the hotel that had been arranged for them, Robert remained silent, brooding over the way the discussions had gone. At the hotel he dropped his suitcase and laptop in his room and headed outside straight away. The others joined him as he waited outside, thankful it wasn't raining.

"What was that all about?" Asked Ellen Prasser.

"I think we should assume we're being spied on." Robert told them.

"The British Government... Spying on people?" Gordon laughed. "Of course they are."

"It only occurred to me when Grosvenor was scanning down that list. Some of the items he seemed to be familiar with, whereas some of the last ones we added really shocked him. Maybe I'm being paranoid but this is the biggest shakeup to the government in my lifetime. I don't want us losing out because they know what we're about to say."

"We need to be able to discuss our strategy outside the meetings." Gordon said.

"You're right. I think we should invest in some tech. Sweep rooms for bugs before we start discussing anything. Carla, could you make some enquiries?"

The next morning, Grosvenor reported back. "I've been advised that the gold held by the Bank of England belongs to the Queen. It is not considered to be an asset open for negotiation."

"With the greatest of respect to Her Majesty, Balmoral is an asset owned by the Queen and it absolutely is up for negotiation."

"I will need to take that back to the Cabinet. Moving onto your requests for ten percent of soldiers, tanks, ships, aircraft, ammunition, missiles, submarines, nuclear missiles etc. etc. I thought the Scottish Government's position was no to nuclear power and no to war. Are you planning invading somewhere?"

"We have always been told the UK Government runs a Ministry of Defence. If ten percent of the UK armed forces – paid for by Scottish taxes and Scottish oil – is too much to defend our little nation... Why does the UK government need ten times as much military might?

"As you well know the UK assists many countries in the world."

"I doubt many on the receiving end of your assistance would agree with you. Regardless, this is our negotiating position. If we want to beat our swords into ploughshares after we get them, what is that to you?"

"I will have to take this back to the Cabinet."

"See that you do. And while there, perhaps you can remind them that Scotland is currently a nuclear power with Trident missiles and the means to develop additional fissionable material, all courtesy of the UK government siting these instruments of death on our land."

"Trident does not belong to Scotland."

"Ten percent of it does."

"You can't cut a submarine into pieces!"

"You know, there are plenty of people in England who would be delighted if we did just that."

By mutual agreement, they decided it was time for a break.

"Do you have to be so hard on him?" Carla asked as they helped themselves to coffee. "We're trying to reach agreement here."

"Stick it to them." Ellen said. "About time someone put Westminster in its place."

"You're not helping, Ellen."

"I've been fighting for the abolition of nuclear weapons since before you were born, Carla. I don't particularly like this myself but from what I've heard, this is how you negotiate – from a position of strength. Westminster thought they held all the cards. Every time young Robert here slaps them down they slowly begin to realise they may actually have to make some concessions."

The afternoon did not go any better. Robert finally had enough when for the twentieth time Grosvenor told them he would have to go back to the Cabinet.

"In that case we're done here for today." He said, rising to his feet. "Run off to the Cabinet if you must but if you do not have power to negotiate on their behalf then tell them to send someone tomorrow who can!"

He strode away from the table leaving his team floundering to catch up.

As they stood outside, waiting for cars to pick them up Gordon asked: "What the hell was that about?"

"I can't sit there day after day having to listen to someone who has no power to make a single decision. It's a tactic, designed to wear us down. After a year of that we'll be begging them to let us pay them to leave the UK." Robert looked round at his team. "I lost my temper. I realise that, but I will not negotiate with someone who has no power."

****

The next day Grosvenor was back but there was a hint of steel in the way he held himself and spoke. "Our Government's position is that any currency union is absolutely conditional on your acceptance of Bank of England interest rates, limits on your spending, your abilities to raise or lower taxes and other terms as laid out in our position paper. That is non-negotiable."

"Why do we need the Bank of England?" Robert asked.

"I don't understand the question."

"It's not necessary, so why is it part of your non-negotiables?"

"Of course it's necessary. How would we print or borrow money without it?"

"You are a sovereign country. You don't need a bank to print money for you. You certainly have no need to borrow money."

"You've completely lost me, Castle. Can we stay on topic please?"

"I am on topic. You have stated that we must accept interest rates set by a bank that your Government does not control as part of a currency union. Now, I happen to believe it's incredibly stupid for a Government to give up the ability to run their own currency. I cannot countenance agreeing to join you in your stupidity."

"The Government does..." Grosvenor trailed off as he

realised what he had been about to say.

"No, they don't. The Bank of England is independent. It's not controlled by the UK Government. What I'd give to meet the confidence trickster who persuaded a previous Government to pay interest just so they could create money. What a beautiful con. No, you can keep your currency if that's the deal you're offering. We'll create our own – at zero percent interest, zero debt and with no borrowing to drag Scotland down with it."

"It's impossible, you'll never manage it." Grosvenor had lost his earlier steel.

"Currency is just an IOU. A fictional notion that only has value when two or more people believe it does. In England some Centuries ago you used wooden sticks as currency. Imagine that, money growing on trees. Yet it worked – at least for a time. We already print our own paper money. There is nothing to stop us expanding that. We can even fix our currency to your pound for a time if we want, though I suspect your currency will devalue at the same rate as you keep borrowing. That's not a mistake we are planning to make."

"How are you going to fund your pensions, your benefits?"

"Haven't you heard? We're scrapping benefits. Though, we are replacing them with jobs which will cost a bit more. On the plus side, people creating and fixing and making will add value to our economy so it should all work out."

Grosvenor shook his head. "You can't really believe this."

"That's not the craziest thing I believe. Shall we continue?"

****

They flew home that evening. Robert spent an hour telling Helen how the negotiations had gone before she told him she'd had enough.

"Just hold me, okay. I've missed you." She curled up next to him and he put his arms round her. "Are you going to have to work this weekend?"

Robert shook his head. "No. But I think I'm going to take Gordon on a field trip tomorrow."

****

"We need to get people out as soon as we can." Robert

looked out over the valley. Clouds were thick overhead, darkening the sky and depressing everything.

"There used to be crofts here. Look, you can see where the grass is a different colour, those irregular rectangles." He walked on forcing Gordon and Carla to keep up with him. "It's October. The earliest we can probably think about starting will be early Spring but even then it's going to take them most of the first summer just to get established. We're going to have to feed people for a year and a half until they get their first harvest."

"Are you sure this is what you want to pursue?" Gordon asked.

"This is what it's all about. What it's always been about. Getting people back to the land. Giving them a chance to build a new future. Getting them working again after years on the dole." He looked back at Gordon. "It can work. We stop paying benefits, we start paying a wage to those people who are willing to work."

"And the people who aren't willing to work?" Carla asked.

"That is their choice."

"You would be willing to let them starve?"

"At some point society has to grow up. We call people adults but then refuse to trust them to fend for themselves. We mollycoddle them with job seekers allowance; housing benefit; tax credits. Give them all the benefits under the sun and then wonder why so many people are unemployed. It has to stop. I don't pay my taxes so other people can sit around and be lazy. If I'm willing to work then I don't see why anyone else should refuse to."

"They will complain. The media will eat it up. I can see the headlines now: Mother of three accuses government of abandoning her." Carla shook her head.

"Two hundred years ago a mother of three would have worked morning, noon and night to keep from starving. She would have worked on her croft; taken a job in mending clothes. Maybe even worked on other crofts to earn money or food. Her children would have worked alongside her. It was hard. People died, but why are we so afraid of that?"

"Of dying? Are you serious?"

"People die. They die because they can't afford their heating bills; they die of cancer; they die in stupid senseless accidents. People still die. And what about suicide. We even have people killing themselves because they perceive there is no hope. What kind of society have we become when people would rather die than find an alternative?"

"You're jumping around too much. Can we go back to the car?"

"Already? We only just got here."

"I'm cold." Carla wrapped her arms around herself.

Robert shook his head and turned round.

"I want to get people out here as soon as possible. Begin planning where to allocate land; start turning over the earth and laying foundations for homes and tracks. If we can get people out here then they will start to have a sense of ownership – will begin to care about what happens."

"What about the negotiations?" Gordon reminded him. "You won't have all the powers you need until they're concluded and we really become independent."

"Does an eighteen year old wait for his parents to tell him when he's ready to become independent? No, ready or not he can move out, get drunk, learn to drive..."

"That's seventeen." Carla interrupted.

"I'm not hearing anything I want Scotland to aspire to." Gordon said.

"The point is that we can walk away at any time. Westminster may not like it, they may even try and stop us but they won't be able to." Robert turned his face upwards, briefly closing his eyes. "The negotiations are not going well."

"You've got to give them time." Gordon insisted.

"I've a feeling they will be a lot shorter than Westminster are expecting. Anyway, I'm handing lead role over to Ellen next week. You the week after, Gordon. See how the two of you get on without me."

"What are you going to be doing?" Carla asked.

"The referendum software needs some management and I think it's time to get the ball rolling up here." Robert took one last look at the landscape before getting in the car.

****

CHAPTER FORTY THREE

He'd rushed the first attempt. That was Tam's conclusion after he'd settled himself down. While the mistake had meant a second attempt was much harder, it did not mean it was impossible. As soon as possible was a flexible deadline. He just needed to pick the right time and place.

Given the level of publicity around the current negotiations, there was plenty of information available on the movement of the negotiating team. One of them, a young lady by the name of Carla, even had her own fashion following in several of the papers.

But it turned out that simple was best. The level of security assigned to the target wasn't consistent. Wasn't even 24/7. It seemed he didn't believe he was at risk, even resented the need for protection. Why would he think he was still in danger when nothing else had happened for two weeks.

Tam walked up to the front door of the house they were staying in, stolen pizza carrier in hand, and rang the door bell. He expected the target would answer and he was correct. Two shots from a silenced pistol in the chest and a third in the head once the target was down and the job was complete.

He took a hurried photo then stowed the pistol in the pizza carrier as he walked back down the path. A text to confirm the kill was his last duty and he disappeared into the night.

****

"Gordon's been shot!"

Robert had a flashback to the attempt on his own life. Unable to attack him, had they struck at his friend and advisor? "Is he alive?"

"He's in theatre now. There's no word from the surgeons but from the description of what happened, it is a wonder he survived at all."

"You can tell me later, what hospital is he in?"

****

Robert, closely followed by his protection detail, ran into the hospital entrance and looked around for a reception desk. "Gordon Taggart was brought in this morning. Gunshot victim. Where can I find him?"

"Are you family?" The receptionist asked.

"This is the First Minister. Gordon is his advisor."

The receptionist studied them and hesitated. "I can only confirm to family members..."

Robert put a hand on the desk to steady himself. "It's okay. If we were family, where would we wait?"

"You need to go to A&E." She pointed down a corridor. "Follow the signs."

****

Robert found Penny pacing anxiously in the A&E waiting area. A female police officer was with her. When Penny saw Robert, she walked over and threw her arms round him.

"They won't tell me." She said. "Just that he's in surgery."

"What happened?"

"The door bell rang. Gordon went downstairs to answer it but didn't come back up. Eventually I went to check on him. Found him on the floor. They just shot him, Robert. Why would they do that?"

She began to sob and Robert held her, looking at the officers around him who were themselves scanning the surrounding room.

When Penny had calmed down, Robert led her to a seat and

sat with her, holding her hand. His phone vibrated and he pulled it out. Carla was trying to call him. He let it go to voicemail.

They sat for an hour with no news. Sat while a mother came in with three children and was taken through to triage; while an older man came in with a gash on his head. They heard nothing until a doctor came out in green scrubs.

Penny stood and walked over to him, Robert following.

"How is he?" She demanded.

"Can you come with me?" The doctor asked.

Penny and Robert followed him, Penny still asking how Gordon was. The doctor led them into a room with sofas. "Can you take a seat?"

"Where's Gordon? Why haven't you taken us to him?"

Robert tried to put an arm round her shoulder but Penny shook him off. "Tell me." She said in a shrill voice.

"I'm very sorry, Mrs Taggart. The artery leading to your husband's heart was damaged in the shooting. We tried to repair it but the damage was too great." The doctor paused, obviously not wanting to continue. "Mr Taggart passed away a few minutes ago."

Penny took a step back. Robert tried again to put his arm around her but she resisted. "Take me to him." She insisted.

Robert followed but stopped outside the operating theatre. He could see Gordon lying on the table, a white sheet over him up to his neck. Around the room he could see evidence of efforts made to save him: metal implements heaped in trays; yellow bags held in hospital bins with red stained cloth or pads evident even through the thick plastic.

He waited for Penny as she stood next to her husband, talking to him, crying and finally kissing him on the forehead.

****

Robert called Helen and told her he was bringing Penny to their house. After he'd dropped her off he told his protection detail to take him to Strathclyde Police Headquarters.

"Thank you for meeting me, Chief Constable." Robert said to Allan Gillies.

"I'm sorry to hear about your advisor. I understand he was a friend?"

"One of my oldest. I need to know what happened. Was this

political? Random? It can't have been random." Robert realised he was rambling. "Did he die because of me?"

"A team was put together to investigate as soon as we heard. As soon as I have any updates I will let you know and of course I'll update you daily, First Minister."

Robert thanked him and left. As he walked out the building onto Pitt Street, he realised he was shaking. In the car he called Carla and updated her.

"The press will need a statement." She told him.

"They always need something, even if it's none of their damn business." He sighed. "Sorry, I shouldn't take it out on you."

"I'll prepare something and email it over."

The streets were unchanged from earlier in the year. Robert looked and was surprised there was no evidence of the new Scotland. People were still walking up and down. Cars and lorries still passing each other on the roads. Should he see any change? He didn't know.

****

CHAPTER FORTY FOUR

Robert insisted the negotiating team go to London as planned the next week. He spoke with Ellen before they went. "Don't let them push you into making rash decisions."

"I'm not a soft touch, Robert. I thought you knew that by now."

"I have no idea what I'm doing." Robert confessed. "This role is supposed to be bigger than one man. I'm supposed to run a country and all I can think about is my best friend has died."

"You need time to mourn. It's probably good you told me last week I was leading the team. I would have had to have you sectioned if you'd insisted going to London after this. Give it time. There are plenty of people who can take the strain for a week or two."

****

Robert called in a group of his MSPs later that day. "I've got assignments for each of you." He handed out packets to them all. "You have one week to visit the location you've been given, research what they are doing there, then report back to me on how we can use it."

The next day he got up early and by Eight AM was in a car with Carla, travelling up to Dundee.

"Do you really think this software is going to work?" She

340

asked.

"It has to. It's probably the most important thing we're going to do. If nothing else works, this has to."

"Why? What's the big deal."

"Have you ever been to Cafe Politics?"

"No."

"You should go sometime. That's the only reason we won the election."

"People getting together and discussing politics?" She looked disparagingly at him. "I enjoy my job, but not that much."

"That's the mistake people make too much. They aren't discussing politics, they're discussing life. All the hundreds and thousands of intricacies that enable us to live and work together. If people can reach agreements then they can make progress. If they could do that without having to write down a law or a rule then so much the better. It requires trust and time but in the end it could be far better than the millions of laws politics have created that kill creativity, kill life."

"But you're proposing that people create new laws, won't that just add to the millions that already exist?"

"Of course."

"So, what's the benefit?"

"They can also replace laws, change laws, even completely remove ones that have no value or purpose. The problem is that we do need rules because we can't completely trust each other. But this system could allow us to go much further. Allow whole communities to govern themselves without need for government intervention."

"Would that be safe? Wouldn't you get strange cults or abusive behaviour?"

"That is a risk but one that can be policed. All communities would still come under the authority of the whole nation. Any that starts to go off the rails can have local authority stripped away." Robert looked past Carla to a village they were passing. "It's an experiment. I can't say how it will turn out but I have hope that people can choose to work together, can reason together. This software gives them a way to do that without having laws forced on them by a government that refuses to listen to its people."

"I have to admit, it scares me."

"So it should. Democracy should terrify any sane person. It

is absolute responsibility. The responsibility resting on the shoulders of every person. But it should also be wonderful, freeing. An opportunity to be seized.

"All the software does is allow people to propose, discuss, amend and ultimately vote. No different to what Holyrood or Westminster does on a daily basis. The difference is that every single person can get involved, if they want to."

"If they don't?"

"We will require everyone to vote on nationwide referendums, within limits. In Switzerland they only have a limited number each year. We may have to cap the number if it gets too unwieldy."

"You're just making this up as you go along aren't you." She gave a half laugh but Robert saw concern in her eyes.

"Some of it. A lot of these ideas have been forming for the last decade. For the software anyway. Developing software is what I used to do for a living. I just never thought I'd have the ability to implement something this big. At the core it's a fairly simple system. I drew up a schema for it one lunchtime."

"Tell me you didn't use a napkin..."

****

"Why do we need a forum?" Carla asked.

"To prevent the media controlling everything." Answered Robert.

"Or to put it another way – to give voters a chance to discuss the issues among themselves without any outside influence." Said Professor Mark Altinham. "At least, that was how the specification put it." He told Robert dryly.

"Well, without much influence. Each proposal will have its own thread, its own mini forum and will be administered by the person who made the proposal. Show us the voting system." Robert said.

Altinham clicked on the Vote now link and they saw another menu appear:
- Referendum on Land Grab
- Referendum on Benefit reform
- Referendum on full employment
- Referendum on electoral reform
- Vote for Altinham

342

• Create Referendum

"Vote for Altinham?" Asked Robert.

"Anyone can create any referendum." The professor said. "I can imagine a fair few worse proposals that will be posted."

Carla raised her eyebrows in a questioning look at Robert. He grinned. "I guess I can too. Show us Land Grab."

Altinham talked them through the rest of the voting system.

"So people just have to click in the boxes to vote?" Carla asked.

"Yes." Professor Mark Altinham demonstrated by clicking on some of the For and some of the Against.

"Why do you have both For and Against?" Carla asked. "Surely it's redundant."

"Including an Against option acts as a safety check. Remember how the voting went in the independence referendum. Many have said they thought there should have been a much higher percentage required for a Yes to succeed."

"Not the majority of people who voted Yes." Robert said.

"For people like myself, well, this system will prevent such a scenario occurring." Altinham continued. "People can either vote For or Against but for a proposal to go to an actual referendum a lead of one hundred thousand votes is required."

"That seems unworkable." Carla shook her head. "What if the proposal never gains that lead?"

"Then it will not be formally voted on. Westminster currently have a petition system and one of the complaints against that system is its one sided nature. There is no debate inherent in the system and you cannot object to a petition, you can only begin an opposing one. The addition of dislikes makes it immediately obvious whether there is a substantial opposition to a proposal. But, in the words of Doctor Seuss, that is not all... There will be a chat/comment facility. Every change proposed will have a thread capability where voters can begin new threads of discussion about the change or add to existing discussions. Built into the system is the ability for voters to communicate directly with each other about the changes being proposed: They can agree or argue, work together or fall apart."

"I'm still not convinced about the one hundred thousand lead. Just say everyone votes. A proposal gets fifty one percent backing from the entire electorate but that is not enough to force a referendum."

"I would say it should not be enough to force a referendum." Altinham said. "If the nation is that divided, no law should be passed until a greater agreement can be reached."

****

Ellen reported back to Robert every evening. They had obtained, at considerable cost, secure mobiles that in theory could not be monitored. Even so, Ellen kept her updates brief and factual.

"More of the same. They want to give as little as they can while holding us in thrall for as long as possible. How they think we could consider what they are proposing to be independence, I don't know."

"Can you stand another week leading the team?" Robert asked.

"It will be my pleasure. I'm beginning to follow your approach to negotiation. It fairly livens up an otherwise dull day."

****

CHAPTER FORTY FIVE

"Robert, wake up."

"What time is it?"

"The baby's coming?"

"What baby?" Robert sat up in bed. "The baby! Are you sure?"

"My waters broke. I've called the midwife. The contractions have started."

Robert stared at Helen. "What should I... Do I... Should we go to the hospital?"

"Could you make me a cup of tea?"

It seemed a strange request but Robert went and started to boil the kettle. Before it had finished boiling there was a knock on the door. Robert checked the clock. It was just after Two AM.

It was the midwife.

"You got here fast." Robert told her. She gave him a strange look.

"Helen's upstairs."

He showed her to the bedroom and the midwife asked if he could get some towels and make them both a cup of tea.

Robert got the towels and topped up the kettle, putting it onto boil. There was another knock at the door. "Surely we don't need two midwifes." He muttered.

It was a paramedic.

"There must be some mistake, I didn't call an ambulance." Robert told her.

"Are you Robert Castle?" She asked.

"Yes."

"The midwife called us. We're here to take your wife to hospital."

"Is there something wrong?" Robert turned and wondered if he should go and check then realised: "But the midwife only just got here. When did she call you?"

"Half an hour ago, Sir. She said to take our time."

"Half an hour... Do you want to step inside?" Robert let the Paramedic in and went back upstairs.

"There's an ambulance here. Did you call it?" He asked the midwife.

"Ah good. Your wife is doing fine Mr Castle. We'll take her into the hospital now."

"I'm happy to take her. Everything is okay, isn't it?"

"First Minister, while everything is fine and I expect there to be no complications, it would be remiss of me to take any chances with your wife's delivery."

"I don't want any fuss. I shouldn't be treated any different to anyone else."

The midwife smiled. "While I agree you should not be treated any differently, the wife of the First Minister deserves all the help she can get. Now, shall we help Helen down the stairs?"

Robert found himself directed, instructed and gently ordered as they took Helen out to the ambulance. The next six hours were slow and tense. They reached the hospital and Robert waited while Helen was checked again. Four centimetres dilated, five centimetres, six. Each slight increase seemed to take an age and in between there were increasingly painful contractions which seemed to come closer and closer together – but never quite close enough.

The midwife advised Helen to keep walking and so Robert and she walked up and down their small private room, then out and up and down the longer corridor until they were shooed back into the room.

And then it changed. Everything speeded up. The midwife said Helen was almost there. Other nurses appeared and a doctor. Equipment appeared and Robert found himself sidelined again, assigned a place at Helen's right hand which gripped his arm or shoulder until he wondered if could sneak some of the gas and air she was hyperventilating.

Helen was told to push. The midwife asked if he wanted to see. Robert declined, happy to stay at the head of the bed. Helen pushed. Against what, Robert wasn't sure but her grip told him it was painful.

And then there was a baby, whisked away to a table before he could properly see it, but definitely a baby.

"It's a girl!" The midwife announced.

Robert found himself blinking back tears. He looked at Helen who appeared so drained she had nothing left.

Then the midwife presented the wrapped baby to Helen and he saw his daughter properly for the first time.

"She's beautiful. Like a prune. But beautiful."

"Robert!" Helen rebuked.

He kissed Helen on the forehead.

"Do you want to hold her?"

He took her, uncertain how to properly hold her but some instinct took over and then he was looking down at her little face. A hand appeared under the blankets, fingers perfectly formed with little finger nails. It was amazing.

"We never agreed on a name." Said Helen.

"No. I still don't know."

"I've been wondering about Robin."

"Robin Castle." It seemed to fit.

****

Even First Ministers got paternity leave it seemed. Every time Robert tried to call to find out how things were going with the negotiations or with parliament, he was gently fobbed off and reminded there were other people who needed his time.

The enforced time away gave Robert more time to think than he wanted. Time to think about Gordon. Time to wonder who had attacked them. He didn't want to believe that Westminster had ordered their deaths but it was the only possibility he could think of. In the end he called Allan Gillies.

"Mr Castle. What can I do for you?"

"The First Minister. The bus crash... Did you investigate that?"

"Yes. Why?"

"What did you find?"

"It was a tragic accident, nothing more. A puncture when the driver was accelerating. The bus swerved before he could apply the brakes and crashed through the bridge wall. There was no evidence of anything else."

"I just... I've been wondering. The crash. The shootings... Are they connected?"

"If it would help I will order a review of the evidence."

"Yes. Thank you."

****

Robert returned to work after two weeks desperate to find out what was happening with the negotiations. He met with the team on Monday morning.

"They're stonewalling." Ellen told him. "With both you and Gordon out of the picture they seem in no hurry to agree anything. They're being canny about it, just insisting on every detail being fully considered."

"Details were supposed to be tackled in phase two. How about everyone else? How do you think it is going?"

The team shared their frustrations and suggestions. Then Robert told them what he was planning for the next week.

"Are you sure?" Carla questioned.

"It's been a month. If they want detail then I think it's time to insist on full disclosure."

****

Robert skimmed through the reports his MSPs had prepared for him. There was good information here but the costs were too high. He'd envisaged the government funding homes being built across Scotland but even a quick calculation showed the cost would be astronomical.

But some of the ideas were intriguing and potentially scalable. The country needed energy and no real agreement on how to resolve the need. Nuclear was expensive to build and maintain, and the long term costs had been lied about for too long – both in terms of finance and risk to the environment.

Coal, oil and gas were hated by environmentalists, but Scotland had a natural abundance of them. Robert wasn't about to kill off the golden goose without a practical alternative.

Renewables were also expensive but some of the projections were just too small. They hadn't fully factored in economy of scale or a government willing to 100 percent commit to the projects.

He sat back and tapped a pencil on the table. It was far too expensive to buy in tech from China or other countries but what if Scottish manufacturing could be rebooted? What if renewables were all manufactured here?

It could lead to further job opportunities, more businesses, more taxes being raised. It wouldn't solve all the problems but it could be a big help. And some of the ideas were worth exploring. If you only built a roof facing towards the sun and tiled it with solar panels instead of standard roof tiles, you saved money on construction and maximized the potential generation of power.

He particularly liked the idea of vertical turbines. Why had these not been developed instead of the massive horizontal wind turbines? Probably just hadn't thought of it. Sometimes you need to go down the wrong path before you realise which is the right one.

He continued reading and then stopped suddenly.

"No way!" He said to himself. He checked back through the document and shook his head, then debated with himself for a few minutes and finally underlined a name. Getting up he went out to the outer office. "Carla, could you get hold of this guy?" He gave her the sheet of paper he'd underlined. "Can we fly him here?"

"When?"

"Tomorrow. If he's available."

"Okay, I'll try and get in touch."

****

"Professor Donaldson, thank you for agreeing to travel here!"

"It's my pleasure. Your young secretary didn't explain why it was so urgent…"

"Carla, my PA." Robert introduced her.

Donaldson bent in close to Robert. "Does she have a loud voice?" He whispered.

Robert saw Carla's eyes widen. He quickly ushered the professor into his office. "Could you ask the team to join us?" He said to Carla.

She raised her eyebrows and turned away.

The other MSPs joined them soon and Robert introduced them to Professor Angus Donaldson, current owner of the Tayvallich Estate.

"As Ed will have told you I wanted to start planning how we're going to make use of the land we're reclaiming."

"Ah yes..." Donaldson's expression took on a distant look. "But not my castle!" He winked at Robert. "That I get to keep."

Robert took a slow breath. "Indeed. The first, most practical way seems to be to re-establish existing crofting communities but then we're looking at building new houses and that's where costs start to skyrocket. Then when I read about the work you've been doing I wondered if we could apply it on a national scale."

"Of course! The work was always meant to be replicable. You should have called me sooner, my boy. I've been working towards this my whole life." Donaldson said.

"Forgive me." Robert said. "I have to ask, you never mentioned any of this when we first met."

"You never asked."

"No... I don't suppose I did. Well, we weren't actually in government until last month. But we are and you're here now. The main issues as I see them are housing, self-sufficiency and energy."

"You also want to enable people to earn an income. Self-sufficiency is fine until you need to repair or maintain and then you run into problems."

"Indeed."

"Left to themselves, people are incredibly adaptable. Look at communities that exist on archipelagos. Generations of people subsisting on fish and the little they can grow but survive they do, and with ingenuity they do well. It was no different in Scotland before people were herded into cities and made dependent on the state. Self-sufficiency should be your first priority."

"I would have thought it would be housing..." Said Edward Sanderson, who'd been elected in the North East.

"People can go without housing but can never go without food."

"You're not proposing…" Robert asked.

"Of course not, my boy. You will provide housing but it is much more important to consider how they will fend for themselves. Otherwise you're just moving people around and still having to provide for them."

"Okay, what do you propose?"

"You plan communities. Scottish communities used to farm together, sharing the heavy work and increasing their output tremendously. People should also have their own gardens but they should be expected to take part in providing for the community as a whole."

"We can't force people to work the land." Said Sheila McCray, who'd been elected in Glasgow.

"No one would have to be forced. Being left to fend for oneself has a way of opening one up to being willing to work. If you have the choice of starving or helping your community to provide food, most people will choose to work."

"We are not going to force people onto the land, Sheila." Robert said. "We're giving them the choice of a new start or providing for themselves where they are. We always promised full employment but there will be new jobs created where people are now."

"At minimum wage. We need to raise that to something we can actually survive on."

"You're right, Sheila. We do." Robert turned back to Donaldson. "Professor, you mentioned hydroponics, I'm not clear what that is."

"A highly efficient way of growing crops that is much less damaging to the environment than using peat or compost. You get higher output and avoid using pesticides. You can either grow in a water rich environment with no bedding material or use something like pumice which is readily available in Scotland."

"Won't that be expensive to set up?"

"There are set up costs but in the long term it more than pays for itself by increased crop yields and sizes.

"I'd also recommend providing some basic materials for cold frames and polytunnels. Teach people to recycle their food waste into the soil and they'll reap the benefits."

"I stood for election believing that we were going to provide jobs for people, I never really understood this determination to reclaim the land." Sheila said. "Isn't there a risk that we're sending Scotland back to the stone ages? Forcing people to subsist on potatoes and turnips. Are we really wanting to send them back to that?"

"Potatoes and turnips!" Donaldson laughed loudly. "My dear, the early crofters always had the ability to produce a wide range of vegetables. If they were lazy or poorly educated they might not use their land to its full capacity but there is no reason a hard working crofter could not take four or more crops out of the soil each year. More if they managed manure.

"While crofters could grow oats, barley and wheat they had better results in Scotland's climate by choosing green crops. But carrots, onions, cabbage, kale, strawberries and lettuce would have been found on most crofts along with herb gardens."

"Lettuce? In Scotland?"

"Of course. And by utilizing cold frames and modern techniques such as polytunnels or hydroponics there is no crop that is out of reach.

"You should also encourage people to keep egg laying hens; for communities to own their own cows or goats and supplement their diet with fish, then they can feed themselves well."

"So you don't think people's health would be at risk?" Ed asked.

"Absolutely not. Compared to the risks of obesity and disease from our modern eating habits it would be possible to re-educate the nation to a much healthier state. Think back to the lessons of the second World War where Britons ended the war – despite severe shortages of food – much healthier than they entered. All down to a carefully calculated ration that gave people what they needed rather than what they wanted."

"This sounds like social engineering on a huge scale."

"We have already been socially engineered to consume too much sugar, salt, fat and artificial additives. All you would be doing is reversing the decline in our nation's health. Giving people a chance to discover how good food actually is.

"Another fact you should consider is that the UK government has allowed itself to become completely dependent on foreign food sources."

"That can't be true…"

"Recent reports have shown that we are only capable – at

this point in time – of producing sixty percent of our needs. Note – needs – not wants. We used to have grain stores across Britain but these have gradually been sold off to provide social housing. If the island of Britain was to be cut off for any reason it would only take weeks before people would starve."

"We're not going to be cut off."

Robert saw the Donaldson's otherwise jolly expression fade and be replaced by something that chilled him.

"History has a nasty habit of repeating itself." Donaldson said in a cold voice. "The time when people say something cannot ever happen again is when they should be preparing for the worst."

Donaldson seemed to shake himself and continued in a gentler tone. "Transporting food half way round the world is expensive and damaging to the environment. If for no other reasons, it would be better for Scotland if we grew more of our own food."

Robert looked round the table and saw concerned looks. "Maybe we should return to this later. How about we look at housing? Professor, no matter how I crunch the numbers I keep reaching a cost far above our budget."

"The first question has to be: what is your budget? Secondly, how many people are you planning to house and in what proportions? By that I mean family size, demographics."

Robert looked round at the others. "Budget is still a major issue. We haven't agreed what share of UK debt we'll be taking on which will have a major impact. Then there are other start up costs, if we can't reach agreement with Westminster."

"It's in their interest to reach a quick agreement, isn't it?"

"You would think so. Anyway, at present I can only expect a maximum of one billion. Way short of what it would cost to house an expected two hundred thousand and their families."

Donaldson picked up a pen and started scribbling away on some paper. He paused, contemplated for a minute and then wrote some more.

"Half a billion." He eventually announced. "That's an initial sum only for housing and doesn't include the families – but you don't want to house families straight away anyway."

"How…? I had a range anywhere from fifteen to twenty billion…" Robert said.

"You want communities, not individual crofters.

Communities need a hall and a hall is the most cost effective way to get started. Build a single dwelling that can be manufactured and churned out as many times as you need it. Build in insulation into the manufacturing process to minimize construction time. Make it big enough to house eighty to one hundred people and flexible enough to be converted into a hall once those people have their own homes to move into.

Donaldson's eyes took on an unfocused look as he continued. "You cut down the design to the bare minimum. A single-sided, sloping roof. We face this South and then use solar panels instead of tiles. Every single inch of roof can generate electricity which can be used by the community. You cut down on construction costs and lose the cost of tiling.

"Over spec the insulation and you could site these buildings in Antarctica and still have to open the window to let the heat out."

"You said manufactured... Do you mean timber frame?" Ed looked concerned.

"Is that a concern?" Robert asked.

"It's just... If we're going to be spending that much money on these buildings, don't we want something that will last?"

"Why do you think timber framed houses don't last?" Donaldson asked.

"Well, they aren't permanent structure like brick or stone."

"Have you never seen a Tudor house? We have timber framed buildings in the UK that are older than most stone and brick constructs. Any building will only last as long as it's maintained, painting or treating cladding, maybe replacing it every few decades."

"Community halls... Could that work?" Robert asked.

The discussion continued for several days.

****

CHAPTER FORTY SIX

"I want to return to the matter of Scotland's share of UK gold reserves." Robert opened his session on Tuesday afternoon.

"As we previously agreed, that matter is not up for negotiation." Grosvenor replied.

"We did not agree that. In fact, there has not been a single agreement in the month we've been holding these negotiations. Does the UK Government want to honour its commitment to these negotiations?"

"Of course. I was under the impression we had made considerable progress."

"Leaving that to one side for now, the share of UK gold…"

"Scotland is not entitled to any share in gold reserves. The gold is held by the UK Government as a reserve and as I keep saying, is not up for negotiation."

"Scotland taking on our share of national debt is conditional on our receiving our share of UK gold reserves. How many tons do you have in the vault?"

"You told me the figure yourself. 310 tonnes."

"You misunderstand me, how many tonnes of actual gold belonging to the UK are held in the vault?"

"310 tonnes."

"I'm not talking about paper IOUs, Grosvenor. How many tonnes, only owned by the UK government; not lent out or held in other countries names is held in the vault?"

For the first time Grosvener failed to reply. Robert noticed members of the UK team looking uncomfortable.

"Well, Grosvener? My team have told me you have been very insistent on detail these last weeks. How many actual tonnes of gold does the UK hold in reserve?"

Grosvenor told him.

Robert coughed a laugh. "Seriously! The only solid asset the UK Government owns and you've managed to sell off ninety percent of it!"

"Gold is far from the only asset the UK holds."

"What assets are you willing to give Scotland ten percent of?"

Grosvener held Robert's gaze but did not reply.

"Ten percent of the army? Ten percent of your tanks? Ten percent of your aircraft?"

"This is ridiculous. This is not the way to negotiate. We are not going to carve up the army in that way."

"Well, in that case, thank you! You make this very easy for us. In truth, many of my fellow citizens despise the military industrial complex you have created. Scotland will establish a more cost effective and appropriate defence system for our needs. How about embassies and consulates?"

"Again, we are not going to negotiate on giving up ten percent of space in every embassy in the world."

"Are you willing to share any of the space? Five percent maybe? Two percent?"

"It's impractical. You may have different priorities to us. There may be conflict."

"Then we shall establish our own network of embassies without your help."

"That's ridiculous. It will cost you a small fortune to buy buildings in capitals round the world."

"It won't cost us a penny. We will offer a reciprocal arrangement. In return for a foreign government providing us with a building we will provide them with an equivalent building in Edinburgh. There is no reason why an embassy has to cost more than salaries for staff and some minor equipment.

"How about transferring Civil Service staff and facilities from England to Scotland?" Robert continued.

"That is a highly complex process that will take months to plan."

"I'm not willing to wait months just for a plan."

"Whether you're willing or not, it will take time."

"No. It won't. Grosvenor, send a message to your masters. As you have been unwilling to agree an equitable distribution of assets in exchange for our taking on our share of national debt, we are ceasing negotiations. If you want to keep all the assets you can also keep your debt. Scotland has declared itself independent. As of January first 2015, we shall be an independent country. If you want to change your position on any of the items discussed you may apply to open an embassy in Edinburgh. We will be happy to offer you a reciprocal arrangement."

By agreed arrangement, Robert and his team rose as one and filed out of the room.

"We never discussed Trident..." Ellen reminded Robert as they boarded taxis to the hotel.

Robert grinned at her. "I expect they will be opening an embassy in the near future..."

****

Barrels had been placed across the road. A sign attached to them read: YOU WILL NEVER TAKE MY LAND.

Robert got out as police officers checked them.

"Filled with sand. We can tip and roll them off the road."

"Do it." Robert looked ahead. The glen they were in wound its way higher into the Highlands ahead. They still had five miles left to drive till they reached the estate entrance, but were about to cross the boundary line.

A few minutes later they were on their way again. Robert wondered if four police cars with eight officers in total was excessive but he'd heard the rumours about this John Anderson.

A mile later on, their way was blocked by large logs. It took all of them, Robert included, to roll those to one side.

Two miles later a skip – filled with rubble – had been placed at a point where the road had been cut through sheer rock on both sides. Traces of an old road could be seen heading up the hill but decades ago this had been blocked off with anti-tank blocks.

"We'll need a crane to move this." Robert was told.

"Very well. We walk from here."

****

"Angus! I can see them walking up the road. Why aren't you here?"

"I told you at the meeting, John. I will not resort to violence over this. There are still legal ways to halt this."

"You saw the way Castle tramped over the High Court. How can you still believe the law can help you?"

"Westminster will place sanctions on Scotland if this goes ahead. There are too many Lords with property here for parliament to desert us."

"They've already abandoned us. I haven't had a single pledge of support. If I don't stand up for our rights they'll take everything."

"Don't do anything rash. At the moment you keep one hundred hectares including the prime part of your estate and hunting lodge. If you're arrested for assaulting or threatening anyone, that will be placed in jeopardy... John... John, are you listening?"

John Anderson allowed the phone to drop to be lost in the heather. He checked his double barrelled shotgun was loaded, the twelve gauge cartridges gleaming in contrast to the walnut grip.

He strode onto the gravelled road that led into his estate garden, standing ten yards back from the open gates. At this distance, with one inch expansion per yard, the shot spread would expand sufficiently to knock a man to the ground when hit in the chest. The damage would be significant but probably not lethal, he told himself. Probably.

He'd sent his servants away the week before. Had hoped they may offer to stay and help defend the estate but they had seemed eager to leave. No loyalty any more, he thought to himself.

Having dropped down to the road he could no longer see the group as they made their way up.

His family had lived on the estate for over three hundred years. They could trace their roots back five hundred more to Kings who had reigned over these lands. This was his land and no upstart politician was going to take it from him.

He heard them before he saw them. Boots clumping up the tarmac. Rifles probably at the ready. Tear gas, batons, whatever the coward could throw at him.

There! He recognized him straight away – the arrogant pretender. John watched Castle walk up to the gate and stop, just outside. The police had not accompanied him. John looked round wondering if they were surrounding him. Was Castle just a distraction while they performed a pincer movement?

"Do you know who I am?" Castle asked.

"Do you know who I am?" John threw back at him.

"John Anderson. Owner of Creigfell estate. Son of Moira and Thomas. You've lived here your whole life."

"That I have and I've no intention of letting you or any other bastard throw me off my land."

"I have a mandate from the Scottish people to reclaim the majority of your estate, leaving you with one hundred hectares. Are you aware of this?"

"I don't recognize your mandate. You are a criminal. A traitor. Those police with you should arrest you and haul you back where you came from."

"Regardless of your recognition, I am here to reclaim the land owned by the Scottish people."

"You'll have to go through me."

"I've no intention of going through you. You are entitled to keep 100 hectares which can include this section of the estate."

"And how long will I be entitled to keep that? You steal most of my land, what's to stop you coming back for the rest."

"I am a man of my word."

"I wouldn't trust you with a penny."

Then Castle sat down. Crossed his legs and just sat down on the tarmac outside the gate.

"What are you doing?"

"I'm not leaving until you acknowledge the right of the Scottish people to settle on your former estate."

"You're going to have a long wait then." John realised he was still holding his shotgun steady. Where it would have shot Castle in the chest it would now tear his head to shreds. He lowered it but still kept it pointing at Castle.

He stood looking at Castle for a couple of minutes and then swore. "This is insane. Get up."

Castle didn't respond.

"Get up you coward!"

Still nothing. John raised his shotgun level with Castle's head then had a second thought and turned. No-one. Where had the police gone? He looked back towards the house.

"Where are the police?"

Castle remained silent.

He couldn't think. This was some trick but what was Castle up to? "Stay there." He said to Castle and turned and walked briskly up to the house. Checking all around as he went he still couldn't see any sign of the police. Had they taken his house while Castle staged his sit-in?

He readied his shotgun but found he couldn't open the door. In the end he had to hold it up against his shoulder then stepped back as the door swung open. The house was dark.

He hesitated before entering. How could they do this to him, turning his own house into a trap?

He jumped in and turned quickly – left then right. Nothing. His anger boiling over, he ran up the stairs, shouting in the hope he would scare anyone waiting.

He searched the whole house but it was empty. Out of breath, he stood back in the hallway, absentmindedly looking around as he tried to work out what they were doing.

He went once round the main house and when he didn't see any trace of trespassers he headed back out to the main gate. Castle was still sitting there but one of the police officers had joined him. What were they playing at?

As he walked closer he realised it wasn't a police officer. Just a boy. Wearing one of those ill-fitting track suits.

"Who's this?" He asked Castle.

"He can speak for himself."

John looked from one to the other. Where had Castle found this boy? He didn't remember seeing him when the group was walking up the road.

"Well? Who are you?"

"Niall Leith."

"What are you doing here?"

"The chief here." He nodded at Castle. "He promised us he'd give us a job. Give us land and a house. Sounded awright."

John shook his head. "There's no job for you here."

"That's awright. The chief said he'd sort it out. Make it possible for us to provide for ourselves."

"There's nothing for you here!" John gripped his shotgun but couldn't bring himself to raise it. Couldn't risk killing a civilian. That was the trick! Distract him and Castle snuck in this boy. "Get out!" John waved his hand at the boy. "Go on, get away!"

The boy just tilted his head. "Nice place you got. Can see why you don't want to give it up. I'd fight for it too, if it was mine."

John turned in disgust and walked back to the house. He headed straight for the drinks cabinet. Began to pour himself a whisky but then smashed the bottle against the wall. He couldn't drink now!

He laid the shotgun on the table and sat heavily on a chair. How long was Castle planning to sit outside his house? Over winter?

He didn't know how long he sat for but eventually took a deep breath and rose. He walked slowly back out and gave a hollow laugh when he saw a third person sitting in the gate. A girl this time. Of course. If the boy didn't persuade him they'd try a female.

He realised he'd left the gun in the house. He stood looking at his empty hands and then carefully sat down in front of the three of them.

"How many more do you have out there?"

"Five million." Castle said in an even tone.

"Is that what this is about?"

"It's about justice. About recognizing that none of us own the land. About sharing the little resource we have with as many people as we can."

"I can't beat you."

"I'm not here to beat you. I want your help. These people with me don't know the first thing about farming. They need your help."

"Why would I help you?"

"I'm not asking you to help me. Help them."

"You're asking too much."

They sat, no-one else speaking until Castle finally stood. "We have allocated 100 hectares to you. If you wish to change the location or boundaries, ask a solicitor to contact us. We will pay all reasonable legal fees. You have one month to request a boundary change or it will become binding.

"We will have people working up here during the Winter and in the Spring will start to move people up here permanently.

"The police will ignore that you threatened me. Do not threaten anyone else or I will end you. Do you understand me?"

John looked up and saw none of the arrogance he expected, just a cold, hard stare. He stood himself, unwilling to show he was intimidated.

"I realise that you have no reason to forgive me…" Castle continued. "But understand that the people who carved up these lands a thousand years ago killed and lied to set their boundaries. The people we will be sending up, like Niall and Aila here, are being given an opportunity to reverse the injustice. To make this land live again. Don't take any anger out on them. If you want to shout at anyone, you know where to find me."

The two young people with Castle stood and the three of them walked away leaving John alone in the middle of his drive.

****

"I really don't know why they insist on you having a protection detail." Mike said to Robert as they walked back down the road. "You seem determined to get yourself killed."

"Balls of steel and a complete nutter." Laughed Liam. "What was all that about sitting down?"

"It worked for Ghandi." Robert said.

"Wasn't that about horses?"

"Horses, landowners with shotguns… It seemed the way to handle the situation."

"And we're within such easy reach of an air ambulance. Your wife is going to kill you for this."

"Helen's not to know."

"Going to be hard to keep this story quiet, Chief." Liam slapped Robert on the back. "Do we need to get you a new pair of trousers?"

Robert ignored him but told himself that would be the last time he went up against a shotgun.

****

CHAPTER FORTY SEVEN

"If there was anything I was dreading – it was this. Right now." Robert told Carla.

They were standing next to his car, looking down the street.

"I don't get it. Why dread this? You're giving these people a new start. A new chance."

"Not all of them are going to want that new start. Some will be too afraid of change and will fight against it – even if it could be better for them in the long term. Basic human psychology. You did study politics didn't you?"

"Must have missed that class. Maybe I was afraid of getting out of bed..."

"Talking to your boss here. I don't need to hear you were lazy at Uni."

"I wasn't lazy. I just chose my courses carefully. Those that started after 11AM..."

Behind them an olive green Army Land Rover pulled up, followed by a series of trucks. Robert walked forward and greeted the General who stepped out.

"Do you have any questions?"

Looking around, the General asked: "Why this street?"

Robert looked back down the row of dilapidated and uncared for housing. Odd wheelie bins lay on their sides, rubbish toppled out. Dog excrement was all over the pavements. Grass grew out of the gutters. Several houses had boarded up windows.

"Unfortunately..." Robert replied. "This street is nothing special. There are many like it. It is one of many where none of the residents is in work — at least — work that the government is aware of. Every single house has at least one person on Job Seekers Allowance. The head of every house receives housing benefit..."

"Received." Corrected Carla.

"Yes. Received. As of today – when we offer them work – they will stop receiving all benefits."

"But we're not going to evict them are we?" The General asked.

"No. None of the houses are owned. They're all rented from the local Council. If the residents do not start paying rent they will start accruing debt. We have some proposals for that but it may not prove workable. For now we just offer them the chance of a job and advise them of the consequences if they refuse it."

"And we are not to use force of any kind?"

"Your men may defend themselves if attacked but no guns and no killing anyone – if at all possible."

Robert had half intended the statement as a joke but looking at the General's steady gaze he wondered if it was a warning that he had needed to make.

"I will tell them to leave their grenades in the vehicles then." The General turned and walked away before Robert fully realised what he had said.

"Did he just out dry humour you?" Carla asked.

"The scary thing is – I don't know." Robert checked his watch. Quarter past Six. "Where are they?"

Robert and Carla watched as the General organised his men. Lining them up the street. They had no body armour on; no stab vests like the police wore. No utility belts with pepper spray or Tasers but they still managed to look intimidating.

Eventually he saw a convoy of three cars turn into the street and approach. They parked behind the Army trucks, away from Robert and Carla. "I may need you as a witness." Robert told her.

He walked up as a group of twelve men and women casually got out of the cars. Several were yawning. One young man looked as if he had not had time to wash – his hair sticking in strange directions.

364

"Which of you is Dorothy Birt?" Robert asked.

"I am. Why did you ask us to be here so early?"

Robert waited until they were all gathered round. "I expected you here at Six AM. Your instructions were clear. If you are late again you will be fired. No excuses. It will take us all morning to move these people and the rest of the day to transport them to their destination. We do not have time for delays caused by you."

"You can't speak to us like that!"

"As of this morning, Ms Birt, no-one on this street will be receiving benefits any longer. Your office was advised of this and that your roles would be changing to Work Program Co-ordinators. You will be training on the job as we do not have time for a full induction program. Your hours and pay will remain the same – as long as the Scottish people perceive you are giving them value for money. Are you aware how much I am being paid?"

Dorothy did not reply but Robert could see from her angry expression she did not care that he was only receiving minimum wage.

"In a few months someone in this nation will realise that some of our public servants are receiving minimum wage but others are earning as much as you – how much do you receive as a salary, Ms Birt?"

"I don't have to divulge that." She replied.

"No, of course not. Though even some of your colleagues may not know your salary banding is forty to sixty thousand. It is strange how as a country we keep these things so hidden. One person earning barely enough to feed their family – another able to afford... is that a Mercedes you were driving, Ms Birt?

"There is no Benefits office any more, Ms Birt. You are being given an opportunity to retrain in what I hope will become a rewarding career – enabling others into useful work. This will be a significant change for you but an even greater change for the people on this street. Some people here have never worked. They have no example except the one that we set them. I don't know if anyone was up early enough this morning to see you arrive late to your work. I was here before Six. The Army personnel you see were here: parked and out of their vehicles at Six exactly.

"If any of you feel unable to assist in the offer of

employment and relocation that we are carrying out today then I will accept your notice now and you may seek alternative employment – do I make myself clear?"

"We don't work for you. You can't threaten us like that!" Responded the young man with the unkempt hair.

"You work for the Scottish people. Have you all forgotten that? Before I started receiving minimum wage – my taxes paid your salary. Your taxes still contribute to your salary! I need to know if you are willing to work. If you are willing to help the people on this street find work. I need to know that you will set a good example for them. If you are able to do that then please join us. You have five minutes. Any delay longer than that and I will have you replaced with someone willing to do your job."

Robert turned and walked away, Carla hurrying to keep up.

"Don't you think you were too hard on them?"

"Life is hard for most people – that's something we forget all too easily. I hope they realise life is better in work than out of it. I need them and their skills and experience. But I can't afford to have people who resent being here persuading long term unemployed to enter the Work Program."

Before the five minutes were up all but Ms Birt and the young man had joined Robert and Carla standing with the soldiers. Checking his watch, Robert saw it was now almost Seven AM. Their five minutes were up and he addressed the assembled men and women.

"Thank you for coming here today. I asked for volunteers but realise that many of you may not have had a real choice. The media will be here shortly so I want to make this brief. We are here to offer the residents of this street the chance to enter the Work Program. I thank the General for his part in organising this stage. You soldiers will be training men and women – most of whom have never worked. You will be giving them useful skills including discipline and belief in themselves, as well as practical survival and construction skills."

"No-one will be forced into the Work Program but we need to make these people aware that they will no longer receive benefits or state handouts of any kind. If they refuse this opportunity – they are on their own."

"We will knock on every door. We will ask the residents to all come to the front door. We will read the prompts from the cards being handed out." Robert nodded at Carla and she began distributing laminated A5 cards to the former benefits team.

"The residents will have two hours to decide if they will join the Work Program and gather a bag of clothes. If they do not have a bag, one will be provided for them. The trucks will leave at Twelve Noon exactly, which may seem like a lot of time but we have the whole street to cover and I expect there will be... difficulties."

Looking at the former benefits team he said directly to them: "The Army is here to assist practically but also to transport the people. If anyone is threatened, withdraw from that house. We will not force anyone to join the Work Program. Do you have any questions?"

"Is that it?" Asked a white haired woman from the former benefits team.

Carla held up a handful of large envelopes. "You will have one of these packs to give each household. The name of the recipient of housing benefit is on the front. The pack explains everything in more detail."

"Can they all read?"

Robert and Carla shared a look. "I hadn't considered that," Robert confessed. "Tell them, how do we put this... We are available to explain anything. Tell them if they have any questions to ask us. Anything else?"

"If they become violent, what do we do?"

"Try not to antagonise them or insult them. Don't let it get to that stage. If you feel at all threatened, walk away from the house. We will work up the street together. Okay. Let's get started."

Robert held out his hand for an envelope and took one from Carla. It was addressed to Mrs Brown at number 2.

The house had no number plate. It had no garden gate. It had a bare plot of earth that might once have had grass but was now strewn with old tins and bottles. The windows were unboarded and the door plain, brown wood with no letter box, but with a peep hole at eye level. There was no door bell. Robert knocked three times, hard.

Above him he heard a window creek up.

"Whadoyawanathistime!"

He translated the stream of words. "I need to speak with every adult in the house." He called up.

"You know what time it is!"

Robert automatically looked at his watch before realising it was probably not worth replying.

"I'm here to offer you all work. Can you please get every adult up and to the front door."

The window slammed shut but there was no sound of movement from inside. Turning, Robert gave a wry grin to the others. "Any suggestions?"

"You didn't think this was going to be easy, did you?" Called the white haired woman. She spoke to Carla who sorted through her envelopes and handed her one. Robert watched as the woman walked up to the house next door. She gave several hard bangs and then stood back.

An upstairs window opened and a stream of abuse came out.

The woman stared up calmly and then shouted: "I'm from the benefits agency. The benefits of everyone in the house have been stopped. I need to speak with you right now!"

Even from where he stood, Robert could hear running and thumping down stairs. The door flung open and Robert wondered if he would have to help protect the woman.

"Whatdoyamean our benefits've been stopped!"

The woman held out the envelope. "Everyone's benefits have been stopped. We're here to offer you paying jobs."

"What's this?" The man asked looking suspiciously at the envelope.

"An explanation of why your benefits have been stopped and an offer of work for every adult in your home. It has all the details."

The man still did not take it. "I got money yesterday."

"Then you are one of the lucky ones. All payments have been frozen."

"Which benefits? Where are you from?"

"All benefits: Job seekers allowance; income support; housing benefit... everything."

"You can't do that."

"I'm not here to argue with you. I'm here to offer you a job and anyone else in your house." She looked at the envelope. "Mr Trent?"

The man looked behind the woman and saw the other benefits staff and behind them, the lined up soldiers. He gave a quick glance to his right and saw Robert. Looking back at the woman he asked: "What is this?"

She pushed the envelope at him and he finally took it.

"Read the information in there. You and everyone in your house have an hour to decide whether you will accept the work we are offering you. It will be paid at minimum wage and will be paid weekly. If you accept this offer you then have until 11:30 to pack a bag with clothes that will do you for a week. You will need warm clothes. The trucks leave at noon. If you are not on them you are on your own." She stepped back and then walked away leaving Mr Trent standing looking puzzled. She gave Robert a quick look as if to say – what are you waiting for and walked up to Carla and took another envelope.

Robert began banging on the door.

****

Irene was awake when someone started knocking on the door. She hadn't been able to sleep for long periods since she hurt her back. Even now, weeks after, she often felt her back ache after lying in bed all night.

She pulled on her dressing gown before she looked at the clock, then she felt a shiver all over. No-one ever knocked on her door this early. She eased open the curtain and looked outside. There were dozens of people on the street. Some standing talking, others walking up to her neighbours houses. She leaned out further and didn't recognise the man standing outside her house. At least it wasn't Neil.

She shouted in at Billy and Colin before going downstairs. She wanted them awake, just in case... Opening the door she saw a tall man with a smart suit holding out an envelope to her.

"What's this all about?" She asked.

"Miss Newlands?"

"Yes."

"The Scottish Government is offering you and everyone in your household a job. The envelope contains details of the offer. As we are providing you with a paying job, we will no longer be providing you with benefits. You have the choice this morning to accept the offer or to reject it. If you accept you will be taken today to a training camp. If you reject the offer then you will have to find your own means of providing for yourself. Do you have any questions?"

"I hurt my back, I don't think I can do manual work."

"That's okay. We will have plenty of different roles for people." He stepped a bit closer, pushing the envelope at her.

"I have a lot of debt. I've some people helping me sort it out but... I need enough coming in so I can pay it off."

The man let the envelope drop as he considered this. "It's my intention that everyone who works will eventually be able to earn a living wage. At the moment we don't have the budget for that but I will be pushing for changes to ensure everyone can survive on what they're paid. As for your debt... If you are paying it off then as far as I'm concerned the government should support you, even if it means you stop paying interest."

Irene folded her arms. "And why should the government listen to you?"

The man put his head to one side. "I'm Robert Castle."

"Should I care?"

"Apparently not." He smiled. "I take it you didn't vote for my party at the election."

"I've never voted for anyone."

"You should start. In fact, I'm going to change the law so everyone has to vote. I want to help you, Miss Newlands. The best way I can think of helping you is to give you a job. But if you have a better way then you need to tell people about it and vote for your plan. Otherwise the government will make changes that affect your life and it will be too late for you to do anything about it.

"Like today..." He held out the envelope again. "Please take it. You have an hour to read and decide if you want to accept the offer. If you accept you have until 11:30 to pack a bag with clothes to take with you for the next week. Make sure they are warm."

Irene finally took the envelope. "You're really offering me and my boys a job?"

"Yes."

She closed the door on the strange man and turned to see Billy and Colin looking down at her from the top of the stairs. "You hear that?"

"They nodded."

"Get packing then." She went to put the kettle on.

Ten minutes later she'd read the letter. It was short and to the point. No more benefits would be paid but they would get a government job including training. The job would be decided based on aptitude. She thought she knew what that meant. They would also get a say in what job to take, though with only two refusals. If they refused three different jobs they would be excluded from the program and have to fend for themselves.

It would be okay though, so long as they didn't try and force her to do a heavy job.

Colin came downstairs. "I don't have a bag."

"Didn't you have a sports bag at school?"

"That's falling to bits."

Irene sighed. "Everything's falling to bits, Colin. If you don't have anything else, use it. Maybe you'll have some money to buy a new one next week."

His eyes lit up. "I can get new clothes!" He dashed back upstairs.

Maybe pay some rent, Irene thought to herself. Though, they would be going away for a week. What was that all about?

She went and got her mobile phone and turned it on.

"Shona? ... It's Quarter past Seven, why? ... Oh, sorry. We've been offered jobs! The man from the government said they're going to stop our benefits but they are going to pay us... He said his name was Castle... No, I'm serious, there's dozens of people out in the street, they're going to every house. He said we've got an hour to accept the offer and then they're going to take us away somewhere for a week."

Irene listened to Shona repeat that she wasn't making any sense. Unsure how to convince her she got up and walked outside. Looking around she saw the man who had knocked on her door standing down the street talking to some people. Walking up to him she offered him the phone.

"My debt counsellor doesn't believe you've offered me a job."

The man turned. "Miss... Newlands?"

"Irene. Will you talk to her?"

"What's her name?"

"Shona Carstairs."

He took the phone and carefully held it up to his ear. "This is Robert Castle, is that Shona? ... Yes, the Robert Castle." He emphasised 'the' while rolling his eyes. "You could turn on your TV. Both BBC and STV were invited here this morning. ... Actually, I've a fair bit still to do this morning so I'm just going to hand you back to Irene." He handed her back the phone.

Irene thanked him and then walked back to her house, chatting to Shona about what she could see.

Then Shona interrupted: "Are you wearing a green dressing gown?"

Irene paused in front of the door. "Yes..."

"You're on TV! No, the other way... That's it! Wave!"

Irene finally saw what had to be a TV camera on a man's shoulder. It wasn't pointed straight at her but seemed to be filming the length of the street. She waved in bemusement before heading inside.

"Is he from the government then?" Irene asked.

"You don't know? That's the First Minister!"

"I thought it was another guy..."

"Well, it's Robert Castle now. I voted for him, well, for his party. Look, don't worry about the repayments. If he's offering you a job then take it. We can sort out the detail later."

****

After Irene had walked out of earshot, Robert turned to Carla. "Make a note of her name, Irene Newlands. I want to keep an eye on her."

"Is she trouble?"

"No, she said she was paying off her debts. She has a debt counsellor. How many people living in this neighbourhood do you think could say that?"

"Okay."

"Also, maybe we need to think about going further with the Jubilee idea. It's one thing to clear a country of its debt, but if our citizens don't get a fresh start then how do they benefit?"

****

At around 8:45 one of the former benefits staff was attacked. Robert was several houses away and heard shouting. He turned and saw one of the team fall back. He left the woman he had been talking to standing in her doorway and rushed over. Before he could get there, two soldiers had grabbed a man and others were surrounding the team member on the ground. One called "Medic!"

Robert pushed through and saw the man on the ground had

a slash across his shirt with a growing red stain along the length. He felt himself be pulled back out of the way as a medic was let through.

"Everyone back off, give us some room." The medic shouted.

Robert watched as he cut open the shirt. "It's not bleeding much but we'll get the wound cleaned and dressed."

The man appeared to be in shock. "Am I going to be okay?" He asked.

"Yes. To be on the safe side, we'll get you taken to hospital and get you some injections."

"I hate injections."

"It's better than the alternative."

"What's the alternative?"

"You don't want to know." The medic expertly dabbed at the wound.

"Has anyone called an ambulance," Robert asked.

"Not yet, Sir" A soldier next to him replied.

Robert pulled out his phone and made the call. As he did he studied the man who had made the attack. He was bare from the waist up revealing tattoos over all of one arm and across half his chest. A mixture of patterns and symbols that meant nothing to Robert. He was still struggling against the soldiers.

When he had confirmed an ambulance was on its way, Robert stood before the man. "Why did you attack him?" He asked.

"The prick said he was talking my benefits away."

"He didn't take them away – you did."

"What the hell are you talking about!"

"Did you vote in the referendum?"

"What referendum?"

"If you didn't vote – then you gave up your rights to your benefits all by yourself."

"What referendum?" The man demanded.

"Last week. We voted to stop all benefits payments. Replace them with a Work Program."

"No-one told me."

For an instant, Robert wondered if he might be telling the truth, then he remembered the instruction that had been sent out that all benefits agencies advise recipients of the referendum. It was possible he had not got the message. Possible he didn't even know about the election... He hardened his heart against the man. If the man did not want to participate in society, did not care about who was in power or what they decided – who was he to complain when they stopped giving handouts.

He dialled 999 one more time.

"What's the emergency?"

"Police." Robert said.

****

"What's the problem?" Robert asked Joe. He had finally begun to remember some of the former benefit staff names.

Joe just gestured towards the woman he was standing beside.

"What's going to happen to my stuff?"

"Your stuff?" Robert could not see any stuff.

"In my house! You're telling me I need to leave my stuff behind. What's going to happen to it?"

"It will stay here, I guess." Robert shrugged.

"You guess? What's going to happen to it?"

"I, well, what do you think is going to happen to it?"

"It'll get stolen! You can't leave anything round here. Don't trust anyone." The woman glared at one of her neighbours who was pulling a heavy suitcase out to the street.

"Do you have insurance?" Robert asked.

"You're kidding right?"

"No."

"Course I don't have insurance! Who do you think I am?"

Robert didn't answer that. "Give me a minute." He told her.

Walking up to Carla who still had a small pile of envelopes in her hands, Robert wondered what was inside the woman's house that she thought was so valuable.

"We have a woman who is worried about stuff in her house being stolen while she is away."

Carla put her head to one side. "Seems like a reasonable fear.

"She doesn't have insurance. I just never considered this."

"What are you going to do?"

"I don't know. Any ideas?"

She shook her head.

Robert walked back to the woman. "What's your name?"

"What's yours?"

He was taken aback. "Robert. Robert Castle."

"That sounds familiar." The woman looked more closely at him. "Have you been on T.V.?"

Robert nodded.

"Do you play the trombone?"

It took a few seconds for the slightly disconnected link to click. "Different Castle. So..." He held out his hand. "Robert..."

She gingerly took his hand. "Margaret."

"Margaret, we are not here to force you to leave your stuff behind. I don't know if you can carry any of it with you..."

She shook her head. "Carry a sofa? Are you out of your mind? It took both my sons to lift the T.V. in. No. I can't carry it."

Sofa and T.V. Robert didn't want to know any more. "This is your choice, Margaret. We are offering you paid work but you will have to leave your home and I'm not sure when you'll next be back. If you stay, then you will need to find your own work. It is quite possible you can do that, but I don't know – I certainly can only guarantee the work I am offering today. You need to understand that you will no longer receive any form of benefit or support from the government, whether your local council or national."

"I'm not leaving my stuff."

"Okay, Margaret. That's your choice. Did Joe give you the envelope?"

Joe nodded.

"Read it. You still have time if you change your mind."

Out of ear-shot, Robert asked Joe: "A sofa and T.V.? How can she afford those on benefits?"

"Do you know how much money people received – are still receiving?"

"Not enough to be able to afford luxury items."

"Yet some of the people on this street will have a large plasma or LCD T.V. and a nice sofa to sit and watch it on. You'll find computers and laptops; they have the latest model mobile phone. Often they dress in tracksuits and might look dowdy to you or me but look closer and it's designer labels they are wearing. There are people here who are poor but there also seems to be a lot of people who apparently are doing well for themselves. How they do it is beyond me. For years we've been told not to look too closely, not to judge. It wasn't worth the effort, wasn't worth the aggravation and assaults when people were challenged. But, you ask me, questions need to be asked. Why should a whole section of society have their luxuries paid for by the state?"

****

At Ten to Twelve, half the street's residents were sitting in trucks. Their suitcases and carry bag between their knees.

"Health and Safety would have a field day if they saw this." Robert said to Carla.

"They will." She promised. "I'm sure you'll deal with them the way you deal with everything else."

"What's that supposed to mean?"

"My way or the highway."

"I'm not like that."

She didn't bother to reply.

Robert walked over to the General. "Are you ready to go?"

"Twelve Noon. On the dot."

"Good. It's important we send a clear message. Do you have a bull-horn?"

Robert took the offered loud speaker and raised it, walking away from the General. There were still scattered groups of people standing about. Others watching from the windows and doorways.

"You have five minutes to board the trucks. If you do not have time to pack, work clothes will be provided for you. If you do not accept our offer of work today, you will need to find jobs by yourself. The Job Centre will still be available and will advertise work but there will be no more signing on for Job Seekers Allowance."

Out of one doorway two young men suddenly ran out chased by an older woman.

"Go on! Get out there. I've had enough of you two lazing about. You can go with them or sleep on the street, I don't care." She turned, went back inside and slammed the door. The two men stood uncertainly on the pavement.

Robert walked up to them. "Get on the truck." He said.

One of them gave him a look but they complied, climbing up into the nearest truck.

"When you are ready, General." Robert called.

Robert headed for his own car, waved at the benefits staff to gather round. "Next street tomorrow. You'll have other staff to train up. Got a lot of locations to cover in the next few months. Later we'll drive you up to one of the camps. It will be good for you to see where we're sending them."

He offered lifts to those left behind by Dorothy Birt. Following the trucks out the street, Robert looked back to see clumps of people watching them go. "You're on your own now." He sighed.

****

CHAPTER FORTY EIGHT

They called it Reboot Camp. For the last month they had been driven to the same location every Monday morning, a gently sloping hillside South of Edinburgh. The first day they had turned up at Four PM and soldiers had been on hand to show them how to erect tents. Each person was given a sleeping bag and wash kit and set of work clothes which included a warm jacket. Irene had hers on immediately.

Then they were all treated to a barbeque. Some of the people on their work gang had complained there was no beer but Irene was secretly pleased. She'd never seen any good come out of men getting drunk.

The wind was cold and most people shut themselves away in their tents before it got dark. Billy and Colin had pitched their tent away from hers and for the first time since they had come into the world, Irene was on her own.

She lay on hard and lumpy ground for half an hour before getting out of her sleeping bag, pulling her jacket on and going outside. The tents were all scattered about with plenty of distance between them. Nearby a woman was standing, the glow of a cigarette red against sky so clear that Irene found herself looking straight up.

After a few minutes, Irene realised someone was beside her.

"Kind of desolate, isn't it. You want a smoke?"

The woman had walked over. Irene shook her head.

"They didn't say we'd be out in the country like this. I only brought one pack of fags with me. Don't know what I'm going to do if I can't get any more tomorrow."

"It doesn't seem real."

The woman lit up another cigarette. "Oh, it's real alright. Clever set up. Get us all away from our homes, isolated and out of our comfort zone. Feed us a good meal... Tomorrow we're going to pay. This ain't going to be no holiday camp."

"We're here to work though."

"And they'll make us work. Will be interesting to see who lasts the week. There're a couple people here who are going to need more than cigarettes to get them through. I'm Vicky, by the way."

"Irene. What do you think they're going to get us doing?"

"I've no idea. I expected to end up in a factory. This has thrown me."

"I've never been out in the country."

Vicky looked as if she didn't believe her. "Seriously? Never?"

Shaking her head, Irene looked away. She could just make out the tops of mountains on the opposite side of the valley, against the sky. "Never had the money. Or any way of getting out here. Can't just take a bus."

"Well, you can but I wouldn't choose to." Vicky took one last deep drag on her cigarette and then dropped it, crushing it into the ground with her boot. "I'm going to try and get some sleep. Can't believe they didn't provide us with any mats."

Irene went back to her own tent. After some experimenting she found she could curl up with the jacket as a pillow. She didn't think she'd get much sleep though. She was right.

The next morning they were all woken up at Six AM, given an hour to eat and wash and were expected to be ready for Seven. The same soldiers who had helped them the previous evening got them to line up in several rows.

Irene shared a glance with Vicky as the senior soldier walked out in front of them.

"I am Sergeant Tanner and my platoon will be responsible for your first phase of training. This is Reboot Camp 72. There are one hundred similar camps around Scotland and the expectation is this number will rise until everyone who needs work, has work.

"We are responsible for training you and for your safety.

You are responsible for learning quickly and working hard. You are responsible for each other. As you learn and master skills you will be taught new ones. After this phase, civilians will be brought in to teach you trades. You will have the opportunity to try and learn many of them. If you want to specialise there will be opportunity for that later.

"We will work you hard every day. There will be no forty hour week here, you will work until the job is done. There will be no drinking or drugs while you are on site and you will present yourselves sober for work at Six AM every Monday. Do you have any questions?"

"What's to stop us leaving?" One man asked.

"Leave any time you want. Edinburgh is sixty miles in that direction, though if you walk out on the job part way through the week you will be treated as having quit. Remember the government is no longer providing benefits. In addition you will not be paid for that week and will lose an opportunity to choose additional training."

"Where's the nearest pub?" Several people laughed.

"As I said, there will be no drinking or drugs on site. Leaving the site for any reason shall be considered a decision to resign."

"Why here? There's nothing to learn a trade on."

"You will be constructing a building. Afterwards there will be additional work including farming."

"Where can I charge my phone?"

At this the sergeant smiled. "If you want to take a selfie, I suggest you do so today."

"What will the building be used for?" Irene felt her heart beating.

The Sergeants smile remained but Irene thought it took on a distant quality. He took a step backwards and half turned away, looking down the valley.

"If you want it to, the building, this valley, could both become your home." He turned back to them. "The government has apportioned areas of land of sufficient size for small communities to become self sufficient. It will be hard work and will take years before you are fully autonomous, but if you want, you can carve out your own destiny."

"Why would I want to live on a hillside in the middle of nowhere?" Another man said.

"That's not for me to answer. However, this is as good a

place as any to learn some new skills. Today we'll be working on foundations... Literally."

And they did. All day digging through heather into peat, lifting ever more heavy shovels into barrows and wheeling those to a growing pile.

Irene worked alongside Vicky who kept a steady stream of banter going with the people around them. They got five minutes rest every hour and half an hour break after three hours. By mid afternoon, Irene was just going through the motions. Her back ached. She could hardly lift the shovel, let alone the barrow. She could see others were also struggling. Eventually she went to speak with the Sergeant.

"We're not used to this sort of work. Wouldn't we be better taking a longer break, or working shorter hours until we're used to it?"

"I've never heard of anyone learning to do something by resting. You're right, this is all new to you but you will learn to cope with it faster than you realise. Each of you has already done more today than you probably thought possible. Take a look."

Irene did and saw the once colourful hillside was black where they had dug into the peat. A massive rectangle with the peat they had dug out piled up further down.

"Why does it need to be so big?"

"The plan is to build a structure big enough that it can sleep eighty people. This will become a temporary home while individual properties are built and eventually will be used as a community hall."

"There's only forty people here..."

The Sergeant nodded. "But some of you have left families back home. Children. Also, there will be other waves of work gangs being sent out and some of them will join you here."

"Will you be training them as well?"

"Maybe you will..."

Irene felt a shiver at that thought. Her training people? She hadn't even been able to train up her boys. But, what if..." She walked back to Vicky.

"What did he say?" Vicky asked.

Irene didn't know how to answer.

That evening they ate late in the evening. When they finished work at Five PM they were led to a kitchen tent and given tasks to help prepare a meal. It took them several hours to prepare and cook the meal. Neither the gang nor the soldiers were in the best of moods that evening. After that they agreed with the soldiers that gang members would take it in turns to prepare the evening meal during the afternoon.

It took them three days to fully clear the peat and dirt from the site. On the Friday morning several trucks drove up as they were having breakfast. The rest of the day was spent unloading tools and materials to start work on the foundations. A huge canvas tent was erected on the flattest piece of ground and the materials and tools carried in to protect them from rain.

Irene was expecting to be driven back that evening but another barbeque was planned and they were told they'd be driven back on the Saturday morning.

"Why not tonight?" Several people asked. They were all sitting on the heather waiting for burgers and sausages to cook.

Irene saw the Sergeant gesture to one of the soldiers who walked off to the kitchen tent.

"Because we are going to celebrate your achievement – your first full week of work. For some of you, the first time you've ever really worked in your lives."

Irene looked across at Billy and Colin who both looked as if they could have slept standing up.

"And..." The Sergeant continued. "You have cleared the way for the foundation and are ready to start work on that next week."

Two soldiers came back carrying plain cardboard boxes and set them beside the Sergeant.

"Now I'm told the First Minister wanted to send you a message." The Sergeant continued. "And I have to say this will be the only time such a message will be delivered."

Irene leaned forward as the Sergeant crouched down and opened one of the boxes. He stood up, two bottles in his hands. "Well done everyone!" He handed over the bottles to the two nearest gang members.

The beer was quickly distributed, just enough for every gang member and soldier to get one bottle each. Irene couldn't normally afford to drink and preferred wine but she clinked bottles with Vicky and Jack, who was on her other side, and took a sip.

She was exhausted, badly needed a shower and had wanted nothing more than to crawl into her bed but as they talked and eventually ate that evening, she began to think that maybe she might miss this.

Mid way through the second week the sky opened and work on the foundations was halted. At one point Irene began to wonder if their tents would wash away but the hillside soaked up most of the water. They sheltered inside a large storage tent for most of that day and were given a chance to look at plans for the building and eventual community.

When the rain lessened they were back out on the hill, learning why foundations were constructed the way they were at the same time as building them.

A farmer was brought in one day to talk with them about growing crops and managing animals. Irene couldn't see herself ever wanting to look after cows or pigs and her first week of digging peat hadn't made her love the thought of working the land, but the farmer had a way of telling stories about life on a farm that had her laughing along with the rest.

When she had a chance she asked him: "None of us have ever worked on a farm, what chance do we have of growing our own food?"

"People have been growing food for thousands of years. It's the most natural thing in the world. That and weeds of course. You plant a seed in the ground and months later you have barley or oats or a beetroot – not all from the same seed. If you choose to stay here then you'll have a lot of people helping you, giving you advice, training. No-one wants you to fail and if you work hard, there's every reason to think you can make a life for yourselves.

"I wish we'd had the support you're going to get. But then, maybe if we'd demanded it sooner we would have received it."

While they let the cement harden in the foundations they dug a deeper hole for a septic tank. Irene was as amused as Billy and Colin to find out they were planning to put something called a fuel cell on it that would provide power from the methane given off.

More trucks arrived carrying massive wooden panels, pre fitted with insulation. They were given basic training in joinery, almost all of it on the job. As with the foundations, everything they did was carefully supervised. They managed to cut plenty of planks of wood to the wrong size but the joiners either managed to find another use for the planks or correct the mistakes.

Vicky had brought a small camping stove and kettle back with her and while they could have used the kitchen tent in the evenings, Irene found she enjoyed the ritual of heating up their own water and brewing tea.

"I don't know how much I'm learning." Irene confessed one evening. "We spend so little time on each phase and by the time it's over, I still don't understand half of what they've told us."

"I don't think that's what you need to worry about." Vicky pulled out a cigarette and lit up.

"What do I need to worry about?"

"Nothing." Vicky laughed. "They're paying us to learn. To work as well, sure, but we are learning."

"I don't think I am."

Vicky took a long pull on the cigarette so the tip flared bright orange. "Why do you think we've got soldiers supervising us?"

"We're on a mountain?"

"Because they understand the need for discipline. Do you think that any of us would get up at Six AM every morning if we didn't have to? They're not training us properly in these skills, just giving us a taster, finding out what we're good at, what we like doing. The real training is making us get up early every morning and working hard every day. Three weeks we've been doing this and we're starting to get used to it."

"So you're saying this is all pointless, what we're doing?"

"No. None of it's pointless. It all has a meaning, just..." Vicky stubbed out her cigarette. "Don't expect to finish this job knowing how to do everything, that's not the point."

"Then I don't know what the point is. They're saying we should have finished work on this building in a few weeks. What am I supposed to do then? If I haven't learnt any skills, what use would I be in a community? If I go back home, I still won't be able to get a job."

"People apprentice for years to become a joiner or brickie or plumber. We've only been here a few weeks and had only days on each phase. What you need to ask yourself is would you like to learn more about anything you've seen or done. Could you see yourself doing that for longer?"

"I don't know. I like being part of this. I'm going to be sad when it ends, I guess."

"Maybe it doesn't have to end. They are creating a community here. We could stay and be part of that. Help building the houses."

Irene shook her head. "I'm not sure. I don't know if I'm ready to do that."

****

CHAPTER FORTY NINE

Back in her own house that weekend, Irene found a letter addressed to her with an official logo saying it was from the Scottish Parliament. After she read it, she called Shona.

"They want to speak to me! Have I done something wrong?"

Shona got Irene to read out the letter.

"No, nothing wrong." Shona told her. "They want to find out how you're getting on. What you think about the training program."

"I feel I'm not learning anything. What if they think I'm not up to it? Would they take me off?"

"Why do you think you're not learning anything?"

Irene told her what she'd told Vicky and what Vicky had said.

"Vicky's right, they can't expect you to learn a trade in only a few days. No, this is an opportunity for you to tell them what you think, maybe even suggest things they could do better."

"Like what?"

"They're paying you while you're on the work gang but you're getting a lot less than you were on benefits. The Council have agreed to waive the rent while you are on the work gang and you don't have to pay council tax either, but you still have bills to pay and you don't know what will happen if the training changes to a permanent job. But that's what I would say. I've not been out there with you."

"I guess I would like a sleeping mat. I don't know. I'm enjoying it but I just don't know what I'm learning."

"Tell them that. Tell them what you're enjoying. Tell them why. That's all they need to know."

****

Monday morning, instead of being picked up by the truck, Irene was collected by a black car. She hadn't known what to wear so had just worn her work clothes. They were muddy and a bit smelly but she never had time to wash and dry them at the weekends.

Driven up to the parliament building she was met by a young woman with straight dark hair, cut at her shoulders. She was wearing a smart dress with black strips at the sides and a cream strip at the front and back that was supposed to make the wearer look slimmer. She didn't need it.

Irene immediately felt out of place though the woman smiled warmly and introduced herself as Carla. She said it was good to meet her again. Irene couldn't think where they would have met.

Walking through the hallways, Irene felt herself tensing up. She didn't want to make a fool of herself but was already worried she looked so out of place with men and women in suits, some woman also in smart dresses. The women all had makeup on and fancy hair styles. Irene had just about managed to brush out her tangles that morning.

Carla showed her into a room with a large desk. "The First Minister will be in shortly." She excused herself.

The First Minister... Not Mr Castle or even Robert. Irene swallowed, closed her eyes and tried to breathe.

"Miss Newlands! Good to see you again." The First Minister shook her hand and gestured for her to sit down. Carla also came back into the room with a notepad and she began writing immediately.

"May I call you Irene?" He asked. "Call me Robert."

She nodded though she didn't know if she could think of him as just Robert.

"You're a month into the work gang programme." He said. "I wanted to ask you how you think it's going."

"Why me?"

He leaned forward. "Because no-one else came out to ask me

to speak to their debt counsellor."

"What difference does that make?"

"You were doing something about your debts before we turned up. That shows integrity, commitment."

Irene thought back. "I didn't do anything. The CAP people offered me help. They looked through my paperwork."

"You said yes. If more people said yes when they were offered help they would have far less problems."

"I guess that's like on the work gang." Irene thought out loud. "I don't know anything so I'm always asking people to show me how to do things again. Some of the men are too thick or too stubborn to ask. They don't get it any more wrong than I do but maybe they would find it easier if they were more willing to ask."

"I would say most men are like that..." Carla said, giving a subtle nod in the First Minister's direction.

Irene waited to see if he would ask her anything else but he seemed content to wait.

"I don't really know what you're looking for." She eventually said. "Why you've brought me here. I don't know how to build a house. I'm not sure I really want to do that anyway. We had a famer in and I know I couldn't look after pigs or cows. I've started enjoying being part of the gang but we're only going to be together for a few more weeks and I don't know what happens next."

"What would you like to happen next?" The First Minister asked.

Irene thought for a minute. She had been wondering about that since talking with Vicky. "They said there will be other communities, other work gangs starting up. I'd quite like to join one of those."

"Why is that?"

"To see if I've actually learnt anything. Maybe to ask all the questions I never thought to ask the first time round. Maybe to see some more of Scotland."

The First Minister nodded. "All good reasons. I'm sure that will be possible. It will be good for the work gangs to have experienced people join them. Our plan is to keep offering people new opportunities. They can move from job to job at a minimum wage for as long as they like. The work gangs are a start but we'll be setting up similar paid training programs with companies around Scotland."

"At the same wage?"

"Yes."

"I'm getting less than I did on benefits. I spoke to my debt counsellor this weekend and she said that if the council starts charging me rent and council tax again, I won't be able to afford food."

The First Minister and Carla shared a look.

"Would you be willing to share what you owe and what your expenses are with us?" He asked.

"Sure."

"Carla, could you arrange a call with Irene's debt counsellor before she leaves." The First Minister sighed. "There are a lot of things I can do and I lot that I can't. The training programs are a risk but at least by paying a minimum wage people are getting a chance to stand on their own feet. There are some families with two children old enough to work, still living at home where they will be bringing in £40,000 a year under this program. That is a decent amount of money. You have two sons yourself, don't you Irene?"

"They didn't rack up my debts."

"No, but they were still living in your home when you started on the work gang. I think it would be reasonable of you to charge them some rent now they are earning."

Irene felt uncomfortable at that suggestion. "And if they move out?"

"I think it would be reasonable to ask them to help. Think about it. I know it's not enough. I can only afford to live on minimum wage because most of my expenses are paid and my wife is working. It needs to change.

"We will be encouraging employers to consider employing people at a living wage. If an employer realises they have someone with the skills and commitment to do a job well, most will gladly pay a decent wage to keep that person.

"But if we feel an employer is just taking advantage of cheap labour then we'll pull out of that contract. Longer term I'm intending to nationalise some industries. That will allow me to employ people at a living wage without risking people's time being wasted by employers like that."

Robert leaned back and stretched. "Anyway. I'm talking too much. I want to hear what you think about the work gangs.

What you think we could do better, or different."

"We've already changed a few things." Irene said. "The second day was awful. None of us got to eat until Nine. It was way too late. We started taking it in turns..."

****

Irene was driven back to the site the next morning, dropped off with a group of electricians. She had spent the trip quizzing them about what they were going to do. Apparently none of the communities were going to be connected to the National Grid. Instead several renewable energy sources were going to be installed as well as the heat pump.

One of the electricians lifted a wind turbine out of its box to show her. "It's a vertical generator. Gives you 200 Watts maximum output. We'll be installing ten of these at your site."

Irene held up her hand and made a mouthing gesture. "I'm hearing words but all I get is you're giving us ten."

He laughed. "Vertical just means it stands upright. Turns round just like those fans you see on the top of vans sometimes."

Irene nodded.

"You've seen horizontal turbines..."

She shook her head. "Words..."

"Big fans, like a desk fan. They have fields full of them in parts of the country. Those can produce Kilowatts. Okay, okay..." He said as she made the mouthing gesture again. "You have a light bulb: sixty watts. One of these..." He pointed down at the turbine at his feet. "Can power three light bulbs and still have a few watts spare. An efficient fridge will use 500 watts but not all the time. However, when you first turn a fridge on you may need a lot more watts. Maybe even five times as much."

Irene struggled to do the maths in her head. "So ten of these wouldn't be enough to start a fridge?"

"Not by themselves. And you'd need some wind. If you have a calm day then you get no power."

"So your food goes off?"

"The fridge keeps cool for a while as long as you don't open the door too much. We'll also be installing twenty solar panels on the roof. Those will also give you 200 watts per unit and will produce that fairly consistently throughout the day. Then finally you'll have the fuel cell."

"Will that be enough?"

Another electrician answered: "You won't be able to install a plasma TV but you'll be warm and have enough power for the essentials. We're also putting in some batteries to store some of the power generated. That should keep you going on calm, cloudy days."

After they arrived, Irene studied the site with a fresh perspective. She had thought the roof of the building a strange design, only angled in one direction. Now she could see this was to the South giving the whole roof available to the solar panels.

Higher up the hill they had cleared more peat and sunk foundations to which the wind turbines could be attached. Irene had noticed it was windier the higher up she went and had wondered why they were working up there. Now she knew.

A large part of the valley would be claimed by the community. While the peat in the hill wasn't great for growing some crops, there was better soil in the valley and the peat could be used for some vegetables. There were also plans to prepare a community garden near the building and for greenhouses and cold frames.

That night she found Billy and Colin outside their tent and sat down with them. "I've been thinking it's about time I started charging you boys rent."

"What for?" Billy asked.

"For paying the bills back home. I can't afford to keep the house on my own."

"We're hardly there."

"The bills need paid whether we're there or not. We can't go to the food bank anymore. I can't afford to keep paying for you both."

"Maybe we should move out then." Billy said, looking at Colin. "They told us we can stay here at weekends if we want. We don't have to go back."

"You would want to do that?"

Colin looked unsure.

"We'll have electricity soon." Billy said. "They're not charging us to stay here."

"I don't think they'll keep paying you if you stay here."

"Then we can live off the land. That's what they're teaching us to do, isn't it."

"If that's what you want... Colin?"

"They said I could learn a trade. They'll keep training me while they pay me. I might have to move around though."

Irene stood. "I might have to as well."

****

CHAPTER FIFTY

"Mr Castle?"

Robert recognised the voice of Allan Gillies on the phone. "Chief Constable. Have you any news?"

"Yes, but it will not be palatable. Can you drive over? I'd rather not speak on the phone."

Robert cancelled his schedule and was at the Strathclyde Police Headquarters in under two hours.

"What can you tell me?"

"It seems Mr Taggart was rather too canny for his own good. I've not yet been able to confirm this for certain but I believe the sources are good. It seems a hit was taken out on Mr Taggart by individuals or organisations who lost rather a lot of money when you won the election and then when you implemented your Land Grab policy."

"But why not target me? Why Gordon? He was hardly a public figure."

"As I said, I have not yet confirmed this, but rumour has it that Mr Taggart placed several high value standard and spread bets – at significant risk to himself. Had you failed to win the election, failed to become First Minister, failed to implement your policies, he would have lost a lot of money."

"Gordon was an elder in our church. I didn't know he had a gambling problem."

"He didn't. He was very good at it. So good that your

victories netted him several million."

Robert whistled. "And if he had lost those bets?"

"I think we could both agree he did. As I said, I still have to confirm this but it seems likely to explain the shooting."

"Any success in identifying the shooters?"

"None so far. It was a highly professional job. We have CCTV of the car from the first attempt but the plates were fake and we have not been able to find the vehicle. It went onto the Motorway and never came off – at least where we have cameras to check."

****

Irene worked on two more community halls that year and stayed in one for several months after it was completed, learning how to grow food. Like the farmer had said, it was the simplest thing in the world to plant a seed. It was everything else that was hard work.

A local farmer drove his tractor up and ploughed two fields for them. As he joined them for their evening meal, they discussed options for bartering use of the tractor for their help as labourers. They also asked him how much it would cost to buy their own plough or tractor. That cost made Irene gasp.

"Though you could possibly get a horse drawn plough made." He told them. "But then you have to look after the horse or hire out a horse. Something to look into."

All of them were conscious that if they stayed in the community, once they were established they would no longer have money coming in. Somehow they would have to pay for new purchases or repairs by themselves.

"I don't know why that worries you all." Said Aaron after the discussion had gone on for some time. "It's no different to how it used to be and communities survived. Some even thrived and became very wealthy."

"How can you become wealthy just growing your own crops?" Someone asked.

"It can be tough as a farmer, can't it?" Aaron directed at the farmer.

The farmer agreed.

"One family on their own will always struggle but we don't have to be on our own. We're building a community here. That's what we used to have in Scotland a thousand years ago. Communities working together. Everybody working for the common good. Men used to leave for a few months to earn money at the fishing or the whaling or to work in a factory and then they'd bring that money home.

"You still see that happening but it's become reversed. People come here from other countries to work and send money home. There's no reason we can't do the same.

"I worked on a Kibbutz in Israel for a couple of years. Those communities have an interesting history. Some of those communities set up their own factories and made themselves millionaires. Whatever you think about Israel or Gaza now, the fact is that small communities of people transformed swamps and deserts into fertile gardens. If they could achieve that, why can't we?"

****

They listened to the radio when they wanted to catch up with the outside world. One evening several of them were sitting outside when they heard shouting from inside the hall.

Irene ran with the others to find out what was happening.

"They're writing off our debts!"

"What do you mean?" Asked Irene.

"The government, they've said that anyone who joins a community can have their debt wiped clean. They get a fresh start. They're calling it a jubilee."

Irene made her way to her bunk and sat down. Almost all the money she'd earned over the past months had gone on paying off the debt and bills for her house. Chris and Shona had made sure she got money for food and clothes but she hadn't been able to save a penny. It would have taken years to pay off the debt at the rate she was going but now she was free.

She lay down so no-one would see her cry, listened to the excited voices in the hall and thought of her strange meeting with the First Minister.

****

The announcement made them all think hard about what they wanted to do. Some people decided to settle where they

395

were. Others wanted to find somewhere better.

When Aaron said he was going to apply to move to a new community on Rannoch Moor that was about to start building houses around the hall, Irene knew she wanted to go with him.

"It's going to be a tough place." Aaron told her.

"I can do tough."

"People have tried starting communities there before but found it too difficult."

"What were you saying about Kibbutz? If they can do it..."

Two weeks later Irene, Aaron and three others travelled the long road North to Rannoch Moor.

"Why do they always site these communities so far from the main road?" Irene asked as the truck jolted from side to side.

"It forces a feeling of independence." Replied Aaron. "If you're on a main road there's a temptation to catch a bus or hitch a lift into town."

"We have to do that sometimes anyway. No community is ever going to be totally independent."

Aaron didn't answer, just grinned at her as the truck continued to bounce.

Building the houses was no less hard work than the halls had been. A hole for the foundations still needed to be dug out for each house; concrete and brickwork was built up; panels had to be erected quickly and the roof attached while wind and rain held off. Every day was tiring but each evening Irene took herself away to work on the community garden, weeding and checking the progress of small seedlings.

One morning Irene woke earlier than normal to bright sunlight. She dressed quietly and went outside for a moment's peace before the community all began to make their usual noise.

Walking round to the garden she saw a roe deer in the middle of the plot, head down, eating at the seedlings. Without thinking she shouted.

The deer raised its head.

Irene took a couple of steps towards it and waved her arms. "Get out of there! Go on!"

The deer lowered its antlers and took a step towards her.

Suddenly, Irene realised she knew very little about deer. She also couldn't think how far it was back into the hall.

From behind her she heard a rushing noise coming closer. Were there two of them? She turned as Aaron charged past her and shouted "ENOUGH!" He was holding a wide broom out in front of him, waving it about.

The deer turned quickly and almost with one bound was out of the garden and then quickly away.

Aaron lowered his broom and turned to her. She saw he was still in his pyjamas. "In some parts of Scotland they only have rabbits to worry about." He stood catching his breath. "We might need to get a deer fence put up."

"How did you know I was out here?"

"I heard you shout."

"You've got no shoes on..."

He looked down at his bare feet. "Apparently not."

"Was that safe, charging it with that broom?"

"Safe? Probably not the best idea but I wasn't really thinking. If that beast had charged you I was afraid I'd have been sweeping up your pieces."

Irene didn't know what to say. In the end she walked over to Aaron and took his hand. "Come on, since you're up you can make me a cup of tea."

"Why you cheeky..." He managed to get out before she kissed him.

****

Robert greeted people as he made his way into the hall. The simple construction had been put up in a matter of weeks with the help of soldiers, local tradesmen and the people who had chosen to join the Work Program.

All around the site he'd seen people working hard. Some showing others how to cut wood; a small group were building a stone wall; some were digging. It was chaotic and messy but Robert could see a sense of purpose in people's eyes.

"Robert!"

He found himself knocked back by Irene who wrapped him in a bear hug. Uncomfortable, he patted her back until she let go. Carla caught up with him and gave him a mischievous look.

"How's it going, Irene?"

"It's amazing! We're working together! We've almost got one home completed. We have planted our first crops and begun preparing the ground for poly tunnels. Some of us are even talking about staying here over winter."

"Are you sure that will be safe?"

"The insulation in the hall is almost too good. We have to have all the windows open during the day or we boil in there. I'm not sure we'd cope if everyone stayed – all cooped up for months, but the way we're going with construction we might have quite a few of the homes ready by then, so maybe we could spread out enough."

"It's good to see you." Robert attempted to shake her hand but got caught in another bear hug. "I need to go, Carla has work for me to do."

Finally free, he went over to one of the tables and sat down by Carla. "Show me then."

Carla adjusted her laptop so he could see the screen. "We're getting weekly and sometimes daily requests now from the communities. Equipment they say they need. Materials. Thousands of communities, each with their own different issues. We said we would help them establish themselves but now they are out there – they're thinking of different ways to do things."

"Over and above what we pledged?"

"Yes! And we just can't afford it. Then there is the work program. We've gone from paying people benefits to minimum wage but entire families were surviving on benefits. Now we have three or four people from the same family each earning a wage and we're paying more now than we were in benefits."

"There should be a payback though. People earn the money and they use it to buy food, clothes, equipment. That feeds back into taxes, right?"

"Maybe, but if so – it is taking too long. We aren't seeing any increase in revenue being raised."

"Then we have to hold a referendum. What do the people want to spend the taxes on? We now have almost four million registered voters, half of whom who never used to participate in any election. This is their chance to have a say in how the country is run. Something that actually affects them directly."

"But we've already cut so much." Carla opened another spreadsheet and pointed at a graph which showed spending going down. "People are starting to complain about the loss of services."

"It's just growing pains. We've allowed ourselves to regress as a nation. People look down on their neighbours when they get into debt and lose their house. But then they think nothing about the government following the same route – just to make their lives easier. The only problem is – it's Scotland we're mortgaging. We don't balance our budget and lose this home – there's nowhere left for us.

"But, okay..." Robert thought for a second. "It should not be one rule for the communities and another rule for everyone else. We have a budget. We make the communities stick to it. They say they need extra material – they only get that at the expense of something else that was allocated to them. If we do not have surplus funds to use then they have to find a way to provide for their own extra needs now.

"Also, we are paying them to build these communities. What are they doing with their wages? I'm not having extra taxes being used if they are unwilling to spend their own money.

"Issue a press release and have it sent to the communities first. We are refusing all requests for changes received up till now. They may submit the requests again but they need to understand there is a fixed budget. If they use it up in one area, they have to provide for the other needs themselves. But even then – I think we should filter the requests. Only ones that will help the whole community. Otherwise they pay for it out of their own wages."

"That is a lot of requests."

"No – it was a lot of requests. How are our staff coping though?"

"There's never enough time or people."

"I guess that's one reason government always seems to grow so big. There has to be a way to cut down though. Every person we employ – even if on minimum wage – is another drain on the budget."

Carla closed her laptop. "Well, if you find a way, let me know."

****

"You have a letter."

Robert gave Helen a kiss and took Robin from her. "A letter? Do I still get those? I have people to read them for me now. How did this one slip through?"

"It's from Gordon's solicitor."

Helen pointed to the kitchen table where a thick and

expensive envelope lay.

"It's addressed to us both." He said.

"I didn't want to open it."

Robert found himself reluctant to do so either. He recalled what the Chief Constable had told him and wondered if there was a connection. He took a knife and slit the envelope open.

"We've been requested to attend the reading of his Will, on Friday."

"Can you go?"

Robert checked his calendar on his phone. "I can change round some meetings."

****

CHAPTER FIFTY ONE

"We've had a call. The Rannoch Moor East village has been cut off. They had over two feet of snow overnight and they lost the phone lines."

"How do we know then?"

"A relative was in the middle of a phone call when the line went dead. She got in touch with the phone company who ran a check on the line. Then she called us. We got your friend Irene in the South village on the line and she told us how much snow they've had."

"How are they doing?"

"Surviving. Most people were in the hall but they have a dozen families in homes now. They were all asleep – at least in the hall until we woke them up. They're warm but starting to get concerned. They'll have to dig themselves out."

"Okay. Give them a call in the morning and check on them. If anyone else phones in let me know but otherwise we'll start phoning round the communities at Seven."

Robert hung up the phone and checked the time. 01:39. He peeled off the duvet and crept across to the window. No snow outside at all. He felt the same disappointment he had as a kid.

He checked on Robin and then got back into bed.

****

"How bad is it?"

"We have a white out across most of Highland Scotland." Carla replied. "Three feet of snow in some locations. We've managed to get in touch with all but three villages. We think the phone lines were brought down. I've asked the village leaders to call in once a day; also to advise us if there's more snow."

Robert turned to his map of Scotland. "Do you think there will be?"

"Who knows."

"When do we leave?"

"You're sure you want to join the rescue team?"

Robert put his hand up on the map. Little green pins everywhere they had established a new community. "How can I sit here when I started all this. If anyone is responsible for these people – I am."

"That doesn't mean you have to do everything. You are not trained for this sort of mission. If you died out there – who would continue your work?"

"You're right. I'm just one man."

"At last you're seeing sense!"

"We need to establish a team who can continue if something happens to me."

Robert could hear Carla sigh over the phone.

"Maybe not then." She said. "Okay. There is a team making their way down from Inverness. You'll need to hustle up to Rannoch Moor. I don't know what the roads are like yet though."

"Find out. I'm going to start putting some supplies in the car."

Robert ended the call as Helen came into his office.

"You're really going?"

"I feel I have to."

"Be careful, okay. You won't do anyone any good if you're stuck in a ditch."

Robert pulled her close. "I'll be back soon."

****

It was Two PM before Robert reached Rannoch Moor. The snow had been building at either side of the road the whole way up. Fortunately a snow plough had already been through cutting a way up the mountain road. The moor was a blanket of white with the road cutting through on its way North. He saw a collection of four wheel drives stopped on the road and pulled up behind them.

A man got out of one and walked over. Robert wound down his window.

"We've been here an hour. Leaves us only two hours of daylight."

"We better get going then."

"I don't take civilians."

"I think I'm probably your boss."

"I don't care who you are. You come with us you take orders from me. You keep up and let us know the instant there's a problem – understand?"

"Okay."

"Pete Jackson." The man offered his hand.

"Robert Castle."

"Okay Robert, we'll need to get your car off the road. Follow us until you're off and then get in with us."

They waited for him while he skidded round and followed into the drift. Robert took out his rucksack then locked his car.

"How do these make it through the snow?" Robert asked once in Jackson's lead vehicle.

"This is fresh, not very solid yet. Once it is gets dark it will freeze hard and we won't be able to."

"You know where you're going?"

"GPS." Jackson tapped a small screen attached to the dashboard.

"I thought that was a Tom-Tom."

"Little bit more advanced. We're looking at four miles up the valley."

"How do you know where the track is?"

Jackson gave him a condescending look. "We don't." As if to prove his point, the vehicle suddenly lurched up and down as Jackson struggled to steady the wheel. "We drive as far as we can and then will have to hike the rest of the way."

Jackson introduced him to the rest of the team. Four other men and one woman in the three vehicles plus Robert. Jackson gave updates to those behind using his radio as he encountered obstacles.

At one point the vehicle dipped down and snow swept up

and over the windscreen. The vehicle stalled, throwing Robert and the others forward. Jackson restarted the engine and slowly reversed backwards. Robert could feel, as much as hear the wheels skidding on the slope. Jackson tried heading forwards again but they quickly ground to a halt with snow again threatening to cover the vehicle.

"Guess that's as far as we drive." Jackson got on the radio. "Get the gear out, we'll be hiking from here."

Looking across at Robert: "We'll give you another jacket. How many layers have you on?"

"Three."

"Let's see your boots."

Robert twisted round and lifted up one leg.

"They look okay. You have decent socks on?"

"I've climbed a lot of Munro's."

Robert held Jackson's stare until he nodded.

Outside, Robert felt the cold air freeze his nose as he breathed. He resisted the urge to breathe through his mouth knowing his nose could cope with the pain better than his lungs if he breathed through his mouth.

Jackson handed him a scarf. "Wear this over your lower face. You have sunglasses?"

Robert pulled a pair out.

"Okay, put them on."

His own rucksack on over his new jacket, Robert followed Jackson as they made their way across the dip. The snow reached chest height and they almost had to swim through it. The ground rose again and they trudged through waist high snow. Robert quickly tired but kept forcing one leg in front of the other. At least it was easier for him, following Jackson, but the team leader never slowed. Just kept a steady pace.

Robert noticed Jackson checking the GPS device every few minutes. He took a look back and saw the team stretched out in a line and something that immediately scared him.

"Is that a snow storm?" He asked.

The team members behind him also turned and then began hurrying to catch up with him. Robert felt a hand on his shoulder.

"You'll need to put this on." Jackson gave him a harness. "We need to rope up."

Robert struggled into the harness. The rucksack off-balancing him, the snow covering his legs, making it difficult to step into the harness. Somehow he managed, aware the low cloud was approaching steadily across the valley.

"We're an hour's hike now from the village. Hopefully it is just a short shower but if it goes on too long we might have to break out the tents."

Robert let Jackson attach a carabiner to his harness and then thread a rope through it.

"I'll stay on lead but I'll need to swap over in fifteen minutes. We'll stay five paces apart and you need to try and match my pace and then just keep going. You bump into me then either you're going too fast or I've stopped. Don't let anyone bump into you, okay? You go too slow and you'll end up with the rest of the team kicking you from behind."

"Wouldn't it be better to tie me in?" Robert asked.

"I'm not going to drag your sorry arse all the way to the village."

Jackson checked the rest of the team were clipped onto the rope and the last man tied on. "Let's move on!"

Jackson set a slower pace than he had before and Robert tried to match it. He tried not to glance behind but realised he could see the clouds catching them up to his left. He adjusted the scarf round his nose and pressed on.

The snow hit with a physical force. One second it was clear blue sky, the next Jackson was lost in a swirl of grey and white. Flakes found their way behind his sunglasses and Robert didn't know if he should take them off or leave them on. He blinked to dislodge the flakes and tried to keep moving with the same rhythm he had before.

He started to lose track of time. Robert was sure it had only been a few minutes but the dancing flakes disoriented him and sudden gusts threatened to push him on his face. He began to wonder if he could die out here. He checked the rope was still attached.

His legs grew more and more tired. Suddenly, his foot hit something solid and Robert felt himself fall. He tried to throw himself back but he went face first into the drift. His sunglasses came loose, digging into his face and as he pushed himself up, his scarf came away and snow began hitting off his nose and mouth. He struggled to stand and had someone catch his arm.

"All stop!"

Blinking away the snow, Robert saw it was the woman –
Andrea. She pulled on the rope to alert Jackson and then picked
up and handed him the scarf.

"Get that back on. Where are your glasses?" She shouted at
him over the wind.

Robert saw she had goggles on. "I lost them."

"Forget them. You'll just have to do without. You ready to
continue?"

He nodded. "Yes."

She tugged on the rope and pushed him round and then on.

Careful to avoid whatever had tripped him before, Robert
marched on. He caught up with Jackson who was standing
looking back.

"Everything all right?"

"I tripped."

"You'll live."

Jackson turned and Robert saw him checking his GPS,
holding the device up close to his face. Then he started walking
again.

The whole world was grey. The wind buffeted him from
behind, snow attacked him from every angle. There was only the
rope at his side, leading off into a swirling future.

Then, for a brief instant, Robert saw the outline of Jackson
in front of him. Robert wondered if the storm was easing but
then Jackson disappeared again. The storm seemed to increase in
intensity and then cleared.

Robert could see Jackson in front. He turned and saw the sky
and behind him the other team members, strung out in a ragged
line.

Jackson stopped and Robert caught up with him.

"I thought that would never end." Robert told him.

"Yeah, it was a long quarter of an hour."

"That was only fifteen minutes?"

Jackson did not bother to reply. He waited until the others
had caught up.

"Let's stay roped in. There are bogs marked on the map and
a small loch. If I do end up walking into one, it would be nice to
know you could pull me out. According to the GPS we have
only half a mile to go. Hopefully we should be able to see the
village soon."

They started walking again, every step a struggle against the weight of snow against Robert's legs and waist. Without his sunglasses, Robert had to look up. The snow was now too bright, even though the sun was behind him.

It might have been another quarter of an hour – Robert didn't want to take his gloves off to look at his watch – when Jackson shouted: "I can see it!"

He was pointing ahead and slightly to his left. Robert looked but could only see snow. He kept walking and noticed black lines appear, as if the ground was raised in places. Then the snow itself started to look more regular. Lines resolving: white, grey and black into houses and a larger hall. Robert picked up his pace. They had made it.

The snow was undisturbed between the houses. As they got closer, Robert saw that some had been cleared outside the hall and some other doorways but it looked like most of the people had simply stayed inside.

Reaching the hall, Jackson untied himself from the rope and banged on the door. Robert reached him and saw a small area had been cleared of snow. Enough for them to sweep the snow from their legs and jackets. The others arrived and Jackson banged once more on the hall door before opening it.

Banging their feet to remove snow from their boots, they clustered in the small hallway, then shut the outer door to conserve heat. Jackson tried to open the inner door but it was jammed.

"Open up!" He shouted.

There was a scraping noise and the door opened abruptly.

"Where did you come from?" Asked a young boy.

Robert looked past him to see the hall was full of people. Some sitting, some lying with blankets over them. Faces turned to them and gradually people began to stand and walk over.

"Where's the village leader?" Robert asked.

"That's me." A small dark haired woman pushed her way to the front. "Who are you?"

"We couldn't contact you on the phone so we came to check you are all alright. Is everybody from the village in here?"

"No. Some people have stayed in their homes. Everyone's fine. I think you've had a long walk for nothing."

"Perhaps not." Jackson answered. "Why haven't you cleared the snow?"

"What do you mean?"

"You've had all day. Why haven't you cleared paths? Even just between the houses. And where is your fuel store? Do you have enough wood?"

The woman looked flustered. "Of course we have enough wood. We've also got peat. We cut that ourselves."

"But where is it? In the hall?"

"We've got enough for today. We will fetch in more tomorrow."

"What if it snows another couple of feet tonight? You need to clear the snow every day or it will bury you." Jackson looked around the hall. "I need all the men here to come outside and help us clear paths between the houses and to your fuel store. We have an hour of daylight."

"They'll get soaking wet! We don't have the fancy clothes you've got on."

"You all have a change of clothes. Your wet clothes will dry out overnight. You should have been told this. It's vital to keep on top of the snow and make sure you can still move around outside. We can discuss it later. Get your jackets and boots on."

Jackson organised the men; finding out where the shovels were kept and sending some of his team to bring those back. Jackson and his team each had shovels in their rucksacks. They took those out and began digging out paths to the nearest houses, taking it in turns to dig. The villagers soon offered to help and Robert joined in, realising it was better to be working outside than standing still.

Soon they had cleared one path, even though the snow kept collapsing.

"It will freeze and then you'll wish you had cleared more as it'll be a nightmare to shift." Jackson told the villagers.

It was just turning dark as they cleared the last path – to the fuel store. Jackson organised the men to carry logs and sticks of peat to the hall and to restock each of the houses.

They all returned to the hall and were greeted with the smell of broth cooking on the hall stove.

As they ate that evening, Jackson and his team explained the lessons they had learnt about survival in snow.

"This could last all winter. You are not going to be able to spend the next three months cooped up in this hall. You'll need to restock: get food supplies in. It took us two hours to trek here through waist deep snow. If you have an emergency – you are going to need to get help faster and that means you need to keep the track clear."

"Or learn how to ski." Andrea suggested.

Everyone turned to her.

"My Uncle always used to tell me of the winter it had snowed like this. He made himself a pair of skis and managed to trek five miles to his work. I never asked him how long it took but you could do the same – or make yourself snow shoes: you know – those things that look like tennis rackets. You spread your weight out and you can walk on top of the snow rather than having to wade through it like we did today. Makes walking so much easier."

"How would we do that?" One of the teenage boys asked.

"You'll find a way." Andrea promised him.

That night they all slept in the hall. Unable to sleep with the noise of people snoring Robert lay in his sleeping bag wondering how he would survive if he was living in the village. The difference between his dream and the reality was enormous. Had he forced these people out here just to suffer?

****

Having used a satellite phone the previous evening to confirm they had reached the village and everyone was alright, Robert promised he would find funding for radios so the villages could still communicate if the phones went down.

They left mid morning after giving the villagers more advice and assistance in how to continue to work with the snow.

Two of the boys came up just as they were about to leave.

"We did it!" They told Andrea, showing her wide snow shoes they had made out of plywood and rope. The boys followed the team out of the village for a mile, showing off their new ability to walk on top of the snow while the team waded through it.

"What do you think?" Jackson asked Robert some time later.

"What about?"

"How they're getting on."

Robert shook his head. "We tried to think through everything they might face. I guess there are just too many variables."

"I think you should be pleased. That was a community we left. People working together. Do you know where they came from?"

"No." Robert realised he had not thought to ask.

"Edinburgh. Morningside. Some of them had been through cold turkey to get off the drugs so they could join the community. They had nothing: no hope; no future except a cycle of drug addiction. You've given them something to work towards; taken them out of that situation and given them a support group."

"They used to be drug users?"

"Some of them, yes."

"I didn't think that was possible. I mean, I knew we were taking people out of those places. Knew that some of them had drug dependencies, but we just couldn't think through everything. I don't know if I should tell you this but a lot of it was not planned. It just took on a life of its own."

"No, you probably don't want to repeat that. But how could you plan everything. When we set out on a rescue mission – we plan for what we know. We train for what we know. But we always go out there knowing that it isn't what we know that is dangerous – it's what we don't know – what we didn't consider. Usually what we couldn't have known anything about at all. Then we just have to rely on our training and wit to deal with the unexpected."

****

CHAPTER FIFTY TWO

Robert made it to the solicitors with only a few minutes to spare. He ran into the building and introduced himself, then was shown up some stairs and into a room where Penny was already seated.

"I'm sorry." He apologised to her, collapsing into the other seat in front of the solicitor's desk.

"Are you alright?" Penny asked.

"Just back. I'll tell you later."

The solicitor introduced himself and then asked Penny if he could begin.

"Gordon's will is very simple. He leaves everything to his wife, Penny – apart from one bequest. He has left a property to Robert and Helen Castle, a number 300 Garrickstone Road, Glasgow. I have instructions to arrange transfer of title immediately. Do you have any questions?"

Robert could only stare at the solicitor in shock. When Penny placed a hand on his, he turned to her. "Did you know?"

She nodded. "He mentioned it. I wasn't sure when he was planning to give it back to you, but probably after you ended your term in office."

Robert clasped her hand. "Thank you!"

****

Late August the next year, Robert and Helen packed their car and carefully sat Robin in her car-seat. She was a quiet child and had worried them as she didn't seem interested in speaking. But she watched everything and as soon as she could crawl had shown tremendous curiosity.

Their temporary house had been abandoned and the three of them had moved back into Castle's castle as soon as the title was transferred.

Helen sat in the back next to Robin for the first part of the journey as they drove North, winding their way round sea lochs and across Glens. They passed several new communities on the way and marvelled at the many simple wooden houses that were being constructed. There were fields with grain and carefully cultivated greenery; and many polytunnels with green leafs hinting at vegetables and fruit underneath.

Helen drove after the first hour and Robert talked to Robin, pointing out sights as they passed.

That night they camped near the village hall. The community held a Ceilidh and Robert and Helen danced for the first time in years. The villagers told stories of how they had survived the coldest winter in recent years and had produced a bumper harvest for their first full growing season.

The next morning they were waved off but before Robert finished packing everything into the car, Irene came running up and thrust a box into his hands.

"What is this?" Robert asked.

"I want you to take it. It's just earth. Good and simple earth, but there's an apple seed in it. You plant that when you get home. You gave us back our land Mr Castle. I just wanted to say thank you."

The End

ACKNOWLEDGMENTS

To my wife and children, thank you for your patience through the long evenings and weekends when I've lost myself to another world.

To Andrew, if you hadn't sent me on that business trip I may never have come up with the idea for this novel – thank you!

To the volunteers at National Novel Writing Month, without you my first draft may never have been. May you continue to inspire people to produce messy first drafts and amazing works of art. Thank you.
http://nanowrimo.org/

To David MacKenzie for a perfectly designed cover, thank you!
http://dmackenzie.com/

To the wonderful people who run CAP Money and CAP Debt – you have helped our family to get control of our finances. Thank you! They can be contacted through
https://www.capmoney.org/

To Michael and Dot, your generosity in sharing your time and knowledge is an inspiration. You have created your own Grand Design in your Zero Carbon House. Thank you for answering my many questions and your kindness and hospitality.
http://www.zerocarbonhouse.com/Home.aspx

To Allan and all at Strathkelvin Judo who shared their knowledge. Thank you.
http://www.strathkelvin-judo.co.uk/

To Frank, you have continued to provide invaluable advice and support. As a life coach you have asked the right questions and given advice that has enabled me to progress faster than I thought possible. Thank you.
http://www.facebook.com/TurnkeyCoach
http://www.turnkeycoaching.co.uk/index.html

To Frank, Peter, Mary, Joy and Norrie, thank you for your insights and help while proof reading the final drafts. All mistakes are mine alone! (If you as a reader do find any mistakes in this version – email me at landgrab@cafepolitics.net)

Finally, to you… Thank you for reading this book. I hope you enjoyed it and would love to hear your feedback – email me at landgrab@cafepolitics.net and review the book on Amazon.

ABOUT THE AUTHOR

Born in Aberdeen, raised in the Shetland Isles and currently living in Central Scotland, Mark Anderson Smith has seen Scotland transformed since oil was discovered under the North Sea. Having lived in England for ten years and worked from 1999 till 2001 in Central Asia he has a unique perspective on what it means to be a Scot at home and abroad.

His two years in Central Asia were spent in the Republic of Tajikistan, a new country that declared independence from the Soviet Union in 1991. Instead of resulting in freedom, independence led to a five year civil war – the consequences of which can still be found today.

Yet despite seeing the destructive power of a country that tried to tear itself apart, he also saw people willing to forgive, willing to work together, willing to fight for the future – without resorting to violence.

As if writing a novel wasn't enough, Mark has 100 goals and you can read about his successes and failures on his blog.

Mark enjoys walking Scotland's mountains and climbing; and will gladly debate the merits of union or independence with anyone.

Twitter: @my100goals
Blog: http://my100goals.blogspot.com
Facebook: http://www.facebook.com/my100goals

Mark would appreciate your feedback:
landgrab@cafepolitics.net

ALSO AVAILABLE BY THIS AUTHOR

As eBook:
The Great Scottish Land Grab
Book One
Book Two
Book Three

The Great Scottish Land Grab
The Complete Trilogy

Dragon Lake

In 2015
100 Crazy Ideas to Fix The Economy
Fallen Warriors

8803111R00248

Printed in Great Britain
by Amazon.co.uk, Ltd.,
Marston Gate.